MEGHAN
QUINN

see me after class

Prologue

GREER

"Before we get started, I've been told I need to ask you a question." Stella sits cross-legged in front of me, a nervous look on her face, water in hand.

"Oh?" I ask, trying to act casual as I bring my glass of red wine to my lips. I have a scary inkling what this might be about.

She glances over at Coraline and winces. "Uh, I feel weird asking."

Oh God . . . I was right.

Shifting, I say, "You know, we don't have to—"

"Then why bring it up if you're not going to propose your query?" Keiko asks impatiently while pushing her green-rimmed glasses up on her nose. "You know the frequency of these meetings is dependent upon staying within the comprehensive itinerary I composed during my lunchbreak."

"Cool your bloomers, Keeks," Coraline says while taking a

large sip from her wine glass. "I want to know what's making Stella so fidgety."

The four founding members of the Ladies in Heat Book Club—aka my mismatched collection of friends—each bring diverse and unique character traits to our group.

Keiko "Keeks" Seymour—resident AP chemistry teacher at Forest Heights High School. Her social etiquette is lacking, her intelligence is off the charts, and she'd rather play with beakers than penises. She wasn't thrilled about the book club name and made a noble attempt to explain why her suggestion, the Austen Empowerment Collaborative, was far more credible. Majority ruled, she lost.

Stella Garcia—Spanish teacher at Forest Heights and my co-coach. Currently single, makes the best tamales I've ever had, and is one stamp away from getting a free donut at Frankie Donuts. Can be shy at times, but when it comes to her family and friends, she doesn't take shit from anyone. Loyal to the core, one of the reasons I adore her.

Coraline "Cora" Turner—recent divorcée and living with her brother, Arlo. Jobless at the moment and couldn't care less about it since both she and Arlo have enough inheritance to last them a lifetime. Often annoyed by her older brother or annoying him, doesn't partake in Twitter—says it's a filthy pool of opinions, and is the first to offer up a bottle of wine.

Then there's me . . .

Greer Gibson—twenty-four-year-old fresh to the teaching scene as Forest Heights's new English teacher and women's volleyball coach. I love running, have a penchant for a man in a cardigan, and can get a little noisy in the classroom while teaching. I currently share a classroom wall with Arlo Turner, Forest Heights most prestigious English teacher, and might have lost my underwear—

"Out with it, Stella," Cora says, snapping at her.

"Please, so we can proceed," Keeks says, straightening her notepad on her lap.

Stella looks me in the eyes and says, '
if there's anything going on between you
ently, Turner won't say a thing, but Broc
strong sexual tension building."

Cora whips her head to me, her c
getting it on with my brother?"

Finger pointed in the air, Keeks lean
proper term amongst company would be coitus."

Rolling her eyes, Cora asks, "Did you have coitus with my
brother?"

"You could also say intercourse if that amuses your
jargon more," Keeks adds. "Or copulating would be sufficient. But if you are inclined toward romantic terminology,
since we are in the presence of the book club, you could say
lovemaking or performing intimate acts. Although, given the
circumstances of when coitus took place—in the work environment—I would deduce that your actions were performed
carnally rather than with the interest of developing a devoted
accord."

"Good God, Keeks," Cora says, irritated. "Who cares
what it's called? We just want to know if it happened." Cora
looks me in the eyes. "Did it?"

Did it . . .

Good question.

I'd like to preface this by saying it was never my intention
to ever get involved in a workplace romance when I was hired
at Forest Heights, let alone get involved with the most surly,
agitating, and pompous man I've ever met.

My intentions were to show students how English and
reading books could actually be fun, bring the volleyball team
to a state championship, and make a new life for myself in the
suburbs of Chicago.

But so far, I've managed to be called into the principal's
office.

Infiltrate the teachers' athletic league.

...ad passionate fights with Arlo Turner over educa-...ecorum, and student-teacher friendships.

Not to mention I've lost my panties to him in my dreams more than I care to admit.

Why did this all happen?

Simple.

The man dresses in a cardigan, that's how.

Arlo Turner. The bane of my existence, annoyance to my sanity, and the only man who's ever made me want to spread my legs in a classroom.

He's torn down my metaphorical walls, strapped on a cottony cardigan—pushed up the sleeves—and has driven me to the brink of insanity, so now whenever I hear the mention of his name, my legs automatically spread, and my heartrate picks up.

Known as Mr. Turns Me On, he's the reason my star athlete is struggling to keep her grades up.

He's the reason I tend to avoid the teacher breakroom.

And he's the reason I might get fired from my first ever teaching job.

Chapter One

GREER

"A master's in English from UCLA is impressive, and your references are excellent. Can you tell us a little about yourself?"

The urge to fidget is painfully overwhelming, but I keep my hands in my lap as I keep my eyes on Principal Nyema Dewitt.

This has to be the weirdest interview I've ever had. We just spent a half hour on my education, my student-teacher experience, and my goals. Nyema has led the charge, but there are a few people behind her, studying the interview, that I can't quite see. Not sure if that's supposed to be less intimidating—faceless laps with clipboards—but it's not. It's more intimidating knowing there are people watching us.

Smiling, I straighten my back and say, "Of course. I grew up in Nebraska on a farm. I'd like to say I helped out a lot, but my dad had hired help, so I spent most of my time playing volleyball and reading. My high school years were filled with volleyball; I was quite obsessed, to be honest. I was so immersed in the sport and my goals to go to UCLA that I forgot to have a social life." I shrug. "I didn't miss out on much, though. I wasn't the party girl. I was the girl whose nose was stuck in a book."

"I like that," Nyema says. "Shows your strong will and ability to make your own decisions."

"Thank you. Never been a follower, really. Always did my own thing. Love to think outside of the box."

"Lovely." Nyema sifts through her papers and asks, "What are some of your favorite books?"

I smile softly. "I'm sure you're expecting me to say something like *Pride and Prejudice* or *Of Mice and Men*, right? Maybe *Fahrenheit 451?*" I shake my head. "Although I do love Mr. Darcy and it's my favorite book to teach, I'm going to be honest, I'm not a huge fan of the classics."

Nyema's eyes widen, and I know it's a risky thing to say, but I feel the need to say it.

"I understand the importance of teaching them, but I also understand the importance of instilling interested reading habits into students. Some of those books come off as . . . stodgy, holier-than-thou, and frankly—boring."

There's a faint snort in the background, and I catch a hand scrawling across the clipboard.

"I see," Nyema says. "What books would you say keep your interest?"

"Honestly?"

She nods.

"I love romance. I grew up reading it and it's one of the reasons I love teaching *Pride and Prejudice* so much. With romance, I get lost in the story and tend to forget everything around me. Now, I'm not saying romance has the educational substance you're looking for when it comes to teaching deep-rooted metaphors and symbolism, but it has offered me the chance to fall in love with reading. For someone else, it could be mystery, suspense, maybe a thriller, or even a fictional story loosely based on something true that happened in history. It doesn't matter the genre, what matters is the escape. The appreciation for getting lost in words."

Nyema smiles and is about to ask something when someone from behind her pipes up.

"So, if you seem to hate the classics so much—"

"I didn't say hate," I say quickly, the tone of the man's voice instantly putting me on high alert.

"Excuse me while I finish my question, Miss Greer."

Miss Greer.

The snap in his voice with those two words—it sends a shiver straight up my spine as I try to make out the faceless voice in the back.

"Pardon me," I say, my leg starting to lightly bounce up and down.

"As I was saying, if you seem to *dislike* the classics so much, how do you intend to teach them? Because Forest Heights has educational expectations; as a teacher, you're required to meet them."

Oh God.

Nyema, completely unfazed by the deep-throated interruption from the back, sits and awaits my answer.

Swallowing hard, I say, "Great question. I would still touch upon all the required literature, but I'd teach it in a way that brings the words to life. I think it's important to do more than just stand in front of a class and lecture."

"Lecturing is an effective and proven way to teach, Miss Greer. Are you saying it's not?"

"I'm saying it's boring." My heart dips, and I quickly search for the words to retract my answer, until I catch the slight smirk on Nyema's face as she stares down at her paper. It's a big enough smirk to give me the confidence to keep going. "Teachers who stand at the front of the class and demand excellence without doing the work are elitist and should possibly reevaluate their way of teaching. I plan on—"

"Are you calling *me* an elitist, Miss Greer?"

Dear Jesus, who is this man in the back?

"Um, are you . . . the lecturing type?"

"I am."

I smile awkwardly and swallow. "Well . . . then I guess I am."

Nyema interjects before I can say anymore. "I think I'll take it from here." Her eyes snap up to mine, and I can't tell if she's pleased, irritated, or horrified.

The smirk is gone.

The air in the room is tense.

And I'm pretty sure I just blew this interview.

———

"THAT'S KELVIN THIMBLE. He teaches geometry and dresses up every Friday as a character from *Star Wars*. Rumor has it he has a crush on Keiko."

"Keiko Seymour?" I ask Stella as we're huddled off to the side, glasses of champagne in hand.

Yes, champagne at faculty night.

Champagne at a backyard barbeque faculty night.

At least that's what it was called when I received the email from Principal Nyema Dewitt.

Yeah . . . I got the job.

Shocking, right?

I couldn't be more shocked myself, but Nyema said she thinks I'll bring a fresh approach to the English department. She's also excited about my coaching ability and immediately introduced me to Stella, the other volleyball coach. We've been hanging out for the past two weeks.

But back to the champagne backyard barbeque. According to Stella, the Friday before school starts, Forest

Heights holds a party for the faculty where the newbies—like myself—can get to know everyone and where we can talk about our summer. When my Uber pulled up to the address on the invite, I wasn't expecting to see to a lake house gated in by seven-foot-tall hedges.

But I did.

After I picked my jaw off the ground and made my way toward the white brick, Tudor-style house, I found Stella, who handed me a glass of champagne and led me to the backyard, where high-top tables were meticulously placed along the large stone patio. A pathway leads to the lower yard, which is covered in pristinely cut grass and at least a dozen lawn chairs that overlook Lake Michigan.

Let's just say, Principal Dewitt is loaded.

"Yeah, Keiko Seymour. Is there another Keiko you know of?" Stella laughs.

"Guess not." I glance around and say, "I thought this was supposed to be a backyard barbeque. This is more like an event thrown by the Great Gatsby himself. I mean . . . look, there's a green light right there."

"That's Arlo Turner for you."

"What?" I ask, facing Stella. "This isn't Nyema's house?"

Stella throws her head back and laughs. "How much do you think a principal gets paid?"

I shrug. "I don't know . . . a lot?"

Stella shakes her head and leans in. "Houses along Lake Michigan are in the millions, Greer."

"Okay, so who's Arlo Turner?"

"Uh, he interviewed you for this job."

"No, he didn't." I shake my head. "Nyema did."

"Were their people sitting in the back of your interview?"

"Yesss . . ." I drag out.

She nods knowingly, a smile pulling up her lips. "Yeah, he was there, and this all makes sense. That's why he wasn't happy."

"What the hell are you talking about?"

"Good Evening." Keiko walks up to us, holding a cup of what I'm assuming is water from the clear liquid. She's dressed in a modest green dress with red roses scattered haphazardly along her bodice. Her black hair is tied up into two pigtail knots with a few wisps framing the front of her lovely face. "I see that you're partaking in adult effervescence during this professional sundown." She sips her water. "Risk takers."

"We didn't sneak the drinks in, Keeks, they're serving them," Stella says.

"Maintaining a constant disposition while amongst colleagues would behoove you. Especially after last year . . ."

Okay, the interview thing could be put on hold for a second. Turning to Stella, I ask, "What happened last year?"

"Nothing. Had a few too many drinks," Stella says, waving her hand in dismissal.

"On the contrary," Keeks says, "she had precisely two IPAs indigenous to Chicago, three margaritas, one buttery nipple, and then schlepped her tongue over Brock "Romeo" Romero's formidable abdomen, which was dappled in salt, right before consuming two tequila shots. She then proceeded to gyrate her exotic undergarments over her head while reciting the Pledge of Allegiance. There's a video of this exasperating occasion if you would like me to procure it for you." Keiko adjusts her glasses and smiles.

"I think we're good—"

"I'd love to see that," I say with a laugh.

"I shall put a note in my phone to remind myself." Right then and there, she takes out her phone from one of the pockets in her dress and types away. I know already Keiko and I are going to be great friends.

"Lovely, thank you, Keeks."

"Yes, of course," she says so seriously it makes me giggle.

"Anyway." Stella faces me again. "I was talking with Gunner and Brock—"

"The physical education teachers, right?"

Stella nods. "They used to be professional baseball players. Both went to Brentwood, both had short careers in the majors. Gunner suffered from Pitcher's Elbow—"

"A commonality among professional pitchers," Keiko interjects. "Formally known as valgus extension overload, it's where the valgus force from snapping your hand and elbow to the lateral side of your trajectory wears out the cartilage in your olecranon bone. Such trauma to your appendage results in swelling and immense pain. The solution would be to change the motion of your pitching arm, though in Gunner's case—one of not being able to 'teach an old dog new tricks'— he failed at expanding his athletic prowess, thereby resulting in early retirement."

"Annnnd Brock snapped his Achilles tendon sliding into home," Stella finishes.

I turn to Keiko, who says, "That's self-explanatory."

Chuckling, I nod. "Okay, so what did they say?"

"They were two of three lucky ones to be chosen to go to the teachers' conference in Denver last week, the third being Arlo. Apparently, he was annoyed that you were hired."

"What? Why?" *Was he the mystery voice in the back?*

"No one really knows what Arlo is thinking at any given time." Stella downs the rest of her champagne.

"Very elusive man," Keiko says. "Brilliant educator, vastly recognized amongst peers, and has a scintillating way of throwing parties that lure the minds of those who are effort-lessly commandeered by sumptuous chattel." Keiko looks Stella up and down. "Like Stella."

"Hey, I appreciate his artistic flair to a nighttime soiree. Nothing wrong with that." Turning toward me, Stella contin-ues, "Anyway, you're standing in *his* lavish backyard, and he doesn't like you."

Just then, with a grand amount of flair, the French doors to the beautiful Tudor house open. It feels like a gust of wind blows by us as a man of stature steps onto the patio. Lifting the sleeves of his light brown cardigan, he pushes them to his elbows, revealing tan, muscular forearms. Beneath the cardigan is a pristine white T-shirt with just the very front tucked in, showing off a brown belt that's securing a pair of dark-washed jeans to his trim waist. Brown boots tap the edge of his cuffed jeans and . . .

Oh.

Dear.

God.

His sharp jawline is covered in a perfect five o'clock shadow, producing a dark and mysterious look, while his hair is styled short on the sides with that sexy kind of messy on top. I'm too far away to tell the color of his eyes, either a blue or a green based on how light they are, but from the overshadow of his narrowing eyebrows, I know they'd be devastating up close.

There's an unlearned swagger in the way he moves around the patio, shaking hands, handing out distant nods of hello with his expertly carved jaw. A smooth quirk to his brow when he spots Gunner and Brock by the buffet of food. And when he finally walks up to us, there's the smallest lift of the corners of his lips as he says in a deep, masculine voice, a voice I'd recognize anywhere, "Hello, ladies."

Oh God . . . it's him.

"Hey, Arlo. Great party, once again. Thanks for having us," Stella says.

"I hope you're enjoying yourselves." His eyes—a combination of blue green, Lord help me—slay me as he gives me a quick once-over. His assessment isn't positive as his face remains neutral.

"We are most satisfied," Keiko says. "We were just conversing about your distaste for Greer Gibson. From her baffled facial expression and lack of response, I've come to the logical conclusion that she was unaware of the foul feelings you harbor for our newest faculty member."

"Jesus, Keeks," Stella grumbles.

Arlo's eyes snap to mine and I quickly look away, downing the rest of my drink.

"Did I say something wrong?" Keiko asks. "I don't quite understand. I stated the facts within relevancy of the conversation. He clearly stated he hoped we were enjoying ourselves, and I perceived that we *were* enjoying ourselves up until the moment you notified Greer about Arlo not expressing fond feelings for her. Although, we haven't explored the core reasoning as to why. I'm still very much inclined to find out."

Arlo nods, and says, "Excuse me. I'm going to say hi to the rest of the staff." He pats Keiko on the shoulder. "Always a pleasure, Miss Seymour."

"Pleasure is all ours," Keiko replies with a brief curtsy.

When he's out of hearing range, Stella says, "What the hell was that?"

Truly confused, Keiko looks behind her and then back to us. "Well . . . I perceived it as a host greeting his guests, but if I read that situation incorrectly, please help me understand what that was."

"No, why did you tell him I told Greer he didn't like her?"

"Because you did," she says with confusion.

Groaning, Stella drags her hand down her face. "That was humiliating."

Staring at his retreating back, I ask, "But why doesn't he like me?" Was it because I called him an elitist? That surely can't be the case.

"The million-dollar question." Keiko shakes her head as if nothing happened and stares at Arlo as well. "If I were to hypothesize—"

"Please don't," Stella says. "Let's just get more drinks."

Taking me by the arm, Stella drags me to the bar, where we fill up on champagne . . . five more times.

―――

"I BELIEVE YOU TWO ARE INTOXICATED," Keiko says, standing above us as Stella and I share a lounge chair and giggle. "May I remind you about the lack of inhibition you possess at this moment?"

"Well aware of the no inhibi—*hiccup*—tions." Stella laughs. "Don't worry, Keeks, I'll keep my underwear on. This bra though . . ." Stella starts fishing around in her shirt. "It's like a torture device. Keeks, help me take it off."

"I will not," she answers, head held high. "Disrobing at a work event is strictly prohibited by standard social etiquette."

"It's just a bra," she whines.

"Still clothes," Keiko replies.

Standing, I wobble on my feet for a few seconds, and then say, "I need to go to the bathroom."

"I believe they're directing all faculty to use the bathroom to the right of the kitchen when you walk into the house."

I pat Keiko on the shoulder. "Thanks, Keeks."

Steadying myself, I take a deep breath and head toward the house, grateful I wore sandals to the event or else I'd be having quite the time traipsing across this lawn in heels. Trying not to look drunk, even though I am—thank you, Stella—I smile at a few people I haven't met, nod toward Romeo and Gunner, who both have huge smiles on their faces, and head into the house where I stumble to a stop from the sight of the kitchen.

Lord Jesus, look at that island.

It's the size of a swimming pool.

A marble-coated swimming pool.

Temptation knocks at my door; the urge to lie across the cool surface and get in a few backstrokes crosses my mind.

Imagine the calories I'd burn swimming on that island.

Maybe sober up a little.

Then backstroke heaven.

Moving toward the island, I consider the best way to hop up on it just as I feel a strong, tall presence walk up next to me.

"Can I help you with something?"

That devastating voice has just the right amount of posh attitude combined with mystery.

Turning around, I come face to face with Arlo Turner. I sway backward only for him to quickly grab my shoulders and right me.

I loll my head to the side and glance at his hands that are gripping my shoulders and then back to him. "You have a strong grip." Oh boy . . . Keeks was right, the inhibitions are gone.

He slowly releases my arms, eyes trained on mine as he takes a step back. Chin high, jaw firmly clenched, he lowers his hands to his side and says, "Do you need something?"

"Yes." I fold my arms over my chest and try not to get lost in the deceiving color of this eyes. What is that? Blue or green? *Make up your mind, man!*

"Well?" he asks with a snobbish lilt.

He's impatient. *Is he like this in the classroom?*

"Why don't you like me? Is it because of the interview?"

Face unwavering, he says, "I don't partake in childish games." He turns to walk away when I grab him by the arm. His eyes shoot to my hand, eyebrows narrowing, and I quickly let go. Sheesh.

"I'm not playing childish games," I say, trying not to slur my words. "I'm trying to make sense of why you have a distaste for me when you've never officially met me. Oh." I hiccup and hold out my hand. "Maybe that's why you hate me, because you've never been introduced. Hi, I'm Greer Gibson and you have delightful champagne."

He stares at my hand but doesn't take it.

"Struggles with socialization, I see." I reach over, pluck his hand from his side and slip it into mine. "My God, your hand is large. Look at it eclipse mine like it's claiming dominance." I give it a good shake and then let go, but not before one more quick examination. "See, was that so hard?" He doesn't say anything, so I continue in a deep voice. "Hi, Greer. I'm Arlo Turner. Nice to meet you. I own this mansion of a house, and, from time to time, I conduct the very satisfying backstroke on my kitchen island."

I press a shocked hand to my chest, enjoying this one-on-one conversation.

"Do you?" I say, answering myself. "I love the backstroke as well. When you perform it, would that be in a bathing suit or a birthday suit? You know what?" I wave my hand about. "Never mind, what's between a man and his island, stays between a man and his island. Am I right?"

Turning to the side, really getting into character, I puff my chest, and in my best Arlo Turner voice, I answer, "Naked, I swim on my island naked. I enjoy the feel of the cold marble against my most heated of areas—"

"Are you done?" he snaps at me, his jaw clenched even tighter, and I truly feel nervous that he might crack a tooth.

"Uh, do you want me to be done?"

"Yes."

"Okay, then I'm done." I smile and rock on my heels, which is an incredibly bad idea. Equilibrium completely off—thank you, champagne—I tumble backward into the island. "Oye." I clutch my back and then pat the top of the island. "Sturdy, very sturdy." I run my hand over the smooth surface. "Fine craftsmanship. Not that I'd know what a good kitchen island is made out of, but, boy, this one sure is nice. Did it come with the house?"

He mutters something under his breath while looking away. Finally, he says, "If you don't need anything, I prefer all guests to linger in the backyard, not inside my private dwellings."

"Oh, dwellings, nice word. Very Mr. Darcy-like." I wink at

him. "Don't worry, I wasn't lingering. Just trying to find the bathroom. Bladder is full," I say, pointing to where I hope my bladder is. "Needs relief."

"I see." He steps aside. "First door on the left."

Tapping my chin, I ask, "And do tell, how many doors do you have in this grand household?"

"Enough."

"Vague answer. What's that about? Is it because you don't like me?"

His tongue runs over the front of his teeth as I notice him exhale sharply. Oh . . . someone is getting annoyed. I guess it's okay since he already doesn't like me.

"I'd prefer it if you don't relieve yourself on my hard-wood floors." He gestures to the bathroom. "Take care of yourself."

"As if I'd pee on your floor. Do you really think that low of me?"

"You've been crossing your legs and bouncing this entire conversation. I don't know much about you, but I do under-stand that's the universal signal that you're about to wet your pants."

I glance down at my legs and . . . well, would you look at that? My legs are crossed and bouncing.

What's going to happen when I uncross them?

Will I . . . wet myself, like he said?

I glance up at him. There's a knowing look in his eyes as he stares back at me.

Peeing my pants in front of him would be positively humiliating.

We can't have that.

With a shaky laugh, I say, "You know, I believe I do have to go to the bathroom, but I can't quite tell where I'm at in the whole 'bladder is about to explode' process. Do you by any chance provide motorized trips to the bathroom?"

"Jesus," he mutters, walking toward the door. "If you pee

on my floor, clean it up." And then he takes off into the backyard.

Calling after him, I say, "I'm going to take that as a no."

The door shuts behind him.

"Yup, that's a no." I sigh and look up at the door. *Twenty feet, you can do this.*

Keeping my legs twisted tightly together, I bunny-hop my way to the bathroom, grateful he left, because, if anything, I need to save a little bit of dignity, and watching someone bunny-hop to the bathroom doesn't necessarily scream "put together."

Although, drinking five glasses of champagne doesn't either.

⌑

"I THINK WE'RE DRUNK," Stella says, resting her head on my shoulder as we share a lounger and stare at the dark abyss that is Lake Michigan.

Keiko left a while ago, stating she needed to get home to ensure she "acquired an adequate amount of sleep." Once Keiko left, Kelvin Thimble left, too. Stella was right, he does have a thing for her, and even though Keiko is completely oblivious, in my drunken state, I noticed. You know . . . since he stared at her from afar for the entire party.

"That was established an hour ago," I say, crossing my legs at my ankles.

"What time is it?"

"Dark," I answer. "It's dark time."

"Is it quiet or is it just me?"

My eyes are drifting shut as I answer, "No, seems quiet. I think it's because everyone saw how much we need a little shut-eye."

"What considerate co-workers."

"With that kind of consideration, I think it very well might be a great school year."

A throat clears above us just as I get comfortable, ready for a brief nappity-nap.

"I think there's someone standing next to us," I say, eyes closed.

"I think that was the ocean lapping against the rocks."

"It's a lake, you dumbass." I laugh.

"That's what I meant." Stella giggles.

"It was neither," a male voice says above us.

Uh-oh . . .

I open one eye and slowly look up to find Arlo standing over us, a displeased look on his face.

Whispering to Stella, I say, "It's the guy who doesn't like me."

She jackknifes off the lounger and sits up, her hair sticking out on the right side. Scrambling to right herself, she says, "Turner, lovely party. Send my praise to the grill master. That brisket was phenomenal."

"The party was over twenty minutes ago."

I lift up as well and look behind us, noticing the empty backyard. "Huh, I guess it is." Smiling, I lie back down. "That champagne was top notch." I snuggle into the lounger. "Thanks for the invite . . . even though you don't like me." I pull on Stella, who sinks back into the lounger, as well. I snuggle to her back and shut my eyes.

"You can't sleep here."

"Why? Is this your bed?" I ask, eyes still closed. "We could make room for you." I pat the small space behind my rear end. "See, right here. Take a seat."

"Did you drive here?"

"Aren't you chatty now?" I sigh and turn to look up at him. "No, I took an Uber. So no need to worry about my car taking up curb space. All good." I wave my hand at him. "We're good, really. You're relieved of your hostess duties."

"Host," he says.

"Huh?" Stella's face twists in confusion.

"Hostess is the female noun for someone presenting an event. Host would be proper in this context since I'm a man. I would expect you to know something as simple as that, Miss Gibson. But alas, you've made the mistake all night."

"Who called the dictionary police?" Stella asks, thumbing toward Arlo.

Even more irritated, Arlo says in a deep, threatening voice, "Miss Gibson, Miss Garcia, you have ten seconds to get up and start vacating my property."

"Ten seconds?" I ask. "Or what?"

"Or I tell Principal Dewitt how extremely unprofessional both of you are."

"Pfft." I jerk my thumb toward him while speaking to Stella. "Look at this guy. Mr. Tattletale." Sitting up, I add, "Snitches get stitches, man." I nudge Stella, but we don't stand; instead, we both sit up on the lounger, trying to steady ourselves.

"One. Two."

My blurry eyes connect with his. "Are you really counting?"

"Four. Five."

"Stella, he's counting at us."

"Seven. Eight. Trust me, you don't want me to get to ten."

"Did you hear that—"

"Nine . . ."

"Okay, okay. We're moving." I grab Stella and stand, my legs wobbly, my brain too tired to even try to calculate the distance to make it out of this mansion. "Man alive, what kind of champagne was that?" I grip my head and stumble forward, landing right against Arlo's torso. My hands planted against his thick chest, I quickly notice how muscular he is under his pristine white T-shirt and cardigan. "Good grief, Stella. This man has muscles." I lift my finger to his jaw where I poke the carved bone. "His angles are spectacular."

"Miss Gibson, I suggest you pull yourself together."

"Ugh, enough of that 'Miss Gibson' crap. We're not at school. It's Greer." I lift off him, but keep one hand on his chest to steady myself as Stella finally meets me at my side, a goofy grin on her face. "Now, if you don't mind helping me lug my body to the front of your abode, it'd be most appreciated."

His jaw tenses, his eyes unwavering as he studies us.

"I agree. A little assistance could really move this process along," Stella says.

Not saying a word, he grabs us both by the upper arms and starts guiding us up the stairs to the patio.

Well, not guiding, more like escorting.

Ehh . . . dragging.

He's dragging us across his lawn, our drunk legs stumbling to keep up.

"Whoa there, horsey." My stomach rolls. "Lit-tle slower, buster. Uneasy alcohol belly over here."

"Same." Stella raises her hand and then asks, "At least I kept my underwear on this time. Progress, wouldn't you say, Arlo?"

"Progress would be not getting drunk at a work function."

"Then why serve alcohol if you don't want people getting drunk?"

"Valid point," I say as we work our way to the side gate. "Frankly, this is all his fault. What was he expecting us to do when serving such delicious bubbly?"

"For such a poised hostess, the follow-through on the thought process wasn't there." Stella hiccups and then laughs. "You'll get the hang of this hosting thing one day, Arlo. Don't give up."

"Yeah, the whole thing was almost a home run. Two minor glitches," I say. "No cap on the booze, detrimental for two uncontrollable lushes. And number two . . . uh . . . oh yeah, number two, not liking me."

"Why is that?" Stella asks, stopping us as she digs her heels into the ground. "Why don't you like her?"

Not showing an ounce of irritation, besides the clench in his jaw and the tone of his voice, he says, "Maybe because she gets wasted at a work event and I'm left dragging her across my lawn when all I want to do is go to bed."

"I hardly consider this dragging," I say, though it's a lie. It's dragging for sure. "And we were perfectly content sleeping in the lounger, so you're the one making this harder on yourself."

"She has a point, Arlo."

Pulling us forward again, he doesn't say a word as we move through the gate and out to his front yard. "I trust you can call yourselves an Uber."

"Sure," I say, reaching for my phone in my pocket. "Whoa, that screen is bright." I look away. "Burned my retinas."

"Spare yourself, you can come to my place. Although, the decent thing would be Arlo telling us we can spend the night in one of his guest rooms." She lolls her head to the side and smiles up at Arlo.

"Set up the Uber," he says without blinking.

"Sheesh, you'd think he'd be more accommodating given the size of his house." Stella types away on her phone, and then says, "They're five minutes away."

"Good." Stepping away, Arlo retreats toward his house.

"Sure, yeah, no goodbye or anything," I call out. "See you on Monday . . . turd nugget." I whisper that last part.

Stella cups her mouth and calls out, "She just called you a turd nugget." The gate to the fence slams and I push Stella, who falls to the ground laughing.

"You ass."

Chapter Two

ARLO

"Good morning," I say as Coraline comes stumbling down my stairs, her hair a goddamn mess, and her makeup smeared under her eyes.

Leaning against the counter in my kitchen, I hold a warm cup of coffee close to my chest as I watch my sister blindly make her way to the coffee pot and pour herself a cup. With a sweep of her hand, she moves her long chestnut-colored hair out of the way and takes a large sip.

Her head falls back as she says, "Praise Jesus."

"I'm gathering you had too much to drink last night?"

"What gave you that impression?" she asks, taking another large sip and working her way to the bar-height chairs at the island.

"The stench you brought into the kitchen."

She lifts her shirt to her nose and sniffs. "I don't smell."

"Hard to smell booze when you've been sleeping in it all night."

"God, what crawled up your ass?"

Lifting off the counter, I rest my hands on the island in front of me. "Need I remind you whose house you're staying at while you get your life back together?"

Her silver eyes snap to mine. "And need I remind you why I'm here? Because until my divorce is final, I'm not allowed to touch any of my finances. Trust me, this would not be my first choice of places to be."

"Why's that?"

"Because you're a stuck-up asshole."

I chuckle. "Tell me how you really feel, Coraline."

She smiles and sighs. "Stop being a jerk and make me some bacon."

"Nice try, sis." I toss a protein bar at her, grateful for our playful ribbing. "I'm heading out."

"Going to go buy your first-day-of-school cardigan?"

"Do you really think I'd wait until the day before to purchase something so important?"

"True." She opens the protein bar, no doubt eager for food and coffee to soak up the alcohol. "Where are you headed?"

"Sporting goods store. Need some new running shirts and shorts . . . maybe some shoes."

"Sunday shopping spree. Don't you want to take your desperate and lonely sister with you?"

I shake my head. "Not when you smell like that."

"Give me ten minutes. I can smell like a flower and look presentable. We can go through the McDonalds drive-thru and get hash browns for my hangover, and then I can help you pick out some supreme workout clothes."

I study her. "Are you going to make me to buy you shit?"

"Yes." She smiles. "But you love me."

"Unfortunately." I nod toward the stairs. "Hurry up, I'm leaving in ten."

"I know I said ten, but give me fifteen." She winces and

then quickly says, "To accommodate for the hangover. I'm moving slower than normal."

"Fine. Fifteen. Hurry up."

"You're the best." She slowly takes off toward the stairs and shouts, "Sibling Sunday!"

Shaking my head, I hold back my smile and drain the rest of my coffee just as my phone buzzes next to me.

With a quick glance, I spot a message from my group text thread with my best friends Gunner and Romeo. I can only imagine what this is about.

I rinse my mug out and put it in the dishwasher, grab my phone, lean against the counter again, and read the text.

Gunner: *So . . . did Gibson and Garcia spend the night?*

Exactly what I thought he was going to ask.

Last night, after everyone left, Gunner was on his way out when he spotted Greer and Stella on the lounge chair. He patted me on the back and wished me luck before he took off. I waited a good ten minutes in the hopes that they would figure out everyone was gone before going over there and kicking them out of my backyard.

Arlo: *No. They stumbled their way to an Uber.*

Romeo: *Why are you asking if they spent the night? Did Turner finally talk to Greer? Solve his differences?*

Gunner: *Did you?*

Sighing, I sink into my position and type them back.

Arlo: *There are no differences to be solved. And they were practically passed out in a lounger. I had to escort them out of my backyard —literally.*

Gunner: *Oh damn. Don't blame them though, I'm not much of a champagne drinker and that shit was good.*

Romeo: *Top notch.*

Gunner: *So nothing happened?*

Arlo: *What do you suppose would happen?*

Gunner: *A passionate love affair.*

Romeo: *LOL. You're such an idiot.*

Arlo: *Something Romeo and I can agree upon.*

Gunner: *Mark my words, you two are going to get it on at some point. I see it in the way you look at her.*

Arlo: *And how is that exactly?"*

Gunner: *You know . . . all growly.*

Romeo: *Growly? Dude . . .*

Arlo: *Good thing you teach physical education. Stick with bats and balls, man.*

Gunner: *You know what I mean.*

Arlo: *We really don't.*

Gunner: *Like you're going to pounce.*

Romeo: *I think he's comparing you to a lion.*

Arlo: *Seems that way.*

Gunner: *You don't have to be dicks.*

Romeo: *You're trying to hook everyone up in a relationship now that you're in one. Be honest, that's what this is.*

Gunner: *No.*

Romeo: *Bullshit.*

Arlo: *As much fun as this was, I'm heading out. See you nitwits tomorrow.*

Gunner: *Did you pick out your first day cardigan?*

Romeo: *What color is it?*

Arlo: *That's not a thing.*

Gunner: *Turner . . .*

Arlo: *Fine. It's green. Now fuck off.*

▯▯▯

"WHY DO you think these hash browns are so good?" Cora asks, mouth full.

"Grease that's probably been reused for months on end."

"Well, good on them." She takes another bite. "They've found the hidden secret to a hangover cure." She leans back into her seat, and says, "Bitching party last night, bro."

"Glad you evicted yourself from your room long enough to enjoy it."

"Are you calling me a hermit?" She licks her fingers.

After turning right, headed toward the mall, I say, "You haven't been social."

"Not much to talk about."

And that right there is why I hate my shit-for-brains ex-brother-in-law. What he did to Cora . . . It burns me watching her act reserved. She's . . . shuttered now. I hate it.

"It's not healthy to hold everything in."

"This coming from the man who's harboring feelings for the newest addition to the faculty."

I stop at a stop sign and turn toward her. "Where the hell did you—" Fucking Gunner. They were hanging out last night. "Don't listen to a goddamn thing Gunner says."

"It was actually Romeo." She chuckles.

"Don't listen to either of them. And don't hang out with them. They're idiots."

"You hang out with them."

"Because they're my only option."

"Doesn't say much about you if your only options for friends are idiots."

Sighing in frustration, I say, "Just don't listen to anything they say."

"Why? Because it's true?" She crumples up her hash brown wrapper and sticks it in the bag.

"It's not fucking true."

"Okay, whatever you say, bro." She picks up her orange juice and takes a large sip. "For what it's worth, I think she's really hot."

Christ.

"From the grip you have on the steering wheel, I'm going to guess you don't want to talk about that though."

"I don't."

"Any particular reason?"

"Because she's inconsequential."

"Ooo, boy, don't say that to her face." Cora shakes her head. "That would be a blow to the old self-esteem. That's something one of those alpha asshole bosses would say." In a hoity voice, Cora repeats, "*She's inconsequential.*" Shaking her head, she adds, "Does everyone at school know what a tightwad you are?"

"Yes."

"Good . . . at least everyone is aware."

"I'm an educator, I'm not there to make friends, Coraline."

"Clearly," she says sarcastically. "Gunner said this new teacher teaches English as well. Does that mean you guys have to work closely together?"

"No."

"Shame. She seems like your type."

"A lush who gets drunk at work events seems like my type?"

Coraline laughs. "If you don't want people getting drunk, don't serve them champagne that tastes like juice. But Greer, she has that whole ombre look with her hair, long legs, pretty lips. Feisty. I could see her giving you a run for your money and you enjoying it."

"I would not," I answer, pulling into the mall parking lot. "Now drop it."

Coraline laughs some more. "Sure, Arlo. I'll drop it . . . for now."

Great. On a deep exhale, I exit the car and wait for Coraline to join me before I lock up. Looking up toward the blue sky, I realize this might be the first time I'm not excited about the first day of school, and it has everything to do with the girl everyone keeps bothering me about.

It's not that I don't like her. I barely know anything about her.

But what I do know . . .

Now that's what's going to drive me fucking crazy. It's why I'll be cold and dismissive.

A turd nugget.

⊏▭⊐

NOSE PINCHED, I bow my head, trying to keep my composure.

Breathe in.

Breathe out.

Do not lose your shit in front of your students.

From the other side of my classroom wall—for the third time today—comes the distinct sound of at least twenty desks being pounded on, followed by a clap as "We Will Rock You" by Queen blares through a bass-filled Bluetooth speaker.

And when the chorus chimes in . . .

For the love of God, I'm going to fucking lose it.

"We will . . . we will . . . rock books."

Boom. Boom. Clap.

"Mr. Turner," Jeremy Whitehead says while raising his hand. "It's hard for me to focus on these chapters with that music."

"I'm aware, Jeremy," I say, unfolding my arms and pushing off my desk. I glance at the clock on the wall and note we have five minutes left in class. Typically, I'd force my students to read until the end of class and pack up when the bell rings, but given the circumstances . . . "You can pack up. Remember the first three chapters must be read by tomorrow. There will be a quiz. If you're in my class, you know we work hard, so be prepared to put in the time."

I round my desk and make a show of writing something on a notepad, when in reality, I'm counting down the minutes in my head before I can march next door and put an end to this godforsaken calamity.

This . . . this is why I didn't want Dewitt to hire Greer

Gibson, because during her interview, she was very expressive about her "offbeat" teaching style. She wants the students to care about the books, rather than just read them. She wants to give them a chance to understand them, appreciate them by using alternative methods.

That interview . . . it was, quite frankly, embarrassing. Watching her falter from confident to ignorant. When she left, I actually laughed, wondering if asking her to come in was a joke, but when Dewitt was serious about hiring her, I had to take a calming breath.

She couldn't be serious.

A teacher who prides herself on using teaching methods like movies and children's picture books to help understand literature? This is a serious high school, not a dainty, hippie-filled educational system.

This is Forest Heights, the most prestigious public school in the country—at least that's what was said last year.

Greer Gibson has no right to be teaching here.

And no . . . this has nothing to do with her saying I'm an elitist.

This has everything to do with her being underqualified, unprofessional, a disturbance, and not the right fit for the Forest Heights English department.

The department I'm in charge of. I will *not* tolerate her making a mockery of teaching high school English.

Slamming on desks and belting out nonsensical lyrics by a seventies rock band is a prime example of her incompetence. And not only is it an elementary approach to learning, it's been a massive disruption to every single class I've had today. Her inability to appropriately teach has taken away my first day intimidation tactics, the same tactics I use every year to set my expectations.

The bell rings. Class is dismissed, and I wait a whole two minutes before I stand tall, lift the sleeves of my green cardigan, and make my way to the classroom next door.

Unfortunately, I share a wall with Greer. I knew going into the school year that was going to be the case. I wasn't aware I'd be making a visit on the first day.

Thankful for lunch break, I charge through her door, only to be slapped in the face with an obnoxious amount of color pinned to the walls. Her room is decorated like it's for kindergartners, not high schoolers. A "reading corner" is in the back. A rainbow of color spans across the walls, one hue rolling into the next. It's ridiculous and childish. Just like the woman standing before me.

"Oh, Arlo. You startled me." Greer chuckles, sitting at her desk, a salad in front of her.

I close the door behind me and set my hands on my hips. "What the hell are you doing here?"

She glances at her lunch and then back at me. "Uh, eating my lunch. What does it look like?"

Through clenched teeth, I say, "During your classes?"

"Oh . . . uh . . . pumping the kids up for the school year. I want to establish a rapport with them, let them know it isn't going to be a stuffy English class of Shakespearean knaves and knaps."

"So you decide to disturb every other classroom around you?"

She faces me now, a look of shock on her face. "You heard my music?"

"The walls aren't soundproof."

She taps her chin. "Hmm . . . I guess I never thought about that."

"Shocking," I mutter.

"Hey." She stands and closes the space between us.

It's hard not to notice the skirt she's wearing and how it clings to her hips, or the tucked-in button-up shirt that leaves no room for the imagination, or the way her hair is pinned up into a bun, highlighting the curves and contours of her face. Coraline might have been right. Greer is slightly my type.

Only slightly and only physically.

With her manicured index finger, Greer pokes me in the chest and says, "What's your problem? Are you this rude to everyone?"

"Just turn it down; some of us have to actually teach."

"As opposed to what I'm doing?"

"I have no idea what you're doing besides being a disturbance in this school."

She rears back. "Wow, you're something else." She shakes her head, moving to her desk. "Principal Dewitt has the utmost respect for you." She gives me a slow once over. "I can't possibly see why. You've been nothing but an ass to me since I arrived."

"Respect isn't just given, you have to earn it," I reply.

"Clearly." Folding her arms, she turns to face me. "So what is it, Arlo? Why are you so hostile around me? Does it really stem from the interview? Because we're fighting and I have no idea why. Did you want someone else to be hired?"

"Yes," I answer.

"Oh, so you're being a petulant child because you didn't get your way. I get it."

"I'm not being a petulant child," I say. "I didn't care who got the job, all I cared about was hiring an individual whose teaching abilities matched the Forest Heights standards. Your predecessor came in with the same unconventional attitude as you did, and do you know what happened?"

"They were well received by the students?" She smacks on a charming smile.

"No, he got caught up in being friends with the students, lost control of the classroom, preliminary test scores dropped drastically, and I was forced to step in and help tutor his failing students. I spent what little free time I had making sure *his* students were prepared. I refuse to let that happen again."

The anger on her face slightly dissipates as she says, "Well, that's not going to be me."

I gesture to her room, and say, "From what I've heard so far, from what I've experienced, and from your lack of professionalism in the classroom, I'd say you're going to be worse."

"Lack of professionalism? Uh, hello, kettle, you're black."

"If I'm showing any hints of being unprofessional, it's because you've driven me past a point of irritation today. You realize you've set a standard today for those students, letting them know they're here to goof off, instead of instilling in them the expectations you're going to have of them? But, then again, you're used to the cacophonous noise of a rowdy gym atmosphere. Your athletic credentials by far exceed your teaching credentials . . ."

Straightening, Greer asks, "Are you saying I got the job because I can coach volleyball?"

"Sure as hell didn't get it because you know how to ceremoniously lead a chant."

"What the hell is that supposed to mean?" she shoots back, coming up to me again, her body now inches from mine as she stands five inches shorter than me.

"This is your first teaching job, correct?"

"Yes," she says, crossing her arms over her chest. Striking the defense, didn't see that coming. *Sense the sarcasm?*

"And you realize Forest Heights is one of the premier high schools in the country, academically, right?"

"Well aware."

"And that since we're so close to Brentwood University and their rich athletic program, we have to compete with the legacy of excellent athletics in the area."

"Your point?" she asks, sounding exasperated.

"You weren't hired because you can convince a group of hormonal teenagers to clap and stomp together about loving books. You were hired for your athletic résumé. Nothing more."

"And why is that a problem?"

"Because you fall under my department," I say, taking a

33

step closer. Her fresh scent of mint and lavender crawl into my space, but I don't allow the sweet smell to distract me. "I don't mess around, Miss Gibson. When the PARCC testing comes around, I hold all teachers in the English department to the same standard. It's why we're the best public high school in the country. I'll be damned if that changes because Principal Dewitt felt we needed a coach over a teacher."

Her lips purse to the side as she studies me, silence heavy, like a vacuum sucking the air between us. "Thou art so easy to judge, Arlo Turner."

My brow quirks up. "Was that your pitiful attempt at Shakespeare?"

"Did it not impress your hoity underpants?"

"No. Now if you'd have said 'Thou art a boil. A plague soul, an embossed carbuncle' like in King Lear, then I'd have been impressed. Alas, you once again disappoint me."

Her eyes narrow. "If you insist on being a prick, I suggest you leave, because I have nothing else to say to you."

Hands in my pockets, I take a small step back. With my eyes trained on hers, I say, "Keep it down, or I'll be sure to let Principal Dewitt know you're distracting my students from their learning."

"Of course you would." She motions two fingers across her forehead. "You have tattletale written all over you." She walks back to her desk and mutters, "Narc."

Without another word, I turn on my heel and head back to my classroom.

I gave her fair warning.

Let's just hope she takes it.

Chapter Three

GREER

"Why didn't you tell me Turner was going to be such an asshole?"

"Mr. Turns Me On is an asshole?" Stella asks sarcastically as she stands next to me, clipboard in hand, assessing the tryout warmups. "Hard to tell when I can't stop staring at his ass in jeans. I mean . . . have you looked at it?"

Unfortunately.

And it's nice.

But not as nice as his eyes.

Or expansive hands.

Or the indent between his pecs that his T-shirts effortlessly show.

"No, I haven't," I lie through my teeth. "I've only been privy to his obnoxious and stuffy personality." Calling out to the girls who are currently doing plyometrics, I say, "Get those butts lower."

"Did you have a run-in with him today?"

"You could say that. He came storming into my classroom during lunch to let me know exactly how he felt about my day one amp up."

"Not a fan?"

"Not even a little. He made it quite clear he's not a fan of me."

"Well, we knew that, but he outright said it? Impressive."

"Yup," I say, clapping my hands, encouraging the girls from the sidelines. "Told me I wasn't hired based on my teaching credentials and he'll be damned if I bring down his precious statewide testing scores. Like . . . get a life, dude, there's more to life than tests."

Stella shakes her head. "Not with Turner. Those exams are his life. And I'm not taking his side, trust me, but now that I think about it, I do remember Brock and Gunner telling me about all the extra hours Arlo was putting in for Gregory Hiddleson, the teacher before you. He was truly annoyed by it, but that's how dedicated he is to it. He'll pick up the slack for other teachers to make sure the students are prepared. I know you probably don't want to hear it, but he's helped bring Forest Heights to its premier status, plus he made the opt-in option for out-of-school-boundaries open to low-income families only."

I pause. "Did he really?"

Stella nods. "Yup. It's important to him that everyone gets a fair shot at a great education. That doesn't mean he takes it easy on anyone, because he doesn't, but he still is quite aware that we're a rich school in the suburbs of Chicago."

"I see." I chew on that information, sort of wishing he was more of a dick. I still feel angry that he judged me so . . . fiercely. I graduated top of my class and received excellent referrals from my student-teaching mentors. For that reason, I'm trying not to take his words to heart. *But . . .*

"He's still an asshole." Stella nudges my shoulder.

Perking up, I nod. "One hundred percent."

"And I think you should continue to teach the way you know best."

"Agreed." I lift my chin. "And if it drives him crazy, then that's his problem."

"Honestly, him coming to your classroom today, telling you—"

"He said he'd tell Dewitt."

Stella pauses and slowly turns toward me. "He didn't."

I nod. "He did."

"Well then . . ." She puffs out her chest. "It's one thing to be an asshole, it's another to threaten my friend. With Gregory, he went to Dewitt as well—I mean, it was justified, but I think we need to get Mr. Turns Me On to loosen up a bit so he's not associating you with Gregory."

"Why do you have that conniving look on your face?"

"He needs to learn to have some fun."

"What's your version of fun?" I ask.

"This means war."

"War?" Uh, that doesn't sound good, and I am the new girl. *Is this a risk I shouldn't be taking?*

"Yup. War . . . and I know exactly who to ask for help."

━━━

"I FAIL to recognize how irritating Arlo Turner falls on my shoulders." Keiko adjusts her goggles before measuring out a blue solution into a thin beaker.

Exasperated, Stella says, "It doesn't fall on your shoulders, Keeks. We'd like your assistance. And we're not irritating him, we're just . . . having fun."

"Why, precisely?"

"Because he needs to learn to have fun, and we're asking you for help, because you're really smart and you have fun things in your lab that we could use to our advantage."

She straightens, and that's when I get a good look at her

slight shoulders in a boxy white lab coat, her safety goggles perfectly covering her green-rimmed glasses, and her long black hair tied into a low ponytail at the nape of her neck. She wears science well. "My lab is meant for education, not for the purpose of a row of the sexes."

"This isn't a row of the sexes."

I'll be honest, what Stella is considering as fun doesn't seem fun for Arlo—it might only piss him off more—but . . . the immature side of me can't help but think he was a mean jerk face and he deserves Stella's version of *fun*.

He might have the school's best interests at heart, but the dude has been a dick to me from the get-go. Instead of getting to know me, he's prejudged me—ahem, Mr. Darcy—and that's not fair.

And also, I've read quite a few research papers about a positive work environment and the effects of a happy teacher in the classroom. A bright, cheery, and relaxed teacher encourages open minds, broadens the comfort level, and helps kids absorb more material. It's time we help pull the stick out of Arlo's ass and maybe show him what loosening up can do.

Leaning on the table with her elbows—we're both wearing safety gear as well, per Keiko's demand—Stella says, "He was rude to our dear friend, Greer."

Cocking her head to the side, confusion laced in her brow, Keiko asks me, "Are we dear friends?"

"Uh . . . aren't we?"

She studies me, and I have this tiny inkling that, in her head, she's calculating my worth. She then turns to Stella. "Are we dear friends too?"

"Hell yeah, girl. We always eat together in the teachers' lounge. And remember that time we went to the bar together after our teacher fun league? You told me all about the gases on planet Earth and I actually learned something instead of going home with another ape of a man."

"I do recall those events but was unaware of the amplified

attachment that materialized post 'bar hang.'" Looking sincere, Keiko says, "We bonded."

"We did, Keeks. Why do you think I always hang out with you?"

"Never gave it much consideration."

From across the science table, Stella nudges Keiko. "Well, consider us bonded. And because Greer is my friend, that automatically makes you friends, too."

Keiko shakes her head. "Not necessarily. There are circumstances to consider when bonding yourself with another human being. Just because you chose Greer to be part of your wolfpack doesn't mean that, by default, I choose her as well."

Isn't that nice?

Turning to me, Keiko asks, "What do you have to offer me in friendship that's different from what Stella offers me?"

Uhhh . . .

"Choosing cronies to associate yourself with is critical in the image you plan to portray to society. If I were to accept the comradery of everyone, what would that say about my character?"

"That you're a people person?" I ask, rather than state, wondering how on earth we got to this point in the conversation.

"Precisely. And I'm not a people person. Therefore, it is within your best interest to acquaint me with your savviest attributes so I can formulate an educated decision if we should adhere ourselves in agreeability."

Exhausted from Keiko's choice of words, I look to Stella, who's now leaning on the table with one elbow, enjoying herself way too much. "Tell Keeks why you're worthy of her friendship."

Okay, didn't think this was going to be an interview, but I guess if I want her help, I'm going to have to convince her why . . .

"Well, I know how to keep secrets. I never gossip about my friends, which is important to me."

"Trust, don't find that often in a world full of social media," Stella says, while . . . oh Jesus, while Keiko is jotting down notes.

When finished, she looks up at me and nods. "Proceed."

"Okay . . . uh . . . I know how to cook."

"Love a good homemade meal, don't you know, Keeks?" Stella asks while rubbing her stomach.

After writing something down, Keiko looks up and answers, "My attempts at being an accomplished hand in the kitchen have been feeble at best. Having a friend who is consummate in culinary dexterity would be quite favorable. What would be your most polished dish?"

"Boxed mac and cheese," I answer. She frowns and starts to write a note. "Wait, I was kidding. That was a joke."

"Ah . . . uproarious." She makes another note.

I hope that's a good funny. She didn't laugh, just let out a soft snort.

"I can make a ton of different things, ranging from enchiladas to the classic meatloaf with accompanying sauce and mashed potatoes, to homemade pasta."

"I see." She taps her chin with her pen. "And how do you fare with desserts?"

"I, uh . . . I fare well. This past weekend, I made a homemade blueberry pie."

"Do you have evidence of this endeavor?" Keiko asks, looking over her notepad at me with a quirked eyebrow.

"Yes. I do. I posted it on my Instagram. Humble brag, you know." I pull out my phone and quickly click on the app, where I find the picture, and turn the screen toward Keiko.

With a studious eye, she gives it a good look over and then writes something on her notepad. "Visually, it stimulates my appetite. But with no hashtag, no filter, how can I confirm the true nature of this picture?"

"I didn't think that was necessary. There's no filter on this picture."

"Is there any left?"

I wince. "Well, actually, I was hungover on Sunday, so I kind of might have sort have eaten the whole thing."

"Total consumption." She nods, writes more notes, and then brings her clipboard to her chest, where she grips it tightly. "From this brief conversation, some quick calculations I've made, along with your admission to consuming your entire pie in one day, I can confidently surmise that we have the potential for friendship."

"Okay." I glance over at Stella, still confused. "So . . . does that mean you'll help us?"

"It does. But . . . Greer, you are currently on a trial basis. If I don't find our individual identities are compatible, then we must sever our coupling."

"Sure . . . yeah. But I really think we could be good friends."

"I concur with your hypothesis." Keiko gives me a curt nod.

I don't know what just happened, but I guess I'm glad that it did. I have another friend, a friend who seems quite loyal once she's attached. I need loyal right now, especially when my classroom neighbor is moody.

"Good. Glad that's solved," Stella says, standing. "Now we need an action plan."

"Something subtle, but also something that says don't mess with us," I add.

"I say we start small, make him question what's happening around him, and then slowly increase the severity of the pranks," Stella says.

Keiko nods in agreement. "Labored manipulation over a certain frequency has proven to be quite successful." She flips the page of her notebook and rests it on the table. Pen poised, she says, "Here's what we're going to do."

Masterfully, Keiko starts laying the groundwork as I smirk excitedly to myself.

Arlo Turner is going to wish he never messed with me.

Let's just hope he doesn't figure out it's me . . . but even if he does, at least I know I have a little secret in my back pocket.

Principal Nyema Dewitt really likes me.

Really, really freaking likes me.

At least that's what I think.

⬚

"ROBOTICS. Are you comfortable with such machinery?" Keiko taps her pen on the desk.

"Uh, I haven't really worked with anything robotic before."

"The only robotics experience I have is with my dildo," Stella says, unwrapping one of the sandwiches we had delivered to school for lunch. "But that's handheld, you know. It's not like I'm using a remote control."

"Phallic mechanics doesn't convert to the type of experience I'm pursuing."

"I played with a remote-control car once," I offer.

Keiko eyes meet mine. "Remember, we're on a trial basis."

Laughing softly, I hold up her sandwich. "Turkey melt?'"

She eyes it and then takes it from me. "Don't mind if I do."

⬚

"EXPLOSIVE BUBBLES?" Stella asks. "That seems a little extreme."

"Although a great idea," I say, treading carefully, you know, since I'm friends on a trial basis. "I think we need to consider what Arlo will be doing in the classroom. He's won't necessarily be playing around with bubbles while teaching AP

English. The man couldn't even stand a little music on the first day. I doubt he's going to be dabbling in bubbles anytime soon."

"Hmm, that does create a predicament." Keiko takes a bite of her sandwich and thinks on it for a few seconds before perking up. "We could fashion an automatic bubble blower in the vents and blow explosive bubbles into his room."

"Can't we just buy those popper things, place them under the legs of his chair, and when he sits, they pop and scare the crap out of him?" Stella asks.

Keiko pauses and hums to herself. Her eyes flit back and forth as if she's solving an equation in her head. When she's done, she looks at Stella. "That could work. Less risk, still great reward. I shall note it."

<hr />

"THERE HAS TO BE A WAY," Keiko says in distress.

I glance at the clock and realize we have five minutes left until lunch is over.

"I think what we have so far is great, Keeks." Her head perks up at me using her nickname. I wait for her to mention it, but she doesn't; instead, she fixates on the one thing she's been fixating on for the last five minutes.

"We can't possibly accumulate the proper conclusion to each prank without inserting a digital monitor inside on his person to audit pulse rate, blood pressure, dilation of the eyes——"

"Keeks, deep breath," Stella says. "For this experiment, we're going to have to fall back to classic observation."

"Such courses of action are for peons." She slams her fist on the table.

"Yes, but unless you have an invisibility cloak and invisible monitors, we're going to have to go with observation."

She sighs. "I'll research the probability of the invisibility cloak."

———

"JUST A FEW MORE, HURRY UP," I say to Stella, who is taking her damn time turning desks around.

When Keiko said we begin small, she meant it. She thought starting the plan too close to the argument would be obvious, so we decided to initiate phase one of a thirty-phase program—yeah, I'm not doing all thirty phases—on Friday, so we could gauge his reaction on a day that would bring him joy, then lead into a weekend.

Keiko wants to consider all factors when we move forward. It's why I had to do some recon work and find his syllabus for the year, so we can see if any of his reactions are environmental. Honestly, the whole concept of conducting experiments on Arlo Turner had me giggling all week. Especially once Keiko showed me the spreadsheet she came up with to keep track of Arlo's attitude. She complained once again about not being able to gauge his vitals and told me she wasn't giving up on the invisibility cloak just yet. She's bound and determined to gather the most conclusive evidence.

"Why do the desks have to be at a precise seventeen-degree angle?" Stella asks.

"I don't know. Keiko said something about just enough of a turn to be noticed, but not enough to be obvious."

"I guess that makes sense."

"Don't question her, just listen to the mastermind."

"I still don't understand why she's not here."

I shrug. "Something to do with not wanting to be caught in the act, even though this was her plan."

"Behind-the-scenes villain. I feel her on that," Stella says, measuring out seventeen degrees. I have to admit, the slight turn isn't obvious. Just annoying. All the desks are turned just enough to face away from where Turner stands at the front of the class.

"Two more and then we're—"

"What are you doing?"

Stella and I both snap to attention and turn toward the door, where Gunner Klein and Brock "Romeo" Romero stand, arms crossed over their bulky, well-built chests.

Crap.

Just from what Stella has told me, the two physical education teachers are good friends with Arlo. Finding us changing his desks doesn't bode well for the plan.

Keiko is going to be so disappointed.

"Uh . . . sweeping," I say, showing absolutely zero confidence in my answer.

"Sweeping?" Gunner asks, stepping into the room, Romeo close behind him. "You're sweeping a carpeted floor?"

"Yes?"

"Without a broom?" He quirks a brow.

"Sweeping with my feet." I start moving my foot back and forth, gathering no dirt whatsoever. Eyes on Stella, I encourage her to join me, but she betrays me and instead sits on a desk and lets out a long sigh. Great help she is. "You know, there's nothing like a faux vacuum line to give the illusion of a clean classroom."

"These carpets don't leave vacuum lines," Romeo says, his eyes following the swing of Stella's legs.

"It's . . . uh . . . the thought that counts?" I shrug, arms out.

Turning to Romeo, Gunner says, "You have to give her credit for sticking to her lie."

"Unlike her friend over there who bailed quickly."

Casual, Stella says, "Rather not make a fool of myself."

"Thanks a lot, Stella," I sarcastically say.

"What's the use at this point? They already caught us, and now they're going to go run to their overlord and tell him that we're messing with his room. There's no use." She leans back on the table and sticks her breasts in the air.

What the hell is she doing over there?

"You really think we're going to run to Arlo?" Romeo says, walking over to one of the desks and taking a seat.

Stella gives him a smooth once-over, taking her time by starting at his Adidas sneakers and working her way up his black athletic pants to his tight-fitting dri-fit shirt, and then lands on his handsome, carved face. "Yes . . . I do."

"Then you don't know us at all," Romeo counters.

"You're right, we don't know you." Stella directs her attention to Gunner and asks, "So, are you going to tell him?"

Walking farther into the room, Gunner says, "Depends. What are you two doing?"

"Vacuuming—"

"Messing with him because he was rude to Greer on her first day, and he needs to learn to loosen up," Stella says. *Where's the girl's loyalty?*

"The music, stomping, and clapping," Gunner says with a slow nod. "We heard all about it."

"Seriously?" I ask. "He was complaining about it? God, he needs to get a life."

"He does," Romeo says with a smirk.

"So you're fucking with his pristine classroom?" Gunner says, taking in the desks. "Well done, ladies."

I perk up. "Well, thank you."

"Subtle, just annoying enough to drive him crazy."

"That's what we were going for," I say with pride, fixing the last two desks. "So, you're not going to tell him?"

"Oh no." Gunner shakes his head. "We're going to tell him."

"What?" I ask, as Stella scoffs and mutters something unintelligible under her breath. "What do you mean you're going to tell him? I thought we were establishing some kind of rapport here."

"You have to give us a reason not to tell him," Romeo says with a smirk.

"Oh Christ," Stella mumbles, pushing her hand through her hair. "You want us to play in that ridiculous teacher league, don't you?"

"What teacher league?" I ask, looking between the two of them.

"We can't have Esther Maximillian and her elderly cohort playing with us anymore—they can barely walk without a cane, let alone participate in the league."

"I told you after what happened last year, never again."

"What happened last year? What the hell are you talking about?"

Stepping in, Gunner says, "The teacher league is a once-a-year competition chosen by the winning school from the previous year. Right before winter break, we engage in an all-out ravenous brawl for the title of best faculty in the area. Depending on what the winning team picks, the sport could range from bowling, to basketball, to badminton . . . to a hot dog eating contest." I wince. Ugh, not for me. "We convene for one sweaty weekend of competition, and the winner takes the pot of cash for their school."

"How much?"

"Ten thousand dollars."

"Seriously?" I ask.

"Don't fall for whatever steam they're about to blow up your ass about helping out the kids and the school," Stella says, clearly bitter. "Keeks and I competed last year, and, come to find out, these two idiots weren't trying to win the money, but trying to beat their rival over at Marjorie Edith High. We were playing volleyball and, somehow, Romeo tripped while trying to hit the ball and used my shorts to try to break his fall, flashing my thong-clad ass to the entire teacher league."

"I said I was sorry," Romeo grumbles. "And I told you, you

47

had a really nice ass. Everyone enjoyed the sight, me included."

"And I told you to go drown in your own bodily fluids." Stella pushes her hair behind her ears. "Keeks was positively horrified when she saw my bare ass. You short-circuited her."

A snort pops out of me before I can stop it, drawing attention in my direction. I quickly wipe under my nose and ask, "So, what are you trying to say? If we join this league, you won't tell Arlo?"

"Exactly," Romeo says.

"I mean . . . I guess—"

"No way," Stella says, standing up and coming to my side. "The league is a long commitment dealing with two narcissistic assholes who think they're God's gift to sports."

"Because we are," Romeo says with a smirk.

"Whoop-de-do, you knew how to throw a ball around a field. The glory days are over, move on." Boy, is Stella spicy right now. There has to be more to this story about Romeo and her that I'm unaware of. "If we agree to do the league, then we have some terms."

"Why do you have terms?" Gunner asks, going to Romeo's side, all of us taking stances, ready to face off. "We're the ones who are helping *you* out."

"That's what you'd like to think," Stella says. "But we all know that's not the case. Sure, whatever, Arlo finds out about the tables. He gets angry, what's new? But if we don't join your league, you're stuck with Esther again."

Romeo and Gunner both clench their jaws, and I know Stella has them. God, I love this girl.

"So, we're going to play it like this," Stella says. Motioning between us with two fingers, she states, "We'll join the league —two division-one, full-ride athletes—as long as you don't tell Arlo about the desks . . . or the rest of the pranks we have planned." Their eyes widen with humor. "And you report back to us with his reaction to every single one of them."

"You want us to spy on our friend?"

"Not necess—" I start.

"Yes," Stella finishes. "We want to know how pissed he is, how annoyed, if he's onto us. Every little detail you can muster up in those pea-sized brains of yours. And in exchange, we'll play in your teacher league."

Gunner turns to Romeo, making a show of it. "They drive a hard bargain."

"Positively evil, if you ask me." Romeo smirks. "But nothing would give me more pleasure than to watch Arlo squirm."

I match his smile.

Turning toward us, the boys close the distance and hold out their hands. "Deal."

As we shake their hands, Stella says, "And that's how it's done."

Chapter Four

ARLO

"Stop fucking with me, was it you?" I ask Romeo, who can't stop laughing as we walk into the Atomic Saloon, our bar of choice that's far enough away from Brentwood University that we don't have to worry about college students and is far too fancy for any high schoolers trying to jump in with fake IDs.

"Why on earth would I move your desks around? Dude, probably the cleaning staff."

That was not the work of the cleaning staff.

That was the work of someone trying to fuck with me, and there are two people dumb enough to do that.

Romeo and Gunner.

"Cleaning staff doesn't move desks mere inches, and all precisely, as well."

"Is he still harping about the desks?" Gunner asks, coming up behind us.

"Yup. Shocking. Arlo can't let it go," Romeo says as we find a booth.

The swanky industrial style bar is dimly lit by low-hanging Eisenhower lights encased in glass globes, giving a warm hue to the room. Encased in deep-red exposed brick, the bar sits center stage, while navy blue leather booths flank the outer ring. In the back, sectioned off by plexiglass garage doors and black trim, are four pool tables with accompanying high-top tables. The space gives just enough room to those who want to be loud, those who want to watch the game, and those who just need to sit back and relax for a drink.

Still irritated by the desks—I know they were the culprits—I pick up the menu and search out a new drink. It was a long first week. Dealing with Greer and her music on the first day, then having to hear about how innovative Greer is from another English teacher, along with the desks, my advanced students who think they know everything—they don't—and then add in my nagging sister, I'm ready for some strong liquid encouragement to start off the weekend.

The first week in a new semester is always hard. You're trying to find your rhythm. Getting to know the students, seeing how far you can push them, how far they're going to push you. The kids always think they're being original in their pranks and smart-assery, but I've been teaching high schoolers for eight years now, so I'm rarely surprised. It's hard not to feel that initial burst of excitement at the idea of molding young minds, believing you can make a difference. In the next few weeks, I expect to establish a solid routine full of expectations that will take us through the winter break. At least, that's what I'm hoping for.

"Why are you looking at a menu?" Romeo asks, eyes on the TV that's just off to the right. The Bobbies are playing the Pittsburgh Steel tonight, so I know we'll be parked here for at least a few hours. "You always get the same thing."

"Changing it up," I answer, even though the whiskey is calling to me.

"Going to get one of those lady cocktails you're always admiring?" Gunner asks, eyes on the TV as well.

Not to sound like a nagging partner that's being ignored, but . . . looks like I'll be spending the night with the sides of my friend's faces.

"Knox has been on fire this year," Gunner says. "His bat is fucking insane."

"I'd be shocked if the Bobbies don't take the World Series," Romeo says. "When offense and defense are both clicking, you're unstoppable."

"Thinking about the lady bird drink," I say, knowing neither of them are paying attention.

"Oh . . ." they both say and then high-five each other like a couple of barbarians. "Nothing gets past the middle infield," Romeo says. "Carson and Knox are unstoppable."

"Or maybe the camel milk cocktail."

"Knox is easily in contention for another Golden Glove Award," Gunner says. "What I wouldn't give to have him and Carson behind me on the mound again."

"Nah, I think I'm going to go with the diamonds are forever cocktail."

"Dude, no one cares what you get," Gunner says, surprising me. "Just shut up about it so I can hear the announcers."

"Why are you here if you could have watched the game at home?" I ask, setting my menu down.

"Because you were crying about your desks, and I figured I'd try to lend some support," Gunner says, turning toward me during a commercial.

"I wasn't crying about the desks."

"You haven't stopped talking about it."

"Because you did it," I say. "Figured if I berate you enough, you won't do it again."

"Do you really think that's going to work?" Romeo asks.

I sigh, knowing the outcome instantaneously. "No . . ."

"Then shut up about the desks," Gunner says right as a waitress comes to our table.

"Good evening, gentlemen, what can I get for you?"

"Three house burgers, two lagers, and a lady finger for this one," Gunner says, thumbing toward me.

Annoyed, I look up at her and say, "Whiskey, neat. Thank you."

"Sure."

Without writing anything down, she takes off. "So how are things with Lindsay and Dylan?" I ask when the waitress is out of earshot.

A few weeks ago, Gunner found out he's the father of an eight-year-old. We ran into Lindsay Nelson, Knox Gentry's wife's best friend—did you follow that?—at a teachers' conference before the school year started, and not only does she have a kid, but it's Gunner's. They have history that dates back to college. I don't know much about it, all I know is Gunner isn't going to let Lindsay slip through his fingers this time, especially since he's the father of her child.

"Slow. Hence why I'm here and not hanging out with them on a Friday night. Trust me, I'd rather be at Lindsay's place watching the game than here with you two."

"I can really feel the love," Romeo says, clutching his heart.

Gunner pushes his hand through his hair. "I wish Lindsay would move a little faster. Hell, Dylan doesn't know I'm his dad yet, he just thinks I'm the cool guy his mom is dating."

"At least he doesn't consider you the douche his mom is dating," I reply. "Like we do."

"Good one." Romeo chuckles.

Ignoring us, Gunner says, "I hate that they're in that small apartment when I have a goddamn house by the lake. I have so much room for them."

"Yeah, but one step at a time, man," Romeo says, growing serious. "You can't pressure her, and you can't move fast with Dylan. You have to make sure you build those bonds first."

"I know." He sighs. "Let's not talk about that shit right now, it'll only depress me. Let's talk about Arlo's obvious attraction to Miss Gibson."

"What?" I ask, just as our drinks are dropped off at our table. "Where the hell did that come from?"

"Dude, it's obvious," Romeo says.

"How so?" I challenge him.

"Uh . . . the way you look at her."

"That's a generalization and not true. I look at her like anyone else would. I also haven't spoken to her since Monday, so how would you observe my interaction with her? Plus, I'm fucking over this conversation. It's like we're on a goddamn hamster wheel."

"Jesus," Gunner says, blowing out a long breath. "Chill, dude. From that reaction right there, it's clear you have a crush on her."

"When did you two become so immature?"

Romeo lifts his beer to his lips. "Always have been immature, you're probably just realizing it now."

"Unfortunate for me."

"You put in the time building a friendship without putting in adequate research before befriending us. Very unlike you, Turner." Gunner smirks.

"It was you two or Kelvin Thimble, and I'm not really into Dungeons and Dragons."

"Thimble is a stand-up guy," Romeo says. "He has a thing for Keiko."

"Everyone knows that," Gunner says. "He practically writes Mr. Keiko Seymour on all of his notepads."

Taking a sip of my drink, I say, "Never said he wasn't a good guy, just not into all of that cosplay stuff."

"But you'd look adorable all dressed up," Gunner teases while tickling me under my chin.

"Get the fuck out of here," I say, pushing his hand away just as I sense two people walk up to our table.

Before I can turn to look, I watch a large grin spread across Romeo's face as he says, "Well, well, well. What brought you ladies here?"

There can only be one reason for that grin.

I look to the side and find Stella Garcia standing next to us, Greer Gibson right behind her. They must be fresh from practice because both of them have their hair pulled up, Greer's in a long ponytail, Stella's in a bun. They're both wearing Forest Heights Volleyball shorts and black leggings with tennis shoes.

The outfit does nothing for me.

Now the blouse and skirt Greer wore the other day . . .

Folding her arms, Stella says, "Needed a beer after a long, torturous practice." She nods toward the TV. "Watching the game?"

"Always, want to join?" Romeo pats the seat next to him and Stella takes it—and his drink—without a blink. And then, just like that, Greer is left to awkwardly stand at the foot of our table while Gunner, Romeo, and Stella all turn to watch the game.

Christ.

I look up at Greer, who doesn't look like she knows what to do.

Neither do I.

I'm not in the mood to keep someone company, but it doesn't seem like our friends are going to be talking much tonight.

"All right, three burgers," the waitress says, coming up behind Greer and shifting around her so she can set the plates down.

"Thanks," Stella says, taking my plate. Uh, what the actual fuck? "I'm starving."

She pops a fry in her mouth while the waitress asks if we

need anything else. "We're good, thanks," Romeo says, waving her off.

Growing irritated, I twist my cup on the table and say, "What the hell is going on?"

Romeo glances up and smiles. "Think I ordered that burger for you?"

"Jesus." I stand from the table with my drink in hand, push past Greer, and go to an empty corner at the bar. I expect Greer to take my empty seat, so I'm surprised when I see the bar-height chair next to me pull out. "Not in the mood," I say, drowning the rest of my drink in one gulp.

"That's obvious," Greer says. "But I'm not about to sit there and listen to the stat brothers talk through the entire game."

"So you think sitting next to me is better?"

"Only marginally. Jury is still out. I might go take a seat by myself."

"Might be a good idea."

I feel her tense next to me and I prepare for an onslaught of "what the hell is your problem" and "why do you hate me" questions. But she doesn't say anything. Instead, when the bartender comes over to us, she orders a simple Blue Moon and a quesadilla. I order another burger and a second drink.

And then we sit in silence.

She pulls out her phone, and she sets it on the bar, tapping away on it.

I stare down at my refreshed drink, turning the glass every so often and then taking a sip.

Our food is delivered and we eat in silence. I admit to myself that her quesadilla looks really good. I even consider saying it out loud but then think better of it. The last thing I want to do is lead her to think I care enough to make the comment.

Because I don't.

Once I'm finished with this burger, I'm out.

But for some reason, I slow down as I eat. From the corner of my eyes, I watch as she spreads salsa over a triangle of quesadilla and then slowly lifts it up to her mouth. Her lips wrap around the food as she bites down, and then her eyes close while she chews, as if she's performing the most erotic act and trying to win an Academy Award for it.

Hell, the way her tongue peeks out to swipe away at the salsa, I'd vote for her. That single movement could easily win awards.

And then, just like that, my mind turns on in the worst way possible.

What would she be like in bed?

Fuck . . . it doesn't matter.

She's young.

She's a subordinate.

She's not your type . . .

Okay, that last one is a goddamn lie. I don't have a type, but I have fucking eyes, and this woman is gorgeous. An innocent face with dangerously seductive eyes. Long, lithe legs that could easily wrap around any man's waist. Beautiful lips, full on the bottom, just a tad thinner on top, but curved and plush, a distraction I could easily see myself getting lost in.

And that's why it's a good idea I'm keeping my distance, because I don't need to get mixed up in some kind of co-worker relationship, especially with a woman whose teaching tactics don't even fall close to my standards. I can't deny her . . . intelligence, given she graduated from UCLA. I won't let a physical attraction derail my purpose of ensuring Forest Heights keeps its academic preeminence. There. *Done.*

Head down, I spend the next few moments focusing on my burger, and once I push the plate away, and take one more sip of my drink, I'm ready to bounce, when Greer turns to me in her seat.

"Was that enough silence for you?"

"What?" I ask, confused.

"Did I shut up enough for you? Is that how you treat your students in the classroom as well?"

What the hell?

She hops off her chair and pulls on my arm, forcing me to get off my chair as well.

"What the hell do you think you're doing?"

"We're playing pool."

I glance over at the empty game section. "Yeah, I'm good. I'm going home."

"Nope." She shakes her head and pulls on my arm, trying to force me to budge. I'll hand it to her, she's strong . . . but not stronger than me. "Jesus, it's not like I'm taking you into lava."

"No, you're just taking me to play pool when I want to go home."

Letting up, she looks me in the eyes and says, "Why are you so crabby all the time? Do you even know what a good time is?"

"I do."

"I don't believe you."

"Do you really believe reverse psychology is going to work on me?"

She glances to the side, her teeth pulling on her bottom lip. My eyes immediately fixate on that little movement. Her white ivories tugging carefully, rolling, enticing me . . .

"I was kind of hoping that it would. Hoping that maybe you know English but not other things."

"I know everything."

"Yeah, sure. Bet you don't know how to play pool," she says, egging me on.

"Told you that wasn't going to work."

"Yeah, you don't know how to play. Instead of using the pool cue, you like to stick it up your ass to make sure you stay uptight at all times."

My eyes narrow.

"I'm right, aren't I?" She nods toward me. "There's one up there right now."

"Are you always this childish?"

"Are you always this soul-sucking?" she counters, crossing her arms over her chest.

I contemplate leaving, not giving her the pleasure of goading me, but then I think about how good it'll feel to destroy her on the pool table. Especially an overly confident athlete like her, now *that* would be soul-sucking.

Without a word, I push past her and head to the empty pool tables. I can practically feel her "winning" grin behind me. She thinks she bested me. She didn't. I'm just back here to teach her a lesson.

Catching up to me, she asks, "So . . . are you any good?"

"Yes."

"You are?"

When we reach the pool cues, I hand her one and grab one myself, then chalk the tip. "Yes." I rack the balls, place the cue ball in the head spot and say, "You break."

"You know, you don't have to snap orders at me. You can be pleasant."

"I know."

Her eyes flatten into small slits. "But you choose not to be."

"Precisely."

"Well . . . aren't you a ball of fun?"

She finishes chalking her cue and then walks around the pool table, her manicured fingers dragging along the siderails. Even though I don't care for her unflattering shirt, when she leans over the table, I catch a small glimpse of her ass in those leggings and, hell . . . that's not a bad view.

Her arm cocks back and she pushes the cue into the cue ball, sending it straight into the racked triangle with enough power to scatter the balls across the table, immediately sending a striped ball into the left corner pocket.

When she looks up at me and smiles, she says, "My dad taught me how to play."

"Doesn't mean you're better than me."

"Aren't you acting a little too cocky?"

"I thought you were an athlete; didn't know you couldn't take it."

Her eyes narrow again. "I can take it." I shrug and wait my turn. "God, you're infuriating."

She moves around the table and angles herself for another shot. She sinks two more balls before missing on the right-side pocket.

I observe the placement of the solids taking in the angles, where I could possibly shoot them. And after a few short minutes, I move to the cue ball and get to work. I feel her eyes trained on me when I lean down, my hand stabilizing the cue as I push it through the cue ball, sending ball after ball into their respective pockets. She doesn't move, only observes, and every time I walk past her, I move closer and closer until my shoulder lightly brushes against hers and I catch her quick intake of breath. I bend in front of her, look over my shoulder and say, "A little room."

She backs up, and I call the eight ball in the corner pocket, before sending it careening inside. Standing straight, I turn toward her and say, "Are you good? Or do you need to play more?"

Her lips twist to the side in consternation. "You're a prick."

I hold back my chuckle. "I had you pegged for a sore loser."

"I'm not a sore loser."

"You just called me a prick after I beat you in pool."

"I called you a prick because you're acting like an arrogant asshole. I'd have been more than happy to accept defeat and praise you on your obvious ability to play pool, but not when you showboat and—"

"How did I showboat?"

She points to the corner of my lip. "Your smug smirk."

"A smirk, that's showboating?" I grip the back of my neck and glance around. "Hell, and I thought showboating would be me flapping my arms around, trying to get the entire bar involved in a chant that praises me and makes you look like a fool. I passed up that idea, trying to save you the humiliation."

Her jaw tightens, and before I know what's happening, she's pushing at my chest. "What is wrong with you?" She pushes me again, but I go nowhere. She might be strong, but not strong enough. Giving up, she tosses the cue stick on the table and says, "God, you're the most infuriating man I've ever met and we've barely shared six words. She grips the edge of the pool table, anger rolling off her in almost visible waves. "Four interactions to be precise—my interview, the party, first day of school, and today. Four interactions and I already hate you. Despise you, actually. What does that say for you?"

When her eyes land on mine, I give her one smooth once-over and then bring my cue stick to the rack where the others are kept. Turning toward her, I say, "It shows that I was right. You won't be the right hire for Forest Heights. If one game of pool tips you over the edge, what the hell are you going to do when you lose control of your classroom? Drill your fist through the wall and call it a day?"

She sucks in a sharp breath and stands tall. "I never lose my composure in the classroom."

"How do you know that? This is your first teaching job."

"I was a student teacher."

"Where you weren't fully in charge," I point out, stepping in close to her.

"I had control of the classroom." She lifts her chin.

"I'm not saying you didn't have control; I'm saying you were in charge for a short amount of time. What happens when you're elbow deep in a semester and everything you've been teaching goes in one ear out the other, the papers you're correcting have nothing to do with what you've taught during class, and instead of learning, the kids rely on you to teach them Tik Tok dances like the first day of class rather than actually learn?"

She glares.

She seethes.

She moves closer, leaving only a few inches between us. "That will never happen, because unlike you, I know how to relate to my students."

"You don't need to relate to them, Gibson. You need to educate them."

With that, I push past her and walk by Gunner and Romeo's booth as they all high-five each other, not paying me a bit of attention. I quickly lay some money on the bar for my meal, and for Greer's, and then, deciding to wait outside, I exit the bar and order an Uber.

The doors to the bar burst open behind me and I glance over my shoulder, where I see Greer standing, her chest heaving, her eyes narrowed, her fists clenched at her side.

If I didn't know any better, I'd think she looks like she's about to punch me.

"As teachers, we're not just here to shove Shakespearean quotes down their throats and talk about the damn green light in *The Great Gatsby* and what it represents. We're here to uplift them, to help them understand the life ahead of them. Do you really think they're going to look back one day and say, 'You know, that Mr. Turner, the way he'd wax poetic about F. Scott Fitzgerald really changed my life'?" She shakes her head, moving closer with every word she says. "No"—she pokes me in the chest—"they're going to look back at high school and think, 'Mr. Turner was an asshole who didn't care about me as a person. He just cared about me as a student. As a number. As a grade.'"

How little she fucking knows me.

I move my jaw back and forth, not letting the crazy sweet smell of her perfume distract me, or the way her passionate eyes flare disarm me, or the press of her finger into my right pec confuse me.

Standing strong, unwavering, I say, "And you think your free-for-all handling of the curriculum is going to change lives?"

"It's not a free-for-all."

I scoff. "Pairing the movie with classic literature, asking them to read the CliffsNotes—"

"That's so they gain a better understanding."

"You're diminishing their ability to read and translate by filling their minds with the cop-out version." I reach out and pinch her chin, now so close I can feel her breath on me. "You want to make a difference? *Teach* them."

I let go just as a silver Camry pulls up to the sidewalk.

"I do teach them," she calls after me, her eyes less passionate, slightly unsure.

"Try doing it without the fanfare." I reach for the door and open it. "If they learn from you by proper instruction, then you're a teacher. Until then . . . in my eyes . . ." I look her up and down. I want to tell her that she's no better than a glorified babysitter. But I can't. Not as her superior. "You need to prove your worth, Miss Gibson. You're there to teach, not babysit."

Chapter Five

GREER

"Are you sure you want to do this?"

"What did I say over the weekend?" I ask. My eyes burn with exhaustion as I cut off the heads of a pack of matches.

"You said full steam ahead."

"Well, that's exactly what we're doing. Full steam ahead."

"Yeah . . ." Stella drags out carefully. "But before, when you wanted to do the pranks, you didn't have this crazy look in your eyes."

"Lack of sleep," I snap. "Where's the ammonia?"

"Keeks is getting it." Stella pulls on my shoulder so I'm facing her. "Hey, can you settle down for a second and talk to me?"

"There's nothing to talk about. Turner is an asshole and he's going to get stink-bombed."

"You know there's nothing more I want than to see Turner being turned out of his classroom because you dropped a stink bomb in there, but something must have happened Friday night that you're not telling me. You have a vengeful look on your face."

"I don't remember swiping on 'vengeful' when I was doing my makeup this morning."

Stella nudges me. "I'm being serious, Greer. Talk to me. What did he say to you?"

Sighing, I sit on one of the desks in my classroom. School starts in forty-five minutes. "What didn't he say, is the question. Not only did he start off the interaction by completely ignoring me, as if I wasn't good enough to even be in his presence, he then proceeded to school me in pool, which was a shot to my competitive heart."

"You're upset because he beat you in pool?"

"No, I'm upset about what he said to me after pool."

"What did he say?"

"He practically called me a babysitter, rather than a teacher."

Stella lets out a low gasp. "No, he didn't."

I slowly nod. "Yup. Said my teaching was frivolous, that I don't actually teach, but lean on cop-out techniques to teach the kids required material."

"Because you help them better understand through visual representation?"

I nod.

Stella laughs. "That's such bullshit. He's pulling his snooty attitude on you, and we won't stand for it." She pounds the desk. "Doesn't he know that not every teacher is the same? Just like every student isn't the same. Ugh . . . what a tool bag."

"Tool bag, a classic insult," Keeks says, entering the classroom. "Derived from the mid-seventeenth century, willingly used to describe a skill-less person, which is quite contradictory given the purpose of a tool is to assist the Homo Sapien in completing tasks." She hands me the ammonia. "*Bag* wasn't added to the insult until recent years, indicating, not only are you a dupe, but you're a whole bag of them." She smiles at us.

"Didn't know there was such a backstory to the term tool bag," I say, feeling a little lighter thanks to Keeks and her unusual sense of humor. "I thought it was something frat boys came up with."

She pushes her glasses up on her nose. "I perceive why you would jump to that hypothesis, but, dismally, the only accomplishments frat boys can lay claim to are the consumption of copious amounts of grain-infused malt liquor, corresponding macho-man-infused Olympics, and the capability of draining said liquor from a funnel straight into the esophagus without an extra cry for breath."

"They're also good at throwing parties," Stella adds. "Not ashamed to admit I've been to a few."

"We all have," Keeks says with a sigh.

Uncapping the bottle of ammonia, I ask, "You've been to a frat party?"

She gestures toward her body. "Contrary to what you might postulate about me, I'm more than a wool skirt and glasses. I've acquired my equitable share of 'fun.'" She brushes her gray-and-purple plaid skirt, smoothing out a wrinkle. "Back at university, I seldom attended a boisterous party. But there was one particularly raucous occasion when I forfeited my sensible brassiere after a riveting game of chess. I exhausted the rest of the evening with my mammaries twisting and turning with bare abandon in my practical party blouse. Quite the affair."

"Keeks, braless, flapping her bosoms in the wind—this is something I'm going to have to see in person," Stella says.

"You should be so lucky," Keeks says with another smile, and I can't help but notice the good mood she's in. I don't know Keeks very well yet, but I do like that, although she sounds so incredibly formal and stilted, she still has a kindness that pulls you in. I wonder if her students see that in her?

Teenagers can be total shits, so I hope they're not mean to her. Well, they probably are, so let's hope she has a thick skin around that superpowered brain.

I drop the match heads in the ammonia and cap the bottle off again, giving it a good shake. It will take a few days for the stink to really build up, so I put the bottle in the bottom of my desk and say, "Did something happen to you this weekend?"

"Why? Do I look different?" Keeks asks, a smile still on her face.

"I mean, you're smiling a lot."

Stella nods while standing next to me, shoulder to shoulder, studying Keiko. "Yeah, you are smiling a lot."

"Do you prefer I frown while promenading around with downturned shoulders, martyring the world with idiosyncrasies?"

"No," Stella says, "but I do want you to give us the scoop about what you did this weekend."

"Hey . . . Keiko," a voice calls from my open door. Stella and I both look up to see Kelvin Thimble standing in the doorway, a huge smile on his face as well. "I assume you had a fair day yesterday?"

"Indeed." Keeks gives him a curt nod. "Rather enjoyable. Thank you, Kelvin."

"Okay. See you at lunch?"

"Affirmative." And then Keeks turns toward us, a blush on her face.

When he's out of earshot, Stella playfully pushes at Keeks's shoulder. "Oh my God, Keeks, did Kelvin finally make a move?"

"If you're referring to Kelvin Thimble approaching me with respect and courtesy to join in a courtship with him, then you would be correct."

"A courtship, how romantic," I say, bringing my hands to my chest. "What does that entail?"

"Exclusive companionship where we delight in each other's minds."

"Not his penis?" Stella asks, causing Keeks to frown.

"Dare I say that's extremely forward of you, Stella. Why on earth would I handle his phallus at the inauguration of a courtship?"

Stella shrugs. "Because they're fun to jiggle."

I snort next to her.

"Sorry to say, but once you hover next to a flaccid penis and slowly drag your finger over it until it's fully erect, it's next to impossible to not want to do it over and over again."

"I agree with that statement. Fascinating stuff, Keeks. Watching how one single flick of a finger can shoot a bout of blood to a man's crotch in seconds."

Keeks takes a pause, her head turned ever so slightly as she processes this information. "I've never considered the implications of experiencing the acts of the human anatomy first-hand. The opportunity to vividly experiment with the phallus permits great intrigue." She taps her chin and moves toward the door. "The possibilities of surmounting the state of erection are endless. Variables such as fingers, hands, feathers all come to mind. What will procure the greatest arousal?"

"Don't forget the female boob. An erect nipple is better than a finger," Stella says.

"Quite right, quite right." She waggles her finger. "I must converse with Kelvin. The theory of a nipple being greater than a finger holds great weight for conclusive evidence."

And with that, she's out the door, leaving Stella and I in a ball of laughter.

"Oh my God, Kelvin won't even know what hit him," I say.

"He won't, but I have a feeling he's not going to mind Keeks experimenting on him at all."

"Depends. Think she'll let him come?"

Stella gives it thought. "You know, Keeks very well might

be the first crossover of nerdy scientist to experimental, phallus-checking dominatrix."

"Is it weird that I picture her in a torn-up lab coat with a beaker as a probe?"

Stella laughs. "No, I have the same visual in my head." Relaxing, she nudges me with my foot. "You good?"

"After that? Yeah, I'm good."

"You better be." Turning serious, she looks me in the eyes and says, "You're a great teacher. You know what you're doing, and Turner is going to rue the day he *suggested* you're a babysitter rather than teacher."

"Don't mess with me."

"Exactly." Stella winks and heads toward my classroom door. "Just don't fall for his charm, okay?"

My nose scrunches. "What charm?"

Stella sarcastically laughs. "Trust me, past the arrogance, there's an even heavier dose of arrogant charm. Just be cautious."

"Yeah, I don't think we're going to have a problem with that. I can barely stand to have a classroom next to the man."

"Good. See you at lunch."

I give her a quick wave and then take a seat at my desk, reviewing my notes for the day.

Be cautious. Seriously? Does she really think she needs to warn me?

The man is positively despicable. I would never see anything but arrogance when I look at him.

⊏⊐

"DID ANYONE UNDERSTAND THAT?" I look around my classroom, noting the bunch of blank faces staring at me. I usually expect that from the first class of the day, given the early morning, but these faces are confused not from lack of sleep, but from the twisty word play from Jane Austen herself. "Are you telling me that it's hard to understand old-timey English? Preposterous." The class laughs, and I hop off my desk and walk over to the whiteboard. "Irony is one of the themes of *Pride and Prejudice*. Just like the very first sentence in the book—"

"Holy God," booms a male voice through the wall. "Evacuate. Single file. Jameson, what the hell have you done?"

My class turns toward the wall that separates Turner's classroom from mine, just in time to miss the giant smile that passes over my face.

I waited until Thursday morning to plant the seed. Gunner and Romeo pulled him from the classroom right before we were supposed to start, I slipped in, uncorked the stink bomb, and planted it in the back. Five minutes from the start of class, just long enough for it to brew up to the front. Perfect.

Turner's class filters into the hall, the cacophonous noise distracting but oh so worth it.

"It wasn't me, Mr. Turner, I swear," a poor kid says in the hallway, and for a brief second, I fear that I might get one of his students in trouble, but then I see Turner step in front of my open door, hand in hair, typing something out on his phone.

"Uh, everyone pull out their CliffsNotes and read the first chapter. I'll be right back."

Going to my door, I peek my head out. "Turner, you're disturbing my class. Mind keeping it down?" His eyes flash to mine, and I add, "If you're going to partake in frivolous field trips, please move your group along rather than staying in the hallway."

His eyes sharpen. "We're not going on a field trip. There's a dead animal in my classroom."

"Are you sure it isn't your lecture dying in there?"

His lips flatten. "Cute."

"Dead animal, huh? Did you kill it with your boring

teaching techniques?" I *tsk* and shake my head. "Death by English teacher, it's a real threat in your classroom. Saw some support groups for your students being posted out on the bulletin boards. Might have been an animal today, tomorrow . . . who knows who's next?"

"Are you done?" he asks, deadpan.

"Believe so." I smile, all too happy with myself.

"Then I suggest you get back to work."

"You're not my boss," I snap-whisper at him.

"I'm head of the department, which means I have a say in who works here."

I smile widely and stand tall; his eyes fall briefly to my chest and then crawl back to my eyes. The brief glance erects a flush of heat up the back of my neck, but I don't let it deter me. "Looks like you don't have too much say, you know, since I work here." I smile widely and say, "Good luck with your rotting lecture—oh, I mean, animal—good luck with your rotting animal."

Shutting the door, happy with myself, I turn to my class, ready to *teach* them the ways of Jane Austen.

———

GUNNER: *Status Report—Anger, fury, kind of smells.*

Greer: *OMG, he smells?*

Romeo: *Like ass. I kicked him out of the teachers' lounge.*

Greer: *That's better than anything I could have hoped for.*

Gunner: *He took a shower during lunchbreak and is wearing his gym clothes, which has only made him more irritable, because, you know, teaching without a cardigan is like touching kryptonite. He needs the cardigan.*

Romeo: *He texted me in between periods and said he's way off his game. The smell is ingrained in his nostrils.*

Greer: *LOL! Did they find the stink bomb?*

Gunner: *Carl, the janitor, located and removed it while wearing a hazmat suit—well, a homemade one.*

Greer: *They're not blaming any kids, are they?*

Romeo: *No. But he has his suspicions when it comes to us, since we pulled him out of his classroom. We need to be careful with the next one.*

Greer: *Roger that. Thanks, boys.*

Gunner: *Our pleasure. Keep up the good work.*

Greer: *Gladly.*

"I DON'T KNOW ABOUT THIS." I look at the assembly of kids all sectioned out by graduating class, our first pep rally of the year about to start.

"This is the perfect time," Gunner says from the corner of his mouth.

"Don't back down now," Romeo adds from behind me.

"There are so many kids here," I say, worrying my lower lip.

"Which is why it needs to be done. He doesn't ever address the school except for this pep rally, where he lists off the honoree students from last year."

"And you know he'll fall for it?"

"He won't know what's happening," Stella adds.

I fumble with the iPad in my hand that Keeks gave me earlier. "I don't know."

Gunner leans in and says, "Now or never, Gibson. He's headed this way."

I glance up to see Arlo walking toward us, glass of water in hand.

"I'm too shaky. What if it doesn't work?"

"It works. We checked multiple times."

"He'll see it all over my face. The guilt."

"We'll distract him. Don't worry. You got this, just keep the iPad hidden," Romeo says.

Arlo closes the space to our group, just as I put the iPad behind my back. His eyes land on me briefly, but in that short glance, he takes me in from head to toe, and I so wish I could read his mind, to know what he thinks of the red sundress I chose to wear today. Does he approve? Am I teacher enough for him? I do have my hair in a tight bun on the top of my head, going for a more studious look, because I want to . . . not because I'm trying to impress him.

"I hate these assemblies, a waste of time," Arlo grumbles, speaking to his boys.

"He's never been a fan of the different dance teams trying to pump up the student body about education. He's rather a throw-a-book-in-front-of-your-face-and-pump-you-up-with-literature kind of guy," Gunner says to me.

"School spirit is worth something," Stella says, jumping in.

"For the underachievers," Arlo mutters, and that comment right there gives me the extra surge of confidence I need to go through with this prank.

When is this man going to learn that we're not teaching in a prison cell, that we're a public school attempting to mold minds, not turn them into classic-literature robots?

Arlo glances at me and I feel my cheeks flame with panic.

Cutting in quickly, Gunner says, "Dude, your pant cuffs are uneven."

That's his distraction? Jesus, that will never—

"Really?" Arlo glances down. "Hold my drink." Gunner takes the drink while Arlo bends down.

Okay, I guess these boys know Arlo way better than I thought.

"That better?" he asks, lifting up.

"Way better," Gunner says, handing him back his drink.

Just then, Principal Dewitt walks to the center of the

basketball court and the students quiet down, showing impressive respect for our leader.

"I know you're eager to get to the dance clubs to see what they've been working on for the past two weeks and over summer, but we have some students to honor first. Mr. Turner, will you please join me at the podium?"

"That's me," he says, walking onto the court.

My nerves immediately hit me harder than expected. "Oh God, I might puke."

"Don't. You're not going to want to miss this," Gunner says, rubbing his hands together. "This is going to be the greatest moment of my life."

"Greater than meeting your son for the first time?" Romeo asks.

"Okay, second-greatest moment."

"Greater than—"

"We're not playing this game," Gunner sternly says, causing Romeo to chuckle.

Principal Dewitt hands the microphone to Arlo, who secures it in the stand on the podium. In his deep timbre, he says, "Thank you, Principal Dewitt. We'll make this short and sweet. We have ten students who made it into the honors program and we're going to call them up to receive their sash and pin." He lifts the cup of water and I hold my breath as he takes a sip. Then I press the preset button.

I hold my breath.

My heart beating a mile a minute.

My lips drying.

My chest hollowing out from pure anticipation.

He opens his mouth and . . .

In the most high-pitched, nasally voice, he says, "Jessica Magnol—" He stops, his face contorting in confusion. "Jessica . . ."

Oh, dear God, it's happening.

The entire assembly breaks out into laughter as Arlo tries

to figure out why his voice is sounding like Alvin the Chipmunk.

Turning to Dewitt, he asks in a high-pitched voice, "Is there something wrong with the mic?"

Nyema taps on the mic and leans in to speak. I press the preset button on the iPad again. "Hello." Her voice sounds normal.

I nearly die.

Oh my God, this is amazing.

Gunner and Romeo are gripping each other, barely able to stand as they roar with laughter.

Brow crinkled. He moves in front of the mic and I press the button again. "It's not the mic?" he repeats, tapping it. He turns the mic off and then back on. Stella grips me in laughter.

"That better?" he squeaks. "What the—what's happening?"

"That's right, keep talking," Gunner says in between a fit of laughter.

The entire gym is engulfed in laughter, and honestly, I'd feel a little bad about the confusion and anger written all over his face . . . if he weren't such a dick to me.

Karma, my friends . . . karma.

Also, a slight tweak of the audio desk's preset characteristics goes a very long way in revenge. Take notes.

⊏⊐

GUNNER: *Status Report: Positively fuming. DEFCON 1 status.*

Romeo: *His face was bright red. I thought he was going to blow a gasket.*

Greer: *Oh God, do you think we should stop?*

Gunner: *Hell no. The next prank is my favorite.*

Greer: *Yes, but we also have to deal with him.*

Romeo: *Yes, we have to deal with him. I might have wanted to* *help you for my own motives, but now I'm invested. Full steam ahead, Greer.*

Gunner: *Agreed. I'm far too invested at this point.*

Greer: *Think he's on to me?*

Romeo: *No way. He thought it was some kid adding shit to the water. You're safe.*

Greer: *Okay, so . . . blue pee?*

Gunner: *Blue pee.*

Romeo: *I need blue pee so much in my life.*

Greer: *Okay, we shall commence blue pee Thursday next week.*

Gunner: *God bless chemistry.*

Chapter Six

ARLO

"Coraline, dinner is ready," I shout to the backyard, where my sister is buried deep in her phone.

"Can we eat out here?"

"If you come help me with the plates and drinks."

She pops up from a lounger and walks inside. I hand her a plate of salmon, rice, and asparagus, and an ice-cold water.

"Water?"

"Your wine consumption has been heavy lately."

"I'm getting a divorce at the ripe age of twenty-seven. I believe I have a pass when it comes to the amount of wine I'm allowed to consume."

"There's no pass, and there's no wine tonight."

Huffing, she walks her plate and water out to the back patio and takes a seat at one of the outdoor tables. I take a seat across from her and hope she's feeling open enough tonight.

Ever since she moved in, it's as if she's reverted back to

teenage Coraline with her moodiness and evasiveness. I worry, because she's exhibiting the same behaviors as before she ended up in the hospital, bleeding out of her wrists . . .

I swallow hard, unable to get the image of my lifeless sister sprawled out on the bathroom floor, blood seeped into her clothing, out of my head.

"Why do you have that look on your face?"

"What look?"

"That concerned, *older brother* look that says 'I'm about to lecture you, so you better listen.'"

I slice my fork through the salmon and scoop up the meat with some rice, not missing the mango salsa I decided to make last minute. "I'm not going to lecture you."

"Bullshit," she says with a laugh. "You fail to realize that I know you—well—and you're about to lecture me, especially after the enforced wine restriction."

Sighing, I push a piece of asparagus with my fork and glance up at my sister. "I'm concerned, Coraline."

"Ah, do I know you, or what?" she asks, placing a piece of asparagus in her mouth.

"Do you blame me? Your behavior is erratic—"

"How so?"

"You're drinking at night, you're never here, you're—"

"And what exactly do you think I'm doing, Arlo?"

Treading carefully, I say, "You're exhibiting the same kind of behavior that—"

"I'm going to stop you right there." She holds up her fork for emphasis. "I might be sad that I'm getting divorced, but I'm also happy that I'm out of that toxic relationship. You don't need to worry about me, Arlo. I know what I'm doing."

"And what is that?"

She sips from her water glass and gently sets the cup down. "I've been seeing my therapist, trying to get my head on straight."

"You've been seeing Dr. Fulkner again?"

She shakes her head. "No. I didn't feel like falling asleep during my session from his boring voice. I found someone new."

"Who is it?"

She rolls her eyes. "You're not going to drop this, are you?"

"No."

"You're insufferable." She takes a bite of the salmon and groans. "Insufferable but knows how to cook one hell of a salmon." I'm rewarded with a smile, which I needed. "I also appreciate you, big brother. I know this isn't ideal, but it's where life has me right now."

I wait a few seconds. "I know I'm badgering, but my concern runs deep, Coraline."

Her fork pauses on her plate and she looks up at me. Sincerity is in her eyes when she says, "I'll never do that again, Arlo."

I solemnly nod. "If it's ever in the realm of your thoughts, you come to me immediately."

She reaches across the table and takes my hand. "I will. You might drive me crazy, but you know I'll come to you."

"Thank you." Knowing that's the best I'll get from her right now, there's no point pushing. Times like these, I wish we had a proper, caring mom here. To be a kinder, more empathetic shoulder to lean on than I am. Coraline deserves the world, as her heart is gold.

God, I hope I never see her so broken ever again. Not sure my heart would withstand that. Twice.

"Is that why you've been grumpy the last few days? I mean, you're always grumpy, but the slamming of kitchen cabinets has been more frequent than normal."

"I'm surprised you've been around to hear the slamming of the cabinets." I smirk.

"Lots of walks," she answers, and I hate that a part of me doesn't believe her. "So, what's going on? A new student driving you crazy? Remember that one kid you used to bitch about all the time? What was his name . . . Needlepoint, or something?

"Neanderpoint. Will Neanderpoint."

"Yes, that's him. He'd spend the entire class contradicting everything you said. That kid was my hero."

"That kid is currently failing out of college. His mom emailed me this past Spring asking if I would tutor him over the summer. I ignored that email."

"Hey"—Coraline tilts her head to the side—"you're an educator, Arlo. You need to help out all kids, not just the ones who nod and smile at everything you say."

"Fuck that. I'm not about to be mentally abused because some dipshit kid doesn't know how to shut up. He's failing because he doesn't believe what the professors are telling him, and he tries to tell them differently. There's ignorance and there's indifference. That kid is indifferent."

"But it'd have been fun for me . . . that's what you're not seeing here." She laughs.

"Glad my suffering is amusing."

"Just a little." She swirls her fork around her plate. "So, what is it? What's driving you crazy? New girl?"

"No." I shake my head, even though immediately I think of Greer. I haven't spoken a word to her since the night we played pool. I see her everywhere, though. Not just outside her classroom, but all around campus. In the teachers' lounge, in the hallways, talking with my friends, in the parking lot, running around in tiny spandex shorts with her volleyball team . . . yeah, that was—hell, that wasn't something I needed to see. I can still envision her tight bubble butt barely covered in spandex, running behind her team, her hair swishing back and forth over her shoulders.

And what's with her dresses and skirts? Does she not own a pair of dress pants?

Her goddamn legs are phenomenal and—

"Hey," Coraline snaps at me. "What the hell are you thinking about?"

"Huh?" I look up and a smile spreads across her face. Shit, she caught me drifting off and if I don't come up with something on the spot, she's going to assume it's a girl. "Oh, sorry, just . . . uh . . . just annoyed. I think the boys are fucking with me."

There, that's true.

Not the entire reason why I'm apparently slamming kitchen cabinets, but a big part of it.

Another big part of it . . . the aforementioned dresses and skirts.

And tiny spandex.

"Gunner and Romeo are fucking with you?" she asks. "How so?"

"Well, the stink bomb."

She chuckles. "Oh God, you were so angry that day."

"My classroom smelled like rotting ass and I had to wear gym clothes to teach, so, yeah, I was mad."

"Heaven forbid." She dramatically fans her hand in front of her face.

"And then at the assembly . . . ." I cut off her chuckling.

"What happened at the assembly?"

I push my hand through my hair, still trying to figure it all out. "Not sure how it happened, but when I went to honor the students who achieved academic excellence the year prior, my voice sounded like I just sucked down ten helium balloons."

"What?" she shouts and laughs at the same time. "Oh my God, seriously?"

"You think this is funny?"

"Arlo, how could you not?" She laughs some more. "And you have no idea how it happened?"

"Not a single clue."

"And you were the only one with the helium voice?"

"Yup." I plop a piece of salmon in my mouth. "Lucky me."

She picks up her phone and starts typing away.

"What are you doing?"

"Seeing if there's a video of it, I need to hear—"

"Phones aren't allowed in the assembly."

"Oh, you clueless man." She shakes her head. "Aha, found it."

"What? Seriously?"

"You'd be surprised what students will do." She presses play and, lo and behold, there I am, standing at the podium, talking as if my balls are being squeezed with a vise.

Coraline roars with laughter, and even though I don't enjoy being the butt of the joke—and *hate* that my hard-earned respect is in jeopardy—I'll admit, seeing my sister with a smile on her face, laughing . . . I'll be okay with it, for now.

Not forever.

But for now, she can laugh.

___

MY LEG BOUNCES up and down under my desk.

Fuck, what is happening?

After what feels like years, Gunner and Romeo open my classroom door with confused expressions.

"Jesus, what took you so long?"

"We were eating lunch," Gunner answers, leaning against the desk directly in front of mine.

"Shut the door," I say to Romeo. "And lock it."

"Lock it?" His brows shoot up. "Dude, you're sweating and you have a weird look on your face. Are you . . . are you losing it?"

I shoot out of my desk and pull on the back of my neck.

I think I'm losing it.

There's no other explanation.

I'm fucking losing it.

My only hope is that Gunner and Romeo are fucking with me again. That's why I called them in here, to gauge their reaction. Because what just happened to me . . . Jesus Christ, please let them be fucking with me.

Turning toward them, I take a deep breath. "I, uh, I have a man issue."

"A man issue?" Gunner asks, a crease in his brow.

"What kind of man . . . ohhhh." Romeo walks up to Gunner and knocks him in the chest with his finger. "Can't get it up."

"You can't get it up?" Gunner asks. "Who's the lucky—or dare I say, unlucky lady?"

"What?" I shake my head. "No, I can get it up just fine."

"When was the last time you tried?" Romeo asks.

"That's not the point."

"Might be. Does this problem have to do with your penis?"

"I mean . . . yeah."

"Okay," Romeo says, "so when was the last time you got it up?"

"That's irrelevant," I snap.

"Seeming more and more relevant to me," Gunner mutters to the side.

"Jesus Christ." I drag both my hands down my face. "This morning, in the shower."

"Hey, me too," Romeo says with a little too much pep in his voice.

"Fuck, me too." Gunner laughs. "It was as if we were all circle jerking together. Like, we could call ourselves the Thursday circle jerkers."

"No," I say flatly. "Don't even say shit like that."

"Don't want to know that I'm pumping my dick at the same time you are?" Gunner asks. "Doesn't give you comfort?"

"Makes me want to never touch my dick again," I answer.

"Given that there's something going on down there, maybe you shouldn't," Romeo says, and I swear to God, I almost scream.

Almost.

This was a mistake. They're going to be assholes, I can feel it.

Hell, they already are being assholes.

"Is it a rash?" Romeo asks. "I've had a rash down there before—well, what I thought was a rash. It was just my balls growing."

"What?" I ask, completely bewildered.

Romeo scratches his neck. "Was it my balls growing? I can't remember. It was back in middle school."

"Tingling sensation in the groin?" Gunner asks Romeo. "Totally ball growth. Did you have a lot?"

Romeo nods. "I think that's why my junk is so massive. Too much tingling in middle school." He shrugs his shoulders.

"Are you two morons done?" I ask, hands on my hips now.

"Hey, we're trying to help you out here. Now . . . is it a rash?"

"It's not a goddamn rash!" I shout.

"Jeez, settle down, man." Romeo crosses his arms over his chest. "Is it . . ." He leans in and whispers, "Venereal?"

"It's hard being friends with you two."

"Hey, I'm not doing anything wrong," Gunner says. "And when you text us '911, penis problems' how are we not supposed to act as if this could be venereally related?"

"I never said penis problem, I said man issue."

"Man issue is code for penis problems. Read the hand-book, man." Gunner rolls his eyes.

"You know what, never mind. Get the fuck out of here. I'll figure it out on my own." I take a seat at my desk and sift my hands through my hair, trying to come up with some sort of reasonable explanation as to why I'm peeing blue.

Straight-up blue.

From my urethra to the urinal . . . bright blue.

I had a blueberry smoothie this morning, but I have them almost every morning and this has never happened before.

Would it be the culmination of blueberries?

Jesus, that's a moronic thought.

Just shows that I really do need new friends.

"Look at him thinking so hard over there. See the steam billowing out of his ears?" Gunner says. I glance to the side to see my two friends, arms crossed, shoulder to shoulder, studying me.

"If he's not careful, he might set off the smoke alarms."

"Be nice," Gunner says. "He looks really distressed. Maybe he needs a shoulder to cry on." Raising his voice, he asks, "Do you need to cry?"

"I need something to punch. Mind lending your head?" I ask, twisting to make eye contact with him.

The idiot taps his chin, giving it thought. "You know, normally I'd volunteer, but I have to see my son this weekend and, even though I hate to admit it, you're strong enough to leave some damage, don't want to scare the little guy. I say you give Romeo that old one-two blow. He has nothing going on this weekend."

"You don't know that," Romeo defends.

"Well, do you?" Gunner challenges him.

"Yeah, I do. I have plans with my Xbox. I've been neglecting him and I promised him some personal one-on-one time."

"You're a grown-ass man, you shouldn't be playing video games. Pick up a goddamn book," I say.

"I did, just yesterday, I picked up a light read about RBI 20, bettering my pitches."

"For a video game . . ." I deadpan.

"Hey, it was reading."

Standing now, I grab my water bottle for a refill before

lunch is over. "Whatever, I'm out. Thanks for nothing."

I try to walk past Gunner, but he places his hand on my chest and stops me. "Dude, in all seriousness, what's going on?"

Sincerity reads in his eyes, and I know if I'm going to talk about it, this is my window.

Letting out a long sigh and unable to look my friends in the eyes, I stare down at my worn brown boots and the cuff of my jeans right above them. "My pee . . . it's blue."

"What?" Gunner asks.

"I went to the bathroom and, well, my pee was blue."

"Are you . . . sure?" Romeo asks, concern growing in his voice as well. "Maybe it was one of those toilet tablets."

"I thought maybe that's what it was, but there weren't any and the pee coming out of my dick was actually blue."

"Huh." Gunner looks to Romeo, Romeo to Gunner, and then they both turn toward me. "When was the last time you had sex? Maybe it's the blue balls leaking out."

Romeo snorts.

Gunner snickers.

And I push past both of them.

"Fuck you both."

I'm halfway out of my classroom when I turn toward them and say, "If I find out you're behind this, you're both dead. Do you understand?"

"What are you going to do? Try to dye our hair with your dick?" Gunner fluffs his short hair. "I'm all for trying something new."

I hate them.

Tossing them the middle finger, I walk out of my room and head toward the teachers' lounge.

From the way they reacted to the look of humor on their faces, I know they have something to do with this.

I fucking know it.

And they will pay.

⊂⊃

"HEY, KELVIN," I say, walking through the teachers' lounge.

"A-r-rlo," he stutters. "G-good to see you."

"Nice start to the year?"

"Y-yes. Thank you." He gives me a flat smile and then takes off. Despite Kelvin's stutter, the students claim him as one of their favorite teachers every year. I'm pretty sure it's because he dresses up every Friday and uses *Star Wars* to help teach geometry. Not quite sure how it relates, but we also have very high math scores.

Greer's teaching techniques come to the forefront of my mind. How is what she's doing any different than Kelvin?

Well . . . she uses CliffsNotes—yeah, I've seen them in her room—for one, a flat-out way to cheat the system.

She also plays movies in the classroom . . .

Yeah, there's a difference.

Kelvin draws a Darth Vader mask using different angles.

Greer sits back and lets the TV do the teaching.

Huge difference.

I walk over to the cooler where Keiko Seymour is filling up her water bottle.

"Keiko, how are you?"

She looks over her shoulder and greets me with a curt nod. "Pleasant, thank you." She studies my face and says, "I'd ask how you fare, but from the corrugation in your supraorbital ridge and the discernable strain in your spinotrapezius, I speculate you're currently labored."

"You could say that."

She steps to the side and screws on the top of her water bottle. "Are you appropriating a satisfactory amount of nocturnal repose?"

Am I getting sleep?

Not really.

Between worrying about Coraline and her health to . . .

hell, to thoughts of Greer and if she's doing a good job, I'm barely getting five hours.

But Keiko doesn't need to know that.

"Good enough."

"Good enough isn't adequate. Eight hours is the recommended amount in order to cultivate favorable brain health."

I slowly nod while filling up my water bottle. "Got it. I'll be sure to work on that."

"We're only as sufficient as the necessities we grant ourselves."

"And what would make someone's pee turn blue?" I mutter to myself, capping off my water.

"Urinating a hue of blue would directly correlate to the ingestion of methylene blue, mostly harmless in a miniscule dose, but not recommended to ingest," she says, just before her eyes widen. "Uh, I . . . I believe class is starting."

"Hold on a second." I step in front of her, watching as she fidgets with her glasses and avoids all eye contact with me. "What would make someone's voice sound like a chipmunk?"

"Changing the presets on a microphone's channel on an audio desk." She slaps her hand over her mouth.

Nostrils flaring, I say, "And the makings of a stink bomb. Would I be able to find them in your chemistry lab?"

"Figuratively, the chemicals capable of generating the foul smell of the aforementioned stink bomb are accessible at any humdrum grocery store."

I fold my arms over my chest. "And would you have shared this information with anyone within our faculty?"

Sticking her chin in the air, she says, "I'm afraid to say this is an abuse of your power and I refuse to partake in it. Excuse me." She blows past me, quick, short steps until she's gone.

Staring at the door Keiko just blew through, I conclude one thing: she's involved. The question is, who's she working with? No. Not just who. *Why? Why have I become the object of ridicule?*

Chapter Seven

GREER

Greer: *Abort. Abort. Keeks cracked.*

Gunner: *What? How?*

Romeo: *When? Did she name names?*

Greer: *Yesterday, teachers' lounge, by the water cooler. Arlo muttered something about blue pee and her incessant need to give facts had her crumbling in seconds. She said she didn't name any names and removed herself as quickly as she could.*

Gunner: *Damn her brilliant mind.*

Romeo: *But no names were listed?*

Greer: *No. But she said he looked really suspicious. I think it's only a matter of time.*

Gunner: *Shit.*

Romeo: *I don't think we have anything to worry about. For being the educated man he claims to be, he's been clueless this entire time.*

Gunner: *That's true. A little Google search would have helped him out with a lot of his problems.*

Romeo: *We're good. Everyone just calm down and, whatever you do, act cool.*

Gunner: *Like we did yesterday when he approached us about his blue pee.*

Greer: *What? You're supposed to report back.*

Romeo: *Sorry, it was at lunch and then we had a PE disaster to attend to.*

Greer: *What on earth could constitute a PE disaster?*

Gunner: *One of the kids got into our sex ed cabinet and was sprinkling condoms all over the gym.*

Greer: *Huh . . . yeah, that does sound like a disaster.*

Romeo: *Boys were laughing, girls were horrified, lewd gestures were made, it was mayhem.*

Greer: *Glad you made it out alive. Now tell me how he reacted to the blue pee. Clearly that's more important. LOL.*

Gunner: *Pissed off and confused. Pun intended. Called us into his classroom for man issues. Romeo and I had to have a good laugh before we went in.*

Romeo: *Pretty sure we'll be winning Academy Awards for our performance.*

Gunner: *It was painful not to bust out laughing from the concerned look on his face.*

Greer: *Was he really distraught?*

Gunner: *Worse than all the other pranks.*

Romeo: *There's always great cause for concern when you mess with a man's prized possession. Anything that deals with the dick and you figuratively have him by the balls.*

Gunner: *Well played, Gibson.*

Greer: *Well, I think that was the grand finale on the pranks because with Keiko on the verge of short-circuiting, I can't possibly do anything more.*

Gunner: *It was a good run while it lasted.*

Romeo: *I think you could throw something in closer to winter break just for the hell of it. Maybe something close to spring break, too, you know, keep him on his toes.*

Gunner: *That's a great idea.*

Greer: *We'll see. In the meantime, thank you, boys, for your service. I couldn't have done it without you.*

Romeo: *Oh shit . . . he just walked into our office.*

Greer: *Abort. Abort.*

Romeo: *From the look on his face, I'm going to guess this won't go over well.*

Greer: *Do not crumble. Protect my name at all costs. Do you hear me? ALL COSTS.*

Romeo: *It was nice knowing you, Greer . . .*

Greer: *Romeo . . . GUNNER!*

Greer: *Do you hear me?*

Greer: *ALL COSTS*

"Oh, sorry, I thought this was Arlo's classroom. Unless, is it?"

Startled out of my intense texting, I glance up to find a beautiful woman in a lovely red sundress with capped sleeves, standing with a bag of food in her hand and a smile on her face.

"Arlo is next door."

"Hmm, that's what I thought, given the jailcell classroom, but he said he was in there and he's not."

"Oh, I think he went to go tell Romeo and Gunner something. You can sit in here and wait if you'd like." I tap my ham sandwich. "Just squeezing in a quick lunch."

"Sure, if you don't mind."

"Not at all." I gesture to the seat in front of me. "Have a seat. I'm Greer. I teach English."

"Ohhh." She smiles. "You're the new English teacher here, right?"

"Yes, that would be me."

She nods slowly, taking the seat across from me. "My brother has said many disgruntled things about you."

"Arlo is your brother?"

She nods. "Yup, I'm Coraline, by the way. Cora for short."

She chuckles and shakes her head. "Arlo's mentioned you. He struggles to—"

"He hates me." I roll my eyes. "I've heard."

"Did he tell you?"

"Pretty much."

She sighs heavily. "That's my uptight brother for you. He has zero filter and doesn't bat an eyelash about it."

Zero filter runs in the family.

"Yeah, he's shown zero remorse for his comments." The night we played pool is still at the forefront of my mind. I'm not sure I'll ever get over that night and the things he said.

"Fortunately, his behavior *doesn't* run in the family."

"So, you're not going to tell me I'm a not an educator but rather a babysitter?"

Her expression morphs into shock. "He said that to you?"

"Yeah . . . which . . . ugh, I probably shouldn't be telling you this. He's your brother—"

She points her finger at me, her eyes stern. "You listen to me, Greer. I love my brother, but he's an asshole. If he's being an asshole to you, I need to know about it, so I can be an asshole to him. Us girls have to stick together."

I chuckle. "I guess so."

"Anyway, I could use some friends. Living with Arlo has taken a toll on my social life."

"You're living with him?"

She waves her hand. "Long story, but yes. I was living in New York City but moved back home a little over a month ago. All my friends are either knee-deep in diapers or have moved away from here. I'm in desperate need to start a book club with a few girls."

"You like to read?"

"Sort of." She shrugs.

"Sort of?" I laugh. "Then why start a book club?"

"Because it's code for let's drink a lot of wine and talk about our lives."

"Ohhh." I laugh some more. "I could use one of those. Right now, all I have is school and volleyball. But nothing outside of school. I bet Stella and Keiko would want to join the club."

"Keiko Seymour? God, I love her so much. She's brought Arlo down a peg or two a few times. He's told me all about it."

"You mean to tell me he actually admits defeat?"

"It's rare." She adjusts the gold bracelets on her wrist. "But when he does admit it, he goes into great detail to prove why someone bested him. And I've heard a story or two about Keiko bringing my brother to his knees. Which means . . . I'm going to need to meet this girl."

"She's amazing. Quirky, but amazing."

"And who's Stella? Wait . . . does she coach volleyball, too?"

I nod. "Yes. Stella Garcia. She teaches Spanish."

"Ahhh." A large smile crosses her face.

"What do you know?" I ask. "I barely know any gossip around here since I'm new, and my two friends tend to stay out of it."

"You're probably aware that Arlo's best friends are Gunner and Romeo?"

"Hard to miss that," I say, picking up my sandwich and taking a bite. Oddly, I offer it to her, but she just laughs and shakes her head. Yeah, didn't think so, but it's nice to be polite.

"The boys come over on occasion, and I like to sit at the top of the stairs and listen to their conversations."

"Like any good sister would." I laugh.

"Obviously. As a little sister, I have responsibilities, eaves-dropping being one of them. Anyway, I've heard Romeo mention Stella a few times."

"Really?" I grow closer to my desk, a huge smile on my face. "Like . . . romantically?"

93

"Well, they haven't done anything, at least not that I know of. All I know is that Romeo has the hots for her."

"The hots." I laugh out loud. "That's amazing." I go to take another bite of my sandwich but pause. "You know, I've noticed a little affection when those two are around each other, but I'm not sure anything is going on. Stella would have told me by now."

"He's totally pining after her. I've never seen her, but all I've heard is what a great ass she has."

"I mean, she does have a terrific butt." Leaning back, I say, "I'm so glad you came into my classroom."

"Me too. This lunch is way better than the one I planned on having with Arlo. And can we point out how rude it is that he's not here? He's standing me up."

"Not sure if he's standing you up. More like trying to get to the bottom of the pranks . . ."

Oh shit, my words trail off and fear immediately creeps up the back of my neck as I slowly look up at Cora.

"Pranks as in . . . the stink bomb?"

I swallow hard. "Uh, yeah, something like that."

"Hold on." She lays her palms flat on the desk in front of her. "Are you telling me you know something about the pranks Arlo has been bitching about for the last three weeks?"

I twist my lips to the side, contemplating what to say. At this point, there's some association with me since I mentioned it, so might as well see how strong this bond can be with Arlo's sister.

"What's your take on girl code? Is it being upheld right now?"

"Are you kidding? I need friends other than my moody brother. Please let me prove to you how strong my girl code is."

I chuckle. "I'm trusting you," I say playfully.

She crosses her heart. "I am your human vault of information. Lay it on me."

On a deep breath, I say, "I'm the one who's been pranking Arlo."

Throwing her head back, she lets out an enormous laugh and then claps her hands, her bracelets jangling against her wrists, making the outburst even louder. "Oh, that's amazing. So, the girl he can't stand, the one who he calls names, she's the one who has been pranking him this entire time? The stink bomb, the chipmunk voice . . . the blue pee, that was all you?"

"I had help, but yes."

"Oh my God, you're my new hero." She laughs some more and then reaches into the brown paper bag, pulls out a wrapped-up sub, and unravels the foil. "Do you realize how much you've aggravated him? He was telling me just last night after the whole peeing blue incident—which, by the way, best thing I've ever heard—that he was starting to worry about going into school."

"He did not say that."

Exaggerating, she nods with gusto. "Oh, yes, he did. Is that why he's with Romeo and Gunner right now?"

"I'm assuming that's the case. Keiko might have let it slip about the pranks yesterday, and he's sniffing out the culprits. I'm hoping the boys take the blame. They were part of it, after all."

"How so?"

"They helped distract him so I could do the dirty work. Had to trade in my time with the teachers' league—"

"Ugh, that stupid thing. Arlo talks about it every year, how they never win and how they could use the ten thousand dollars." She haphazardly waves her hand in the air. "He ends up donating the money anyway."

That gives me pause.

"He donates ten thousand dollars to the school every year?"

"Don't think that's any of your business," Arlo snaps from the doorway of my classroom.

Crap.

Heat floods through my veins as embarrassment washes over me from being caught talking about him without him being present.

"There you are," Cora says, wrapping up the sub and plopping it in the bag. "Way to stand your sister up after you begged her to bring you lunch."

Eyes trained on me, irritation clear, he says, "I didn't beg you, and I had some business to take care of."

"Well, that business forced me to start eating without you."

I quiver under his stare as he says, "Coraline, meet me in my classroom. I won't be long."

"Uh . . ." She glances between the two of us. "You're not going to be mean to her again, are you? You know she's more than just a babysitter." Cora's eyes widen and she turns to me quickly. "Oh shit, that wasn't part of the girl code, was it? I swear I'm better than that."

"No, he knows he said that already."

"Okay, good." She picks up a pen off my desk and jots a number down on a Post-it note. "Call me, Greer. I'd love to hang out some more."

"You two are not hanging out," Arlo seethes.

Calm and collected, Cora walks up to her brother and pats him gently on the cheek. "You're cute, thinking you can control our lives. Don't be long, brother, I might just dive into your sandwich as well."

Cora gives me a quick wave and then is out the door, shutting it behind her.

Trying not to wilt under his stare, I stand from my desk, round it, and sit on the corner. His eyes travel my body, not hiding the blatant once-over. And even though I wish I could say the way his eyes travel up my body—greedy, hungry, angry —doesn't affect me . . . it does.

It causes my chest to quake, my throat to tighten up, and my palms to break out in a sweat.

Under his stare, I flatten my hands down the front of my dress, wishing I could read his mind. Wishing I knew how to change this hate-hate relationship to something that isn't so volatile.

But from the determination in his eyes to speak with me, I'm going to guess we're continuing down the hate-hate path.

He closes the distance between us, and the intoxicating smell of his leather and spice scent pushes into my breathing space, taking up unwanted room. His deep, intimidating voice seethes through the dense quiet of my classroom when he says, "I know it was you."

Oh crap.

Did the boys give in? Throw me under the bus?

Damn it, I wish I could check my phone for any warnings from them.

Then again, maybe he's testing me. Maybe he's bluffing. Maybe he doesn't know anything and is just taking a guess. In that case, go with the evasive technique.

"Know what was me?" I ask, gripping the edge of the desk while I lean against it, trying to look as casual as possible, even though my heart is thumping rapidly in my chest and I can feel sweat start to accumulate on the back of my neck.

"Don't fuck with me, Greer," he says, his voice so menacing that I feel like all the air around us is being used to fuel his anger.

"I'm not fucking with you," I say, my voice wavering.

And of course, he catches it as he takes another step forward, his intimidation tactic seriously outdated, but God is it wreaking havoc on my nerves.

Looking down at me, his chin still held high, he says, "Do you think it's a good idea to poke the bear, Greer?"

"I mean, if this has to do with my teaching techniques—"

"You know damn well this has nothing to do with your teaching," he says, pushing forward so his hands land on either side of the desk and I have to lean back so our faces don't touch. My teeth roll over the bottom of my lip, keeping it from quivering while I hold my breath, attempting to show how unaffected I am by his closeness but failing miserably.

He's insufferable.

He's rude.

He's brash and holier than thou.

But God, is he handsome.

Chiseled jaw, just enough five o'clock shadow on his face to leave a mark, but nothing that's going to be bothersome. His eyes are downright devastating, especially when angry, and his body . . . even under a cardigan, I can tell just how carved he is.

With every second that goes by when I'm close to this man, I can feel my defenses lower, my intrigue spike, and my desire to drive forward causing me to forget all the reasons why he's the most unbearable man I've ever met.

"The pranks stop now," he says. "Do you understand me? They stop. Now."

"I, uh, I don't know what you're referring to," I say, avoiding all eye contact with him.

"What did I say about fucking with me, Greer?"

"Do it?" I ask, adding a cheeky smile.

He doesn't flinch.

Doesn't even consider laughing.

But instead, his jaw clenches tighter as he lowers his mouth to my ear, the scrape of his scruff barely grazing over my cheek as his lips hover right by my ear. My entire body breaks out into a wave of goosebumps as he speaks.

"This is your one and only warning. Fuck with me again and you won't like what happens."

My breath catches in my throat and I wait for him to lift up, to turn away and join his sister for lunch, but he doesn't move. Instead, I feel our breaths sync, an unusual desire I wasn't expecting swirling between us.

I pull back just enough to catch his eyes. They study me.

Intense. Deep, with a hint of vulnerability. The type of vulnerability that isn't offered over a cup of coffee, but the kind that's spoken about once trust has been established.

There is no trust between us.

But inexplicably, a small piece of me wants to establish that layer of trust so I can dive deep into the vulnerability that lies just beneath his tough exterior.

"Are you planning retaliation?" I ask.

His eyes drop to my lips before focusing back on my eyes. "Retaliation? No." He licks his lips. "Punishment . . . always."

Oh.

My.

God.

I suck in a sharp breath as he pushes off the desk and stares down at me. Unmoving, put in my place, I'm unsure if I want to slap the man for invading my space, give him a piece of my mind and tell him exactly where he can put his punishment, or tear at his cardigan and shirt and dig my fingernails deep into his toned muscles.

Either way, I don't have time to decide because he turns away and heads out of my classroom, leaving me breathless, annoyed, and unfortunately . . . horny. *What the fuck was that?*

When the door closes behind him, I scramble to my phone, pick it up, and read the text messages from Gunner and Romeo.

Gunner: *Alert. Alert. Romeo cracked. Arlo is coming your way.*

Great. I press my hand to my forehead. And here I thought I could trust these two.

Romeo: *In my defense, he twisted my nipple. I had to go to the bathroom and try to eliminate the pucker of my shirt he made right over my nipple with some water and the hand dryer. It was not pleasant. I got my penance.*

Romeo is such an idiot.

I can't even think about him and Stella, because if he ever did make a move, I'm not sure he'd be able to handle her.

She's a firecracker, and apparently he cracks under the pressure of a nipple twist.

I guess if something does ever happen between them, I have some vital information for Stella so she knows how to get her way. A good nipple tweak and whatever she wants is hers.

I type them back.

Greer: *He just left my classroom.*

They must have been waiting for me to type back because they immediately respond.

Gunner: *Oh shit, was he angry?*

Romeo: *Did he try to give you a nipple twist?*

Greer: *Was he angry? What kind of question is that? He's always angry. And no, he didn't try to twist my nipple. I think he knows better than to attempt to do something like that.*

Then again, would he?

The way he said *punishment* . . . full of promise, full of dark, twisted thoughts, I wonder if he really would be into something like that. Just from his overall demeanor, I could easily see Arlo being the domineering asshole in bed you read about in books, the damaged one, the one with secrets that make you fall head over heels for him.

Not this girl.

Nope.

No way.

Never going to happen.

He may be handsome, but I'm not that easy.

Gunner: *True, you're feisty. I think he might be afraid of you.*

Romeo: *Was he afraid of you?*

Greer: *Uh . . . not necessarily. More confident in his intimidation tactics than anything. Brought his A-game.*

Gunner: *Oh shit.*

Romeo: *What did he say?*

Greer: *Let's just leave it at there won't be any more pranks. He's made his intention clear.*

Gunner: *Although I haven't laughed as hard in a long time as I* *have in the last few weeks, I think that's smart. Arlo might be quiet, but he's vengeful, and we've both seen it firsthand.*

Romeo: *Best to keep your distance.*

Greer: *Sure, that's easy, with him being my classroom neighbor and the head of my department.*

Gunner: *Just steer clear and when we start practicing for teacher league, we can make sure we keep you two separated.*

Greer: *Uh . . . he's on the teachers' league?*

Romeo: *Did we fail to mention that?*

Greer: *Yep. Also, I'm not doing that league. You cracked. You didn't hold up your end of the bargain, so I'm not going.*

Gunner: *Wait a second, we did everything we could to keep your name out of his mouth. If it wasn't for Keiko, he never would have even sniffed around your classroom.*

Romeo: *Truth. Keeks was the leak. I just happened to almost lose a nipple because of it.*

Gunner: *You will be required to show up.*

Greer: *Really think I'm getting the short end of the bargain.*

Romeo: *Not our fault your bargaining partner failed to work out the fine print.*

Greer: *Which reminds me, word on the street is you have something for Stella. That true?*

Romeo: *Word on the street is you have a thing for Arlo. That true?*

Greer: *Well . . . guess I'll be on my way.*

Romeo: *Smart.*

Gunner: *I'll send you the details about Sunday.*

Greer: *Sunday?*

Gunner: *You're killing me. The teachers' league. Come on, Gibson.*

Greer: *Okay, yeah, sure. I'll be there.*

"COACH GIBSON, can I talk to you?" Blair, my setter, asks.

Practice is over, I'm tired after running sprints with my

athletes, and I want to go home and soak in the tiny tub that I can barely fit my tall body in.

I sprint with the girls, because there's no reason they shouldn't be able to beat me. If I do beat them, they have to complete two more full-court pyramids before they go home. I've beat them once, and shockingly, it's never happened again.

"Sure, Blair, what's up?"

Blair Venezuela has been on varsity ever since her freshman year. She's played club volleyball since middle school and has developed into a key player, essential to our team. She's small, quick, and has no fear when it comes to diving for the ball. Her sets are always perfect, and she can dig just about any spike from the opposing team. This summer she signed a full-ride scholarship to UCLA, my alma mater, and she couldn't be more excited. I spoke with my coach back at UCLA and she gave me some things to work on with Blair to prep her for the college level. Like the hard worker she is, Blair has taken everything in her stride and proven to me how she's become the athlete she is. She's hardworking and never gives up. And yes, I can see the similarities between us. I was just as driven at her age, and it served me well.

She takes a seat on one of the bleachers while I pack up the rest of my things. "So, I'm having a bit of trouble in one of my classes, and since you teach English, I thought maybe you'd be able to help me."

"What class?" I ask, my brow furrowed. Blair doesn't have a hard time in class. Stella and I looked through all of the athletes' grades to make sure they weren't just talented on the volleyball court, but also had a handle on their academics, and if they didn't, they were required to sign up with a tutor. As I found out pretty quickly, as a female in sport, yes, you can get your college paid for, but unless you're Venus and Serena Williams, you're not going to be compensated well for your athletic prowess. The grades have to be there. The degree, the education—they matter. Grades are just as important, especially given the chances women have at moving their sport along past college.

"AP English."

My heart flips.

Shit.

"Uh, who's your teacher?" I ask, even though I know exactly who it is.

"Mr. Turner." She sighs and reaches into her backpack. She pulls out a paper encased in a clear binder, typed and professionally put together. Red ink is splashed all over the white paper, and at the top is a giant letter *F* circled at the top.

Oh hell.

"We turned in papers this week. He worked on mine last night. Today during class, he called me to the side and handed me my paper, saying that he was disappointed in my work, and reminded me of his class policy where he gives each student one chance to change one of the grades on his papers by rewriting it and taking his notes into consideration."

What an arrogant ass.

I quickly flip through the paper, skimming over *The Great Gatsby*, and already rolling my eyes. What is it with that man and that book? It's not that great.

I know, I know. I'm an English teacher. I should appreciate the written word. I mean, sure, it's an okay book, but I don't understand how the schooling system decides what books we have to teach. What qualifies a book as a classic? What makes that book soooo special?

I understand I should care about this. But I don't. I care about my students having a passion for books and leaving here not just with an understanding of how to construct a proper paper, but to be a master at it.

"What if I fail another paper? I really thought I did a good job on this."

"Did anyone else fail?" I ask her.

She shakes her head and chews on the inside of her cheek. "I, uh . . . I worked on my paper with Sonia, my best friend, and we didn't copy each other, but we went through all the symbolism, talked about it, and considered how Mr. Turner would want us to interpret it when writing our papers."

"What was her grade?"

Looking ashamed, she says, "She got a *B*."

Lips flattened together, I slowly nod my head. "Does he know you're on the volleyball team?"

She nods. "Yeah, I always change into my practice clothes before class so I can go straight from class to the court."

"And he told you he graded this last night?"

She nods. "Did I . . . did I do something wrong?"

I shake my head. "Not at all." Demeaning my skills as a teacher is one thing, but jeopardizing a student's future to *discipline* me? That's completely unfounded and unethical. And, if I'm honest, I'm surprised he'd even consider doing that. It makes me furious, though. *None of my pranks threatened a student's future.* Trying not to show my anger, I say, "Do you mind if I keep this paper and look it over this weekend? See where the mistakes were made. We can go over it Monday. How does that sound?"

"You don't mind?"

"Not at all, Blair. That's what I'm here for, okay?"

She nods and stands, zipping up her backpack. "Thank you, Coach Gibson. I really appreciate it."

"Sure." I nod and once she walks away, Stella comes up to me.

"What was that about?"

Staring off at our retreating player, I say, "Turner is going to die."

"Uh-oh, that doesn't sound good."

I curl the plastic-covered paper into a tube. "It's not. He should fear for his life."

"Should I sound off the metaphorical sirens?"

I shake my head. "No." He deserves to be taken to task about this, but I'll read Blair's essay first and hopefully find that he didn't really mark her down intentionally. *I have to take the higher road.* But . . . "This will be a sneak attack. Exactly what he deserves."

"When?"

"Sunday, at teachers' league," I answer.

"Oh boy . . . things are about to get interesting."

Indeed they are.

Chapter Eight

ARLO

"It's fun watching you run around, trying to make sure everything is perfect," Coraline says, sitting on the kitchen island, cross-legged, picking at the fruit platter I put together earlier today.

"I'm not trying to make everything perfect."

"Uh . . . you balled a melon." She picks up a piece of cantaloupe and plops it in her mouth. "I didn't even know people balled melons anymore. I thought the proper procedure for serving melon was just cutting it up. And you even put it in a separate bowl."

"People don't like the melon juice touching other fruit," I say, straightening the bowls that she keeps messing up.

"When did you become the hostess with the mostest?" She looks around. "Fresh flowers, make-your-own-mac-and-cheese bar, balled melon—who the hell are you?"

"These are my colleagues. Presentation needs to be proper."

She chuckles. "When the hell did you go to finishing school? From what I can remember, we both were put into private school, which was more of a detriment than anything. The need to break rules was heavy in our blood."

"Your blood, not mine." I shake my head.

"Uh, pretty sure you dated Tiffany McCrae because she was sporting that whole Avril Lavigne punk vibe and you wanted to horrify Nana and Pops when you brought her home. I can still remember the look of abhorrence on Nana's face when she asked why Tiffany was wearing a man's tie loose around her neck and Tiffany replied, 'Why aren't you?'" Coraline laughs and I pause, chuckling slightly.

"Pops begged me to break up with her to appease his wife."

"Wasn't she your first blow job?"

I raise a brow in her direction. "Why is that something you know?"

"Think I heard you talking about it with one of your friends. Or . . ." Coraline taps her chin. "Did Tiffany tell me? Hmm, I can't remember. Either way, she was your first. Daring man, given she had braces."

"Yeah, well, we all make bad decisions. It was shortly after that we broke up."

"Metal mouth eat up your dick?" Coraline smiles widely.

"No, she was eating up other guys' dicks at the same time."

"What? Really? She was cheating on you?"

"She labeled it as experimenting. I didn't see it that way. We broke up." I set out the napkins and the silverware along with my plates.

"And then that's when you started dating Gemma and lost your virginity, right?"

"Why are you detailing the timeline of my sexual experiences?"

She rocks on her butt, looking like she's having far too

much fun. "Bored. Nothing better to do. Now, were you short on the trigger?"

Turning my back to her, I say, "What do you think?"

"Given I've taken two virginities in my lifetime, I'd say yes."

"You've taken two virginities?" I ask, knowing my sister is pretty much the only one I would have this conversation with. She's the only person I feel comfortable around. I don't have to wear a shield of armor around her because she knows everything about my life. We don't share the same father. We don't have a stable mother. And we were both raised by our grandparents, thankfully, who tried to keep even heads on our shoulders, while our mother ran away and took her shot at acting.

She was in a few commercials, but never hit her stride. She still lives in Los Angeles, picking up odd jobs here and there, living off one-eighth of our grandparents' inheritance, while Coraline and I obtained most of it. We say Merry Christmas to each other, but that's the extent of our communication, and I'm okay with that, because I have Coraline.

She's my family.

She's all I need.

Even if she's incessant with her needling conversation about my personal life.

"I'm pretty sure it was three, but Bobby swore he'd had sex before. To this day, I don't believe him, he barely got it in before he was coming."

"Jesus." I place my hands on the island and lower my head. "Okay, we're not talking about this anymore."

"Uncomfortable?"

"How did you guess?"

She smooths her hair behind her ear. "I'm good at reading people."

Sighing, I lean against the counter and ask, "So, where did you go off to yesterday? You were gone for quite some time."

"Wouldn't you like to know?" She winks and plops another melon ball in her mouth.

"I would, actually."

"Well, that's my personal business, just like you said whatever is happening between you and Greer is your personal business."

That's exactly what I said to her Thursday night, when she wouldn't stop badgering me about the encounter with Greer during lunch. Hell, I don't even know what happened—how would I explain it to Coraline?

One minute I had Romeo's nipple pinched between my fingers, and then, the next thing I knew, I was inches from Greer, about to lay her across her classroom desk and pull her nipple between my teeth.

That goddamn dress.

Those innocent eyes.

The lightest of smirks on her face, knowing she'd bested me.

The combination pushed me over the edge, and I wanted to punish her, maul her . . . fuck her.

After I retreated from her classroom, a wave of awareness washed over me.

I don't do that shit.

I don't lose control, let my emotions get the best of me, but there I was, acting rather than thinking.

And I can still smell her, feel her chest barely reaching up to mine from her heavy breath, hear the quiet, whisper-like sound of her voice.

She's all I've been able to think about for the past few days and it's driving me fucking insane.

What's driving me insane? The gall she had to prank me.

After I already laid down the groundwork for a civil teaching environment, she blatantly disregarded that and decided to not only get back at me tenfold, but to rope in my unapologetic friends, as well.

It's obvious in a few short weeks she's been able to irritate me and get in the good graces of my friends. Which means only one thing—I need to be ready for whatever is thrown my way today.

Coraline hops off the counter and comes up next to me. She pokes me in the arm. "Thinking about Greer?"

"What?" I shake my head. "No."

Coraline lets out a belly laugh. "Liar. Isn't she about my age?"

I shrug, even though I know for a fact she's twenty-four.

"That means you're about eight years older than her, since you're ripe with age and all."

"I'm thirty-two, that's not ripe with age."

"Still, leer at someone your own age."

"I'm not leering at her. I'm not . . . anything with her. You're the one who keeps bringing it up."

"Fine." She crosses her arms over her chest. "Then tell me that this food fanfare you worked on for the better half of the day isn't for her."

"The fuck it is." I walk over to the pantry and grab a bag of sour cream and onion chips, thinking maybe I should put out one more side. "Just making sure people are fed."

"Uh-huh, we'll see about that."

The doorbell rings and I glance over at the clock—ten minutes before people are supposed to arrive, which means that's Gunner and Romeo. Thanks to the strict regimen they went through as student athletes at Brentwood University, they're programmed to arrive ten minutes early to every function.

Moving past Coraline, I answer the door to my two friends, finding nervous looks on their faces. They should be nervous. I haven't spoken to them since the nipple twisting.

"Hey . . . buddy," Gunner says, waving his hand.

"Best friend of all time," Romeo says, arms wide, walking toward me.

"I dare you to hug me right now."

Romeo's arms automatically fall to his side. "Maybe another time."

"Might be a good idea."

"Are we, uh, allowed to come in?" Gunner asks, holding both hands over his nipples as a shield.

"Not if you're going to walk around like that all night."

He drops his hands and I let them in. Coraline catches them in the hallway and starts slow clapping. "Really, boys, valiant job with the pranks. I know you were just doing the grunt work and you weren't the masterminds, but still, well played."

"Maybe we don't talk about that," Romeo says from the side of his mouth.

"Smart man," I say, walking past them and into the kitchen. They follow.

"Holy shit," Gunner says, taking in the island. "This looks fucking good . . ." His voice trails off as his eyes land on the melon. "Dude, you separated the cantaloupe for me? You know I hate the taste of it all mixed together."

"Oh, you're right, you do." Picking up the melon bowl, I dump it in with the rest of the salad and then mix it all together. "Couldn't remember who it was who didn't like melon. If it's just you, then who cares?"

"Dude," Gunner says, hands falling to the island. "You did that on purpose. That's cold."

"Want to talk about cold?" I ask, brow raised.

"Drop it," Romeo says. Pointing to the ambrosia salad I know Romeo loves, he says, "I'm going to guess you put mandarin oranges in that because you know I hate them and they ruin the dish completely for me."

"Oh, that's what I forgot." From a drawer in the kitchen island, I take out a bowl of canned mandarin oranges and dump them on top of the ambrosia salad. "There, better."

Coraline chuckles from the side. "It's the simple things that can truly ruin someone's day."

"That was the point." Pointing to both of my friends, I say, "You know better than to fuck with me. Do it again and the consequences will be way fucking worse. Got it?"

Romeo lowers his head to the island, his forearm acting as a pad between him and the marble. "I can't believe you added mandarin oranges—in front of me. That's fucking cruel."

Gunner pats his back. "We deserved it, man." Gunner clutches his heart. "I'm just glad Dylan and Lindsay didn't have to see me go through this."

"Were they going to come?" Coraline asks, picking up a chip and shoving it in her mouth. I told her about Gunner and Lindsay a few weeks back and she couldn't have been more excited to meet them. She's been wanting Gunner to bring them over for a while, more to drill Lindsay about Gunner's inadequacies than anything.

"That was the plan, until Thursday went down. I, uh"—he pulls on the back of his neck—"told her maybe it wasn't the best time to come over, given Turner's mood."

"Good call. He's been very unpredictable lately," Coraline says.

"Pot calling the kettle black," I mutter next to her.

"My whereabouts have been unpredictable, not my attitude," Coraline counters. Coraline turns to my friends, Romeo still nursing the loss of his ambrosia salad, and asks, "Do you guys know if there's anything going on between Arlo and Greer?"

Gunner's eyes flash to mine and I silently tell him to tread lightly, not that he knows anything.

There's nothing to know. Nothing is going on.

"Uh, not that I know of."

Good, he's teachable.

"Even if there was," Romeo bemoans and lifts his head up, "I wouldn't say a goddamn thing at this point."

"Ugh, you all are annoying."

The doorbell rings and before I can take off to get it, Coraline walks to the front door.

From the hallway, I hear, "Greer, hi, we were just talking—"

"Where's your brother?" she snaps.

Gunner and Romeo's eyes both widen and travel to mine.

"Oh shit," Gunner mutters.

"What the hell did you do to warrant that tone of voice?" Romeo asks just as Greer steps into the open kitchen and living room space.

Wearing a pair of leggings and a long sleeve T-shirt, her hair braided into two tight French braids, she locks eyes with me and . . . *oh shit* is right.

If looks could kill, I'd be dead and buried six feet under with that one glance.

But because I don't tend to show emotion outwardly, I keep calm as she approaches me, guns blazing.

"I need to talk to you, in private."

"Ooo, someone is in trouble," Romeo sing-songs, and I glance over Greer's shoulder to flash him a withering look. He shuts up quickly.

"Do you truly believe this is the time to air whatever childish grievances you might be harboring, Miss Gibson?"

"Oh, the condescending tone isn't going to get him anywhere," Coraline says, lining up with the boys, bowl of chips in hand, watching us carefully as if we're a movie playing out in front of her.

"Terrible move on his end, but then again, he doesn't have a knack for diffusing a situation. Let's see how this plays out," Gunner whispers, grabbing a handful of chips and shoving them in his mouth.

Standing tall, Greer slaps a paper on my chest and says, "We need to talk. Now."

Not moving, I say, "Try that request again, but without the

demand in your voice. You catch more flies with honey, Miss Gibson."

Her eyes flame, nostrils flair, and fuck, it feels good to be on this side of her pissed off.

"Uh, is anyone else fearing for their lives?" Romeo asks.

"You know, my balls aren't feeling safe right now and I'm not the one she's mad at."

"Is it weird that I'm oddly turned on by this entire interaction?" Coraline asks.

"Yeah, because it's your brother," Romeo says. "But, hell, I think I might be turned on too."

"Will you please shut up?" Greer says, whipping around to them. All their eyes widen as they take a step back.

Maybe it's time to take this elsewhere.

Stepping to the side, I walk past her and toward my office.

"Where do you think you're going?" she yells at me.

"To my office. I'd rather not be mindlessly badgered in front of an audience."

"Dude, watch it. I think she has the ability to cut you down with one roundhouse kick. Stella said she's feisty," Romeo calls out as I disappear down the hall and toward my office.

Calling out to Coraline, I ask, "Please make sure when the others arrive they're directed to get some food and then head out back."

Greer stomps behind me and just as I turn to shut the door to my office, she slips in. Casually, I go to my desk and sit on the front.

"Care to explain to me why you're yelling at me in my own house?"

She holds up the paper again. "This is why." She tosses the plastic-covered paper with a giant *F* circled on the front onto the desk. She then folds her arms over her chest and asks, "Care to explain why you took your anger with me out on one of my athletes?"

"What on earth are you talking about?"

"Blair Venezuela. She's my setter and she brought this paper to me. You failed her."

I glance at the paper, immediately remembering what was so awful about it. "Very good, Miss Gibson, you understand what an *F* means. Now if that's all, I'd like to get back to my guests."

"Do not play that asshole game with me. You're failing her because of what I did to you."

"As much as I'd love to play into your self-absorbed thoughts, that isn't the case here."

She points at the paper and says, "I read through it. Yes, there were some grammar errors and some misguided thoughts, but it didn't warrant a failing grade."

"Maybe not in your eyes, Miss Gibson, but I'm not seeking out mediocrity. I demand excellence, and this paper missed the mark. It was mindless drivel, random thoughts, and nothing cohesive that actually explains the symbolism in the book. It was as if she was paraphrasing what her friend wrote. Which is exactly what she did."

"You don't know that."

"And neither do you. Did you read Sonia's paper? Because Blair's is a misguided version of it. Now, why don't you stick to your musical chairs classroom where nursery rhymes are taught to understand the intricacies of a well-written novel, and I'll stick to my classroom where higher education isn't only demanded, but expected."

I stand from my desk and start to walk past her when she cuts me off, her body moving into my direct path to the door.

"It was not a failing paper, Arlo," she says through clenched teeth.

"It wasn't a pass. If you don't believe me, then I'll be happy to expose you to a passing paper, one that actually has great thought put into it, not ramblings built from Internet searches."

"You're going to mess with her life."

"Are you suggesting I give her a free pass?" I shake my head, closing what little space we have between us. "She's attending UCLA next year. You're aware of their academic excellence. Why would you want to provide her with a shortcut?"

"I don't want to provide her with a shortcut, Arlo." She sticks her chin up, her eyes trained on mine as she speaks. "I don't want you picking on her because she's my athlete."

"You really think I'd do that?"

"I do."

Unbelievable.

I don't have to stand here and listen to these accusations. Pushing past her again, our shoulders bumping, I head for the door, only for her to swoop in and stop me again.

"You're going to stand there and tell me that while grading her paper, you had no intentions of giving her a bad grade just because she's my athlete? Because you were mad at me?" She pushes my shoulder, trying to grab my attention, which I don't want to give her. "Because you thought it was one way to get back at me."

I take a long, hard look at where she pushed my shoulder and then I look at her.

Eyes furious, raging.

Neck flushed, a vein twitching on the right side.

Chest rising faster than before.

Hands curled into fists at her sides.

The anger washing over her is mirrored in me, and before I know what I'm doing, I press one hand against her hip and back her against the closed door. The other hand lands against the wood next to her head. She gasps from the quick movement but doesn't falter.

She holds strong.

Stands her ground as I battle with roaring animosity and unbridled arousal.

Fuck.

Even though her beauty strikes me in the pit of my stomach, it doesn't overshadow the resentment I have for her implications. I would never jeopardize a student's future by failing them unnecessarily. For eight years, I've worked relentlessly to enable my students to perform to the best of their ability, to attain the GPA required to gain entry into their desired university. *Blair's grade was deserved.*

In a voice that comes out menacing, I say, "You might want to rethink your accusations, Miss Gibson. If brought to Principal Dewitt, there could be major implications."

"Maybe they should be brought to her."

My thumb drags along her hipbone, she sucks in a sharp breath, and her tongue wets her lips.

"I wasn't speaking of implications for me . . . I was talking about you."

"Wh-what do you mean?" she asks, her voice wavering as my thumb slips under her shirt. Just the pad of my thumb presses against her bare skin.

"Principal Dewitt takes complaints seriously. If you told her I was punishing your athlete, my student, because I was mad at you for pranking me, not only would she investigate the pranking and the harm you could have imposed on a faculty member, but she'd also have the paper sent to a review board where they'd run it through a plagiarism program first and then grade it from there. Not only would you possibly lose your job over mindless pranks that disturbed the environment of the school, but your athlete could also be punished for possible plagiarism, resulting in suspension. How do you think UCLA would like that?"

"You . . . asshole."

She raises her hand. I grip it, pushing it against the door, above her head. She's pinned in place.

I lower my mouth to her ear once again. Speaking softly but firmly, I ask, "Is that a risk you're willing to take?" My thumb slides a little farther under her shirt, and she lets out a harsh breath, her torso twisting as her lungs seek more air.

"You . . . don't know she plagiarized," she says as my nose grazes the side of her cheek.

Fuck, she smells so good. Her skin's so soft. Her fiery disposition's turning me on more than I care to admit.

This isn't how I handle conversations or disagreements. But this girl is making me lose my mind. Being around her causes me to forget how to hold a civil conversation. Instead, I have this urgent need to be next to her, touching her, so close to her that my lips can practically taste her. And I hate that. I hate that she can overrule my common sense and self-control. *Maybe I should hate her.*

"There were some unoriginal thoughts in her paper." My breathing slows down, anticipation building heavy in my chest as I move my head so we're looking each other directly in the eyes.

And when our pupils connect, the air stills around us. The rest of the guest arrivals fade into the background, and what's left is this moment, with Greer, temptation knocking me in the dick, pulling me closer and closer until I don't think I can stop myself . . .

Knock. Knock.

Greer jolts up but I don't move, keeping her pinned against the door.

"What?" I seethe.

"Uh, should we start eating?" Romeo asks.

"Yes," I snap.

"Okay, uh, sounds good."

When he steps away, Greer whispers, "We need to get out there."

"You were the one who wanted to have this conversation."

"Well, I can't have it when . . . when you're this close to me."

"And why's that, Greer?"

"Because . . . you're . . ." She groans as I lower my mouth to her ear and capture her lobe while my hand slides up her stomach a little higher. "Fuck, Arlo," she gasps, and it's like an aphrodisiac, hearing her say my name with capitulation.

And when I think she's going to push me away, her hands slide up my chest to my shoulders.

"Admit it," I say while her hands drag up my neck to my face, where she maneuvers my forehead to press against hers. Our noses touching, our breaths mixing. "Admit that I'm right."

"Never," she says so softly that I almost don't hear her over the pounding of my heart. Her hand slides up to the side of my face, cupping it. "You're an arrogant prick who believes the world revolves around his agenda." Her thumb passes over the scruff on my jaw, the movement igniting the flames in my stomach to a roaring inferno. She turns my head, brings her mouth to my ear and whispers, "Well, it doesn't." And then she drags her mouth along my cheek until she reaches the corner of my mouth, where she stops.

I hold my breath.

Waiting.

Anticipating what I know will be explosive.

What I know will be a passionate kiss full of hate.

Full of distaste.

Full of unadulterated emotion that neither of us seems to be able to control.

And as she sucks in a sharp breath, I prime myself, get ready for her lips on mine . . .

"We need to go," she says, pushing at my chest and slipping out from under me.

Stuck in my position, one hand still leaning against the door, I look to the side and catch the flush of her cheeks, the fidgety movements as she attempts to right herself.

Pushing off the door, I drag my hand through my hair and

try to calm the rapid beat of my heart. "You're going to go out there like that? Flushed? Turned on?"

Her eyes widen. "I'm not turned on."

"You're not?" I ask, brow raised, moving closer again. "So if I feel your pulse, it wouldn't be pounding just as hard as mine?"

She shakes her head, backing up until she reaches the wall.

"And if I moved in closer, you wouldn't feel the need to reach out and touch me?" I leave nothing but a few inches between us.

"No," she answers, keeping her hands at her sides as her body remains rigid, but her eyes give her away.

Moving in the last few inches, I drag my fingers down her neck and across her collarbone. Her head rolls to the side and her mouth parts.

Her hand falls to the waistline of my athletic shorts, her fingers slipping against the elastic, dipping in just enough to drive me fucking crazy with need.

Swallowing hard, I catch my breath as I say, "And if I were to drag my hand between your spread legs . . . would you be wet?"

Her eyes flash to mine with lust in them. Hunger. Need.

Whatever answer she gives me, I know, right here and now . . . she wants me, just as badly as I want her.

"Arlo, I . . ." Her breath catches, she licks her lips, and her fingers rub against my skin.

Fuck . . .

I take her jaw in my hand, angle it up and stare at her luscious lips. Pink, wet, ready.

I lower.

Foreheads connect.

Noses brush.

Lips seconds away—

"Arlo, where's the mac and cheese?" Coraline yells from

the kitchen. "I can't find . . . Oh, it's in the oven. Don't worry, everyone, it's in the oven."

"Jesus Christ," I mutter in frustration and push away from Greer. Back turned toward her, I grip the back of my neck with both hands and catch my breath.

What the hell am I doing?

There are people in the other room, and I'm seconds away from taking Greer up against my office wall. This isn't who I am.

Not even close.

We were discussing a student—how did it turn into this, seconds away from kissing a woman I despise?

Blowing out a heavy breath, I turn around to find Greer staring back at me, her nipples hard, her eyes crazed, almost as if she's trying to discern what just happened as well.

We stand there staring at each other, both trying to catch our breath, both with arousal evident in our body language.

She takes a step forward, and I quickly say, "Don't."

Her eyes widen.

"Don't fucking come near me, Greer."

"Excuse me?"

"You heard me. I said don't come near me." I pull on my hair, telling myself to stay in place, to not go over there and kiss the confusion off her face.

Getting involved with her would be an epically bad idea. Not only do we seem to be at each other's throats whenever we get the chance, but she's younger than me, a new teacher in town, and I share a wall with her at school. It all screams bad decision.

Ignoring my request, she charges toward me and pokes me in the chest. "You're the one who made the first move. What am I supposed to do, sit back and let you play with me like that?"

"It was a mistake."

"You're damn right it was a mistake. Jesus, Arlo."

Standing tall, I glance at her lips one last time and then smile, which only turns up the volume on her anger.

"Why are you smiling?"

"Nothing."

I walk past her toward the door and once again she stops me right before I can exit. "No, not nothing. Why are you smiling?"

"Your nipples. They're perfectly hard, begging for my mouth."

She glances at her breasts and then quickly covers them up with her arms. "You're an asshole."

"So you've said before. Doesn't mean you don't want me."

"You are unbelievable."

"Imagine what you'd be thinking if I actually drove my tongue into your mouth." On that, I let myself out of my office and head to the kitchen, where Coraline is the only one left filling up a plate. Everyone else is outside.

She lifts her brow at me and I ignore her, collecting a plate and filling it up, only for an irritated Greer to follow closely behind. She picks up a plate and bumps me out of the way, helping herself to the mac and cheese before me.

Coraline laughs and mumbles, "Oh, tonight should be fun."

"WHACK THAT COCK," Stella yells.

Romeo reaches back, swings his racket with all his might, and wallops the shuttlecock straight into the net.

"Ugh, and you call yourself an athlete." Stella tosses her hands in the air. "Embarrassing, Brock." It's funny to me when Stella uses Romeo's actual name. She's the only one I know who calls him Brock, and it's as if his mother is yelling at him by the way he straightens up.

After dinner, which I ate silently off to the side while

Romeo, Gunner, Stella, Greer, and Coraline all sat together, we set up the badminton court—the game of choice this year —and started going over strategy.

Since there are four people allowed on each side, and we only have five people right now, we're playing two on two. Romeo told us we'll get people to fill in as opponents and play us as we near the tournament. I've been sitting out, watching Stella and Romeo argue, while Greer avoids all eye contact with me besides the few snide looks she sends my way in between volleys.

"I have to go to the bathroom," Gunner calls out, tossing his racket to me. "Take my spot. Participation is required."

Sighing, I stand, and Greer quickly says, "We should switch teams. Get used to other players."

"No way," Romeo says, shutting that idea down quickly. "Not when Stella is yapping at me about my athletic prowess."

"What athletic prowess? I have yet to actually see you do something on this court, unless . . ." She turns to Coraline, who's holding a rule book. "Cora, does it say anything in there about hitting the cock into the net for extra points that we're unaware of? Because if that's the case"—Stella slow claps— "you should be in the hall of fame for badminton."

Coraline makes a show of flipping through the pages. "Nothing about netting the cock, but I'll keep you posted."

"Fine, until then, hit the damn thing over the net." Stella pats him on the back and gets into position. "Come on, Turner. Greer won't bite until after the game."

Great.

I step into the marked-off space with Greer and keep my distance as Stella serves the shuttlecock over the net, straight to me. I get ready to hit it, only for Greer to step in front of me and hit it back.

"Uh, that was in my area."

Romeo hits it over the net and cheers for himself.

Stella mutters a "finally."

Once again, the shuttlecock flies toward me, and, with her hip, Greer bumps me out of the way to hit it.

"What the hell?"

She doesn't answer me, but instead bounces on her feet like a tennis player at Wimbledon, waiting for the next hit.

Stella hits it this time, Romeo congratulates her, and I move in front of Greer, only for her to hop up and hit the shuttlecock back over the net.

"Greer, you can't play by yourself."

"Looks like she can." Coraline snickers from the sidelines.

"Oh, nice hit," Stella says to Romeo, the shuttlecock heading to the back corner of our court. Greer and I both back up, and before I know what I'm doing, I reach out and push her to the side, sending her into the grass, and hit the shuttlecock over the net.

"You bastard," Greer says, hopping up and pushing at my chest.

The game is ignored as Stella hits the shuttlecock back over the net, where it drops between me and Greer as we stare each other down.

"You started it." I poke her leg with my racket.

Her eyes widen and she pokes me back with her racket. "You were a dick to me way before I was to you. So, you started it. You can't count previous experiences. This was a clean slate."

"Oh, is that what that was back in my office, wiping the slate clean? I don't recall that. All I can remember is you accusing me of punishing your athlete as vengeance."

"You did. Admit it."

"I have better things to do with my time than fuck with another faculty member and her student athletes. That's more than I can say for you." I look her up and down.

Greer opens her mouth to reply, only to look to the side, where Gunner—back from the bathroom—Stella, Romeo, and Coraline are all standing together, watching us.

"You know, I, uh, I think we did enough practicing tonight," Romeo says. "I think we should call it a night."

"Good idea." Stella hands her racket to Gunner, who collects Romeo's as well. "I was getting tired anyway."

"Yeah, me too," Gunner says.

"Ditto," Romeo adds.

Coraline looks at all three of them and says, "Are you mental?" She waves toward me and Greer. "We've front-row seats to this nightmare unfolding, and you want to leave now?"

"I'm nervous of what might happen and would rather not be an accessory to murder." She takes Coraline's hand and says, "I'll treat everyone to ice cream while these two figure out their issues."

Greer tosses her racket and says, "I'll join you."

Stella puts her hand up and halts Greer. "You know I love and respect you, but no. You aren't invited." She motions between me and Greer. "You need to figure this out, because now that I'm involved in this stupid teachers' league, I won't let your petty fighting make a mockery of us. So, air out your grievances, figure it out, and when we see each other again, you two better have smiling faces, even if you have to fake it."

"Stella, I don't—"

"Hey." She snaps her finger at Greer, who rears back. "We helped you with the pranks, now it's your turn. Fix it."

"You know, it's a huge turn-on that you're so into the teachers' league," Romeo says, heart eyes practically spilling out of him.

"Shut up, Brock." Stella charges past him, Gunner and Coraline following closely behind.

"I'm going to call up Lindsay and see if she wants to meet up with us, take Dylan out to some ice cream."

"Great idea," Coraline says, her voice trailing off. "I can't wait to meet them."

And then they're gone, leaving me alone in my backyard with Greer.

A very angry, irritated, and less-than-excited Greer.

This should be fun.

———

"HERE," I say, handing Greer a water with slices of cucumber.

She looks at the drink and then back up at me. "Did you poison it?"

Rolling my eyes, I take a big gulp and hand it to her. "No."

After the rest of the crew went to get ice cream, Greer angrily stormed off down the stone steps of my backyard that lead to the bottom half, where I have lounge chairs looking out over the lake. She took a seat and that's where she's been since.

Given the immense amount of anger in her eyes during badminton, I thought it would be a good idea to let her cool off, so I went inside, did dishes, and then took her some water . . . and cookies. But she hasn't seen those yet.

"Move your feet," I say sternly.

"Why?" she asks, staring at the lake.

"So I can sit down."

"There are a lot of other chairs. Pick one."

Huffing out in frustration, I push her legs to the side and take a seat on her lounge.

"Insufferable," she mutters, bringing her legs into a criss-cross position.

I hold the plate of chocolate chip cookies out to her and say, "Here, eat one of these. Maybe you'll be less crabby."

"Less crabby? Don't you think you're the one who should be eating the cookies? Or do they not fix bastard? Also, it's extremely offensive that you think a cookie will change my attitude." She picks up two cookies and takes a bite of one. "Damn it," she whispers, reaching for the plate and taking another. When I quirk a brow at her, she says, "This has nothing to do with my crabbiness or need for sugar as a woman and everything do with how incredibly soft these are. Got it?"

"Sure. Whatever you need to tell yourself."

"See, that right there," she says, pointing at me, mouthful of cookie. "That attitude, that's what's making me want to jab my fist through your eye socket. So condescending all the time. Ever consider not acting like a total motherfucker?"

"Never gave it much thought." I plop a cookie in my mouth.

"Maybe you should. You'd be more likeable."

"My goal in life isn't to please everyone. I don't have to make the world around me happy in order to be happy."

"Wouldn't kill you to not be a dick, though."

"Contrary to what you might believe, I'm not a dick."

She sips her water. "Oh, I know, you also suck ass really well."

I run my tongue over my teeth and, in a deeper tone, say, "Wouldn't you like to know?"

Her eyes narrow and she stares at me while taking a bite of cookie. She chews, swallows. "Whatever happened in your office was a lapse of judgment."

"Nothing happened. At least not for me. You were the one with the hard nipples."

"And you were the one with the . . . well . . ." Her lips quirk to the side. "Were, uh . . . were you hard?"

Fuck, I almost laugh out loud from the confused look on her face.

Almost.

"No," I answer. "I'd have to be remotely interested to be hard." I was so fucking hard I could have hammered nails with my cock. But I refuse to be goaded.

She's mid-bite of her cookie when I say that, causing her to sputter crumbs all over me with her outburst. "Remotely interested? Are you kidding me right now? You were the one with the hand up my shirt."

"I wouldn't have qualified that as up your shirt. My fingers barely touched your skin."

"Well, there was touching, and caressing, and you . . . and you nibbled on my earlobe."

I shrug. "Doesn't mean I was interested."

"You're so full of yourself, you know that?" She washes her cookie down with water and then removes the plate of cookies from my hand, setting them on the side table next to the lounge.

"What are you doing?"

"Proving a point," she says, standing, only to push me back on the lounge and then sit on my lap.

Seeing where she's going with this, I place my hands behind my head and look up at her. "Enjoying yourself?"

She rolls her eyes and scoots up so her pelvis sits right on top of mine.

There's no doubt in my mind that I can best her in this, that I can look away, think of other things, make for damn sure that I don't get turned on.

But then . . .

She moves her hand over her neck, rotating her head to the side.

Eyes closed, she massages her shoulders, little wisps of her hair floating over her face.

Her top teeth roll over her bottom lip, sucking and pulling it in, and fuck . . .

Once again, her nipples are hard.

And I want to suck on them and fuck them.

Focus, Turner.

"Do you have a point to this nonsense?"

"I do." Her eyes open and her hands tumble to my chest, where she very softly runs them up and down my sides.

"Then get to the point, I have better things to do than see

your pitiful attempt at trying to turn me on. Keep in mind, we have to work next to each other, so I wouldn't embarrass yourself if you can avoid it."

Not saying a word, her hands travel up my stomach, over my pecs and to my shoulders, which she gives a little rub.

There's something about another human's touch, the kind of touch I haven't felt in a while. It paralyzes my thoughts, blinds me to what's happening.

Little flashes of getting lost in her touch blank out my mind sporadically as she continues to move her hands over my torso, always with a barrier of clothing between us, but nonetheless, it's doing the job.

She's doing the job.

Fuck.

I bite down on my lower lip and concentrate. Focus on anything that—oh fuck.

She rolls her hips.

Shit. Now I'm biting on my lip, trying to keep it together. But it's not working. A tingling sensation travels up my legs and hits me straight in the groin. I grab her wrists and twist her so fast off my lap and onto the padded lounger that she has no clue what's happened until I'm hovering over her, pinning her hands just above her head.

"Wh-what are you doing?"

"Putting an end to this. It's massively inappropriate."

"Inappropriate?" she asks, her neck flushed, her cheeks pink, a light sheen of sweat dotting her hairline.

She's turned on.

Just that little movement, it got to her, too.

Fuck, it got to both of us.

"You've been inappropriate since the moment I met you, and now you're throwing down that card? Can't have it both ways, Arlo."

"You think I want this? You?"

Her jaw clenches and she tries to free her hands, but I

have them pinned tight, not wanting her to touch any part of my body, because I know that's what she wants to do. I can see it in her eyes. But I won't let her. I'm fucking thirty-two years old, and I don't have time for this sort of immature shit. Especially after her claim that I marked Blair's paper incorrectly. *It was plagiarism.*

I pull away and roll off to the side, placing my head in my hands, feeling that tension creep back up to my shoulders. This is so fucked.

"God, Turner," she growls. "You drive me insane. What was the point of me staying here if you're going to be a closed-off jerk the entire time?"

"We were supposed to work out our differences, and you were trying to work over my dick."

"You would be so lucky. I was trying to prove a point, which clearly I made because you're trying to hide the proof."

"I'm not hiding anything."

"Fine. Stay away from me. Just stay away." I watch as she gets up, angry, shaking her head as if I'm a lost cause. "I don't give a fuck that you hate me, by the way. I don't understand it, as I'm a damn good teacher, but whatever." She takes a few steps away, then pauses. "I just wish you were more real with me, rather than putting up constant walls."

"I don't trust many people."

"Why not?"

"No one gave me reason to growing up," I answer honestly.

Her head tilts to the side ever so slightly. "You're just going to toss that out there as if this is a casual conversation?"

"Isn't it?" I ask.

"I don't know."

"Me neither," I say, just as confused. I look over my shoulder and see . . . compassion. *Fuck that.*

"Arlo, I—"

"Just leave."

"Arlo . . ."

"Leave," I shout. "Okay? Fuck . . . just leave."

I'm so messed up in the head and I have no idea why.

She's making me think about shit. She's making me question my professionalism. She's accusing me of punishing students to get back at her.

And . . . hell, she's making me wonder just how wet she was only moments ago.

Chapter Nine

GREER

I take a few deep breaths and convince myself that everything's going to be okay.

That I'm not about to embark on another journey through the black hole that is Arlo Turner.

Since the weekend, I've felt confused, even more irritated than before, and . . . well, and horny.

Honestly, I have no idea what's happening when it comes to Arlo. Out of the blue this man dislikes me, then he turns me on, then pulls away, then turns me on even more while arguing, and fighting, and . . . Jesus, anyone else confused here?

Show of hands?

Either way, I have to talk to him about Blair, and it needs to be a civil conversation, despite the war of turmoil wrestling inside my head.

His door is open and he's sitting at his desk, looking over papers. School let out two hours ago, and I came as soon as I could from practice. I'm thankful he's still here. I didn't want to drive to his house to have this conversation. Lucky for me, Gunner said Arlo stays late on Mondays to catch up on work.

And he was right.

With a sigh, I lift my hand and give his door a knock.

His head turns toward me, and I'm struck by his brilliant eyes first, then the chiseled features of his handsome face.

If I were a student of his, there's no way in hell I'd be able to concentrate. I'd be infatuated. I know this because, even as a grown woman, I'm taken aback by just how good-looking he is. It can be distracting, getting caught up in his eyes, in the way his cardigans are perfectly pushed up to his elbows, revealing tanned and muscular forearms, or the way they lay over his carved shoulders. And his dark hair, mixed with the dark scruff on his face . . . It only highlights how symmetrical his face is.

Positively devastating.

Turning back to his papers, he asks, "Can I help you with something, Miss Gibson?"

Ahh, back to Miss Gibson now. Fair enough.

After the confusion, taunting, and angry confrontations on Saturday, I agree that's for the best.

I step into his classroom and ask, "Do you have a minute?"

Not answering right away, he finishes reading the paper in front of him, flips it over, and circles a *C* at the top. God, so automatic, no thinking it over. A grade, just like that.

A part of me wonders how well I would have done in Arlo's class if I were his student. I'm starting to believe not well with my ability to barely focus when I'm around him.

Pushing back from his desk but staying in his chair, he asks, "What's up?"

I study him for a second, gauging his mood. No furrow in his brow, no clenched jaw. He actually seems . . . reserved, emotionless, and I don't know what's scarier—Arlo Turner emotionless and shut down, or Arlo Turner charged up and ready to destroy any walls I may have erected around my libido.

From my back pocket, I place Blair's paper on his desk and then sit on the edge, looking down at him while I speak. "Can we have a civil conversation about Blair's paper, please? Without yelling at each other or pointing fingers?"

"Sure," he answers, leaning back in his chair and folding his hands over his stomach. "What would you like to talk about?"

Okay, he's starting to scare me now. He's too casual.

Did someone slip him a tranquilizer and not tell me? Whenever I've been around him, there's always been some sort of emotion grappling at him, but not today, not now, and I truly don't know how to handle it.

"Okay, um . . ." I clear my throat, trying to gain my bearings. "Can you explain to me what you're looking for—"

"Can I ask you a question?"

"Uh, sure," I say.

He picks up the paper and flips through it. "Why is it that you're in here talking about this paper, but Blair has yet to come to me and discuss it herself?"

Oh God, here we go, I can feel the condescending attitude rearing up and ready to go.

"I thought if I gained a better understanding of how to assist her, it might be more beneficial. She did come to me for help."

"I see." He rocks in his chair. "Did it ever occur to you that maybe your advice should have been 'See Mr. Turner, talk to him, and maybe he can assist you'?"

"Frankly, you don't seem like the approachable type," I say, keeping my voice even.

"And yet, you're stepping out of your day to approach me."

"Because I can handle my own."

"Don't you think she should learn how to do that?" he

asks, making a point that I don't want to admit could be right. "She's not going to have you in college. What happens when a professor fails her? Think she'll ask her college coach to do the heavy lifting for her?"

"No, I just thought—"

He tosses the paper on the desk and says, "She's about to cross over into adulthood. Let her." He leans forward in his chair but keeps his eyes trained on me. "It's nice that you care, though."

And then he turns back to his papers, starting on the next one.

Uh, was that . . . a compliment?

Did I hear him right?

There was no sarcasm in his voice.

No hate.

Just a plain old compliment.

When he sat back in his chair, did he push a button that slipped me into some kind of alternate universe?

"Is that all, Miss Gibson?"

"Uh, yeah," I answer, unable to move from the spot on his desk.

He looks up at me. "Then will you be going?" He nods to the door.

"Yeah." But I don't move. I sit there, stunned, wondering what made him have a change of heart.

Was it a change of heart?

Or was he just appeasing me to get me out of his room?

His pen drops to the desk and he leans back in his chair again.

"What?" he asks, his voice growing annoyed now.

Turning so my legs are now parallel with his body and I'm facing him, I say, "You gave me a compliment."

"I was merely stating a fact. No need to get emotional about it."

"I'm not getting emotional, I'm just a little shocked."

"Well if that's the case, I'll be sure to never do it again."

"Stop." I playfully push at his shoulder. "Lighten up, you know you want to."

"I was having a perfectly fine time grading mediocre papers."

"Sounds riveting." I smile at him and nudge him with my foot. "You know it wouldn't hurt you to smile."

"Give me a reason to smile and I will."

"Is that a challenge?" I ask, liking this lighter side of him.

"It's however you take it."

"Fine, challenge accepted." I rub my hands together and realize I have the perfect story. "I have a policy in my class-room that if a student's phone rings in class, they have to give it to me to answer."

"Uh-huh."

"Well, yesterday, someone's phone rang. I immediately stopped my lecture and found the culprit. Joe Wallace. I held my hand out and he gave me his phone reluctantly. I answered it, and found out his mother wanted to tell him she found the superhero underwear he loves so much in his size at Costco, and she got him two boxes of them."

He doesn't crack a smile, doesn't even flinch.

"Oh, come on, that's funny."

"Barely comical."

"You're such a liar." I nudge him with my foot again, only for him to grab my calf and move his hand up my leggings to my thigh. God, his hands are big . . . strong . . . enticing. "Back to this, huh?" I ask.

The corner of his lip tilts up and I nearly gasp.

"That, you smirk at? Not the superhero underwear?"

"I'm not easy."

"You seem easy."

He gives my leg a squeeze and pulls away, going back to his papers. "Well, I'm not. Now if that's all——"

I don't know what possesses me—maybe it's from him not

yelling at me today, or the tiniest of smirks to ever cross some-one's face—but I reach out and push a wayward strand of hair off his forehead.

His eyes lift up and focus on mine, head tilted, those blue-greens staring up at me as if I could possibly hold his happi-ness in my hands.

"Who do you get your eyes from? They're gorgeous."

Wetting his lips, he says, "My mom."

"Does she have long eyelashes too?"

He nods.

"Were you close with her?"

"Not even a little."

I smooth my fingers over his jaw and he leans into the touch.

"Was she the one you were talking about when you mentioned no one gave you the opportunity to trust anyone?"

"Yup."

"What a nice gift for her to give to you," I say, trying to lighten the mood. And it does just that, because the furrow in his brow recedes.

"She's a thoughtful one." His eyes search mine and then he turns back to his papers. "I should get these done."

"Can you talk to me for a second?"

He leans back and rolls his eyes—without the normal disdain. "What, Miss Gibson?"

"Don't sound annoyed or anything." He's about to open his mouth with a reply when I point at him and say, "Don't say anything snarky or that will piss me off."

"Don't tempt me."

I wait for a smirk, I know he wants to, but he holds strong and gives me all his attention instead. I'll take it.

"So, if I'm getting this straight, you're more than happy to speak to Blair about her paper, you're not punishing her because of me, and we could possibly be friends."

"Yes, if Blair comes to me during lunch, I'll help her with

her paper. I can be an asshole, but not at the expense of a student. I invite you to remember that. And acquaintances will be just fine."

"Acquaintances? You think we're mere acquaintances?"

He sighs. "What do you want from me, Greer? You want a relationship?"

"What? No." I shake my head, my cheeks flaming. "I wasn't even thinking about that. I just thought it'd be nice to . . . I don't know, be nice to each other."

"I can be cordial."

"Heaven forbid anything more." I take in his whiteboard and wonder what I want from him.

"This past week got the best of me." He clears his throat. "Don't expect that mercurial behavior anymore. Which means, I think it's best we keep things cordial, but nothing more. I have no interest in the way you educate, nor do I have interest in your volleyball team or any other extracurricular activities."

"Wow, okay, tell me how it really is." I stand from his desk and start to walk away, when he stands as well, grabs my hand, and spins me back toward him. I catch my balance with my hand to his muscular chest, which I quickly remove.

"You want to know what I really think?"

"Yes, please. I want you to be real."

"Real. Fine." His eyes grow darker. "Those dresses you wear are my undoing. The skirts, well, they're a bonus. I envision peeling them off you over my desk after class. Your eyes—they're unlike any color I've ever seen, caramel-colored with a hint of green on the outer ring. Enticing, curious. They bother me but intrigue me at the same time, making it hard not to give you the privilege of being looked in the eyes. And your perfume . . . it's dizzying, mystifying, causes me to lose my frame of mind and puts me in a headspace of lust. Demanding lust."

Oh God.

My stomach clenches, the thought of him peeling my clothes off is extremely tempting. What would it feel like to have his large hands roam over my body, cupping my breasts, playing with my nipples? Would his mouth be just as delicious as I expect it is? Just as demanding and rough? Would he expect me to listen to him? To his commands?

Would I?

Searching his beautiful eyes, I know I would. If, right now, he told me to take my shirt off, I'd oblige. I'd be desperate for his direction, knowing he'd be an expert at bringing me pleasure. And that's *not* me. I'm confident in myself, in my brains and looks. I don't *need* a man to make me feel good. And yet with this man . . . I feel desperate and needy. *But why?* I've been around handsome men before. I've been around demanding men before too. How is it one charmless, incisive man can untether me? He's arrogant. Unyielding. But maybe . . .

It's the way he carries himself, the confidence he exudes, the broody attitude with the peekaboo charm that shows itself every once in a while.

He's devastating, and I'm very quickly realizing that.

I'm also realizing I'm starting to have this need to see him. To be near him. To gather his attention even if it's just for a few short seconds.

I enjoy how he stops me from walking away, that those moments spur on vulnerability from him.

I enjoy how unhinged he looks when he's near me, how his hands itch to touch me.

His fingers come to my chin and pinch it while tilting the angle of my head up a few more centimeters. A firm grip, one that has me shaking in my shoes, waiting, anticipating what he might do next.

"This can't happen," he says, his voice cracking.

"Why not? Admit it, Arlo, you want to fuck me."

"Of course I want to fuck you. I've wanted to fuck you since your interview. Your beauty has no bounds, Greer."

I wet my lips. "Then why won't you? Is it against school policy?"

"No."

"Do you already have a fuck buddy?"

He shifts. "No."

"Are you a virgin?"

His eyes narrow.

I chuckle and smooth my hand over his chest. "Just making sure. So, what's the hold up? Does my teaching technique really trouble you that much?"

"No."

"Are you—"

"I have other things I need to focus on," he says, cutting me off before I can guess again. "Important things. I can't afford the distraction."

"What important things?" I ask, feeling my eyebrows pull together.

"Nothing you need to know or worry about." He lowers his hand and takes a step back.

"Okay," I say, feeling defeated, and I really don't understand why.

I hate the guy.

I like the guy.

He irritates me.

He digs deep into my soul.

That kind of toxic behavior should be dropped and left to die on its own. No need for it to take up space in my head, but as he backs away, a small piece of me calls out to him.

Let me help you.

Let me be a shoulder for you.

Let me be an escape . . .

He picks up his papers and puts them in a folder, then he

gathers his shoulder bag and tucks the folder into it. Turning to me, he says, "I'm leaving."

"I gathered."

"So . . . you can leave."

"Okay." And as I start to turn away, I catch him give me one last look, almost as if he's hoping I'll say something else, that I'll push him a little further, ask him to share with me.

But I won't.

I won't push it now.

But I might later . . .

⸺

"YOU LOOK QUITE LOVELY TODAY," Kelvin says, coming up to the table Keiko, Stella, and I are all sitting at. Every Friday, we order from the Italian restaurant down the street for lunch. Today, we bought two calzones and divided them up amongst the three of us. One pepperoni and pineapple, the other sausage and spinach. Both equally fantastic, both terrible for the hips.

"Thank you for the compliment," Keeks replies rigidly, scanning Kelvin up and down. "I'd share the same sentiment, but unfortunately an ungodly shade of mustard besmirched your tie, causing your appearance to be quite off-putting."

"Keiko," I say sternly under my breath as Kelvin lifts up his tie and examines it.

"What? Is it not the truth?" She gestures to poor Kelvin. "The seedy condiment splotch is arresting against the light blue of his paisley cravat."

She's not wrong, but, good God, does she have to point it out?

Tucking the tip of his tie through one of the spaces between buttons on his shirt, he nervously says, "I had a soft pretzel for lunch. Good thing I took off my Obi Wan Kenobi robe, or else I'd be a mustard-smothered Jedi." He laughs. He snorts. My cheeks flame with secondary embarrassment.

"Yes, bravo, Kelvin," Keeks says before wiping her face and standing. "Care to escort me to my classroom?"

"I'd be honored," Kelvin says, standing taller. "Do you want me to remove my tie?"

"No, what you have done is sufficient." Keeks nods to us and then takes off, keeping her arms crossed at her chest as Kelvin walks next to her.

Once they're out of earshot, I chuckle and shake my head. "Oh God, I love them."

"They're so overly polite, it's hard to listen to," Stella says, picking up a piece of her calzone. "I can't believe they went on a date."

"And he tried to kiss her, and she went into a ten-point list as to why it wasn't the right time to be sharing a first kiss."

"I wonder if we should contact her parents somehow and see if she came with a handbook to give to Kelvin."

I shake my head. "I think Keeks is writing the handbook as she goes. God, I love her. I wish I had the same balls of steel as her, able to tell it like it is."

"Yeah? Who do you want to knock down with the truth?" Stella dips her calzone into the accompanying marinara sauce.

"No one in particular." At least that's what I tell her. "Living your life freely like that must be nice though."

"True."

"Hey, ladies," Gunner says, coming up to our table, Arlo at his side. "How were your calzones?"

Stella turns in her chair. "Watching us eat, Gunner?"

"Everyone was," he answers. "The calzones smell amazing. I think we were all hoping there would be leftovers."

"Have you seen Keiko's appetite after a saucy round of teaching? She's ravenous. Greer and I are just grateful we were able to get our fair share."

I glance up and catch Arlo staring at me. When our eyes

meet, he doesn't look away; instead, I watch his eyes rake me over. I chose a simple blue sundress with yellow polka dots and capped sleeves. I paired it with yellow high heels and a tiny yellow bow tucked into my low bun. Nothing special, but from the dark look in Arlo's expression, he appreciates the outfit.

Which seems odd to me, because I make sure that my dresses are never revealing, for obvious reasons. I keep the necklines high and the hems longer, over my knees. They do accentuate my waist, but that's about it.

Men—not sure I'll ever understand them.

"What did you have for lunch, Arlo?" I ask.

"He always has a steak salad, no dressing, tons of veggies. That's unless his sister brings something in. He prefers a certain structure in his life, isn't that right?" Gunner knocks Arlo in the arm, but it doesn't shift him from looking at me.

"I can answer for myself," Arlo says.

"Sheesh, no need to get sensitive about it," Gunner says.

"So, you like routine?" I ask, something clicking in the back of my head.

"Loves it, thrives off it, hates when his routine is thrown off," Gunner answers again.

I smile. Gunner doesn't seem to have a clue.

"Ahh, so let's say a new teacher comes into your life and starts playing loud music in the classroom and disturbing your peace, you'd find that . . . disruptive?"

"Nah, he was just saying—"

Arlo whacks Gunner in the stomach, causing him to buckle over slightly. "Enough, let's go."

They start to walk away, and I call out, "Wait, what were you just saying?"

"Nothing that concerns you," Arlo says, retreating with Gunner.

Once they're gone, Stella picks up another piece of calzone and says, "I bet it had a lot to do with you."

"I think so too," I say, staring at the door. I just don't know what to do with that information.

———

"THAT'S A GREAT IDEA," Evelyn Barney, one of our ninth grade English teachers, says. "It'll be fun for the students and bring more life to the curriculum."

Arlo sits on the edge of his desk, nose pinched, head tilted down, clearly in distress . . . from me.

Once a month, we have a department meeting to go over our curriculum, where our students are tracking, and suggest any new ideas we might have to help liven up the classrooms. The last part is courtesy of Principal Dewitt, not Arlo. If it were up to him, we'd all be teaching a strict regimen of stuffy literature with accompanying papers.

"We are not dressing up as literary characters," Arlo says, lifting his head, obviously exasperated.

"Why not?" I ask. "The students will love it, and hey, you could dress up as Jay Gatsby. All your dreams will come true."

He flashes his scowl at me. "There's no point in dressing up as a literary character other than to make a mockery of ourselves."

"I disagree." Turning toward our colleagues, I say, "All in favor of dressing up next Friday, please raise your hands." Everyone raises their hand except Arlo. "Then it's settled. We're dressing up." I pound my fist on my desk. "Meeting adjourned." I stand from my desk and so does everyone else.

Arlo stands tall and calls out, "Meeting is not—"

"I have kids to feed, Turner," Evelyn says. "Can't be here all night. Greer, will you send us the details and requirements for dressing up?"

"I'd be delighted." I smile. "What's for dinner?"

"At this point, beanies and weenies."

"Oh, that's . . . uh, yummy." I give her a wave, feeling a little sorry for her kids. "Goodnight."

The teachers file out, and I start packing up as well, ignoring Arlo's blatant stare down. Once packed up, I shoot him a quick smile and say, "Successful meeting. Well, I'll be on my way—"

"Greer," Arlo says, his voice full of malice.

I wince and turn toward him, plastering on a large smile. "Yes?"

His nostrils flare and I brace myself for the tongue-lashing that I know is coming. I overstepped. I pushed him past his comfort zone and created an English teacher mutiny, all in a matter of minutes. I'm sure he's not happy about it, if his face is any indication.

"Do you have plans for dinner?"

Ehh . . . what?

Did I just hear him correctly? He said *plans for dinner*, right? Is this some sort of trickery?

Like he gets me to say no, and then he throws down an insult, like . . . uh . . . well, you can, uh . . . eat my dick for dinner.

Hmm . . . Arlo doesn't seem like a "eat my dick" kind of guy.

But he also doesn't look like he wants to share dinner plans with anyone, not with the way he's steaming with anger, so I tread carefully.

"Well, I was probably going to stop and pick something up on the way home. Not much of a cook when I'm tired." I shrug.

"Where do you live? Close?"

"Just off Johnson Boulevard. Why?" I tilt my head to the side. "Are you planning to murder me with a hoagie?" I chuckle.

"That would be far too easy." He grabs his bag and says, "Let's go."

145

"Uh, go where?"

"Your apartment. We have things to discuss and I'm hungry."

"But . . . I didn't invite you over."

"Yes, and I didn't invite you to run my faculty meeting either, but I guess that didn't stop you." He reaches the doorway and nods at me. "Move it, Gibson. I've been known to get hangry."

Well, at least he's honest.

Chapter Ten

ARLO

On the way to our cars, we decided on Thai food. I placed an order to be delivered, Greer gave me her address, and we left. She hopped into her black Honda Civic and I got into my Tesla—which she commented on jealously.

When we pulled up to her apartment building, I was surprised.

Good area, but I know from Coraline looking over apartments that these are all studios.

Our teaching staff isn't paid what they deserve, but they're also not salaries that would require you to rent a studio apartment.

"You know, I still think this is weird," Greer says, getting out of her car. "Why couldn't we have just had dinner at a restaurant?"

Because I want nothing more than to spank you after that meeting.

Because I feel like yelling and screaming my frustration.

Because I'm desperate to have you alone.

"You really want to fight in public?" I ask.

She pauses, halfway up the stairs to her apartment complex. "We're going to fight?"

"What do you think?"

"That we could have a civil conversation."

"When has that ever happened?" I counter.

"There's no time like the present to change." She gives me a giant smile, and fuck, I want to kiss it right off her face.

Given my stance on keeping my distance where this girl is concerned, I'm going into this dinner with plans of keeping my hands to myself, eating, talking to her about insubordinate behavior, and then moving on with my night.

That's it.

She leads us to her apartment and just as I suspected, when she opens the door, I'm welcomed into a cozy studio apartment with a lake view. Kitchenette to the left with a two-person table pressed against the wall. An unmade bed that lines up with the large floor-to-ceiling window. No curtains, no privacy, just the hope that no one is able to look into her apartment. Across from the bed is a dresser with a small TV on top, and then to the right is a closet and what I assume is the door to the bathroom.

The space is small, colorful . . . and messy.

Clothes are draped over every surface, including . . . small string thongs.

Hell.

She tosses her purse to the side and says, "Wasn't expecting company. Want me to straighten up for you?"

"Might be nice to sit somewhere."

"It's not that bad, and they're all clean clothes. I like to save money on drying." She picks up a laundry basket and starts tossing her clothes inside. Picking up a neon-yellow thong, she swivels it on her finger and says, "This one is my favorite."

"Don't need the commentary on your underwear. Thank you."

"But it's more fun that way." She picks up a black lace bra and says, "This barely contains my tits. I only wear it on dates."

My jaw clenches. "Does that mean you've been on a date recently?"

"Only with myself." She winks, and I swear, she's fucking with me right now.

Just then, there's a knock on the door, and I stand to get it, but she waves at me. "I got it." Bra in hand, she goes to the door and opens it. "Yum. Thank you. Smells amazing."

"Sure," a male voice says. "Uh, do you need anything else?"

"We're fine," I call from my chair.

"Oh, okay. Yeah. Have a good one."

"Bye," Greer says in a cheery voice before shutting the door. "He was nice."

Rolling my eyes at how oblivious she is, I lean back in the small wooden chair, trying to get comfortable.

There's no couch.

Just two small, child-sized chairs and a bed.

I really should have thought this through.

She brings the food to the table, sets it down, and then grabs us plates and silverware. I open up the to-go boxes and wait as she pours us both a glass of water.

"This is all I have, sorry."

"Water is fine."

We both serve ourselves and dig in. For a few moments, we're quiet, simply enjoying the food. But it doesn't last long, because Greer glances up at me and asks, "So . . . when are you going to start yelling at me?"

"Do you mind if I eat first? It will benefit you if I'm fed."

"Oh, right. The whole hangry thing. Got ya." She winks,

then picks up a giant scoop of noodles and shoves them in her mouth. While she chews, cheeks puffed, she smiles at me.

Shaking my head, I turn back to my plate, trying to figure out what I'm going to say to her, how I'm going to approach this conversation without—

"I think there's steam coming out of your ears."

I look up at her. "What?"

She motions at me with her empty fork. "You're thinking awfully hard. I think smoke is coming out of your ears."

"Think you're funny?"

"Not just me, a lot of people do. Gunner and Romeo. Stella, Coraline . . . Keeks—well, she has her own sense of humor, but sometimes I can get a chuckle out of her. Oh, and Kelvin thinks I'm a hoot, as well as—"

"I don't need the rundown."

"I mean, you sort of asked for it."

I set my fork down. "When you woke up this morning, was it your primary goal to annoy me?"

"No, but it became my secondary goal at the meeting. Is it working?"

"What do you think?"

"From the throbbing vein in your neck, I'm going to say yes." She smiles again, and I swear, I'm seconds away from tipping this table over and doing something about that smile. "Ooo, I can feel your anger from all the way over here. Maybe we should have an icebreaker or something. You know, a way to loosen up before you tear me a new one."

"Were you a camp counselor?"

"No, why? Do I have the spirit of one?"

"Unfortunately, yes."

"Good for me."

Of course she'd say that. She lives in chaos, so how is she always so happy and cheerful? I'm not the most . . . let's face it, I'm a grumpy bastard a lot of the time. *Why is she like this? Why does it fucking annoy me?*

She finishes up her plate and takes a large gulp of her water. She shifts in her seat and says, "While you finish up, do you mind if I get out of this dress? It's usually stripped off my body by now."

"Do whatever you want," I say in a grumpy tone.

"You're an absolute doll." She winks and stands, taking her empty plate to the sink and putting the leftovers in her empty fridge. She plucks a few things from her laundry basket, then goes into her bathroom and shuts the door.

Jesus.

Why does it feel like I'm holding my breath?

Maybe because I'm extremely uncomfortable.

Maybe because I want to know what she chose from that laundry basket.

Maybe because my mind and dick are fighting an epic battle of who to listen to.

Once finished, I take my plate to the sink and then pull out my phone from my back pocket to text Coraline.

Arlo: *Late night. Be home in a bit. You okay?*

She texts back right away.

Coraline: *I'm fiiiiiine, Arlo. Stop worrying about me.*

Arlo: *Where are you?*

Coraline: *At home. Where are you?*

Arlo: *Not home. Do you need anything?*

Coraline*: Not home . . . hmm, why does that seem suspicious? And no, I don't. I'm a grown woman.*

Arlo: *Who is going through a divorce.*

Coraline: *Best decision of my life. Now will you leave me alone?*

Arlo: *Okay, well, I'll be home in a bit. We can watch a movie if you want.*

Coraline: *Will you braid my hair too?*

Arlo: *Don't be a smart-ass.*

Coraline: *Stop being overprotective.*

Arlo: *I care about you.*

Coraline: *I know and I love you for it. Now go back to being elusive. See you later, bro.*

Sighing, I stick my phone back in my pocket, just in time for Greer to open the door to her bathroom and walk out wearing a silk spaghetti-strap tank top and matching silk shorts.

That's what she chose to wear?

That?

She takes a moment to release her hair from her bun and shake it out, letting the long ombre-colored tendrils float around her shoulders.

Fucking . . . hell.

"Okay." She claps her hands together and sits on her bed. "Let's have this conversation."

She's not wearing a bra.

Her nipples are poking against the fabric.

Her shorts are riding high between her legs.

She looks so goddamn fuckable right now, I feel my dick starting to win the battle with my brain.

Leaning against her counter, I say, "What are you doing?"

She smiles wickedly at me. "Getting comfortable."

"You're fucking with me again."

She holds up her hands in defense. "You were the one who wanted to come to my place. I'm just getting comfortable for whatever you have to say to me." She pats her bed. "Come, sit. Let's gab."

"No way in hell I'm sitting on your bed."

"Oh, it's not a bed right now." She shakes her head. "Only a bed when I'm under the covers. This is a couch currently. So have a seat." She pats it again.

"I'm good where I'm at."

"Suit yourself," she says while shifting. Her foot hits her nightstand and all of a sudden, a buzzing sound rattles in the drawer.

Oh . . . hell . . .

"Uh." Her face pinkens and before she can move, I walk over to her nightstand, open up the drawer, and find a jiggling purple vibrator. "Finicky power button." She chuckles and reaches for it, but I grab it first and switch it off.

"Use this often?" I say, holding it up.

"You do realize you're holding my vibrator, right?"

"Well aware."

"And you know where that goes, right?"

My eyes flash to hers. "Between your legs, maybe up against your clit." I examine the length. "Inside of you. Maybe you tease yourself, rubbing it against your nipples before you slowly lower it over your stomach and then to your cunt."

She blinks slowly, her mouth falling open.

"Do you come quick, Miss Gibson? Or can you hold out, not letting yourself fall over until every muscle in your body is bunched up and ready to explode?"

She swallows . . . hard. Her eyelids are heavy, her lips wet.

I place it back in the drawer and shut it. I don't sit on the bed but instead stand in front of her, my cock pressing against the zipper of my jeans, starting to grow painful with need.

"What is it? Do you come hard?"

"I . . ." Her hand floats up her neck. "I highly doubt this is what you came here to talk to me about."

"You're right. I came here to lecture you."

"Yes, so let's just, uh, get that over with so you can be on your way."

"Fine." Stepping closer, I press my finger to her chest, forcing her to lie back on her bed, then I pull her legs off the edge and lower my hands so they straddle her body. I can make out her hard nipples as the swell of her breasts nearly fall out of the loose silk top. "Care to explain to me why you thought it was necessary to take charge of my meeting?"

"You know, maybe we could have this conversation at the table."

"Nah, I'm good here." Wetting my lips, I say, "Explain."

"I, well, I wasn't trying to cause a disturbance."

"Hmm, but you did. I don't take well to disturbances, Miss Gibson."

"I thought it was a good—"

"I like to run the meetings myself with very minimal input."

"But that's not how—"

"And I don't appreciate a newbie rallying the troops to overturn one of my decisions," I say, growing sterner with each sentence.

"I wasn't trying to cause trouble."

"And yet, you did."

With my foot, I kick her legs open, then reach into the nightstand to grab the vibrator. When I switch it on, her eyes widen.

"What were you trying to do exactly?" I ask, bringing the vibrator close to her chest.

She sucks in a harsh breath, her eyes immediately turning hungry, needy, and on her next breath, her pelvis rises and she spreads her legs even more.

"I was . . ." She gulps. "I was trying to—"

"Undermine me?" I bring the vibrator to her right nipple. Her teeth fall over her bottom lip and her eyes squeeze shut.

"No."

"Make me look like a fool?" I run the vibrator to the other nipple, loving how the sensation seems to drive her mad.

Just like she drives me mad.

"No, Arlo. I was—"

"Offering a suggestion?"

On a sharp exhale, she nods. "Yes."

I lower even closer to her face and move the vibrator down her stomach to the waistline of her silk shorts. "Guess what, Miss Gibson?"

"What?" she says, her hips rocking up as I move the vibrator even farther south, right to her pubic bone.

"I didn't want your suggestions."

Another inch, and then . . . I switch it off and stand, my cock aching in my jeans, but wanting to teach her a lesson. I toss the vibrator to the side and turn away from her.

With a disgruntled gasp, she says, "What are you doing?"

When I look over my shoulder, I catch her flushed cheeks, her heaving chest, and her pleading eyes.

"Leaving. Our conversation is over. I think I got my point across."

"Arlo," she calls out as I'm halfway to the door.

"Yes?" I ask, turning toward her.

"You realize I'm just going to finish when you're gone."

"You're right." I walk back over to her and she smiles. Instead of finishing her off, I snag the vibrator and stick it in the back pocket of my jeans.

"I'm aware you can still finger yourself, but you and I both know it won't be nearly as satisfying, especially when you know my fingers could do a better job."

"I don't know that," she says with defiance.

That defiance is going to be the death of her.

Leaning over the bed again, one hand next to her head, I lower the other between her legs and drag my finger over the silk of her pajama bottoms. Her eyes nearly roll to the back of her head as I find her slit and feel how wet she is through the silk. I slowly slide my finger over her arousal as she lightly moans and arches her back. *God, her scent.* I want to bend down and taste her. Devour her pussy until she's screaming my name and coating my tongue with her release. *Fuck. I need to get laid.*

I make one more pass before pulling back, snapping my hand away.

Looking her in the eyes, I say, "Now you know." Lifting up, I take off toward her door, and I don't look back. I leave.

Leave her in a state of need.

Leave myself in need of a cold shower.

When I reach my car, I lower my head to my steering wheel and take a deep breath.

Fuck.

I think I just ruined myself.

It was worth it, but I definitely ruined myself with that one torturous touch.

———

"HEY, BRO," Coraline says, walking into my classroom with a to-go bag and two drinks.

I could not be more grateful for her perfect timing.

I'm starving.

Irritated at the lack of intelligence my students possess so far today.

And even though it's Monday, I'm still feeling a pent-up need from last Friday. My hand wasn't nearly good enough. It got the job done but that was it. My body is craving so much more than just getting the job done.

My body is craving warmth. Challenge. Defiance.

"You look like you're in a good mood," Coraline says, setting the subs on my desk as I give her my chair and grab a spare one for myself.

"Rough day dealing with morons."

She chuckles. "If only your students knew you speak about them with such high regard."

"Maybe they should, might pull their heads out of their asses."

She hands me my meatball parm and unravels her chicken, bacon, and ranch sub, filling the classroom with the smell of food instantaneously.

"What have you been up to today?" I ask.

This past weekend, Coraline and I hung out and had a

movie marathon. We watched a range of movies from *Indiana Jones* to *Bridget Jones*. I fell asleep multiple times, and she poked me with a broom she kept next to her. We ate shit, and she wouldn't let me work out either day, which meant this morning I drilled my body . . . only to eat a meatball parm for lunch.

If I didn't know any better, I'd think she's trying to get me to eat my feelings, feelings she doesn't know I have.

So maybe I'm the one doing it, eating my feelings.

That's most likely the actual scenario.

"Had a two-hour conversation on the phone with my lawyer. Can't wait to see that bill. I cleaned the house because I'm a good sister like that, and because I might have dropped a bowl of brownie batter on the floor, scattering it all over the hardwood and kitchen counter. But don't worry"—from her purse, she takes out a single, wrapped square of brownie—"there was enough in the bowl still to make a small loaf-pan-sized brownie." She taps the brownie. "There are marshmallows and almonds inside, just the way you like it."

Groaning, I say, "What are you doing to me?"

"That six-pack of yours is annoying. I want to see it gone." She chuckles and lifts up her sandwich, taking a bite.

"Well I *don't* want to see it go. So stop giving me sweets." I grab the brownie. "But I'll take this."

She laughs out loud. "Sucker." She winks and then says, "I started a book today."

My brows raise. "Oh yeah? What did you start reading?"

"A filthy romance. Found it on your library shelf." She taps a wondering finger and says, "Why do you have a filthy romance on your bookshelf?"

"I'm an English teacher. I need to understand all forms of literature."

She pauses, studies me, and then says, "What a load of bullshit." She shakes her head and laughs just as there's a knock at my door.

I glance to the side to find Greer standing in the doorway, wearing a pair of black skinny jeans and a red blouse and her hair styled in waves around her shoulders.

Hell . . . and I thought the dresses were devastating.

"Sorry to interrupt. I was headed to the teachers' lounge but heard your voice and wanted to say hi, Cora."

Coraline waves her hand. "Come in, have lunch with us."

Uh, I don't think so.

"Oh, that's okay, you two need your time together." Well, at least she has a sturdy head on her shoulders.

"I hung out with him all weekend. I want some girl time. Come, sit."

Greer's eyes fall to mine and I know she's not going to sit without me agreeing to it, and if I deny her a seat at our table, I'm going to have to hear about it from my badgering sister, so I stand and grab another chair.

"Sit," I say rather gruffly.

She walks over, takes a seat, and as she sits, my hand skims her back, my ability to not touch her failing within seconds.

Her eyes slightly widen as she looks up at me. "Thank you," she says quietly. God, the red of her lips entices me.

What would that red look like pressed all along my body?

Would it come off?

Would it smear along my length?

Would it mark me as hers?

"How are you?" Coraline asks, breaking me out of my reverie.

"Good. Tired. Didn't get much sleep this weekend."

"This lump of muscle over here did," Coraline says, thumbing toward me. "We had a movie marathon and he slept most of the time."

"Not most of the time," I correct her.

"He snored at one point."

"She exaggerates for a living. Don't trust a thing she says."

"Ahh, so are you going to deny the sleeping, the snoring . . . the filthy romance?"

I feel Greer's questioning gaze on me, waiting for an answer.

But I don't give it right away. I take a sip of my drink, lean back in my chair, and study the two women looking for answers.

After a few moments, I say, "Did I fall asleep? Occasionally I drifted off. I did not fucking snore, and you know that."

Coraline tilts her head back and laughs.

"And as for the filthy romance, yeah, I have one. I actually have three, because they're a series."

"You read a series?" Coraline's eyes nearly pop out of their sockets. "Oh my God."

"I'm nothing if not thorough in my research."

"Greer, these are the kind of books that get your motor revving. Trust me, I started one today and already found myself hot and bothered."

I feel Greer's eyes on me again and instead of turning away, I turn toward her, making direct eye contact. She's the first to look away, which is exactly what I wanted to happen.

"Did you get hard reading them?" Coraline asks.

Of course she would.

And if she thinks she's going to embarrass me, she's wrong.

"I did," I answer honestly, causing Coraline to howl and Greer's cheeks to redden. "There's a scene with a vibrator in one of them that was inspiring."

Greer clears her throat and shifts in her seat. There's no doubt in my mind she's thinking about Friday, about how close how I was, how close she was to coming. How my fingers felt sliding between her legs. How bad she wanted me to finish her off . . .

"Ew, why did you say it with a deep tone like that?"

I glance at my sister. "You asked."

"Yeah, but I didn't ask for the tone." She gives me a side-eye and turns to Greer, who finally opens her lunch bag and takes out a small salad. "We should form that book club I mentioned. We can read Arlo's naughty books first and try to guess what parts made him hard. My guess—all of them."

"You're disturbing," I say, taking a bite of my sub.

"Come on, I need a girl group. You can come over to my place Friday night."

"You have your own place?" Greer asks, finally saying something after a bout of silence.

"Well . . . Arlo's place."

I chuckle quietly and Coraline tosses a balled-up napkin at me that I catch with ease.

"Anyway, we can have drinks and go over our first reads. What do you say?"

"I'm all for a book club, and I'm sure Stella would be interested. I think we'd have to convince Keeks with something other than reading and friends. There'd have to be something that—" Greer snaps her fingers. "The girl loves Nilla Wafers. If we tell her there will be a box of Nilla Wafers, she'll be there."

"Really?" Coraline asks. "That's the blandest cookie ever."

"She's obsessed with them."

"Okay, that can be arranged." Coraline taps her finger in front of me. "Did you hear that? We're going to need Nilla Wafers by Friday."

"Looks like you're going shopping then," I say, glancing over at Greer, catching her looking at me as well. Her eyes snap back to her salad.

What is she thinking?

I'd pay a good amount of money to see what's going on in that head of hers.

"So, it's a date, then. You'll let Stella and Keeks know?" Coraline asks, and even though I'm annoyed that she's going to have a book club meeting at my house, I feel grateful that

Greer wants to hang out with my sister. Not for my own selfish reasons, but because I know Coraline needs this, a friend, some real people in her life. And even though Greer drives me to distraction, I keep thinking about how she wants me to be real with her. *Like she is with your sister. Someone she barely knows, yet she's prepared to get her group together to include Coraline.* That deserves my respect.

"Yes. I'll message them later. They'll be so excited."

"Fantastic." Coraline sips from her water and asks, "What are you dressing up as this Friday? Arlo was telling me about how you took over his meeting and got everyone to agree to dress up as their favorite literary character. Made my day, my weekend, actually."

"Uh, I haven't decided yet," Greer answers.

"That's hard to believe, given the ridiculous notion was all because of you." I wipe my mouth with a napkin and then stare Greer down.

"Ugh, he's still bitter about it. You can hear it in his voice."

"I think he's bitter about a lot of things," Greer says, giving me a sharp once-over.

"So true. He told me he isn't dressing up."

"Coraline," I say sternly.

"What?" She shrugs. "That's what you said. I think it's fair that Greer knows."

Turning toward me, arms folded, Greer says, "You're not dressing up?"

"Wasn't planning on it."

"You have to."

"I actually don't have to do anything," I say. "Those who want to participate can participate. I am not one of those individuals."

"Arlo . . ."

"Greer . . ."

We stare each other down. Our eyes flitting back and

forth, our jaws clenched. Tension rises, sucking in the air around us, and I'm almost positive if Coraline weren't here right now, I'd be pushing Greer onto this table to help her better understand.

"Uh . . . as much fun as this staredown is, you two look positively pained," Coraline says. "Maybe we should stop before someone bursts a blood vessel."

Ignoring my sister, Greer says, "You'd set a horrible example if you don't dress up."

"How so? The students don't know about it. It's not like they're looking forward to me throwing together a mindless costume just for the hell of it."

"It isn't for the hell of it," Greer defends, scooting to the edge of her seat. "This is a way for you, as an educator, to teach your students about the importance of character description, of bringing a piece of their literature to life, to not look like a freaking robot at the front of the classroom all the time."

"I can do that without dressing up like a fool."

"Whoa, that's harsh, Arlo," Coraline says. "Maybe chill a bit."

"I'm chill. I'm just not dressing up."

Greer's lips twist to the side. "You realize you look like a child, right?"

"Actually"—I smile—"you're the one dressing up, so you're the one who's going to look like a child." I scoop up my wrapper and crumple it up. "I'm going to the bathroom before lunch ends. Thanks for bringing lunch, Coraline."

"Yeah, sure, thanks for bringing down the mood."

I wink at my sister. "Anytime."

And I leave a steaming Greer behind me.

―――

"ARLO, do you have more than two wine glasses?" Coraline asks from the kitchen, where she's been rummaging around all night, prepping for the book club at the end of the week.

"No. I don't have the need to accumulate excessive things."

"This coming from a bachelor who lives in a six-bedroom mansion by himself."

"It was about location, not the house," I say, looking up from my phone, where I've been catching up on some current events.

"Sure, that's what all the rich, single guys say. Do you even plan to have a family?" she asks, coming over to the couch, where she takes a seat on the armrest.

"Someday," I say casually.

"Really?" she asks, excited. "Like kids and everything?"

I glance up at her. "Maybe."

She clutches her heart. "Aw, I never thought you had a heart big enough for kids."

"Is that supposed to be a compliment?"

"Umm, I think just a statement. Wow. So, I'll be an aunt someday, that's exciting. Almost as exciting as book club on Friday." She slides down onto the couch and clutches a throw pillow to her chest. "But I can't be a good host for book club without an adequate amount of wine glasses."

"Then go get some."

"I'll have to." She nudges me with her foot. "Hey, thanks for letting me invite the girls over. I'm really excited about it."

"You don't have to thank me, Coraline. My house is your house, too."

"Either way, thank you. I'm so glad I met Greer. She's pretty awesome and real. God, is she real." Yeah . . . Greer is real all right. Coraline lifts up and places a quick kiss to my cheek. "I'm going to check out the lighting in the backyard during this hour. I think that might be a good place to hold the meeting."

"Or just have it here in the living room, like I've said a million times."

"Like you know everything." She waves her hand at me and then bounces toward the backyard just as my phone buzzes with a text message.

Gunner: *Dude, are you really not going to dress up Friday?*

Romeo: *When I heard the English teachers were all dressing up, I felt a pang of jealousy I wasn't invited to the dress-up party, but then I realized, you'd be dressing up. Quit playing games with my heart.*

Arlo: *Don't you two have something better to do with your lives?*

Gunner: *Lindsay and Dylan are at his basketball practice. I'm not allowed to go just yet.*

Romeo: *I don't have a baby mama, or a child, and I already finished my workout. Not really doing much but catching the Bobbies game. So, no, needling and annoying you seems fitting.*

Arlo: *Who told you?*

Romeo: *Stella. She was hoping I could talk to you and convince you to dress up.*

Arlo: *What? Why?*

Gunner: *You're so oblivious.*

Romeo: *He really is. *Sighs* Greer was really excited about getting the entire department to dress up, and the head of the department isn't going to be involved. Kind of a blow to the tit, you know?*

Arlo: *She doesn't care that much. She just suggested the idea to grate on my nerves.*

Gunner: *You sure about that?*

Arlo: *Yes. Trust me. Since she arrived at this school, she's done everything in her power to annoy me. This is another one of those moments.*

Romeo: *Yeah, I don't think that's the case this time. Stella said she was really upset.*

Arlo: *How do you know Stella wasn't just saying that? How do I know this isn't another one of your stupid pranks?*

Gunner: *I knew that was going to come back and bite us in the ass.*

Romeo: *I swear, dude. This isn't one of those moments. I really think she was upset about it.*

Arlo: *Well . . . then she shouldn't have suggested it. She knew I wasn't going to be pleased. Her problem, not mine.*

Gunner: *Harsh.*

Romeo: *Some might say cruel.*

Arlo: *It's reality. I'm not that kind of teacher, never will be.*

<hr />

"GOOD MORNING."

I look up from my car and catch Greer locking up her Honda. It's early Thursday morning, the fog still heavy in the air, a crisp reminder that fall is right around the corner.

There are only a few other cars parked in the teachers' parking lot, one of them being Principal Dewitt's. She's always early, but I've never seen Greer come in this early.

Shutting my car door, I lock up and say, "Good morning."

And since we're going to the same place, we fall in line together, both carrying our bags, a long day of teaching ahead of us.

I haven't really seen her since Monday, just randomly here and there in the hallway, but I do know she'll be coming over tomorrow night after practice, because Coraline asked to borrow some money for the book club. I was more than happy to hand her my credit card and told her not to worry about paying me back, but I know she's been keeping count of every last dime, because that's the considerate person she is.

But what has put a smile on my face the past few days is how excited Coraline has been about Friday night. She's put together booklover bags with bookmarks, wine glasses, and bottles of wine for everyone. She also spent time moving around the house, finding the perfect spot to hold the meeting. She ended up sticking with the living room like I suggested. Imagine that.

Besides her running around the house like a madwoman, I have to admit, I'm grateful for it. Seeing that spark in her eye, the excitement—it eases me.

When we reach the entrance of the school, I open the door for Greer and she gives me a small nod before entering. And even though our last conversation was awkward at best, I feel the need to say something to her about Coraline.

"Uh, I wanted to thank you," I say, feeling uncomfortable.

Greer slows down her pace. "Thank me for what?"

"For, uh, doing this book club thing with my sister. She's really excited."

"Oh. Yeah, sure. You don't have to thank me. I like Cora, she's fun."

"She is fun. She's also going through a rough divorce and this book club thing is putting a smile on her face, something I've struggled with lately. So, thank you."

"Like I said, no need to thank me. I like Cora, and I'm excited to get to know her better." We walk up the stairs to our classrooms, our steps falling in unison, the halls dim and quiet before the crowd of students pour in.

"Why are you here so early?"

"Couldn't sleep. Figured I'd just come in." We reach her classroom, and she gives me a curt smile. "Have a good day, Arlo."

And that's when I notice the bite in her voice and lack of enthusiasm. There's no sassy schoolteacher trying to tell me how to properly educate my students. There's no sexified vixen, ready to tease me, tempt me, throw me off my game.

It's almost as if someone or something has sucked the spirit out of her and left her with minimal personality. My text conversation with Gunner and Romeo floats to the front of my mind. Is she really upset? Am I being an ass and don't realize how much this actually means to her?

"Are you, uh . . . are you ready for tomorrow?" I ask, not quite ready to say goodbye.

"Of course." She unlocks her classroom door, and as usual, I'm assaulted by gaudy brightness and blazing color. "If anything, I'm always prepared. Oh, by the way, Blair told me she got her second paper back. A *B-* is a big jump from an *F*."

I shrug. "She earned it. She put in the time, she learned, and she wrote a compelling essay, one I hope to see her improve on throughout the year."

"Glad to hear it." She gives me a soft smile and then says, "Well, see you around." And then she disappears into her classroom.

On a sigh, I let myself into my classroom and take in the drab space, the lack of color and character. It's cold . . . almost prison-like.

And for the first time since I've been a teacher, I wonder . . . is it enough?

When my students leave my classroom and go on to college, they're prepared, they're educated, they're ready to take on a college essay and excel at it, which is what my goal is as a teacher. To foster these students and make sure they're gathering the tools they need to move on. Blair is a great example of that.

I forced her to put in the work, to speak to me during lunch, to learn a constructive way to interpret literature, and she came out better for it, so why am I questioning myself?

Shaking the thoughts out of my head, I set my bag on my desk and pull out the questions for today's pop quiz on the reading from last night. I spent a great deal of time thinking about them. Thirty questions, each class has to answer different ones, so there's no cheating in between periods. They have one minute per question and must answer thoughtfully.

It's challenging.

It's what my advanced placement students need.

They don't need frills like dressing up.

They need structure.

A schedule.

They need to be kept on their feet, never complacent.

Picking up my whiteboard marker, I uncap it and get to work on writing my questions on the board. *Stop questioning yourself, Turner. You know what you're doing.* Just because it looks like you sucked the life out of one of your colleagues doesn't mean you need to rethink your entire teaching process.

Chapter Eleven

GREER

"Oh my God, I love you so much," Stella says, coming up to me in the parking lot. "Don't even tell me—you're Elizabeth Bennet, right?"

I curtsy and say, "You are quite correct."

"God, let me get a good look at you." Stella takes my hand and forces me to twirl. "Honestly, you could be a doppelganger for Kiera Knightley in this getup."

"That's what I was going for. Some of the other dresses I considered were a little too . . . booby, and I didn't think that was appropriate."

"Yeah, good call." She claps. "Seriously, I love this so much."

Despite Arlo's reluctance to participate in today's literature dress up, everyone else is participating. I know we'll have at least one Harry Potter, Lennie from *Of Mice and Men*, Juliet from *Romeo and Juliet*, and a Huckleberry Finn. We'll see what everyone else dresses up as. There were still a few teachers trying to make up their minds.

But I knew from the beginning who I wanted to be.

The queen of *pride* . . . and *prejudice*.

I found a brown frock with an empire waist and long sleeves resembling the one Kiera Knightley wore in her representation of the book. I even styled my hair to look like hers as well. Since I've been showing clips of the movie throughout the reading of the book, I know they're going to understand it immediately, which puts a smile on my face.

Today is going to be a great day, even if I couldn't count on everyone to support the idea.

"I need to get the foreign language department to participate in something like this. Have a war-of-the-countries type thing. It'd be fun."

"That would be fun. Have you spoken to them about it?"

Stella shakes her head as we make it to the school entrance. "No, we have our meeting next Wednesday. I think after they see the English department, they'll be into it. We're all pretty easygoing."

"Well, hopefully they don't notice Arlo."

"I can't believe he's not dressing up. Makes me want to punch him right in front of his students. A fist to the eye. He won't even see it coming."

"I'd love to see that."

We chuckle and climb the stairs to the second floor of the school. When we reach the top, she turns left and says, "Good luck today. Enjoy it—and, hey, book club tonight."

"Remind Keiko."

"No need, she already texted me this morning making sure there were going to be Nilla Wafers."

I roll my eyes. "There will be plenty."

"It's what I told her. See you at lunch." She waves and we part.

Turning down the English hallway, I take a deep breath,

preparing myself for the day, just as a tall, dark figure steps out of my unlocked classroom.

I pause, let my eyes focus, and then . . .

Oh. God.

Dressed in a tuxedo, hair slicked back, looking so damn sexy I might hike up my skirt right here and now is Arlo Turner.

There's no way.

He didn't dress up, did he?

Then again, why would he be dressed in a tuxedo?

Stunned, I close the distance between us.

He doesn't smirk.

He doesn't make any sort of gesture of acknowledgement as I approach him. He stands regally, just like Jay Gatsby.

"Arlo . . ." I just about whisper in shock.

"I was just leaving some donuts on your desk. Coraline wanted me to give them to you."

Giving him a small once-over, I take him by the arm and bring him into my classroom, where I set my things on my desk.

"Why . . . are you . . . are you dressed up?"

He shrugs. "Wasn't too hard to put on a tux."

I cover my mouth with my hand. This man. This unruly, surly, arrogant ass dropped his guard for today and put on a tux.

The sentiment is too much for me to handle. It's a sweet gesture, a kind one . . . a detrimental one. Because now, instead of hating him like I've been doing all week, he's cracked a hole in my heart.

He's making me think sweet things about him.

He's causing me to . . . oh dear lord . . . he's causing me to swoon.

I take his hand in mine, and I softly say, "Thank you, Arlo."

Clearing his throat, he steps away and says, "Don't think I'll do it again. You're lucky I had this tux in my closet."

"I wouldn't dare ask you to expose your true, nerdy self ever again."

Backing away some more, he looks me up and down and says, "You make a great Elizabeth Bennet. Your prideful personality is a rare match."

"Maybe you should have dressed up as Mr. Darcy. Your prejudice would have been quite fitting."

He straightens his tux and says, "Have a good day . . . Miss Gibson."

"You, too, Arlo," I say, breathless as he retreats from my classroom.

Turning to my desk, I grip the edges and take a deep breath. I was not expecting that at all. I was expecting a cardigan-clad man next door, not a devil in a tux, looking positively stunning with his scruff and slicked-back hair.

Look out, Leonardo, there's a new Jay Gatsby in town, and he's stealing hearts with every devastating glare.

———

"I STILL CAN'T BELIEVE he dressed up," Stella says as we walk up Arlo's driveway, cookies in hand, and freshly showered after practice. Thankfully, my hair has a natural wave to it, so I'm letting it air-dry, and since Cora said to come casual, I dressed in a pair of leggings and a tank top.

"I can't believe it either," I say, trying to hide just how much it meant to me. "The students were talking about it all day."

"I even got wind of it. The entire school was buzzing. There was an excitement in the air. It was a good day."

"I couldn't agree more. Arlo Turner has a reputation for being serious and, frankly, a scary teacher, so seeing him dressed up, playing along, the students were buzzing, loving it.

He thinks it doesn't make a difference, but it does. It makes a huge difference."

And as we step up to his door to ring the doorbell, my stomach flips around from the knowledge that he's on the other side of the door. Will he talk about the day? Will he mention how much the students loved him dressed up? Or the monologue he memorized for every start of class?

Oh yeah, I heard about it all. He didn't just dress up, he went all out.

Then again, I don't think I'd expect anything less from Arlo Turner. He's not the one to half-ass something. If he goes in, he goes all in.

Stella rings the doorbell, and the door is quickly opened by Cora, who looks relieved. "Thank God you guys are here," she says quietly. "Keeks is telling me all about her bunion and I'm pretty sure I'm dying a slow death inside."

"Did she tell you its name?"

"Baptista. Beautiful name for a hideous thing."

We chuckle and walk inside Arlo's grand house. The entryway alone gives you a rich, homey vibe, but when you walk into the grand living room and kitchen, it's impossible not to gawk and fall in love with the space. The back wall of the house is covered in windows, giving you a beautiful view of the lake, and the kitchen, with its large island and marble countertops, is absolutely to die for. If I were a cook, I'd be drooling to get in there and make something.

"Good evening," Keeks says, greeting us with a nod. Dressed in a pair of sweatpants that cinch at her ankles and a T-shirt with the Periodic Table of Elements on it, Keiko looks the part of relaxed chemistry teacher, despite the stiff set of her shoulders.

"Hey Keeks," Stella says. "What did we say about sharing your bunion story?"

"I was short of conversation. It was what came to mind at the time."

Stella takes a seat next to her. "Weather is always a safe topic."

"I spoke about the weather patterns. Cora struggled with input, so I changed topics."

"You asked me if I knew the variables that fluctuate the jet stream."

"An integral part of the conversation when speaking of weather patterns," Keeks says, confused why Cora doesn't get it.

Cora holds up her glass of wine. "Needless to say, I started drinking early."

I take a seat on a large, comfy chair and take in the spread on the coffee table. A bowl of Nilla Wafers is directly in front of Keiko, while the rest of the table is covered in appetizers ranging from mini sliders to pizza to fries. It's a decadent smorgasbord, perfect to delight in with good friends.

"Wow, this spread is incredible," I say. "Arlo doesn't mind that we're going to eat in the living room?"

Cora waves her hand. "He doesn't get a say in the matter because he's not here. Out with the boys doing lord knows what."

"Darts," Stella mumbles while shoving a mini quiche in her mouth. When we all look at her with questioning expressions, she says, "Romeo asked if I wanted to be his partner. Told him I had book club, which then resulted in him asking a million questions I didn't feel like answering."

"Very well, no ill-mannered masculine assumptions to dishearten our intentions of pursuing literary comradery," Keeks says, shoving a Nilla Wafer into her mouth.

"Nope, we're on our own." Cora holds up an open bottle of wine. "Anyone want a drink?"

Stella holds up her hand. "I'm picking up a few freelance conditioning classes tomorrow. Can't be hungover."

Cora moves to the wine glass in front of Keiko, who vehemently shakes her head. "Alcohol does not negotiate in good health with my gastrointestinal tract. Symptoms of abhorrent flatulence accompanied by death-gripping defecation wreak havoc on my person. Thank you, but I shall pass."

Eyebrows pinched, nose turned up, Cora faces me, and I gladly hold out my wine glass. "Fill her up."

"No flatulence issues?"

I shake my head. "No, I can handle my liquor just fine."

"Thank God for that." Cora fills up my glass, and when she's done, I give it a good swirl and take a sip.

"Wow, this is great."

"It's one of Arlo's expensive bottles." She chuckles. "He never drinks it because he never has company over, so I figured he won't mind."

Oh, now I feel guilty. "Are you sure?"

"Positive. He always says what's his is mine."

"Arlo is an attractive man," Keeks says out of nowhere. "Is he presently courting anyone?"

I nearly spit out my wine. Why on earth is she asking that?

"You interested?" Cora asks, brows raised.

"Oh no. My counterpoint of attraction currently is Kelvin Thimble. But he is frequently out of sorts and clammy with nervous perspiration whenever I'm around. Makes the act of growing intimate difficult, as I'm not fervent on apprehensive bodily fluids."

"Understandable," Stella says. "But what does this have to do with Mr. Turns Me On being single?"

"Oh God, do not call him that." Cora grimaces.

It's true though. That nickname could not ring truer.

"I came up with a hypothesis that if Arlo was courting someone, he could instruct Kelvin how to court properly as well."

"That's not a job for Arlo," Stella says. "That's a job for Romeo. He's the king of getting women to fall for him."

"Is that coming from experience?" I ask, smiling over my glass of wine.

"No." Stella rolls her eyes. "But I've heard enough stories from his college and baseball days that claim him as very skillful in the topic."

"Would he converse with Kelvin?"

"Want me to ask?"

"Yes," Keeks says with a nod. "Thank you."

"Why are you worried about that right now?" I ask, curious as to where her mind is wandering to.

"This is a romance novel book club, is it not?"

"It is," Cora says, handing out giftbags. Inside is a small clipboard with attached book suggestions. All read like a romance novel.

"That's what I gathered from the invitation. According to an avid Google search, romance novels include graphic coitus, bringing fictional characters to completion. Research proves that acts of pornography, written or recorded, can lead to an increased level of arousal, tapping into the reptile part of the human brain and reflecting in physical wakefulness. In street terms, one can become horny. Although, I have an extensive amount of maturity in beguiling myself—"

"Oh dear God," Cora mutters, leaning back in her seat and drinking her wine. I take a large sip myself.

"I have obtained someone of interest of the opposite sex and would prefer for him to bring me to completion. Therefore, he needs to prepare himself for the ravenous behaviors I'm anticipating taking over me once I dive deep into erotic literature."

The three of us find ourselves silent. All of us blinking. All of us unaware of how to respond.

When I signed up for book club, I didn't think we'd be talking about Keiko masturbating or training her boyfriend to be a suave man of the sheets rather than sweating all over her.

And we haven't even picked out a book yet . . .

"BEFORE WE GET STARTED, I've been told I need to ask you a question." Stella sits cross-legged in front of me, a nervous look on her face, water in hand.

"Oh?" I ask, bringing a glass of red wine up to my lips.

She glances over at Coraline and winces. "Uh, I feel weird asking."

Uh-oh. I hope this isn't what I think it's going to be. "You know, we don't have to—"

"Then why bring it up if you're not going to propose your query?" Keiko impatiently pushes her green-rimmed glasses up on her nose. "You know the frequency of these meetings are dependent upon staying within the comprehensive itinerary I composed during my lunch break."

"Cool your bloomers, Keeks," Coraline says while taking a large sip from her wineglass. "I want to know what's making Stella so fidgety. Out with it, Stella," Cora says.

"Please, so we can proceed," Keeks says, straightening her notepad on her lap.

Stella looks me in the eyes and says, "Brock wants to know if there's anything going on between you and Turner. Apparently, Turner won't say a thing, but Brock thinks there's some strong sexual tension building."

Cora whips her head to me, her eyes wide. "Are you getting it on with my brother?"

Finger pointed in the air, Keeks leans in and says, "The proper term amongst company would be coitus."

Rolling her eyes, Cora asks, "Did you have coitus with my brother?"

"You could also say intercourse if that amuses your jargon more," Keeks adds. "Or copulating would be sufficient. But if you are inclined toward romantic terminology since we are in the presence of the book club, you could say lovemaking or performing intimate acts. Although given the circumstances of when coitus took place—in the work environment—I would deduce that your actions were performed carnally rather than with the interest of developing a devoted accord."

"Good God, Keeks," Cora says, irritated. "Who cares what it's called? We just want to know if it happened." Cora looks me in the eyes. "Did it?"

"What? No." I shake my head, feeling the wine sloshing around in my body. "With Turner, no way. He's an ass." I wince. "Sorry, Cora."

"No, he is an ass, you're right." She sighs. "Ugh, how fun would that have been though? You and my brother. You might have been able to change his horrible mood. He can be such a dick."

"Isn't he allowing you to gather your comrades in his house to discuss literature?" Keeks asks.

"Yeah . . ." Cora answers and then with a smile says, "He can still be a dick."

Hear, hear.

At least, that's the kind of attitude I try to convince myself of.

My attitude hasn't changed because he dressed up . . . nope.

He didn't penetrate my armor at all . . .

And thanks to Mr. Turns Me On Especially In A Tuxedo, I don't even have my vibrator to help me with any type of penetration. Infuriating, insufferable man. *Ha. I sound like Elizabeth Bennet.*

———

"SO, it's between the teacher romance and the historical with the Scot on the front and the burly man chest," Stella says, looking over the printed-out options Cora provided us with.

I'm one bottle of wine deep, feeling pretty damn good, and I've been able to black out the first part of this meeting when Keeks went into great detail about the clitoris and proper stimulation needed in order to orgasm.

It was disturbing and educational all at the same time.

We devoured the food, delighted in some cookies, sent texts about Kelvin to Romeo, who said he'd rather not be the "Hitch" to Kelvin Thimble, and now we're finally zeroing in on the book to read.

It's been a fun night.

A relaxing night.

One I really needed.

"Both are alluring," Keeks said. "Both I believe will bring arousal."

I think she's missing the point about book club, but hey, there's always one in the group, right?

"At first, I thought you girls would like the teacher book since you're teachers. Thought it could fulfill a fantasy for you, but then you referred to my brother as Mr. Turns Me On . . . several times." She gives a pointed look to Stella, who laughs. "And now I think I'll picture my brother when reading and I really don't want that. So, my vote is for the Scot."

"I vote teacher," Stella says with a smirk.

Cora playfully tosses a pillow at her.

"That would leave you to decide," Keeks says to me.

Smiling broadly, I pull my knees to my chest and drain the rest of the wine in my glass. I say, "Although the teacher book is enticing, I'd rather not think of Cora's brother either. I vote for the Scot."

"What? Come on," Stella whines. "But there was promise of sex on a desk."

"As if that would ever really happen," I say. "No teacher in their right mind would ever have sex on a desk, in a class-room, where anyone could walk in."

"It's fiction, Greer. You should know a thing or two about that."

I motion to Keiko. "Yes, but think of our poor Keiko. She's impressionable. Who's to say what she'd do if she read that book and she started taking it to heart? Next thing we know, she's riding Kelvin Thimble on one of her chemistry tables, twirling her granny panties over her head like a lasso."

"Valid concern," Keeks says, adjusting her glasses on her nose.

"Keiko is smarter than that. She can decipher the difference between reality and fantasy."

"Stella," Keeks sighs with exasperation. "Need I remind you about the reptile part of the brain again? When arousal spikes—"

"Okay, okay." Stella tamps Keeks down with her hand. "Yes, I remember. Please, God, let's not go over it again. But if you read this book, are you going to try to find a Scot to make out with in the Highlands?"

"Don't be absurd," Keeks answers. "Clearly that's a preposterous notion."

I chuckle. "Am I drunk, or is this not making sense at all?"

"This is not making sense," Stella says with a shake of her head.

"Doesn't matter." Cora lifts her empty glass of wine to the air. "We have our very first book. Yay."

I lift up my empty glass as well. "To the sisterhood of the book pants."

"Oh, are we naming our book club?" Keeks pulls a slip of paper from her purse. "I took the liberty of developing some fastidious names for us. I ran them through a series of linguistic tests and discovered one to be the most superior of the three."

"I have a name too," Cora says, sitting up. "Shall we take a vote?"

"It would be the democratic thing to do," Keeks says.

Stepping in, Stella says, "Cora, since you hosted, let's hear yours first."

She nods, the room growing serious as Cora clears her throat. "I was thinking we call it the Ladies in Heat Book Club."

Stella and I both laugh as we nod. "Oh, that's amazing," I say.

"Preposterous," Keeks says. "Such a name degrades us in a manner I'm not comfortable with. We're not feral cats, strutting with our tails up, searching out a male suitor to ease the ache in our loins."

"You might not be . . . but I am," I say, realizing . . . huh, maybe I'm drunker than I thought.

"We could always call it the Reptile Brain Book Club," Cora deadpans.

"Mockery isn't a pleasant shade on you, Coraline," Keeks says, causing Stella to snort and Cora to laugh as well. "But that was a well-placed burn, so I offer my compliments."

"Uh, thank you?" Cora asks with confusion.

"Okay, Keeks, what was your well-thought-out and researched book club name?"

Sitting taller, chin jutted out, Keeks says, "The Austen Empowerment Collaborative."

Silence . . . as everyone stares at Keiko.

"Austen, as in Jane Austen?" I ask.

She nods. "What a woman of her time."

"It's . . . nice," Stella says.

"Very womanly," I add.

"Yup, both those things," Cora says while tapping her chin.

"Shall we take a vote?" Stella asks. "All in favor of The Austen Empowerment Collaborative, please raise your hand." Keeks raises her hand with pride, but that's it. No one else. "Okay and all those in favor of the horny book club name—"

"Ladies in Heat Book Club," Cora corrects her with a smile.

"Yeah, all those in favor of the Ladies in Heat Book Club, raise your hand."

Unfortunately for Keiko, Cora, Stella, and I raise our hands.

"Blasphemy," Keeks says, fist hitting the armrest of the couch.

"Sorry, Keeks," I say, "But the other one is funny and I had a lot of wine."

"Shall we vote when two of the members haven't lost control of their faculties?"

"No," we all say at once.

"Very well. We shall be referred to as the Ladies in Heat, I hope you are delighted with yourselves."

"Oh, quite delighted," Cora says and yawns, stretching her arms over her head. "Okay, ladies, I think our first meeting must come to an end." She points at me. "You're not driving. You can stay here."

"I can take her home," Stella offers.

"Nonsense. She'd just have to come back here and pick up her car. Arlo has a great guest room full of everything you'll need."

"He won't mind?" I ask.

"Nope, and he's not even home to vote. Keeks, are you okay to drive?"

"I didn't consume any alcohol."

"Yeah, but from the way you've been stroking the cover of the Scot book, I wanted to make sure you're not accessing the reptile part of your brain."

"If I was accessing the reptile—"

"Please, for the love of God, no more," Stella says while standing. "Enough arousal talk for the night. A girl has to return home alone, after all."

Laughing, Cora stands as well and starts gathering empty plates. "Can you ladies just help me clear the coffee table so Arlo doesn't lecture me in the morning about leaving dirty dishes out?"

"Of course," we all say.

Together, we clean up our mess, wipe the table down, and leave the kitchen and living room spotless, as if we weren't even there. We say bye to Keeks and Stella at the door, making sure everyone has each other's phone numbers, and then Cora, with another giant yawn, shows me to the first-floor guest room, fully stocked as promised, and the attached bathroom.

"Are you sure Arlo won't mind? I feel kind of weird staying at his place without him knowing."

"I'll text him, let him know. Don't worry. He'd rather you stay than drive home."

"Okay." I give her a smile and then pull her into a hug. "I'm so glad you accidentally walked into my classroom."

She hugs me back. "I'm glad I did too." When we pull away, she gives me a soft smile. "I really needed the friendship, so, thank you."

"No, need to thank me. I needed a girl group. You made that happen."

"Nothing some sliders and mini quiche couldn't accomplish." She sighs. "Okay, you all set?"

"Yup. I have everything I need. Goodnight."

"Night."

Chapter Twelve

ARLO

Cora: Don't freak out if you see a random person in the house. Greer is in the guest room. Wine was consumed tonight.

That's the text that greeted me when I got home a little past eleven.

Now that it's one in the morning, I still can't seem to get it out of my mind.

Greer is sleeping in my house.

Downstairs, in the guest room, she's sleeping.

Normally, I wouldn't think twice about a guest, but something has shifted in me and I can't seem to turn it off.

Awareness of whenever she's around.

This need to . . . hell, to make her smile even though it goes against my basic principles.

An overwhelming sense to talk to her.

Today was my undoing. I don't know what possessed me to acquiesce, sure as hell wasn't peer pressure, because I got my fair share of looks from other English teachers when they knew I wasn't going to dress up. But when I noticed how sad she was, how reserved . . . hell, it snapped something inside of me this morning, and before I knew it, I was putting on my tux and slicking back my hair.

I blame it on the soft spot I have for my sister. Unbeknownst to Greer, when she took my sister in, befriending her without a blink of an eye and bringing her into her girl group, it fucked with my ability to detach. It's weakening me. Softening me. It's making me do stupid shit like think about Greer in a whole other light. One that paints her even more brilliantly beautiful, with a heart of gold and a caring soul.

She's torn down one of my well-constructed walls, and I can feel my will slowly slipping away.

It's why I find myself gravitating toward her. Needing to touch her. Smell her. Please her.

It's why I dressed up. Why I have this sense, this urge to make her happy.

And I'd never say this to her . . .ever . . .

But it was . . . fun, bringing life to Jay Gatsby. It was great timing with my lesson plans, another reason I was okay with my decision.

I wasn't expecting much when I ran into her this morning. I was more or less expecting her to rub it in my face, give me a little told-you-so attitude.

That's not what I got.

Instead, there was gratefulness in her eyes.

Appreciation.

Pure joy.

I made her smile. Made her happy, brought her spirit back.

Dragging my hand over my face, I sit up and swing my feet to the side, setting them on the rug beneath my bed. I need a drink, something to ease my mind, help me relax.

The lights are out, the house is quiet and still, so I quietly make my way down to the kitchen in just my boxer briefs. The guest room is on the other side of the house so I'm not worried about waking up Greer.

I turn the corner going into the kitchen and head to the cabinet where I keep the alcohol but then think better of it. Drinking at one in the morning isn't something I do, and it's not something I'm going to start.

Instead, I grab a glass from the cabinet, open my fridge, and pour myself some apple juice. A far cry from a glass of whiskey, but it will have to do for now. Leaning against the counter, I bring the glass to my lips just as a movement from the corner of my eye gives me pause.

"Jesus, I didn't see you there," Greer says, holding her hand to her chest.

Wearing nothing but a tank top and what I can only imagine is a thong from how thin the fabric is, Greer steps into the kitchen with wild, wavy hair and a sleepy look in her eyes.

"What are you doing up?" she asks.

"Thirsty," I answer, not wanting to tell her the truth.

She walks up to me and that's when I get a better view of her practically bare tits in a thin, threadbare tank top. Damn.

"What are you drinking?" she asks, completely oblivious to the way my eyes are eating her up.

"Apple juice."

She chuckles. "You don't seem like an apple juice kind of guy. Where are the cups?"

"Cabinet next to the stovetop," I say.

She moves past me and my eyes stay fixed on her, and when she passes me, I'm granted a fucking gorgeous view.

High, tight, and round, her ass is exposed to the chilly night air, only a thin string of black falling between her cheeks. I spend too much time taking in her backside, and when she turns around, she catches me, realization dawning on her.

"Oh God, I'm not wearing pants."

"Nope," I answer, bringing my glass to my lips.

"You just saw my ass."

"Correct."

"You were just staring at my ass."

"You can keep saying it in different ways but it's not going to change the fact that, yes, I saw your bare ass."

"Well, this is embarrassing."

"Only if you make it." With one hand, I grip the counter behind me, keeping myself from reaching out and pulling her in close so I can smooth my hand over her perfect rear end.

"Right." She smiles and goes to the fridge, where she opens the door and pulls out the apple juice, my eyes attached to her backside the entire time. Firm hamstrings lead to her glutes, giving her a very athletic look, a look I can appreciate.

When she's done retrieving her drink, she joins me at the island and takes a sip before asking, "Do you drink apple juice often in the middle of the night?"

"Frist time," I answer.

"Well, I'm glad I could be a part of such an historic occasion."

I tip my drink back then take the empty glass to the dishwasher. Turning toward her, I say, "Do you need anything else?"

She shakes her head. "No, I'm good. The guest bed is really comfortable."

"Okay, well . . . have a good night, then."

I start to walk past her when she stops me, placing her hand on my bare chest. I suck in a sharp breath and then stare at her, my blood immediately pooling in my groin.

Innocent eyes look up at me as she says, "Thank you for letting me stay here."

"No need to thank me," I say. "It's better than you driving."

"I know. But still, it must be weird having me here."

I shrug. "Didn't think much of it."

What a fucking lie, but she doesn't need to know that.

"Yeah, I'm sure I'm the last thing on your mind." Her hand drags down my chest and over my abs before dropping to her side. The light scrape of her fingernails over my skin just threw gasoline on the flame I have burning for this woman.

"Do you want to be on my mind?" I ask, my voice heavy, deep.

Her eyes flash to mine, indecision weighing heavily in them. "Thought maybe I was," she says, turning away from me and leaning against the counter, her pert ass inches away from me. Did she just grant me an invitation?

Jaw clenched, my hands itching to reach out and touch her, I ask, "Why would you think that?"

She looks over her shoulder, and that's when I catch it: seduction in her eyes. "Since you dressed up for me."

She shifts, her ass so goddamn tempting that I feel my mouth go dry as I tell myself to stay still, not to reach out, not to fall under the spell she's trying to cast.

"I didn't dress up for you," I say, keeping still, but hell . . .

She shifts again, and I'm fucking dying.

I want to touch her. I want to toss her up on the counter and get lost in her scent, in her wild hair.

I want to punish that mouth of hers, make her think twice before tempting me.

"Then why did you dress up?" she asks, turning toward me.

"Turn around."

"What?" she asks, her brows furrowing.

"Turn. Back. Around."

"Arlo—"

"Don't make me tell you again," I say, my will slipping.

I feel it drain out of me, the wall she's cracked inside me slowly crumbling.

The resistance falters, and I blame it on the lack of sleep

and pants in this kitchen, because when she turns back around, my hand falls to her lower back as I step in behind her.

"You think I dressed up for you?" I ask, spanning my hand over her back and slipping it under her shirt. I feel her muscles bunch up along her spine as I move my hand higher.

"I can't come up with another reason."

"So you assume it's for you?" I move my hand back down, loving the sharp intake of breath I hear.

"Wasn't it?"

I lean over her back, my arousal pressing against her leg as I whisper, "It was for you."

Her head twists to the side and she says, "Thank you."

"Don't make a thing of it," I say, my lips brushing her ear. "And don't ask me again."

"Can't make that promise," she says, her voice breathless. "I have so many things I want to do with the English department."

"Jesus, Gibson," I curse and move my hand to the waistband of her thong. "Is it your personal goal to annoy me?"

"I don't know," she whispers. "Is it your personal goal to turn me on and leave me horny and begging?"

My hand snags the string of her thong and I yank it down, letting it fall to the ground. She steps out of it without being asked and then sticks her ass out as if begging for my touch.

"Tell me," I whisper, stepping to her side now and taking in the arch in her back and the curve of her bare ass. "Are you begging now?"

"No, I'm propositioning."

I bring my hand back to her spine, where I drag her shirt up to the bottom of her shoulder blades and then leave it there, knowing the weight of her breasts won't let it go any farther north. Then I glide my hand down until I reach the globe of her ass. My finger slides over the divot between her cheeks and then to the other side.

"God," she grumbles, "you make me so hot, Arlo."

"Are you wet?"

"The minute I saw you shirtless in the kitchen, I got wet."

I smooth my hand over her ass, so fucking firm it drives my cock wild with need. "Did you think staying here would lead you to run into me?"

"No, but I'm glad I did."

"So, you're telling me, you walk around people's houses in nothing but a thong and a tank top?" I run my finger down her crack, causing her head to fall to the counter in a deep exhale, as her ass pushes against my hand.

"Never."

"So then this was for me?" I smooth my hand down her crack, and her legs are spread just enough where I can reach to her arousal.

Fuck . . .

She is so wet.

"Oh God," she moans against the counter, and I quickly pull my hand away. In seconds, she lifts up and turns toward me, eyes awake now, needy. "Don't." Her voice is stern. "Don't tease me, Arlo."

"What were you expecting me to do? Finger you on my kitchen counter?" I glance down between us, unable to see the luscious spot between her legs in the dark, but well aware of how hard her nipples currently are.

She brings her hand to my stomach, where she drags her fingers down the divot in the middle of my abs to the waistline of my briefs. I don't waver, I don't stray from eye contact, and I sure as hell don't let her know how fucking satisfying it is to have her hand on my skin.

"I don't care what you do to me, Arlo. As long as you do something."

"I told you I wouldn't get into this with you."

"Then let's just call it sleepwalking," she says, moving her hand down a few more inches. My cock surges forward. Her fingers connect with my erection, just the lightest press, but the look in her eyes and the way her teeth fall over her bottom lip is my undoing.

I stall her wrist and say, "No touching."

"Arlo—"

I grip her hips and lift her onto the counter, where I spread her legs and step in close to her. Her hands fall to my shoulders and her chest nearly scrapes against mine from the heaviness of her breath.

I smooth my hands up her thighs, to her sides, and then all the way to her breasts. I pull her tank top down, exposing them.

Fuck . . . they're perfect. A handful, firm, sexy as shit, just like her. Her nipples—hard and ready—beg to be pinched, and when she puffs her chest closer, I take one between my fingers, rolling the little nub. Her head rocks to the side as her mouth falls open.

"You're not teasing me, are you? I . . . I don't think I could take it." *Neither could I. I'm burning for her. From her scent. To her wet, dripping arousal.*

I bring my mouth to her neck and kiss along the column. "Are you saying you need release?"

Her hands pull on the back of my head, keeping me in place. "Desperately."

I bite the spot just under her ear and she lets go of me, only for me to pull away a few inches, our noses almost touching, our breath mixing as I play with her nipple, rolling it consistently, never letting up.

"How do you want this release? With my fingers? My mouth?"

"I want you," she answers, her legs locking around my waist so I feel her arousal on my stomach.

"You want my dick."

"Yes."

"You can't have it," I say, moving my head back to her

neck, "but you can have my fingers, or you can have my mouth."

"Why not—"

"Those are the terms," I say, lifting away and looking her in the eyes.

She looks away and nibbles on the corner of her lip. Finally, she asks, "Can I have your mouth and your fingers?"

"Greedy." I unlock her legs from around my waist. "Get on all fours."

"Here? On your counter?"

"Yes. Quickly, or this offer expires."

I let go of her and snap the towel off the oven and fold it lengthwise for padding. When she turns over, I help her place the towel under her knees.

"Now lean your head down and stick your ass out at me."

"Arlo—"

"That or nothing," I say, smoothing my hand over her ass right before I smack it, the sound ringing through the quiet house.

"Oh . . . Jesus," she cries into her arm.

Smoothing my hand over the sting where I slapped her, I say, "It'll be in your best interest to be quiet and not wake up my sister. If you get too loud, I'm pulling away and leaving. Do you understand?"

"Y-yes."

"Do you want something to bite down on?"

"That seems aggressive."

"You've never had my mouth on your pussy before." I slide my fingers down her center and press against her entrance. She moans, and I repeat, "Do you want something to bite down on?"

"Yes," she says, her voice shaky with a hint of embarrassment.

Grabbing another towel, I hand it to her and say, "Don't make a sound. Got it?" She nods and I move in behind her, taking in her pussy and how fucking wet she is. "When was the last time a man fucked you?"

"I don't know——"

"*Never* is the correct answer, Miss Gibson. Because you've never been fucked by me." *You never will be, and my cock will hate me for that.*

I place my hands on her ass, spread her, and lower my mouth to her pussy, where I press a gentle kiss. Her back tenses and then she melts into the counter, a moan getting stuck in her throat.

I play with her for a few breaths, dragging my tongue over her lips, along her inner thigh, back to her center. She writhes beneath me, her pelvis turning, reaching, begging to hit her in the right spot. I clamp down on her hips and say, "Move again and I'm done. I'm in control. Not you. Got it?"

"Y-yes," she groans. "Sorry . . . Mr. Turner."

Holy.

Fuck.

My dick grows even harder, if possible, from the way her breathless, raspy voice just said my last name.

That deserves a reward.

I move my mouth from her inner thigh to her center and flick my tongue against her clit. She moans and quickly muffles herself with the towel. I bring my hand inward, keep my tongue flicking quick and short on her clit, and then stick a finger inside of her.

She moans even louder, and I pause.

"S-sorry," she says. "Please don't stop. Please."

I don't move, instead I wait a few breaths and when desperation laces her voice with another *please*, I bring my mouth back down onto her clit, where I intensify the pressure.

Harder.

Faster.

More forceful.

My fingers move in tandem with my tongue.

Her muffled sounds grow faster, louder.

My cock juts against the counter, seeking relief as well.

Her legs tense.

My tongue fires over her sensitive spot.

My balls tighten and fuck . . . fuck, my entire body is ignited.

Her torso quivers.

Faster.

Harder.

Flick. Flick. Flick . . .

"Ohhhhh," she cries out, her legs tensing, her back arching, and she comes.

Fuck . . . yes.

My tongue flies over her clit at a relentless pace, pulling out every last ounce of her orgasm until I hear her surrender, and watch her lower to the counter.

Mother of God, I'm hard. It's painful, as my cock juts against the fabric of my briefs, aching for relief.

I pull away and help her to the ground. Taking the towel that supported her knees, I wipe it across my face and then set it on the counter where she lies, sated, trying to catch her breath. I take a moment to pick up her thong and stuff it in the waistband of my briefs, so it's not discovered by Coraline tomorrow morning.

Smoothing my hand over her ass, I give her a few more seconds and then turn her around, adjust her tank, and lift her up into my arms. She rests her head against my chest as I carry her through the first floor of my house and to the guest room. I push the door open with my foot, then take her to the bed, the entire walk fucking painful from how turned on I am.

I move the covers over her body and consider sitting next to her, but think otherwise, knowing that will only result in me crawling into bed with her.

"Goodnight, Miss Gibson."

"Arlo, wait." She sits up. "Come here."

I take a step back. My erection's quite obvious in my briefs, begging to be freed and buried in her beautiful mouth.

"What are you doing? Let me give you release."

"Not necessary." I take another step away. "Get some rest." Looking her dead in the eyes, I say, "And do not follow me. Do you hear me? You're not to leave this bed until the morning."

"Why are you being like this?"

"My house, my rules."

"You didn't even kiss me."

"Were you looking for intimacy or release, Miss Gibson? Release I can give you, intimacy should be sought out with someone else."

Her eyebrows pull together. "Why are you against intimacy?"

"I'm not here for a therapy session." Reaching the door, I ask, "Do you need anything else?"

"Your dick in my mouth," she answers. *And God, do I need that.* Her. Sucking my cock down her throat.

Five steps. That's all it would take for me to be in her hot and filthy mouth.

But I won't. *Can't.*

Gripping the doorway, I say, "You should be so lucky." I'm lying. I would be the lucky son of a bitch.

But that's not who I am. *Lucky.*

And then I leave before I lose my damn mind.

Chapter Thirteen

GREER

"Good morning," Arlo says, walking into the kitchen, freshly showered and in a pair of jeans and plain white T-shirt. Hair still wet and smelling incredible, masculine—he's every bit of a fantasy I had last night.

I woke up this morning thinking what happened last night was a dream, that is, until I found my thong on my nightstand and a note next to it. In his sharp handwriting, all it said was "You taste like fucking honey."

I then proceeded to throw myself back against the plush white pillows and drape my arm over my face.

It wasn't a dream.

It was all real.

I was on my hands and knees on top of Arlo's kitchen island while he ate me from behind.

It was erotic.

Something I've never done, nor thought I'd ever do.

And it unleashed something inside of me, a carnal need

that's never been tapped into before. That man is provocative, seductive, demanding, and even though I've had a few boyfriends, none of them compare to Arlo Turner. He seems so strait-laced, but God, is he not. *You taste like fucking honey.* My mouth was literally salivating, desperate to wrap around his cock. *Another first.*

And yet he denied me. How can a man so virile—*amorous* —have such crazy self-control?

"When was the last time a man fucked you?"

"I don't know—"

"Never is the correct answer, Miss Gibson. Because you've never been fucked by me."

Just from the memory, I reached between my legs and attempted to ease the growing ache until I came. But it wasn't satisfying. It wasn't even close to what I needed. It was a means to an end. What I need is him.

Arlo.

I want his hands.

His tongue.

His mouth.

His cock.

I want it all.

"Ugh, wine always gives me the worst headaches," Cora says, as she stands next to a glass of orange juice on the counter, the exact spot where Arlo fucked me with his tongue last night. "It was a feat on its own prying my eyes open this morning." Turning to Arlo, she asks, "I'm going to get some breakfast burritos from around the corner with at least a dozen hash brown patties. Want anything?"

"I'm good," he says casually. Barefoot and godlike, he goes to the fridge, where he pulls out the apple juice and pours himself a glass.

"How are you not completely hungover right now?" Cora asks me.

Because your brother fucked me sober with his tongue last night.

197

"Not sure. Had some apple juice in the middle of the night, so maybe that was it," I say, glancing at Arlo, whose eyes are fixed on mine as he tilts his glass to his mouth.

"You're telling me you mixed sweet wine with sweet apple juice?" She clutches her stomach. "That makes me want to vomit right here." She shakes her head, completely oblivious to the stare down I'm having with Arlo.

Those eyes, so penetrating, it's as if he's stripping me bare and reading my thoughts with every breath I take.

"Sleep well, Miss Gibson?" Arlo asks me.

"Miss Gibson?" Cora scoffs. "Where are we, in the classroom? Call her Greer, you weirdo."

But he doesn't flinch, he just raises a brow, and I know exactly what he's trying to convey by calling me Miss Gibson. He's trying to remind me about last night, as if I need reminding. What happened . . . that will be imprinted on my brain forever.

From the command in his voice, to the way he brought me to the hilt, let me ride out my orgasm, and then tucked me in after—I will never forget the feeling of complete ecstasy followed up by caring warmth.

"I slept great. Thank you for letting me stay here last night."

"Glad I wasn't the only one drinking." She presses the palm of her hand to her forehead. "Keeks kept talking about being aroused last night, right?"

"Correct."

She nods. "That's what I thought."

"On that note, I'm going to leave you two alone," Arlo says.

"Don't bother. I need a breakfast burrito. Do you want anything, Greer?" Coraline asks.

I shake my head. "I'm going to take off and get back to my place. I have frozen waffles calling my name."

"I'm not one to get in the way of a girl and her frozen

waffles." Cora comes up to me and gives me a quick hug. "Mama needs a burrito. I'll catch you later." Cora turns to Arlo and points at him. "Be nice to her, understand?"

Arlo doesn't respond, just drinks his apple juice casually.

How could he possibly look that laidback when I'm vibrating with so many emotions?

"Bye." Cora waves behind her, grabs her keys off the entryway credenza, and takes off, the door shutting behind her.

A few seconds roll by before I turn to Arlo, whose eyes are trained on me.

The air around me shrinks as he eats me up. After I got myself off in bed, I took a quick shower, piled my hair on top of my head, and changed into the clothes I wore last night, minus the thong. That's stuffed into my purse.

"So . . ." I say, feeling awkward and unsure of myself. "Did you . . . uh . . . did you masturbate last night?"

He sets his glass down. "What do you think?"

"I think you did." Growing a little courage, I add, "And I think you did it with my name on the tip of your tongue."

"Wasn't your name on my tongue; it was the taste of your pussy on my tongue that got me off."

Good God, I shiver in my seat, unable to control the involuntary shudder from the rumble to his voice.

I lick my lips, my heart thudding in my chest as he rounds the kitchen island. I twist in my stool so I'm facing him when he steps next to me.

He reaches up and gently draws his thumb over my cheek. Quietly, he asks, "My scruff didn't hurt you, did it?"

He doesn't want intimacy, but this right here, asking if he hurt me, feels more intimate than a kiss, especially the way he's cupping my cheek.

"I'm a little sore, but in the best way possible. Every time I move, I love knowing it was you who was between my legs."

His eyes darken and then he slowly tilts my head to the

side, moving his thumb down the column of my neck, to the spot right below my ear. "I marked you," he says, his thumb rubbing over what I'm assuming is a bite mark.

"You can see it?"

"Only if you know it's there." He comes back to my eyes. "I bit you hard enough to remind you who took you last night."

"Once again, don't need the reminder."

His hand falls to my chin, where his thumb tugs on my bottom lip. "I fantasized about these lips sucking my cock last night. I couldn't sleep until I got off at least twice."

"You could have had the real thing, you know."

"I could have, but I wasn't the one in dire need."

"Coming twice in order to sleep seems like a dire situation."

His hand floats down my neck, to my collarbone. "I'll let you know if it's ever a dire situation for me."

"Will you, or are you going to forget this happened come Monday?"

"Isn't it easier that way?" he asks, his hand floating to the strap of my tank top. Slowly he pushes it off my shoulder, along with my bra strap.

"Not when you touch me the way you are. You're going to make me want you even more."

"You're going to have to learn to control your urges, Miss Gibson."

He slips the other shoulder of my top off and then flips my tank top and bra down, exposing my breasts.

Hunger fills his eyes as he scans me in broad daylight.

With any other man, I'd be self-conscious to be topless in the kitchen, the harsh morning sun exposing my bare breasts. But Arlo brings out that carnal, palpable desire that would permit him to fuck me against a window and have me not care if one of his neighbors witnessed the act.

"Your tits are exquisite." He reaches out and squeezes one, his thumb rolling over my nipple.

"I hope you plan on finishing whatever you're starting."

Pausing, he looks at me and says, "You're right. And I have no plan to finish you off." He flips my bra and tank back up and steps away. "You have waffles waiting for you."

When he steps away, I quickly hop off the chair and go up to him, my skin crawling, tingling, needing to feel him.

Even though he's much stronger than I am, I push him against the wall and press one hand to his chest, warning him not to move, and because he's the teasing bastard he is, he smirks, as if my sheer force is comical to him.

With my other hand, I cup him through his jeans, feeling how hard he is, just from those little touches.

"Who are you kidding, Arlo? You want this just as bad as I do. Why are you denying yourself?"

"I'm not denying myself," he says, reaching down and pulling my hand away. A wave of embarrassment washes over me, but it doesn't stay for long, because he unzips his jeans and presses my hand against his length, the only barrier being his black boxer briefs. "I'm prolonging the inevitable."

He strokes my hand up and down his length, his head falling to the wall, his teeth pulling on his bottom lip.

"Why prolong it when you can have it now?" I ask, my thumb hitting his tip.

He sucks in a sharp breath. "Because the inevitable can still evolve."

"That's a contradiction."

"Not in my book." He removes my hand and buckles back up. Gripping my chin, he tilts my head back and says, "Get out of here, before I make you regret overstaying your welcome."

"How could you possibly make me regret that?"

"Bringing you to the point of orgasm, but denying your release. That's how."

"You would never."

"How you underestimate me, Miss Gibson. I was able to avoid your offer last night, even though my cock was aching for your lips. There's no doubt I could edge you out, despite wanting to feel you come on my tongue again."

God, he's so dirty.

Stepping away, he turns me around and brings me against his back, his hand splayed over my stomach, his mouth dropping to my ear, a feeling I'm starting to become addicted to. I'm not particularly short, but Arlo is the perfect height—his whole body encompasses mine. His delicious scent, the weight of his strong arms, the strength of his chest surrounding my back . . . *I want him. More than—oh . . . that feels good.*

His hand travels down my stomach and rests just above my pubic bone. "Now, be a good girl and leave my house. If you listen, you might be rewarded later, when you're least expecting it." He bites down on my earlobe, causing me to gasp.

"Arlo," I say, hearing how breathless I am from his proximity. "What . . . what are you doing to me?"

"It's called karma, and it's coming back with a vengeance."

"Karma from the pranks?"

He nods against me. "I told you not to fuck with me. Now, I'm going to fuck with you, on my clock, not yours." He brings his hand to my breast and gives it a squeeze before stepping away. "Have a good day . . . Greer."

Moving back around the island, he snags a banana from the kitchen counter and heads to his backyard. I watch him get comfortable in a lounger and, God, what I wouldn't give to crawl into that lounger next to him, or maybe on top of him, anything to feel his touch one more time.

But if I've learned anything in the last twenty-four hours, it's that Arlo means what he says. If I don't listen to him, I have a feeling I'm not going to like the consequences. So, reluctantly, I gather my things and head out the front door. I hop into my car and lower my head to the steering wheel.

I've read so many books where the heroine describes this feeling of being . . . controlled, and I've always rolled my eyes and thought they were contrived only through authors' boundless imaginations. Where the hero is like a conqueror of lands, where he hegemonizes and controls the heroine's thoughts and actions. And I, of course, have likened myself to Lizzie Bennet—determined to stay my course, be comfortable in my skin—and yet, one alluring man has somehow pushed me beyond my boundaries. And I've let him.

"I told you not to fuck with me. Now, I'm going to fuck with you, on my clock, not yours."

And I crave it.

What the hell is happening to me?

———

GREER: *Why do I feel like I'm in trouble? Am I in trouble?*

Stella: *How the hell do I know? Principal Dewitt never calls me into her office.*

Greer: *My pits are sweating.*

Stella: *Mine are sweating for you.*

Greer: *Okay, I'll text you when I'm done.*

I pocket my phone and take a deep breath as I round the corner to the main office. When Principal Dewitt said she wanted to see me during lunch, I was instantly nervous that she somehow, by an act of God, found out about Arlo and me having sexual relations on Arlo's kitchen counter.

Far-fetched, I know, but still, it was the first thing that popped into my head.

"Did you get called in too?"

That voice.

Oh God.

I look to the right, where Arlo is sitting in one of the chairs just outside of Principal Dewitt's office. I haven't seen him in two days, and I started to worry that maybe he was regretting what happened Friday night or technically Saturday morning, but before I can second-guess that assumption, he smirks at me, easing my mind.

"I did." I press my hand over my stomach, watching how inconspicuously Arlo takes in my dress, his eyes eating me up like a rabid beast. "Do you know what this is about?"

He stands and says, "Probably about what happened between us this weekend."

"What?" I shout-whisper. "But how? I didn't say anything. Did you?"

He chuckles, the sound so alluring and comforting that I want to snuggle into his side and ask him if I can stay there while Principal Dewitt speaks to us.

The door opens to the principal's office and Nyema Dewitt steps out. "Arlo, Greer, thank you for stopping by during lunch. Come, have a seat." She directs us to the chairs in front of her desk. Arlo and I both take a seat, but while he leans back and crosses one leg over his knee, I fidget in place and try not to throw up.

"I don't want to keep you from your lunch break, but I wanted to get this settled so I can move on to other things."

Settled?

Oh God.

Does this have to do with the dress-up day?

Arlo did say he'd report me to Nyema if he needed to. Did he report me, then go and butter me up over the weekend so I wouldn't hate him for getting me fired?

I think he's conniving enough to do something like that.

"I do have a salad waiting for me in the fridge," Arlo says with charm.

Charm.

The man has charm that doesn't entail ripping your panties off to appease his demands. Who knew?

"Steak with gorgonzola?" Nyema asks.

"Always." He winks, and I nearly throw up right there on the spot.

Suck ass much, Arlo?

Good God, man.

"Well, I won't keep your salad waiting. I wanted to talk to you about the homecoming dance."

Homecoming?

"We're short two chaperones, and I was hoping you could fill in."

From the corner of my eye, I see Arlo grip the armrest tightly, but that's the only evidence of his displeasure. "Of course, I can be there."

"Wonderful." Nyema turns to me and says, "Newbie is always the first to be thrown to the wolves. Are you available, Greer?"

"Of course. Haven't really established a life outside of school just yet, so I'm your girl. Plus, I'm super great at making sure students stay in line while also having fun. Because you know, high school has to be full of fun. So much fun . . . and rules. There must be rules, too." *God, stop rambling, Gibson.* "But, yes, no social life, so I'm here for anything you need."

"I wouldn't say that," Arlo says, picking a piece of lint off his pants, a diabolical pull to his lips. "My sister was telling me all about your Ladies in Heat Book Club."

Oh.

My.

God.

My face burns with embarrassment as Nyema raises her brow in my direction.

Uhh . . . things I don't want my boss knowing about me—
not when I'm trying to impress her, solidify a job here.

Awkwardly chuckling, I say, "Um, yeah . . ." I swallow. "I
do have that."

"Ladies in Heat?"

I thumb toward Arlo. "His sister's idea."

"Ahh, but you voted on it. Keiko Seymour offered the
Austen Empowerment Collaborative, which I thought was
more fitting. More respectful."

What the hell is he doing?

Asking to be murdered?

Because that's exactly what's going to happen when we
leave this office. I don't care if he made me come harder than
any other man.

Murder . . . total murder.

"Well"—Nyema uncomfortably shuffles some papers on
her desk—"seems like a fascinating club."

I lean forward and place my hand on Nyema's desk. "I feel
like I need to clarify that we're not really in heat."

"Could have fooled me," Arlo says on a chuckle. "With all
that talk about arousal and the reptile brain."

"Would you look at that," I say, standing from the chair.
"Time to go eat that salad of yours." I grab Arlo by the arm
and try to lift him out of his chair, but he doesn't budge.
"Arlo . . . salad."

"Don't be rude. We haven't been dismissed yet."

I narrow my eyes at him just as Nyema says, "You are
excused." She waves a pen between us. "I see why the English
department is raving about the new addition to the faculty.
You two sure have a spark."

I quickly turn to Nyema, horrified. "No, we don't. There's
no spark."

Arlo stands. "Wouldn't want her to think that we get
along, now would you?" He adjusts the sleeves on his forest-
green cardigan.

"We don't . . . I mean, we do. I just mean, there's nothing going on. No spark."

"Okay." Nyema looks at me, confused. Jesus, I'm making it worse. I can sense that's what's happening. I need to shut my mouth and leave. "Anyway, homecoming, sure. Whatever you need, I'm there. I have no life so I'm available. I mean, besides the book club, but that's once a month, nothing to worry about. And you know, I wasn't even sure I was going to participate."

"That's not what—"

"Your commentary isn't welcome right now," I say, hand up to him. Smiling maniacally, I say, "Lunch is calling, thanks for this meeting. Oh, and did I mention, that top on you is stunning?"

"Thank you, Greer," Nyema says with a smile while looking at her pink shirt. "And great job with the volleyball team. We've been impressed with the progress you've made."

"Thank you."

I give her one more smile and as I walk out of her office, I hear her say to Arlo, "Go easy on her, Arlo." They both chuckle, and the hairs on the back of my neck stand straight, anger boiling in the pit of my stomach.

How could he possibly talk like that in front of our boss? Embarrass me like that?

Not looking back, I charge toward my classroom. Without even turning around, I know Arlo is hot on my heels, because when I reach my classroom and try to shut the door, he stops it with his hand and squeezes inside, only to shut the door behind him and lock it. *Fuck. Fuck. Fuck. Why the fuck did he do that? Making me look like a fool in front of the woman who controls my position here. Why?* Pranks are one thing, but this is pushing the envelope.

Spinning on my heels, I look him in the eyes and say, "That was absolutely humiliating."

"Wasn't for me." Zero emotion crosses his expression, and

it takes everything in me not to wipe that blank look off his face.

"That's because you weren't the one being picked on. She's our boss and I'm a new teacher. I don't need her knowing about the Ladies in Heat Book Club. I need her to take me seriously. Arlo, you humiliated me."

"She's a person, too, you know. You walked in there with a stick up your ass. Thought I'd loosen you up."

"I don't need you to loosen me up."

"Really?" he asks, taking a step forward. "Sure seems like it."

I look him up and down as he approaches. "What are you doing?"

He moves in—*silently*—and I back up until I hit the edge of my desk.

"Don't think you can touch me and I'll forget what just happened."

Closing the space between us, his hands land on my hips and he lifts me up on my desk.

"I'm serious, Arlo. Don't you have a salad to eat?"

His eyes practically turn black when he says, "I'd rather eat you."

In seconds, he's leaning forward, and his hands are crawling up under my dress to the waistband of my thong.

"You are not about to go down on me in my classroom."

"Are you sure about that?" he asks, slipping my thong off before I can stop him. He takes the thin fabric and stuffs it in his back pocket, then pushes me back so I'm leaning on my elbows.

"Arlo—"

He lifts my skirt up and exposes me as he squats down. Looking up at me, he says, "Tell me now, right now. Tell me you don't want this."

I mean . . . I am mad at him, but if he were to rub his

finger between my legs right now, I know he'd be extremely happy with how turned on I am.

"That's what I thought," he says with such cockiness, that if his head wasn't dipping between my legs, I'd kick him in the chest.

But damn my body and my need for this man. I let him pull me to the edge and spread my legs just before his face falls between my legs, his fingers part me, and his tongue finds my clit.

"Oh God," I say quietly, sifting my hand through his hair. "This . . . this shouldn't be happening."

He pulls away. "Then tell me to stop."

Not saying a word, I press his hand to my center, then hear a light chuckle before he goes back to work, and it's the most glorious and erotic thing I've ever done.

It doesn't negate the fact that I'm still mad at him, or that I want to rip that cardigan off his body and smother him with it, but if I can get a little pleasure before I perform my act of murder, then it's worth the wait.

He moves his fingers to my entrance and presses two inside, scooping upward, making stars burst behind my eyes.

"Arlo," I whisper, shifting my hips, my body already humming, buzzing, climbing to the apex of my orgasm.

Is it really that easy for him? For him to pull pleasure from me in seconds? It shouldn't be possible. Moments ago, I was livid. Desperate to be left alone. But now . . .

Pushing at my legs, spreading me even more, he drives his tongue harder against my clit, the sensation rocking me to my core.

"Oh shit," I say breathlessly as his tongue flicks softly, only to drive down again.

My legs quiver.

My stomach bottoms out.

A wave of numbness washes over me and pools between my legs.

"I'm going to come," I whisper, just for him to pull away. "Arlo," I whisper yell, aware that we're still in the classroom. "What are you doing?"

"Do you forgive me?"

"Wh-what?" I ask, my chest heaving, my legs shaking.

"For what happened in Nyema's office—do you forgive me?"

"That's unfair," I say.

"It's not. I'm apologizing, I'll finish you off if you forgive me."

"What? Why?"

"Because you want to come." He presses his fingers upward and my head falls back.

"Oh . . . fuck."

"God, you're sexy." He leans down and presses kisses along my inner thighs. "Doing this in the light, where I can fully see you, it has me so fucking hard."

"Arlo, please," I beg, my clit throbbing, my mind crazy with need.

"Forgive me, and I'll make you come harder than the other night."

"Not possible."

"Try me," he says, his eyes determined when I look at him.

"Fine, I forgive you."

"Good."

He lowers his mouth to my clit and presses a few soft kisses before he flattens his tongue and moves long strokes along my slit. It's not what I want; it's just teasing me, dangling me off the edge but never letting me fall over.

"You're . . . oh God, you're frustrating me."

"Then I'm doing it right," he says, right before flicking his tongue lightly against my clit.

Over and over and over . . .

The pleasure builds.

It wraps around me, warming my body.

Igniting an inferno in the pit of my stomach.

"Yes . . . yes," I breathe heavily. "Yes, Arlo."

I clench his hair. My legs cling to him, pulling him closer, and then . . . I come.

A cry falls past my lips as my hips jackknife against his face, my body racing with such euphoria that a wave of tears hits the backs of my eyes.

"Oh my God, yes, Arlo," I say, riding out his tongue, dragging out every ounce of pleasure until I have nothing left to give and collapse on the desk, looking at the ceiling of my classroom.

I drape my arm over my eyes as I attempt to catch my breath. I cannot believe he just did that. *The rule follower. The cardigan wearer. The it's-my-way-or-the-highway man.*

What. The. Hell. Just. Happened?

And how?

Arlo lifts up, pushes my skirt down, and then helps me into a sitting position. Cupping my cheek, he looks into my eyes and says, "Have a good rest of the day, Miss Gibson."

"Wait," I say, still trying to recover. "You can't just leave like that."

"I can."

"But . . . what about . . ." I look down at his crotch, where I catch his bulge.

"Not your concern."

"So, that's it? You're going to make me come and then leave?"

"I don't see why this is an issue. You got what you needed, correct?"

"Yes." I press my hand against my hair, making sure it's flattened. "But what about what you need?"

He glances at my crotch and then licks his lips. "I got mine, don't worry about me."

And then he's walking out of my classroom, making me question the last ten minutes. Because what man, who showed fierce dislike for me and made derogatory remark after derogatory remark, suddenly deems it his purpose to make me feel *sated?* Yet deny himself. It doesn't make sense.

I'm physically sated, yet does that mean I forgive him for acting in ways that were truly cruel and manipulative?

Should I?

Chapter Fourteen

ARLO

To: Faculty_All
From: Dewitt, Nyema
Subject: Promiscuous Students

Dear Faculty,

As some of you might have heard, there was a neon-pink thong found just outside the English department wing. Our goal as a faculty is to make sure within the walls of our school, we keep it to education. Given the raging hormones we're dealing with, we're bound to run into something like this. But we have a no-tolerance policy, which requires you to report any information you might have acquired through gossiping students. Feel free to stop by my office with any leads.

Our school holds the lowest teenage pregnancy ratio in the country and I plan on keeping it that way.

Thank you, and keep educating.

Nyema

THE DOOR to my classroom slams, and I look up casually to find Greer standing by the door, a horrified look on her face, a printed piece of paper in hand.

I don't need X-ray vision to know what's on that paper.

"Have you seen this?"

Returning to my computer, I continue to enter grades. "I did."

"Uh . . . don't you have anything to say?"

Eyes trained on my computer, I say, "You apparently wear the same kind of underwear a high schooler would wear."

"Arlo," she practically yells, coming toward me and slamming the paper on my desk. "What if my initials were on that underwear?"

"Do you usually have your initials on your underwear, as if you're going to summer camp and don't want to lose them?"

"No, but . . . it could have been a possibility."

"I'm busy, Miss Gibson. I don't have time for your hysterics."

"Hysterics? Are you insane? Arlo, that was *my* underwear that was found."

I tap the printed email. "Which means, you better deliver the information about the underwear, since you know details. Don't want to disappoint her."

"Stop being so casual about this."

Sighing, I turn toward her in my chair and take her in. Black skinny jeans, purple blouse, hair pinned on the top of her head, and high heels on her feet. She looks fucking good and I'm feeling hungry again.

"What do you want me to do?"

"Uh, not drop my underwear around school? Maybe try that to start. Or how about don't steal my underwear at all? Who does that?"

"You didn't seem to mind until just now."

"Well, I do mind. Don't take my underwear."

"Okay." My eyes land on her breasts.

"Eyes up here," she snaps at me. I glance up at her. "We need to have a conversation."

"What kind of conversation?"

"A serious one." She crosses her arms over her chest, and I have to admit, I like her irritated and angry like this.

"Okay." I rock back in my chair. "Converse, Miss Gibson."

"Fine. I will." She shifts; her eyes look to the side. "So . . . uh—"

"Kids these days," Gunner says, busting through my door. "Underwear in the hallways—don't they have any class?" He pauses and looks between us. "Am I interrupting anything?"

"Miss Gibson was just conversing with me. Would you like to continue?" I ask, brow raised.

"Oh . . . uh, no." She shakes her head. "I think I'm all done."

"Are you sure? It was about the underwear, was it not? I believe Miss Gibson might have a lead."

"Really?" Gunner asks, rubbing his hands together. "What's the lead? Is it that punk Caleb and his girl Raquel? I saw them making out against the lockers several times the other day, and I kept poking them with a baseball bat to break it up."

Greer purses her lips, shoots me a look, and then says, "No. I don't have a lead. I was just . . . disgusted that someone would believe it's acceptable to not only take someone's underwear, but then display it to the school. Don't you think that's disrespectful? And something that shouldn't happen near the English department, especially on Arlo's watch?"

"She's got a point," Gunner says with a knowing look. "How are you letting that kind of behavior slip by you?"

"How do we even know it was promiscuous behavior?" Arlo asks, rolling his knuckles over his desk. "Could have been someone accidentally losing their underwear after changing from gym."

"Plausible, but the gym is on the other side of the school.

She'd have been fumbling with her books a lot to lose her underwear."

Arlo points his finger. "Can't guarantee the underwear belongs to a girl, either."

Gunner taps his chin. "Right, right. Good point." He turns to Greer. "Are you sure you don't have a lead?"

"I don't."

He studies her, and she fidgets under his gaze. Gunner is good at reading people, and funnily enough, Greer is giving off all the wrong body language. "You look like you're hiding something."

"She does, doesn't she?" I say, finding too much comfort in how uncomfortable she is.

"I'm not hiding anything. I'm just . . . thirsty. I need a drink. Excuse me."

Gunner steps into her path, breaking off her retreat. "Hold on a second." He lifts her chin and studies her eyes carefully. I smirk behind her, loving every moment of the squirming Greer. "Yup, there's a secret she's holding back. So, what is it, Greer?"

"Care to share with the class?" I encourage.

Her shoulders tense and her head lifts. Finally, she says, "Fine . . . I heard the underwear belongs to you, Gunner, and that there's some trend of male teachers wearing thongs."

Gunner shakes his head. "Stopped wearing thongs after I graduated from college. Sorry to disappoint."

"You wore thongs in college?"

"Easier for the long runs our coach made us go on."

"Oh, well . . . that's what I heard. Okay, bye." Greer pushes past Gunner and exits the classroom before either one of us can stop her.

When she's out of sight, Gunner turns toward me and says, "I don't believe that."

Chuckling, I say, "Yeah, me neither."

"So, Sunday Funday this weekend? Your place still?"

"We're practicing, right?"

"Yeah, but figured we could make it a little more fun. Jason has the day off and he was going to come over with his wife, Dottie, and I was going to bring Lindsay."

"You're going to bring your girlfriend to Sunday Funday? Think that's a good idea?"

"Dottie's her best friend from college. She can handle whatever we throw her way with her friend by her side. Plus, I think Lindsay could be good friends with Cora. They got along when we had ice cream last time."

"You don't have to reason with me, just wondering if you're ready."

"I am." He smiles and takes a seat on a desk. "Dude, I really like her. And Dylan, fuck, he's amazing. Sweet and funny. And smart. So freaking smart."

"Does Dylan know about you being his dad yet?"

"Not yet." He looks downcast. "Lindsay isn't ready. She wants to make sure we're in a solid spot before she tells him. Bringing her to hang out on Sunday could be a good next step."

"Then bring her."

"You don't mind the extra people?"

"Have I ever?" I ask, raising a brow at my friend who is notorious for bringing extra people to my parties.

"You've gotten butthurt before."

"Don't fucking use the term *butthurt*."

Gunner chuckles. "You know what I mean. But if you're cool with it, then I'll bring her along. And Jason is a lot of fun. He's ready to take some people out in badminton."

"Looking forward to it."

"Okay, well, I'm going to hit up the teachers' lounge, see if anyone knows any info about the thong. I really want to bust Caleb. He's such a little bitch."

"Is a seventeen-year-old really getting the best of you?" I ask.

Gunner stands and stretches his arms over his head. "He is, the little fucker. He's really getting to me."

———

"DEAR MR. DARCY, IT WAS A PLEASURE—"

"What are you doing?" I ask from the doorway of Greer's classroom.

Her head snaps up, and when she sees me, her eyes narrow and she lays the paper in her hands flat on the desk.

"None of your business."

"Ah, still mad about the other day?"

"No." She turns away from me.

"Liar." I walk into her classroom and shut the door.

"Don't even think about it," she says, holding up her finger to me. "I've got news for you—whatever is going on in that thick head of yours isn't going to happen."

"What do you think is going on in my head?" I approach her desk.

"Sexual things." She turns back to her paper, reading it over.

I slip the paper from under her and bring it to my eyes to read.

"Hey, give that back."

I scan it and then ask, with a confused brow, "Did you write a love letter to Mr. Darcy?"

Head held high, she says, "I did. Do you have a problem with that?"

"No, I'm just wondering why."

"We're writing letters to fictional characters next week and I wanted to use this as an example."

"Love letters? Are you going to bring out the construction paper and markers as well?"

"Hey." She snaps the paper out of my hands. "Don't be

rude. This is a great way to help the readers connect with the characters."

"Bet you they hate it."

"Bet you they think I'm fun and exciting and always creating new, interesting ways for them to learn, unlike your stodgy approach on the other side of the wall."

"Not getting into that debate with you again," I say. I have other things on my mind.

"Okay, then why are you here?"

"I wanted to check something under your desk. I'm looking for a symbol to see if it's an original."

"Seriously?" she asks. "That's what you're doing on your lunch break? Checking the authenticity of the desks?" Shaking her head, she pushes away from her desk and motions to the large opening. "Have at it."

God, that was far too easy.

Moving around the desk, I get on all fours and crawl under the spacious opening. I haven't seen many desks likes ours that offer so much room, but when I was sitting in my classroom looking at it, I knew it'd be perfect. Especially since the sides of the desk are flush with the floor.

"What's that pink thing in your back pocket?"

"A flashlight," I lie, then turn around and pull at her chair, bringing her closer to me.

"What on earth?"

My hands find her thighs, and I switch on the vibrator I stole from her apartment and rub it against her inner thigh, grateful for the skirt she's wearing today.

"Oh my God," she says. "Arlo, you can't be—"

I press it against her pussy for a second and then run it down her other leg.

"Oh Jesus. Oh God, this is not happening." She says the words but spreads her legs at the same time. I smile to myself. She's way too fucking easy.

What I can't believe though, is that I'm doing this to her in the first place. This is so out of character for me, and yet, I can't seem to stay away. I've had fucking partners, women who knew that there would never be intimacy between us. Mildly satisfying. But Greer is so expressive. Volatile in every way.

And although I could be noble and say that my *sexual attacks* on her are solely for her pleasure, they're not. I like the control. I like causing her to buckle. Perhaps, to push her beyond her normal boundaries. She's addictive, but I know I won't let it go any further than this.

"I've thought about doing this to you ever since I stole your vibrator. I've just been waiting for the right moment."

"What . . . what made that moment today?" she asks, spreading her legs even wider.

"This dress. I saw you walking down the hallway and I knew I needed to fuck you in it."

"Well, you're not really fucking me, now, are you? A vibrator is."

I turn up the speed, and she jolts when I bring it closer to her center.

"It's still me controlling it, knowing when to turn it up, when to turn it off, when to torture you." I slip the vibrator under her thong and rub it against her slit.

"Dear God, please forgive me," she says.

"I wish I could see your face. I want to know what you're feeling."

"Turned on. Breathless. Useless."

"Do you wish this was my cock?" I ask, moving the vibrator away, only to push it back on her clit.

"I wish I was able to touch your cock," she says.

"Are you saying you're greedy for it, Miss Gibson?"

"Yes," she says, just as there's a knock on the door and it opens. Greer sits straight up, but I don't move . . . and I don't turn off the vibrator.

"Greer, do you have a moment?"

"Principal Dewitt," Greer says as I turn off the vibrator.

She doesn't move—she can't, or else she risks the possibility of exposing me. "Of . . . of course."

I switch the vibrator on, the buzzing sound easy to hear in the quiet classroom. Her legs clench and I smile so hard, my cheeks start to hurt.

"What's that buzzing sound?" Nyema asks.

Greer laughs awkwardly. "Yeah, I . . . uh . . ."

I turn it off; her legs relax.

"I think it's the air conditioner."

"Oh, okay, how annoying. I'll put a word in with maintenance."

I turn it back on and press harder against her clit.

"Oh, there it goes again," Greer says, her voice strained. "Darn that air conditioner. Keeps us c-cool, but . . . oh God." She swallows hard. "Sorry, I have a . . . um, my back. Oo, it's . . . hello, it's cramping up. Old volleyball . . . wooo"—she blows out a long breath—"injury."

I switch the vibrator off.

"Oh, maybe you should get up and stretch."

"Nope, good . . . I'm good."

"Okay. Well, I wanted to talk to you about the volleyball team."

I turn on the vibrator.

"Oh, dear God . . . what about them?" she asks, her voice attempting to sound casual. "Sorry, little hyped up from the buzzing." Technically, that's not a lie. "It's been driving me nuts all day."

"Understandable. Anyway, we've a bit of a bus issue for the game tonight. There aren't any available. Could I ask you and Stella to drive two twelve-passenger vans to the game?"

"Umm, yeah. Sure." Her legs clutch around my hand like a vise. "Do we have permission to do that?"

"Yes, the permission slips the parents signed at the beginning of the season cover that."

I ramp up the vibration.

"Yes!" she says loudly. "Yes, that would . . . uh-huh, yup, we can do that."

"Wonderful." Nyema pauses and then says, "I'll send maintenance over after school, get that fixed for you."

"Th-thank you."

"Okay, I'll leave you to it. Thank you for being flexible."

"Of course."

"Door shut?" Nyema asks.

"Pl-lease," Greer stutters.

The door clicks shut, Greer exhales, and I dip the vibrator closer.

"Oh fuck, oh fuck," she whispers. "Oh, fuck, Arlo." And then she's coming. From under the desk, I watch her convulse, her entire body shuddering as she rides out her orgasm.

When her legs fall open again, I take that moment to remove the vibrator and press my mouth against her arousal, lapping up every last drop. She lets out a long moan. I push her away from the desk and crawl out to observe her.

Cheeks red.

A light sheen of sweat on her upper lip.

Completely sated.

"I hate you," she says, her beautiful eyes opening up to me.

"No, you don't." I reach over, place the vibrator in one of her drawers, and then turn to leave.

She grabs my hand, though, and stands on wobbly legs. I help steady her, but once she's set, her eyes go from hazy lust to pure anger.

She pushes at my chest and asks, "Are you insane?"

"No."

"Arlo, you could have gotten us in serious trouble."

"Maybe. Good cover with the air conditioning." I tip her chin up. She swats my hand away.

"Stop acting like what you just did was nothing."

"It wasn't nothing." I grip her hip and pull her in tight so she can feel me, how heated and turned on I am. "It very much was something."

"You could have gotten me fired."

I shake my head. "A mere slap on the wrist."

"She doesn't like promiscuous activity."

"Was that promiscuous?"

"Ugh." She nudges me away and pushes her hands through her hair. "You're infuriating."

"Normally, people are calmer after having an orgasm like you just did."

"And normally, people have those orgasms in a safe environment, not a classroom. And I can't believe you didn't lock the door. Were you hoping for someone to walk in?"

"More fun like that." I wink. "Didn't think it'd be Nyema though. That was entertaining."

Greer points her finger at the door, undeniably upset. "Get out. Get out now. Do not come in here again, do you hear me?"

I move, but not toward the door. I move toward her and back her against her whiteboard. I reach up and cup her cheek, angling her jaw up.

"Don't be mad at me."

"I am."

"Don't be."

"I can't just switch it off like that, Arlo. I'm trying to prove myself at this school, and you're making that hard."

"You're making me hard."

Growling, she says, "Are you even listening to me?"

I slowly nod and lick my lips. "I am. And I'm sorry. It won't happen again."

Her brow furrows. "Really?"

I chuckle and stroke my thumb over her cheek, trying to tell myself to walk away, that this hold right here, the way my thumb loves rubbing her cheek, it's too intimate. It's too much.

But I can't stop myself. I hate that she's upset with me, that anger resulted from this, rather than lust.

"I won't fuck you under your desk again. Now, on top of your desk, that's another story." I step away and stick my hands in my pockets. I give her a small once-over and say, "You look beautiful today, by the way. And when your face is flushed like that, freshly fucked, it simply adds to your beauty."

I start to walk away, when she calls out, "Arlo?"

I look over my shoulder.

"You're forgetting your vibrator."

"That's yours, Miss Gibson. I suggest you take it home. You don't want the air conditioner acting up in the middle of class, do you?"

She purses her lips. "I don't. But, hey, we need to talk."

I smirk. "Good luck tonight."

"Arlo, I'm serious."

Yeah, I can hear it in her tone, but I'm not ready to talk, so instead, I leave, thinking how that was more satisfying than I thought it'd be.

Chapter Fifteen

GREER

"Didn't expect to see you here. I saw that you guys won tonight," Gunner says, breaking the silence in the gym.

From the bleachers, I give him a soft smile and then turn back to my notebook, where I've been writing down notes for class, notes that have morphed into realizations . . . feelings . . . and emotions.

I'm conflicted, and there's only one person to blame: Arlo Turner.

He has me convinced that I want more from him than secret orgasms. He has me feeling like . . . like I could possibly start something more.

And I honestly don't know how I feel about that.

He's been so cold toward me, and now, he's soft at times, dedicated, leading me to believe that he cares about me.

He's mercurial.

He's unpredictable.

He's addicting.

And he's toying with me.

I desperately want to talk to him, ask him what his intentions are, because even though I've been a more-than-willing participant in these one-on-one orgasmic interactions, I also know this is not who I am. I've never been the girl to sneak around and search out pleasure, and only pleasure. For me, sex goes hand in hand with intimacy, with a relationship, and even though Arlo makes me feel out of this world, his refusal to let me touch him, hold him, kiss him . . . it pains me.

I'm a lover, a feeler, the girl who not only deserves to be intimate, but demands it when physical attraction crosses over to more.

As Gunner approaches me, I say, "Hey, yeah, we did. I dropped off the van and thought I'd try to catch up on a few thoughts." I snap my notebook shut, not wanting him to see anything.

"Looks like more than just thoughts. You okay?" He presses his finger between my eyes, smoothing out the furrow in my brow.

"Yeah," I sigh, but I sound less than convincing.

"Sounds like it." He bumps his shoulder with mine. "Come on, you can talk to me."

Ha, yeah, okay.

Let me just talk to one of Arlo's best friends about how the underwear in the hallway was mine, thanks to Arlo and his sinful mouth.

"I'm really fine." I shove my notebook into my backpack and zip it up. "I should get going. I'm starving, and that game has taken every last bit of strength from me."

"Perfect. We were just headed to the bar for some dinner. Why don't you join us?"

"Who's *we*?" I ask, a lift to my brow.

Gunner chuckles. "Just me and Romeo. Don't worry, you're safe. Turner has retired to his *abode*. I know this because that's what he texted me when I asked if he wanted to grab a beer. Pretentious ass."

"Just you and Romeo? Does that mean you'll dish the goods on your best friend?"

A large smile spreads across Gunner's handsome face. "Anything you want to know, we're here to hand out all the details."

"In that case, I'm in."

———

"THESE GARLIC FRIES are hitting the spot," Romeo says, picking one up and shoving it in his mouth.

"I don't think I've ever been more grateful for food," I say, wiping my truffle-coated fingers on my napkin.

Romeo arrived at the Atomic Saloon before us and, like the amazing man that he is, had drinks and an appetizer of truffle garlic fries already at the table when we arrived.

"You know, I'm happy Gunner ran into you at the gym," Romeo says, bringing his lager to his mouth. "I don't think we get enough time to sit down and chat with you."

"Because your overlord is always bogarting you two," I say with a grin.

"Overlord? You think Turner is our overlord?" Gunner asks.

"Uh . . . yeah."

Gunner and Romeo exchange glances, playful smirks on their faces, and then they both shrug. "Yeah, that's an accurate description," Romeo says. "But he had his chance tonight of breaking up the prank band and he missed it."

"We should take a picture and send it to him."

I shake my head. "Or we can keep it a secret and be in cahoots, you know, like the good old peeing-blue days."

Gunner rubs his chin. "I do like being in cahoots." He smacks the table. "We keep it a secret."

227

"That way we can talk about him and he won't be the wiser about it." Romeo lifts his glass and says, "To gabbing all the gossip."

I can toast to that. I lift my glass, and we all clink right before we tip back and drink.

When we set our glasses down, Gunner picks up a fry and says, "What do you want to know?"

"Oh . . . uh . . . I mean, we don't really have to talk about him."

"Where's the fun in that?" Romeo asks. "Is he still being a dick to you?"

Hmm . . . what a complicated question.

After what happened under the desk, I'd say no, but then again, he runs so hot and cold, I honestly have no idea what's going through his mind. *And then he said I looked beautiful.* It's moments like those that have me wondering, craving more.

"Uh, not really," I answer. "He's calmed down, but then again, we haven't been poking the bear, and I haven't rallied the troops to bang on their desks, so I'm pretty sure he's content with himself."

"Sounds about right," Romeo says. "I swear, that guy needs to loosen up."

"Oh?" I ask. "What, uh, what do you suppose would loosen him up?"

"Getting laid," Gunner says, picking up another fry.

"That's such a man thing to say," Romeo scoffs.

Gunner raises his brows. "Last time I checked, I have a penis. Therefore, I am a man."

I chuckle as Romeo says, "Yeah, but show some class, dude." Turning to me, Romeo says, "In the words of Keiko, Arlo needs coitus."

I snort.

Gunner scoffs. "How is that different than what I said?"

"Has hints of maturity and refinement."

"Sure, if that's what you want to call it."

Chuckling, I ask, "So, how come you two don't help the poor, cardigan-wearing man out?"

Romeo finishes off the last fry, dusts his hands off on his napkin, and says, "Ever since I've known Arlo, he hasn't been one to talk about relationships, or even getting some, for that matter. I think the only reason I know he's not gay is because of the way I've seen him check out women. Other than that, he's very private when it comes to that part of his life."

Huh, that's interesting.

I can guarantee he's not gay. I think that was debunked the moment he took me on his kitchen island . . . and on my desk . . . and under it . . .

"Huh. Now that you point it out, I don't think I've ever even heard him talk about a"—Gunner looks me in the eyes— "excuse the indecency, but I've never heard him talk about a conquest. Or a one-night stand. Or . . . anything, for that matter."

"He seems very proper," I say, trying to add something to the conversation.

"His upbringing made him that way. Rich grandparents, boarding school, all that fun stuff."

"He went to boarding school?" I ask, not realizing that at all.

"Oh yeah, him and Coraline. When they were old enough, their grandparents sent them to a boarding school in New Hampshire. They came back for holidays and a portion of summer, but they spent a good amount of their lives living far away from home and were demanded to be excellent in everything they did. Found that nugget out one drunken night in his backyard. He had a few too many drinks and was talking about his childhood. No clue why."

"I brought Hot Cheetos. He said he'd never had one before, and we both took offense," Romeo cuts in. "We demanded to know why, and that's when he went on a rant about his childhood."

"Oh yeah." Gunners nods as my mind starts to whirl, connecting the dots.

Why he's so proper.

Why he feels like he's holding on to something when I'm near him, as if he doesn't want to lose control.

Why he's so adamant about excellence.

Why he's so closed off.

"If he weren't giving off strong Alpha vibes, I'd consider him a virgin." Romeo takes a sip of his water.

Gunner laughs. "There's no way in hell Arlo Turner is a virgin."

Yeah . . . he's not.

"But hey, he's not rude anymore, right?" Romeo asks.

"Uh, yeah, I mean . . . he's fine." I pick up my beer and take a giant gulp, hoping they can't read me.

"Do you know what that tells me?" Gunner says with a knowing look, and I slowly begin to panic, thinking he might see through me. "That we need to pull some more pranks on him."

Romeo smacks his hands together and says, "I couldn't agree more. What do you say, Greer?"

I look between the two, noting the excitement in their eyes. "I, uh . . . I think I barely scraped by without the true wrath of your overlord. Pretty sure I'm going to stay out of this one."

"Ugh, come on. You were perfect to plant the seed."

"Yeah, and guess who he's going to come to first if his pee is blue again?"

"True." Gunner taps his chin. "We're just going to have to think of another way to annoy him."

Laughing, I say, "I love how your friendship works."

———

"SO . . . tell us, Greer, are you seeing anyone?" Romeo asks.

Feeling a little loose from my three beers, I say, "Why? You interested, Romeo?"

His eyes widen and he scrambles. "No, I mean, you're hot, but no, because well, you know . . . uh . . ."

I laugh and shove his shoulder. "I'm just playing with you." I'm tempted to ask him about Stella, but I refrain. I don't want to know, actually, because then I'd feel obligated to say something to Stella, and from the uninterested vibe I get from her when he's around, I'd say that's not information she wants to obtain. Better if everyone is uninformed. "No one for me right now," I answer, being honest, because even though I've received quite a few orgasms from Arlo, I think that's all they are, orgasms.

"So I'm the only attached one at the table?" Gunner asks, and I can't help but chuckle. Who knew these two would be so invested in talking about love and relationships? But here we are, drinking beer and gabbing it up—like they said.

"Looks like it," Romeo answers.

"Okay." He rubs his hands together. "Then as the one currently in a relationship, it's my duty to pry. How about some rapid-fire questions? You both have to answer."

"Dude, you know everything about me," Romeo points out.

"Yeah, but Greer doesn't, and it's only fair if she divulges information, so do you."

I glance over at Romeo. "He has a point."

"Fine. Let's get to it."

Looking far too excited, Gunner considers his questions. "Greer, you answer first, then Romeo." We both nod and then all three of us lean on the table, as if we're in an interrogation room, a single light swinging above us. "Relationship or fling?"

"Relationship," I answer.

"Both," Romeo says.

"Both, really?" I ask.

He shrugs. "I'm not desperate to be in a relationship, but think it'd be cool to be in one if I find the right person, and I'm totally into a fling if it means zero strings attached."

Huh, I wouldn't have guessed that.

"Okay, men or women?"

"Men," I answer.

"Women, duh."

"Okay, just checking. It'd be cool either way, but, you know, in case I run into someone who might work for either of you, as your friend in a relationship, it's good to know what side you play for." Clearing his throat, he asks, "Last time you had sex?"

"Uhh . . ."

I can feel my face flush, but before I can answer, Romeo says, "Four months ago, and my dick hates me for it."

"Four months. Dude."

Romeo holds up his hand. "I know . . . I fucking know."

Then they both turn toward me, and I slowly draw a circle on the table with my finger. "What, uh . . . what qualifies as sex? Like . . . coupling? Oral? Vibrators?"

"Good question. Let's say dick-in-the-vagina penetration," Gunner says.

"Oh, okay, then I don't know, a while."

I can feel their eyes on me, trying to read my facial expressions, most likely taking in how red my face feels.

"Is there another form of sex you've had recently?" Romeo asks.

Yes. Multiple kinds, with your best friend, your overlord.

"Nope," I squeak out and bring my beer to my lips.

Romeo sits taller and turns to Gunner. "How come I don't believe her?"

"Because she looks more satisfied than both of us combined," Gunner says.

"Do I?" I smooth a hand over my hair. "Must be all that chocolate I've been eating. Just as good as an orgasm."

"Sorry to break it to you, babe, but if chocolate is just as good as an orgasm, you're not having sex with the right guy," Gunner says.

And that couldn't be more true.

"I've had chocolate and sex at the same time," Romeo interjects, "and it's not the same. Chocolate is great, but an orgasm is mind-blowing."

Gunner leans in closer, staring me down. "What do you really want, Greer?"

"What do you mean? And how did this turn into a relationship conversation?"

Gunner points to his chest. "Remember, currently in a relationship, which means I want everyone in a relationship."

"He's been on my case, too. You're not the only one," Romeo mutters while bringing his beer to his lips.

"We'll get to you in a bit, but I want to know what you want, Greer. You said *relationship*. Is that what you're looking for?"

I think back to my notebook, the feelings I wrote down, the emotions I was thinking. My mind wanders to this "thing" with Arlo and how exciting it is, but how it's missing something for me. And I know exactly what it is. Intimacy—that I crave desperately.

I stare at the wood grain in our table and say, "I'd like something intimate. A relationship where I not only feel special, but where I make someone feel wanted, needed, cared for. I want to be able to go on dates, hold hands, take long walks at night under the stars. I want passion and spontaneity, but I also want reassurance that there will always be comfort and routine within a relationship. I want something sweet. Something naughty. Something that rocks my world and changes the colors around me. I want . . . love."

Gunner sits back in his booth, his shoulders slumped forward. "Damn."

Romeo drains the rest of his beer. "Yeah . . . damn."

"Is that too much?" I ask, feeling self-conscious.

Gunner shakes his head. "Nope, it's exactly what I want too."

"Hell, I think I might want that too," Romeo says.

And then we sit there, in silence, considering my words.

Yeah . . . that's exactly what I want, and not what I'm getting from Arlo. I don't need him to love me. But these peek-a-boo orgasms and heated moments aren't going to fulfill me.

I want the promise for more. And I know it's not a possibility with Arlo. *So that draws a proverbial line in the sand.*

<hr>

"THANK YOU FOR INVITING ME OUT," I say as we step outside the bar. I drove over with Gunner, so I called an Uber to take me home.

"I'm glad you came. I liked getting to know you better," Gunner says, pulling me into a hug. He's such a nice guy. If I didn't know he's emphatically obsessed with his girl, Lindsay, I'd consider flirting with him.

Romeo comes up to me and pulls me into a hug as well, my cheek pressing against his well-built chest. Hell . . . if Stella EVER considers anything with Romeo, I'll have to tell her about his hugs, because this is nice, really nice.

"It was a blast, Gibson," Romeo says, pulling away. "I feel more connected to you than ever."

Gunner grips Romeo's shoulder. "Now I have this overwhelming sense to find you a man."

"Why do you say that?" I chuckle.

"Because, you're a good girl." He reaches out and boops my nose. "And after that whole speech about wanting someone to lean on and hold your hand and be your person, you deserve that."

"She does." Romeo clutches his chest. "Shame Arlo is such a douche. They would be perfect together."

My breath catches in my chest, the mere mention of Arlo's name putting me on high alert.

Gunner shakes his head. "Nah, he would never. Not because he doesn't find you attractive, but because he's too closed off. Greer deserves better. Let me ask around, I'll find you someone. I'll talk to Jason."

"Oh, that's not necess—"

"Don't worry." Gunner holds up his hand. "We've got you covered. Now go home and get some sleep. We've some practicing to do this weekend."

He winks, and just as I go to say something, my Uber pulls up behind me. Gunner opens the door and helps me in. With a quick wave, I'm being taken back to my apartment. And although it was a great night with the boys—total sweethearts—I feel a pinch in my chest about their last words.

"Shame Arlo is such a douche. They would be perfect together."

"Nah, he would never. Not because he doesn't find you attractive, but because he's too closed off. Greer deserves better."

They're right. I do deserve better. I like warm, open-hearted men over closed-off counterparts.

Chapter Sixteen

ARLO

Gunner: *Fuck, Greer is amazing.*

    Romeo: *A real champion among women.*

    Gunner: *The whole package.*

    Romeo: *So damn sweet, I feel like I need to see a dentist now.*

    Gunner: *Dude, that didn't make sense.*

    Romeo: *It did in my head. And, hey, I thought we were in cahoots.*

    Gunner: *Oh shit, you're right. Shhh . . . maybe he won't see these text messages.*

    Arlo: *What the hell are you two talking about?*

    Romeo: *Damn it. He saw. What do we do now?*

    Gunner: *Pretend someone stole our phones.*

    Romeo: *Good idea.*

    Romeo: *Oh, hey, Arlo, someone stole our phones.*

    Gunner: *Yup, travesty, but we got them back.*

    Arlo: *You are fucking morons. You were still texting in the group thread.*

    Gunner: *Ah, hell.*

Romeo: *Damn you, beer. *shakes fist**

Arlo: *What the hell is going on?*

Gunner: *Should we tell him?*

Romeo: *I think we should. He's onto us.*

Arlo: *Get to the point.*

Gunner: **sighs* We went out to dinner with Greer and, dude, she's fucking phenomenal. The total package.*

Romeo: *We told her if you weren't such a douche, you two would be perfect together.*

Gunner: *You would. So . . . care to shake the douche off and give it a go with her?*

Arlo: *Stay the hell out of my business.*

Gunner: *^^^that's the kind of douche we're talking about.*

Romeo: *Yeah, wouldn't kill you to be a touch nicer.*

Gunner: *Maybe smile a little.*

Romeo: *Chortle every so often.*

Gunner: *Lighten up.*

Romeo: *Pull the stick out.*

Gunner: *Act like a civilized human . . .*

Arlo: *Did you want to practice and eat at my place?*

Gunner: *Yes!*

Romeo: *That's rhetorical, right?*

Arlo: *Then stay out of my personal life.*

Romeo: *Sheesh, what crawled up his ass?*

Gunner: *Dude, I was thinking the same thing. He's being ruder than usual.*

Arlo: *Still in the group thread.*

Gunner: *Mother of God!*

Romeo: *Beer, you tempting mistress.*

"IT SMELLS AMAZING IN HERE," Stella says, walking into my house with Greer trailing behind her. "My stomach is starting to crave your house."

I shut the door behind them, everyone else is already here.

I've had quite the fucking weekend so far, thanks to Gunner and Romeo's texting. After their Friday night drunk texts, they texted me again yesterday and continued to tell me how amazing Greer is. After a while, I stopped responding, because I didn't know what to say.

Yeah, she's great.

She makes me feel things I'm not sure I'm ready for—hell, I know I'm not ready for.

She makes me smile when she walks into a room, and that's concerning.

Because I don't know how to react to that response. I don't know how to react around her.

Hence why my shoulders currently feel stiff and the air in my lungs feels clogged as I catch a whiff of her perfume.

Pull it together, Turner.

"Congrats on your win Friday," I say, running my eyes over Greer quickly.

Short denim shorts, frilly white tank top, brown high-heeled sandals, and her hair tied up into two buns on the top of her head.

Fuck, I want her.

Again.

"Thank you," Greer says and turns toward me. "Arlo, I need to talk to you about Blair again, can we have a moment?"

"Sure," I say, confused. Nothing should be going on with Blair. Her last paper was *B-* material and needed a little work, but nothing we need to talk about.

"Stella, let everyone know we'll be right out."

"Sure, but, you know, teachers get breaks, too." She takes off down the hall, and Greer leads me to my office.

She shuts the door behind her and points to my desk. "Sit. Now."

"Do you really think you're about to take charge?" I ask.

"We're not doing anything sexual, but I need you to sit and listen to me."

Sighing, I walk over to my desk and sit on the edge while crossing my arms over my chest. "Make it quick. I don't like keeping guests waiting." And I can't possibly be in here with her alone for too long. I don't trust myself.

"Heavens to Betsy, we couldn't have that," Greer says, clutching her chest. She's in rare form today.

"Taking the sarcastic approach today?"

"I suggest you watch what you say, Arlo. I've had time to think, and I'm itching to get it off my chest, and instead of walking away or pushing it to the side, I'm going to talk to you."

Fuck . . .

"Okay, talk," I say, trying to remain as casual as possible.

"Okay," she says, shaking out her arms and pacing my office.

Fuck, she's adorable. Angry and geared up to give me a piece of her mind.

"I'd like to start this out with a general statement." She turns to face me, hands on her hips. "You're really good at oral."

I chuckle. "Thank you."

"I mean . . . really good."

"So far, I like how this conversation is proceeding."

"And your ability to turn me on with just a push of your sleeves up your forearms is ridiculous."

"Glad I can oblige." I smirk.

"But . . ." She pauses and takes a deep breath. "I'm not the type of girl who just . . . messes around. Nor do half the things you've made me do these last couple of weeks."

"I haven't made you do anything. You went into it willingly."

"You know what I mean," she says, sounding exasperated. "You're all kinds of tempting, and it scares me a little. I have a job to worry about here. You know first-year teachers are on probation and they have to prove themselves at Forest Heights. Any misstep could ruin this opportunity for me. And this is one hell of an opportunity."

"Okay, so you've stated the obvious. Is there a point to this conversation?"

"You don't have to be rude."

"Not being rude. You don't have to be sensitive."

"You're so annoying," she says, turning away from me. "I can't believe I'm actually about to ask you this."

"Ask me what?" I say, pushing off the desk and walking up behind her. She's facing my window, which looks out over my front yard, and I take that moment to move my hand around her waist and press against her stomach, bringing her back against my chest. I bring my lips to her neck and kiss up the column until I reach her ear. "Nervous?"

"A little," she answers honestly, twisting in my arms so we're facing each other. "I don't want you to think I'm getting all clingy, but . . ." She bites her bottom lip and blurts, "I'm looking for a relationship, not a fuck fest. I want to know what your intentions are with me."

"Oh." I take a step back and pull on the back of my neck while I stare down at her.

"From that one move away from me, I'm going to guess your intentions don't involve such titles as boyfriend and girlfriend."

"Yeah, not . . . really," I answer. *Hell, where is this coming from?*

She nods. "That's what I thought you were going to say."

"I don't do intimate—"

"I know." She takes a deep breath. "I'm glad I know where we stand."

"Okay." Feeling uncomfortable, I ask, "Are you okay?"

"Yeah. I am." She smiles. "So, I guess I'll be going."

"Okay."

She turns to leave but pauses and faces me again. "You realize this means I won't keep doing this, right?"

"Doing what?" I ask.

She motions between the two of us. "This. I can't have you touching me anymore, not if it doesn't mean anything. I came here to start a new life, Arlo. That involves a serious relationship that leads to marriage and a family. I know that seems like a lot, but it's my hope. My dream. If I keep fucking around with you, with no promise of going anywhere, I won't reach my dream. I would just be putting it on hold."

My jaw clenches, my heart rate picks up, anger starting to form at the back of my neck, spiking me into a tense ball. I have no right to be mad about her choice. She's looking for something I don't want to give. I can't blame her. And yet, I don't fucking like it.

"Do you understand?" she asks.

"Yes, I understand."

"No more touching, Arlo. Strictly colleagues, that's it."

"If that's what you want."

"I want other things, but you're not in a position to give them to me, so this is how things have to play out."

I stick my hands in my jeans pockets and rock on my heels. "I get it."

She smiles sadly. "Thank you for understanding." She thumbs toward the door. "Guess I'll get going."

"Be right behind you," I say as she walks out of the office.

I don't follow right away. Instead, I back up to my desk, where I contemplate what just happened. Greer isn't a girl who can keep feelings out of the mix. I was lucky I got as much out of her as I did.

The only problem is, I never got to feel her mouth on my cock, on my body . . . on my lips. I never gave myself the opportunity to strip her bare, hover over her, and then plunge myself so far deep inside of her, she'd be imprinted for life. *That's ridiculous talk, Turner. Imprint. I'm not a fucking werewolf.*

Well, no harm, no foul. I don't really have time to torture—*pleasure*—Greer, so now's a good time to put an end to that immature game anyway.

And that weird feeling inside me *isn't* an ache for her. *For her cries of ecstasy. For her cries of my name as she submits to my seduction.*

No. For the first time since I met Greer Gibson, I agree with her one hundred percent. Now my life can go back to its normal rhythm and structure and order.

As it should, *right?*

Chapter Seventeen

GREER

"No, no, no," Jason says, shaking his head. "You have it all wrong. Mr. Darcy wasn't prejudiced against Lizzie. He could not care less about her rank in society."

"Are you insane?" I ask. "Did you even read the book?"

"Uh . . . *did you?*" Jason Orson, the starting catcher for the Chicago Rebels, asks.

"More times than I care to admit."

"Then you should know that he was never prejudiced. He was scared."

"Oh Jesus." I rub my temples. "Where in the book does it ever say he's scared?"

"The great thing about Jane Austen is she doesn't have to write it; she portrays it in the mood."

"You're giving me a headache."

"Quit now," Dottie, his wife, says while leaning in. "He can go all night."

"Trust her, my stamina for Mr. Darcy is fierce."

"Oh, I could go all night and into tomorrow," I counter, taking a sip of my wild berry seltzer. No drinking for me tonight. No way in hell am I staying here for the night, especially with school tomorrow. I don't need to be rolling into the parking lot with Arlo Turner driving, one eye barely open while I second-guess all my decisions from the day before.

"She's annoyingly persistent," Stella says.

"I don't think you know Jason," Gunner cuts in, taking a seat at the outdoor table. "He created the term *annoyingly persistent*."

Jason smiles gleefully at me, the large brute of a man entirely too adorable for his own good.

"You're proud of that?" I ask him.

"Very. I take my annoying habits to heart. I wouldn't be the man I am today without them." Jason tilts his drink toward me and then sips from the can. And I have to admit it, I might have started this party feeling pretty upset from the conversation with Arlo, but spending time with Jason has cheered me up, even if he acts like an emotional idiot.

"How about this? We both agree we have passion for P and P and leave it at that?" I say.

He mulls it over, giving the pact some serious thought, making a show of it. At this point, I wouldn't expect anything less from him. "I guess I can agree on that, under one condition."

"What's that?" I ask.

"You tell me—right here, right now—who is your Mr. Darcy?"

I roll my eyes. "As if that's even a question. Colin Firth."

"God, I knew I liked you. If only Kiera Knightley was Elizabeth when Colin was Mr. Darcy. Talk about dream cast."

"My heart would have been moved." I laugh.

"Mine too." Jason studies me and then leans forward. "Are you seeing anyone?"

Uhh . . .

Dottie chimes in, tapping his ring finger. "I understand your passion has overcome you, but remember, you're married."

Jason huffs and turns toward his wife. "Not for me. Jesus. You think I worked as hard as I did to win you over just to throw it away like that?" Jason looks at me. "No offense."

"None taken."

"I was thinking she'd be perfect for Walker."

"Walker Rockwell?" Gunner asks just as Arlo and Romeo join the group. Lindsay and Dylan are late, so we're waiting to break out the badminton until they get here.

"Yeah," Jason says.

"Walker, as in . . . the catcher for the Chicago Bobbies? Your rival team?" Romeo asks this time.

"Uh, yeah. Is there any other Walker I might know?"

Gunner and Romeo both give me a glance and then turn back to Jason. "She's too feisty for him."

"Feisty is what he needs," Jason says. "The guy is in need of some happiness in his life. Greer would be perfect." Facing me, Jason asks, "How do you feel about blind dates?"

And just like that, I can feel Arlo's heated gaze.

This just got exponentially more awkward.

"She loves them," Stella answers for me, completely oblivious to the war playing out in my head. Only an hour ago I was being turned down by Arlo Turner. And now I'm being set up? With a professional baseball player, nonetheless.

Normally I'd be ecstatic, but I'm still feeling . . . blah about everything with Arlo.

I thought maybe I'd made more of an impact on him, that he'd consider the idea of a relationship, but he didn't even flinch. He could not have distanced himself quicker.

Which means he isn't right for me.

He's not the man I should be spending my time or thoughts on.

"Do you love them?" Arlo asks standing from the right of the table, holding an IPA close to his chest.

My eyes connect with his, and I swear I spot a flash of vulnerability, but it's gone before I have time to dissect it.

Clearing my throat, I say, "I'm not opposed to them, as long as the match is good."

Arlo's jaw clenches, and I realize he's not happy about this.

Well, guess what, buddy? You had your chance. *I'm worth more than a short-term, directionless fling.*

With a renewed sense of courage, I say to Jason, "Tell me more about Walker."

"WHAT KIND of game are you trying to play with me?" Arlo says when I set a few plates in the sink and rinse them off.

The rest of the group is outside playing badminton. Dylan and Lindsay are finally here, and they're having a blast.

Watching Gunner with his son has surprised me. He's fun and has a good head on his shoulders, but he morphs into a different person around Dylan, and it's incredibly sweet to watch. And the look Dylan gives Gunner when he encourages him—God, my heart can't take it.

"I'm not trying to play any games with you, Arlo. That's exactly what I'm trying to avoid."

"You spent half an hour talking about Walker. You're telling me that was unintentional?"

"What does it matter?" I ask, turning toward him and gripping the edge of the counter. "You don't want a relationship. I do. Walker apparently does, or at least something like it. Why shouldn't I ask questions about a potential date?"

"It matters because I've had my mouth all over your pussy."

I laugh. "Okay, so that means you've claimed me? Get a

life, Arlo." I push past him, but he grips my arm, halting me in place.

"I don't have claim over anything you do. But be goddamn respectful in my house."

I flash my eyes up to his. "Respectful? It's not like I was humping the table, telling Jason to bring the meat to me now. I asked a few questions. And if we're going to talk about being respectful, try not getting me off with a vibrator while our boss is only a few feet away."

I pull my arm away, and I'm about to walk away, but then say, "And you have no right to even an ounce of anger over this situation."

"I know," he says curtly.

"Then back off."

He takes a step away and I head to the backyard, where I find Romeo hoisting Stella up on his shoulders and parading her around the yard. She has a huge smile on her face, and I honestly wonder when those two are going to hook up, or if they've hooked up already.

"They're cute," Dottie says, coming up next to me.

"I was just thinking the same thing."

"Are they together?"

I shake my head. "Not that I know of."

"They should be," she groans. "Ugh, before Jason, I was never this girl, the one who would look at two people and think how romantic it'd be if they were together. Jason has ruined my jaded heart."

I chuckle. "I could see how something like that would happen. He's quite the catch."

"He's quite the handful," Dottie counters. "And seriously, if you don't want to go out with Walker, let me know. I'll let Jason down easily. He can be pretty aggressive when he puts his matchmaker hat on."

"Aggressive and persuasive."

"Very much so, and honestly, I got the feeling that maybe something was going on between you and Arlo."

"What?" I ask, trying to act as cool as possible. "Why would you think that?"

"Just the looks you two gave each other while we ate. Seemed like there was something there."

I chew on the side of my cheek, my mind a fuzzy mess of uncertainty at this point. "There's nothing there," I answer. *He's made that quite clear.*

"Huh. Could have fooled me." She lifts her drink to her lips as Dylan and Gunner perform a game-winning dance on the badminton court, while Romeo sulks next to Stella, who is patting him on the back. "Walker is a sweetheart, though. Rough around the edges, but I think you'd like him. Plus, you guys have the whole athlete thing in common, something I could never relate to with Jason."

"Were you guys close in college?" I ask. I found out they went to the same college earlier.

Jason, Gunner, and Romeo were all in the same graduating class. Jason went the long haul, while Gunner and Romeo for various reasons hung up their cleats and became teachers. But they're still very close.

That much is obvious from the playful banter they have with each other.

"Me and Jason?" Dottie laughs and shakes her head. "No. I admired him from afar but never did anything about it. It wasn't until years later that we reconnected, and not by my doing, but thanks to my meddling friends."

"Oh, I love meddling friends, as long as they're not meddling with my life."

"Agreed. Acting as a meddling friend, now that's a good time. Which reminds me . . . about Walker."

"You're starting to sound worse than Jason."

"I only ask because Jason is going to pester me the entire way home about whether I think you'll give Walker a chance.

Save me the grief of the 'I don't knows' and give me an answer."

"And, as we learned, he's annoyingly persistent."

"Exactly."

Laughing, I see Arlo move around from the corner of my eye.

Why not go out on a date with a professional baseball player? For all I know, we might actually have a great connection.

"Dottie, if you think Walker is interested in a long-term relationship, then, yes, I'll go on a blind date with him. I'm not a fling girl. I hadn't realized how vital that was to me until recently. So, if you see potential, then, yes, I'll go on a date with him."

Dottie clutches her chest. "Oh, God, Jason is going to cry. You have no idea how much this will mean to him."

"I think as long as Walker doesn't cry, we'll be okay."

"IMPRESSIVE RÉSUMÉ." Keeks flips through her phone. "Offensively, he's been a key component for the Bobbies over the last few years. Although, it seems that the past two years he's struggled to achieve the same batting average."

"Who cares about the batting average? Look at his pictures," Stella says, also on her phone. "Hubba-hubba. Love the whole dark and mysterious look."

"Can you two please stop?" I say, picking away at the couscous meal I made for myself last night while meal prepping. The recipe sounded good, but the finished product needs a little help.

"Ah, I recognize your conjecture. His facial structure quite accurately resembles those of a Greek demigod. I would hypothesize a precise merger of Apollo and Zeus."

"Well, mazel tov to Apollo and Zeus for birthing Walker,

their human child." Stella sighs. "I haven't been able to catch the last few games."

"Although a boring sport to examine, I wouldn't mind scrutinizing an inning or two just to observe how authentic these pictures are, as well as see the man squat."

"You want to see him squat?" Stella asks.

"For scientific purposes, of course." Keeks adjusts her glasses, but the stain on her cheeks gives her away.

"How are things with Kelvin?" I ask, wanting to send her a gentle reminder that she is, in fact, involved with a man.

"Kelvin Thimble caressed my breast last night," Keeks says, eyes still scrolling through her phone, acting as if the information she just delivered isn't mind-blowing to me and Stella.

"What?" Stella asks, setting her phone down.

"Uh, we're going to need a lot more information than that. Like, where were you, what were you doing, were you naked, or was it above clothes?"

Keeks looks up from her phone and glances between the two of us. "Is this one of those gentlelady showdowns where we speak of one's sexual prowess and conquests?"

"Yes," Stella and I say at the same time.

"Ah, I see." She sets her phone down, folds her hands together and says, "Kelvin and I participated in a sexual rendezvous last night, masqueraded as dining in his motor vehicle for an experiment. Given that we both lacked sexual partners in our teenage years, we were never granted the chance to act with promiscuity in Lovers Lane. Feasting on burgers from the burger king himself, Kelvin asked point-blank if he could hold my breast. Given the variables of the night, I conjectured there was no night like tonight for Kelvin Thimble to, in street terms, cop a feel. With ketchup-coated hands, he reached out and pressed his palm to my breast."

Oh, dear God.

"How was it?" Stella asks.

Keeks adjusts her glasses again, clears her throat, and says, "An inner carnal beast erupted from the bowels of my soul, and before I could figure out where it originated from, my tongue was haphazardly licking Kelvin's mouth while his ketchup-covered hand clutched at my hair."

Too much detail . . . way too much detail.

"I tapped into my reptile brain. Arousal spiked, milkshake was scattered over Kelvin's lap, and I used it as lubricant for—"

"I think I'm good with the rest," I say, cutting her off. "Really, I can imagine where this went."

"I can't," Stella says. "What did the milkshake lubricate?"

If she says *vagina*, I'm going to die.

"The coarse wool of my skirt over the corduroy of his dress slacks."

My nostrils flare, and I beg the high heavens to please help me not make a grossed-out face.

"Well, that's . . . an interesting mesh of fabrics," Stella says.

"The milkshake assisted with the velocity of friction."

Just then, the door to the teachers' lounge opens and Kelvin walks in, Arlo close behind him. I haven't spoken to Arlo since Sunday, even when passing each other in the hallway. Apparently, now that he's no longer pawing after me, there's no need for interaction.

"H-hi, Keiko," Kelvin says nervously with a giant smile. He gives her a short wave.

"Kelvin, pleased to see you. Were you able to remove the milkshake from your corduroys successfully?"

"Indeed. They are quite clean."

"Wonderful. I was just conversing—"

"About Greer's date with Walker Rockwell," Stella cuts in, shooting Keeks a warning look, and for the first time since I've known the girl, she understands the social cue. No need to embarrass poor Kelvin Thimble. No, we can just throw me under the bus in front of Arlo instead.

In their defense, they've no idea anything has been happening between me and Arlo.

"Who's Walker Rockwell?" Kelvin asks as he shifts closer to Keiko.

Arlo walks to the fridge and answers for everyone, "The starting catcher for the Chicago Bobbies."

"Oh." Kelvin looks over his shoulder. "I d-don't follow sports much. Bobbies is baseball, right?"

"Yes," Stella says. "And he's dreamy, Kelvin. They're going out Saturday night after his day game. Want to see a picture?"

"Oh, sure," Kelvin says, leaning over.

Stella flashes him the screen just as I hear Arlo crack a soda open behind us. I keep my eyes on Kelvin, not wanting to give Arlo any reason to think that I care he's in the room.

"I've seen his face around Chicago. H-he was on a billboard near a comic book store I frequent."

"Dark Night Comics?" Keeks asks.

"Indeed. Do you frequent there?"

"On the occasion."

"Maybe we can go this Friday."

"I'd enjoy that. Maybe we can share another milkshake."

"Just don't spill it," Stella mutters, and I kick her shin under the table.

"T-too bad your date is Saturday night. We could have gone on a double date," Kelvin says.

"Well, you can always change your date to Saturday," Stella suggests, and I kick her under the table again. This time, she glares at me.

"You know, I think Walker would probably just like a one-on-one at first. Double date later."

"If there is a later," Arlo mumbles, walking by.

"What's that supposed to mean?" I ask, folding my arms over my chest.

"It means, he might not like you. Focus on the first date, then the second."

"Hey, of course he's going to like her," Stella says in my defense. "Greer is a catch. Just because you find her repulsive, doesn't mean other men will."

"Thanks," I sigh.

"We'll see," Arlo says, pushing through the door and leaving.

"God, what crawled up his ass and died?" Stella asks, leaning back in her chair.

"According to the circumference of the anus, there are quite a few creatures that could have—"

"Metaphorical, Keeks. Christ," Stella says, pressing her hand against her forehead.

"Ahh . . . but if it wasn't metaphorical—"

I stand. "You know, I should get back to my classroom before the bell rings. It was a lovely lunch. Thank you." I turn to Kelvin and say, "Good seeing you, Kelvin."

"Y-you, too." He awkwardly smiles and then helps Keeks stand. It's a sweet gesture, one I'm sure Arlo has never made in his life. He's better at laying people down where he wants them rather than lifting them up.

Another reason why I'm going on this date. A change of pace. A way to get my head in the right space.

A moment to be treated like a lady. And maybe a moment where I get a sense of a happy, relationship-filled future. *Maybe.*

Chapter Eighteen

GREER

Greer: *I feel like I'm going to throw up.*
    Stella: *Don't. You brushed your teeth.*
    Greer: *That's not helpful.*
    Stella: *That's solid advice. No one likes puke mouth.*
    Greer: *Stella, please . . .*
    Stella: *You know, when I befriended you, I didn't think you were going to be a high-maintenance friend, but boy, was I wrong. *Sighs* You know that dress is killer on you. The red is fantastic and your boobs look spectacular. I'm quite jealous of your rack. And of course, your hair and makeup are on point. He's going to think he just hit a home run.*
    Greer: *Baseball lingo, really?*
    Stella: *Did it work?*
    Greer: *A little.*
    Stella: *Good, now knock him dead.*

With a deep breath, I stick my phone in my pocket and head toward the restaurant, walking around the corner and running straight into Arlo Turner.

Startling back, I clutch my purse to my side and say, "What the hell are you doing here?"

He holds up a bag of food. "Picking up dinner. You?"

My eyes narrow. "You know exactly what I'm doing." I glance around. "Were you just waiting around for me to show up? That's creepy, Arlo."

"I have better things to do than stalk you, Miss Gibson."

"So, you're saying this is purely coincidental?"

His eyes eat me up as he scans over my dress and pause briefly at my exposed cleavage.

"No, I'm here with Gunner and Romeo."

All of a sudden, they both come out of the restaurant and say, "She's not here—" Their voices fade when they spot me. "Oh, there she is," Romeo says. "We were just—"

"Spying on me?" I say, hand on my hips.

"No . . ." Gunner says. When I stare him down, he answers, "Fine, Jason sent us to see how the initial greeting went. We dragged Arlo with us, hoping we could use him as a spy, because Walker would know what we're doing. But he refused to go inside the restaurant."

The bored, *I told you so* look on Arlo's face makes me want to punt him in the leg.

"Well, I don't want you here. You're going to make it more awkward, so leave."

"I agree. This isn't particularly how I want to spend my night," Arlo says. "And since I drove and I have the food, you two better be moving your asses."

"What are we going to say to Jason?" Romeo complains.

"Tell him it looked like sparks flew from the very beginning," I say, laying it on thick. "That when I walked up to him, as a greeting, not only did I smooth my hand up the lapel of his jacket, but I also pressed a soft kiss to the scruff on his face while his hand very delicately slid around my waist, just above the swell of my ass."

Gunner scratches the side of his face and turns to Romeo. "I think Jason would totally buy that."

"Easily. Romantic and detailed." Romeo claps me on the shoulder. "Thanks, Gibson."

"You're welcome." I smile and start to walk toward the door of the restaurant. "And if you two need a picture, I'll have the waitress take a candid shot of us without Walker knowing."

"God, that would be a dream. Thank you."

"Anything for you, boys." I twiddle my fingers at them as a goodbye. "Enjoy your food." Just as Arlo turns the corner, he shoots me a quick look, a look so devastating, so vulnerable, that I have a sudden need to chase after him.

But I don't.

Why? Because he's been an asshole all week, back to his normal self, and, if I'm honest, I think I dodged a potential bullet. Do I fantasize about him sexually? *God, how could I not?* As I told him, he does oral *very* well. But a long-term relationship can't be all about sexual satisfaction. Apart from those sexually charged moments with Arlo, he gave me nothing. In fact, I still know nothing about him. He's a closed book—yes, a great pun for an English teacher—and that's not me. I want to be with someone warm and funny, an equal. Surely that's not too much to ask for.

This date isn't about him.

This is about me.

If he wanted a chance, he had it. And if he couldn't work out that I like openness and honesty—*sharing*—then again, I'm glad we're through.

Exhaling, I walk into the restaurant and tell the hostess I'm here to meet Walker. She takes me back to a private area immediately, where I find him hunched over at the table, on his phone, wearing a slate-gray button-up and black pants. When he spots us, he quickly tucks his phone away and stands.

And good God is he massive.

Tall.

Muscular.

Larger than life.

"Your waitress will be with you soon," the hostess says.

"Thank you," Walker responds. Holding out his hand, he says, "It's nice to meet you, Greer."

Jason would be so disappointed with this greeting. I shake his hand and say, "Great to meet you, Walker."

Like a gentleman, he pulls out my chair, helps me into my seat, and then sits across from me.

Immediately, I feel awkward. Not because of Walker, but because blind dates are incredibly uncomfortable.

"I saw that you guys won your game. Congrats."

"Thanks." He shifts in his chair, attempting to get comfortable.

Okay, not much of a talker. "So, how do you know Jason? Besides the whole baseball thing?"

"We work on same non-profit things together." Walker picks up his menu and examines the choices. He looks . . . distressed, almost as distressed as I felt when Arlo gave me that last look. He sets the menu down and says, "Hell, Greer. I'm sorry. I . . . my head is with someone else. I don't want to lead you on, but Jason begged me to go on this date."

I reach out and press my hand to his arm. His eyes lift up to mine, and I say, "Don't apologize, I'd be lying if I didn't admit to the same thing."

He perks up. "Really?"

I bite my bottom lip and nod. Although, his comment really does nothing for my self-esteem. *Jason begged me to go on this date.* Yep. But, I'm also glad he's upfront and honest. "Unfortunately, even though he's everything wrong for me."

Walker seems to think on that and says, "Should we talk about it?"

I chuckle. "I mean, you're the only neutral party I know that I could talk to about it. What about you?"

"Same."

"Did our date just become a therapy session?"

"I think it did."

"Does this mean we can order all the food, and dig deep into our feelings?"

"Food, yes. Deep feelings . . . maybe."

"Fair enough." I hold up the menu. "Let's make a dent in this menu, Rockwell."

⸻

"HUH," I say, tapping my chin and lifting my glass of wine to my lips. "That's quite the pickle."

"It is." He takes a sip of his water while we wait for our food. We just shared an appetizer of ceviche, cleared that out pretty quick, but it did a good job curbing the hunger that was starting to set in.

"And there's no possible way she can date you unless she's not working for the Bobbies?"

"There's a zero-tolerance policy for staff."

"Huh, and I thought my situation was bad. You have it way worse."

"Let's talk about you, then."

"It's the classic story," I say waving my hand. "Girl meets boy, boy . . . fiddles around with her, girl wants more, boy is emotionally unavailable."

He nods in understanding. "I can see that," he says quietly. He's very reserved, doesn't speak much, I've noticed, but what he does say usually packs a lot of punch. "I've been emotionally unavailable, and it has nothing to do with the girl and everything to do with me unable to break through that barrier. Doesn't mean he doesn't want you. Just means he doesn't know how to want you."

I think back to Arlo's expression tonight, the dejection in his eyes. "The want is there," I say. "And this might be too much information, but he's been very adamant about making me feel good. I have yet to do anything sexual to him. Even a kiss. Nothing."

Walker scratches the side of his face. "Sounds like something I'd do, but he has a stronger will than me."

"Why?"

"Not wanting to give in to temptation and getting lost in it," Walker says automatically, his eyes drifting to something over my shoulder. "One taste, one feel, and it could ruin a man like me, like him. Someone who's holding back. He's reserved, and there's a deep-rooted reason. But there's a reason why he won't go there with you, and it's because he sees you as a threat."

"A threat?" I ask, my brow creasing. "How so?"

"Because, he's probably spent a great amount of time putting up the wall that's guarding his emotions, and with one look, you cracked it."

"I don't think—"

"Let me ask you this," Walker says, turning toward me completely and leaning in. "Does he touch you a lot when he gets the chance?"

"I mean . . . yeah. He always has a hand on me."

"Does he leave abruptly after pleasuring you?"

"Yes, and it's really annoying."

"Do you find yourself being tracked down by him? Like a wolf to the prey? Eyes always on you?"

"Yes . . ."

Walker nods. "He wants to claim you but won't let himself."

"Well, that's bullshit, then," I say, crossing my arms. "Why do I want to be involved in his emotional instability?"

"You don't." Walker tilts his drink back and sets the glass

on the table. "You did the right thing, walking away, going on this date with me."

"It's not really a date." I smile at him.

"He doesn't know that. All he knows is that you're out with another man. A man who could possibly encroach on his territory. If I were him, I'd be pacing my goddamn house right now, vibrating with anger."

"He doesn't have a right to be angry."

"Nope, he doesn't. But that doesn't mean he won't be." Walker shrugs. "Don't try to think on it too much, because it won't make sense to you. Unless you live inside our heads, it'll never make sense."

He's not wrong. Guys are weird creatures. Walker is really sweet, and despite his tough-guy façade, I like that he's showing me inside his mind. *Although, as he noted, I pose no threat.*

"So what do I do, then?"

"Nothing."

"Nothing?" I ask as our food is delivered to our table. Walker went with the filet and a side of vegetables, while I chose the salmon on mango rice.

He picks up his fork and knife. "Yup. Nothing. From experience, I can tell you, pushing him for more will only push him away."

"So what am I supposed to do? Just sit back and wait until he pulls his head out of his ass? What if he never does? I'd be wasting my time."

Walker pauses mid-cut of his meat and looks up at me. "Is that how you feel? Like he's wasting your time?"

"Is he not? Dragging me along with no thought of even exploring a relationship? That's stringing someone along, Walker. Is that what you're doing with your girl?"

He sets his silverware down on his plate and moves his hand over his jaw. "No, I don't think so. If she was teasing me like this guy is teasing you, *knowing* it could go nowhere, I'd be pissed off. And I certainly wouldn't do that to her. We haven't done anything intimate. Just work side by side."

"But you can't stop thinking about her?"

"Yeah."

"And you think there's attraction on her side?"

"I believe there is."

"So, you both are at an impasse right now."

"Seems that way."

Chuckling, I drive my fork through the salmon, scooping up some of the meat. "Aren't we a pair?"

He shakes his head in laughter. "We are."

———

"CHOCOLATE MAKES ALL the worries temporarily go away," I say, scooping up some of the fudge from the lava cake and bringing it directly to my mouth.

Even though he's on a strict diet, Walker indulged tonight as well, splitting the lava cake with me. "So, what are you going to do?"

We spent the entire night talking through our options, discussing our different situations, how we could possibly make them work or not work. How we'd feel if they didn't work out. Would we be upset walking away? Or would we get over it? I don't know about Walker, but I have my answer.

"Walking," I say, before pulling my fork past my lips again to collect any leftover chocolate.

"You're not going to wait?"

I shake my head. "No. I'm glad you helped me understand his possible motives, but honestly, I'm not here for *complicated*. I came to Chicago to start a new chapter, to be the best teacher I can be, and to help my volleyball team win a state championship. Even though I think I could like Arlo, his mood swings are unpredictable. And . . . I'm not sure he'd ever offer a deep, emotional connection. I don't think I'm ready to take on anything that's going to reduce my emotional wellness."

He nods.

"Does that answer scare you?"

He shakes his head. "I'm at a stalemate with my situation. She works for the Bobbies; I'm a player. The only way we can be together is if she gives up her job, and I'd never ask her to do that."

"Is she willing to do that?"

"It's not an option," Walker says matter-of-factly, and I don't argue.

"So, then . . . should we have given this a shot?"

He laughs and so do I. "I think we're too far gone on emotional humiliation to even consider it."

"I wouldn't say what we went through was emotional humiliation. More like bonding." I hold up my wine glass. "To new friends."

He smirks. "To new friends."

We clink our glasses and then finish our lava cake. Continuing the gentlemanly act, Walker pays for dinner even though I incessantly asked him to split it with me. He shut me up when he told me that he probably earns my entire paycheck for the year when he plays a single game. So . . . he paid.

We gather up our things and head out of the restaurant. Once outside, I turn to him and say, "Even though this isn't how Jason hoped for things to go, I'm really glad we went out. It's given me peace of mind. I haven't been able to talk to anyone about this."

"Me neither." He stuffs his hands in his pockets. "I appreciate you wanting to listen."

"I know this may be weird, but do you want to maybe exchange phone numbers, that way we can continue to help each other if need be?"

"Glad you asked." He pulls his phone out. "I could use the friend."

"Me too. My friends are teachers or Arlo's sister. Can't quite communicate about this with them."

"Not so much." He hands me his phone and I plug in my info. He then sends me a text and I save his contact information. "Jason is probably going to cry when he finds out we're just going to be friends."

"That's the second time someone mentioned Jason crying. Is he overly emotional?"

"You could say that." Walker shifts. "Would it be weird to send him a picture of us together? Maybe to ease his mind, and then I can break the news to him later?"

"As long as you don't tell him what we talked about."

"That shit's between us," Walker says in a serious tone. "You don't have to worry about me mentioning that to anyone."

"Thank you." I snuggle against him and say, "Let's take that picture."

Holding out his phone, he turns it to selfie mode and we take a quick picture that Walker sends to Jason. His response is immediate.

Emoji heart eyes.

"He's going to be crushed," I say.

"Yup." He gives me a quick hug, and then we're on our way.

Even though it wasn't a love connection, I still feel lighter, happier, than when I first arrived. In fact, the time with Walker has given me hope. There are good guys out there, who, like Walker, are essentially reserved. Arlo's reserve is a deliberate choice. A controlling choice. I take a deep breath, knowing I'm going to be okay.

Chapter Nineteen

ARLO

"Good morning," Gunner says, strolling into my classroom. "How was your weekend?"

Painful.

Miserable.

A goddamn agonizing two days.

"Fine," I answer, opening my laptop and firing it up for the day.

"Just fine?"

"Yeah, just fine. What do you want me to do? Perform a dance number associated with my weekend?"

"I mean, I wouldn't mind it." Gunner laughs. "I took Dylan and Lindsay to the Bobbies game this Sunday. Dylan was living his best life in the box seats and went home with a massively sick belly from how much he ate, but he had one hell of a time. Pretty sure he's going to be a Bobbie for life. Jason will try to convert him over to a Rebel, though. No doubt about it."

"Glad you had a good time," I say curtly.

"Dude, you okay? You look really tense."

"Yeah, fine."

"Morning," Romeo says, walking into my classroom as well. He sets a pastry box on my desk and says, "Stopped by Frankie Donuts this morning. Made the extra trip because they started this new donut-of-the-week promotion and I couldn't resist this week's." He flips the bakery lid open, revealing the best donuts in Chicago. The smell alone makes my mouth water. "Piña colada. Coconut and pineapple frosting, yeast donut, with a cherry and coconut flakes to top it off. How I waited to eat one until now is beyond me." He reaches in, grabs a donut, and takes a massive bite. After a few moans and groans, he says, "Fuck, this is good."

Gunner picks one up and says, "This isn't on the pyramid of health we're talking about today, but to hell with it, I'm an adult." He takes a large bite as well and moans, then they both stare down at me, waiting for me to indulge.

Hell, might as well, given my current state of high-level irritation.

I pick up a donut and take a bite.

Yup, that's good.

That's really fucking good.

"I'm contemplating between putting the rest in the teachers' lounge or keeping them for myself," Romeo says. "After I deliver one to Stella, of course. She'd murder me if I didn't give her first dibs."

"Don't forget Greer," Gunner says.

"Oh, shit, I almost forgot. Guess what Jason sent me last night?" Romeo takes his phone out of his pocket and scrolls through it for a few seconds before turning the screen toward us.

On the screen is a picture of Walker and Greer, snuggled in close, smiling at the camera.

What the fuck . . .

"Looks like they had a great time and hit it off well. Jason tried to pry for details, but didn't get anything from Walker, just the picture. I told him I'd ask during lunch today."

"He must be squealing with excitement," Gunner says.

"He told me he was full of emotions last night and couldn't quite work through them."

"He's such an idiot." Gunner chuckles and they go on about Jason, but I tune them out, because all I can think about it how comfortable Greer looked in the picture.

Are they going out on another date?

Did he kiss her goodnight?

Fuck . . .

If he kissed her, I'm going to fucking lose my goddamn mind.

I haven't even tasted those lips.

But that's entirely on me.

And even though I don't want to admit it, I'm fucking regretful.

I wish I knew what her mouth felt like on mine. I wish I knew what it felt like to hold her hand. To snuggle in and take a picture with her, but that emotional block is there. The one impeding me from going any further with her.

She put a crack in it, began to knock it down, and instead of embracing it, I fled.

I got scared.

Worried.

She was right to push me away. She's someone who deserves to be cherished, worshipped. A relationship girl.

I barely know how to be emotional with my sister, to care for her. How could I care for someone else?

How could I be the man she deserves when I've never had an example of what that looks like?

"Uh, where did you go?" Gunner asks me, poking me in the shoulder.

"Huh? Oh, sorry. Was thinking about Coraline," I lie.

"Everything okay with her?" Romeo asks.

"Yeah." I shake my head. "I should get some shit done before the teenage pukes get here."

"Same," Gunner replies.

"I'm going to deliver donuts unless you guys want one more."

I shake my head, but Gunner takes another.

Looking between us, he says, "I have a girl, and I'm a dad. I think it's about time I take this chiseled body to dad-bod mode."

Romeo groans. "Fine, but when you complain to me about your pants not fitting, I'm going to remind you of this comment."

Gunner has the donut halfway to his mouth when he replies, "Yeah, I'll run extra tonight."

On their way out, Romeo says, "Meet us in the teachers' lounge for lunch. I'm going to get the scoop on Greer's date. Maybe there's love in the air."

Nauseated, I set my donut down and slump in my chair as they both depart my classroom.

There's no way in hell I'm going to the teachers' lounge for lunch. You couldn't pay me enough to listen in on the date that had me agonizing, tossing and turning, and not getting one ounce of sleep.

Nope, not happening.

I'll stay here and grade papers.

Hell, I'll grade other teachers' papers. Anything to avoid hearing the sordid details of Greer's date.

I'M HERE because I'm retrieving my salad, that's it.

No other reason.

And I'm reading the bulletin board in the teachers' lounge because I want to catch up with the current events.

A 5K to benefit Special Olympics. I'll do that.

Oh, and look, Jamie Marino got engaged. She teaches . . . history, right?

And, shocking, the underwear still hasn't been claimed, but Dewitt is still taking leads.

"Oh, I should not have eaten those three donuts," Gunner says, holding his stomach as he walks into the teachers' lounge.

"I thought you had two," Romeo says, trailing behind him.

"I snuck another in and now I'm regretting it."

The door opens again, and this time, Stella, Keiko, and Greer walk in. "Romeo, those donuts were so good," Stella says. "Are there any left?"

Romeo goes to the pastry box and flips open the lid, revealing nothing. "How fucking rude." He lifts it up. "Who takes the last donut and doesn't throw out the box? That's just giving teachers false hope, and that's the last thing we need when dealing with hormonal nitwits all day." He tosses the empty box on the floor and stomps on it.

"You okay?" Gunner asks him, hand on his shoulder.

"I think all the sugar is getting to me." He lets out a deep breath and spots Greer. "Hey, how was the date?"

Now this is the moment where I should leave, because I don't want to indulge my curiosity about Greer's date, but you just saw the violent outburst from Romeo. He's on edge, and I'd be a terrible friend if I didn't stay through this and make sure he's okay.

Greer and Stella walk over to the fridge and retrieve their lunches. Keiko claims a spot at one of the tables, and Greer and Stella join her.

"Why are you prying into my personal life? Jason not give you what you want?" Greer asks, unpacking her lunch.

I turn away and examine the bulletin board some more,

trying to look casual, not interested, really just here for my friend.

"No, he didn't give me any information. Walker didn't talk. Jason was hoping I could pull something from you."

"And why would I tell you about the date?" she asks. I can practically feel her raised brow.

"Because if I don't deliver, Jason will continue to ask incessantly. Remember what I told you last night?" Romeo clasps his hands together. "Please, just something."

"According to the 'girl gab' we shared this morning, they exchanged contact information," Keiko announces to the room.

"Keeks, what the hell?" Greer asks.

"I'd prefer to eat my lunch in peace, not listen to Brock beg for morsels of a night over which he has no claim. Now he can take that information to his friend and be done with the badgering."

"You exchanged numbers?" Romeo asks as I turn around.

Greer eyes me quickly and then turns to the wrap she packed for herself. "We did."

"Does that mean a second date?" Romeo asks and, honestly, I've heard enough.

I grab my salad and take off, leaving everyone in discussion over Greer's date.

Romeo doesn't seem to need my support anymore.

And even if he did—I roll my eyes at myself—I'm not the friend he'd expect help from.

No. It was the right decision Greer made, and she should look for her future husband. Or whatever.

Fuck.

And I'm the one who has to act like everything is normal.

―――

KNOCK. *Knock.*

I look up from my computer and see Greer standing in my doorway, wearing a pair of leggings and a Forest Heights Volleyball T-shirt. Her hair tied up into a high ponytail.

Remember when I said this outfit does nothing for me?

I lied.

"Hey, we're all going to grab a beer and strategize about badminton. Gunner and Romeo request your presence."

"Busy," I say, turning back to my laptop, where I'm checking on my Amazon Subscribe and Saves.

"I don't think *busy* is an option with them. They were adamant about you coming."

"Then why did they send you to come get me?"

"They raced to the bar to grab good seats since the Bobbies are playing tonight. Stella is with them already."

Vitamins and toilet paper are all coming in on time, thankfully. I shut my laptop and stuff it in my messenger bag.

"I should get home to Cora—"

"She's meeting us there." Greer crosses her arms over her chest. "Any other excuses? Need to check your vitamins again?"

Hell . . .

"How about this? I don't fucking feel like it."

"At least that's honest."

I stand from my chair and sling my bag over my shoulder. I move toward the door, but she doesn't move.

"What?" I ask, exasperated.

"Everyone says you're cranky. You're unbearable to be around unless Romeo gives you a donut."

I've had five this week, which is unheard of.

"And that you're being a dick to your students."

"I'm not being a dick to my students."

"Blair said you handed out two pop quizzes yesterday, and everyone failed the second one."

"Then they should pay attention more when they're reading, shouldn't they?"

"Arlo."

Pushing my hand through my hair, I say, "What's the point of this conversation? To tell me I'm in a bad mood? I don't need you to tell me that, I'm living it. So, unless there's something constructive you want to inform me of, please move the fuck out of my way."

She moves to the side. "Excuse me for wanting to see if you're okay."

"Really? Is that why you're here? To see if I'm okay? Because you sure as shit didn't start the conversation like that."

"Why are you so hostile? I did nothing to you."

She's right, she did nothing. This is all on me, and yet, I can't seem to control my anger.

Do I want to taste her again? Abso-fucking-lutely. But I hadn't realized how much I liked passing her in the hallway and teasing her. With snark. It was banter she reciprocated, and because of her fucking smart mouth and sassy attitude, it challenged me. The fight. The tease. *Her.* Occasionally, I saw her smile, but that's gone now too. And I've missed that. *Her.*

Seeing her, in my classroom, beautifully flushed with anger, the feelings I've tried burying arise. *Want. Need.*

"If I keep fucking around with you, with no promise of going anywhere, I won't reach my dream. I would just be putting it on hold."

She did nothing but tell the truth. It's agonizing. I know what my body wants, but my head is fucking with me. Which makes me angry.

"Just leave me alone, Greer."

"Oh, so now you call me by my first name?" she asks, her voice sounding menacing. "But when your tongue is between my legs, I'm Miss Gibson?"

My lips purse, my eyes narrow, and I take a step closer, getting in her face. "Do you miss my face between your legs?"

She doesn't flinch, but stands tall. "I miss the feel of a man's hand holding mine." She steps in closer. "I miss the feel of someone calling me just to hear my voice." One more step. "I miss the feel of a man holding me while I drift off to sleep. Anyone can make me come, Arlo, but it's the one who makes me feel special that I miss."

"Walker not giving that to you?"

"That's none of your business." She steps away and says, "I'll let the guys know you're too much of an asshole to join tonight. I'm sure they'll understand. They've known you long enough." Then she walks out of my classroom, her ponytail swishing over her shoulders.

Shit.

―――

"HERE," Coraline says, handing me a beer and taking a seat on the large lounger I'm stretched out across.

"Thanks," I say, staring out at Lake Michigan, the sun setting over the horizon, lighting up the sky in beautiful shades of pink and orange. "How was the other night at the bar?"

"Fun. The guys bitched about you for a bit."

"What's new?" I ask, bringing the beer to my lips.

"Greer was in a crap mood. Kelvin and Keeks were there, too. They sat at another booth, though, and compared notes on a recent article they read about wind propulsion. Or something like that. I can't quite tell you what it was, but at one point, I looked over and they were holding hands across the table. It was adorable. Keeks then went to the bathroom with me and told me her arousal was spiking so she was going to go make out with Kelvin behind the bar. Things I didn't need to know."

A light chuckle comes out of me.

"Hey." She pokes my side. "You do know how to laugh."

"What are you trying to say?" I ask her.

"Just confirming what the guys think. That you're a grump."

I watch the small waves of the lake lap at the rocks that jut up against the body of water. "Can I ask you a question, Coraline?"

"Always."

"Do you think we're incapable of affection?"

She doesn't answer right away, but rests her head on my shoulder. "No. But I do think it comes to us less naturally. It's one of the reasons *He Who Shall Not Be Named* wanted a divorce. Called me cold and frigid."

"He was a dick."

"He was right. I was never into PDA despite his many attempts to get me to loosen up. It was hard for me to stop what I was doing and remember that maybe he needed a hug. As time went on, I forgot to kiss him at night, he didn't kiss me goodbye, and we drifted apart. He cheated on me, and now we're in the middle of a messy divorce. Yes, his cheating was the reason for leaving him, but I didn't help the situation. I didn't participate in my marriage like I should have."

"You never said that before," I say, surprised. "You just told me he cheated on you."

"Because I wasn't ready to face reality." She sips from her drink and says, "You know how you always ask where I am?"

"Yeah."

"Well, I've been going to marriage counseling."

"With—"

She shakes her head against my shoulder. "No. Not with him. I've been going on my own. I've been trying to figure out where I went wrong and, when the time comes, how I can be a better partner. It's how I came to terms with my lack of affection, and it's something I've been working on."

"Why didn't you tell me?"

"I was embarrassed. I think the lack of love in our household growing up really fucked with me, and from the sounds of it, it fucked with you, too."

"Yeah, you could say that," I say with a heavy breath.

"Is there someone you're not telling me about?"

Without going into detail, I say, "There was, but she wanted more, and I couldn't give her that. I didn't really know how to without feeling completely lost."

"Is that why you've been cranky lately?"

"Something like that," I answer.

At first, I was so angry at Greer, how she'd made me feel. But what she said the other afternoon was spot-on. She knows what she wants in a partner. She knows what she misses. And in that moment of anger, as she turned for the door and left, my first thought was *I want to try.* My second thought was *That's stupid, asshole. It's beyond you.* And the anger kicked back up a notch.

And here's my sister, *telling me* that she thinks counselling will help her be warmer. Is it right to lay all the blame for my prickly persona on the family environment I was raised in?

Is there any other answer? But I can't do this with Cora right now. I need to think. "I'm also irritated that Romeo keeps bringing in Frankie Donuts. I've had to kick up my cardio more than I care for."

She chuckles. "I think a few donuts aren't going to kill your figure." I pinch her side and she giggles, swatting me away. "Seriously, though, do you want to go to marriage counseling with me?"

"Marriage counseling with my sister—pretty sure that would be an ultimate low."

"We'd be really clear that we're not interested in marrying each other."

I laugh. "I don't think I'm at that point. I just need to take the plunge."

"Do you need me to push you?"

"Maybe," I say.

"Honestly, Arlo, what do you have to lose? If it doesn't work out, at least you tried. It's better than sitting around, being angry all the time."

"What if I'm not good enough?"

"You can't think of it that way. You have to give yourself the chance at least. You can't set yourself up for failure before you even give it a shot. That's not fair to you or to her." She elbows me and says, "Plus, who wouldn't want to be with my brother?"

"You'd be surprised."

"Well, your arrogance can be quite off-putting at times."

"Thanks." I chuckle.

"Just trying to keep you grounded." She twists her head and kisses my shoulder. "See? Affection. It's easy."

"I'm your brother."

"Doesn't matter. It's still progress. Now, stop making excuses and go after the girl. Then report back to me. I'm going to find out who she is soon because I'm nosey like that. The only reason I'm not asking right now is because you opened up. But next time, I'm going to need a name and a picture."

"Don't push your luck."

"Initials?"

I chuckle. "Maybe."

"I'll take that for now."

Chapter Twenty

GREER

Greer: *Pleeeease, Stella?*

   Stella: *No way in hell. I did my duty last year.*

   Greer: *I don't feel good. I really need you to fill in.*

   Stella: *Liar.*

   Greer: *I'm not lying.*

   Stella: *Then what's wrong with you?*

   Greer: *Headache, stomachache, legs ache.*

   Stella: *The stiff air of the gymnasium will make you feel better.*

   Greer: *Did I mention I have the poops? I can't possibly chaperone with a situation like that.*

   Stella: *I'll bring you some Imodium on the way to the bar. That should help.*

   Greer: *Ugh, why are you not a good friend right now?*

   Stella*: Me? You're the one not being a good friend, trying to guilt me into chaperoning the homecoming dance.*

   Greer: *You're more experienced. I think pregnancies are going to happen on my watch. That's not something I can have on my conscience.*

Stella: *But, there is the possibility they might name the baby after you in nine months. That's an honor.*

Greer: *Stella, I'm begging you. I'll buy you lunch every day until the end of the semester.*

Stella: *Your attempt to bribe me with food is commendable. Unfortunately, I'm watching the game with Romeo tonight. He got tickets and invited me and Cora since Gunner and Arlo are chaperoning with you. I'm about to get a footlong hotdog and shove it down my gullet. Don't worry, I'll think of you the entire time.*

Greer: *You hate me.*

Stella: *I love you. But this is something you have to do on your own. Good luck. Have fun!*

Ugh. I shove my phone into the pocket of my dress and step out of my car. I tried Keeks, too, but she texted back "reptile brain" and that was it. I didn't dive deeper, because, good God, I could see her thinking it's okay to show pictures since she's into evidence and all.

No luck.

I'm stuck chaperoning with Gunner and Arlo. I'm just hoping Gunner can be a good buffer.

I cross the threshold of the school and hear the music thumping through the halls. God, I already feel uncomfortable. From what I can remember from school dances, you're either on the dance floor, grinding against each other, or you're one of the nervous high schoolers sitting to the side, watching everyone grind on each other.

Unfortunately, I was a grinder growing up.

I decided to dress nicely though. A simple black dress with pockets that flares at my hips and black heels. My hair is pulled back into a high ponytail, and I added a touch of red lipstick, something I never wear at school, but I felt like I needed to make an effort.

"Greer, hold up." I turn to find Gunner jogging up to me. He's wearing a pair of dark jeans and a navy button-up shirt, tucked in, and a brown belt wrapped around his waist.

"You look nice," I say.

Proudly, he plucks at his top and says, "Lindsay got me this shirt."

"Aw, really?"

"Yeah, she brought it over right before I left. I think it was just an excuse to get in some lovin' before I had to leave."

"Well, that's sweet. It looks nice on you."

"I'll have to tell her other teachers were hitting on me."

"Uh, I wasn't hitting on you. I said you look nice," I say as we push through the gym doors to a decorated space of black and silver stars, multiple tables and chairs, and a dance floor with disco ball hanging overhead, which makes me chuckle. That had to be a teacher who put that up, not a student. There's dark purple uplighting along the walls, making the gym look less like a sweaty place where sports take place and more like a magical oasis for the student population.

"She doesn't have to know you were just being complimentary."

"Sure, do that. Make her feel insecure, see where that gets you."

Gunner taps his chin. "Hmm, you might be right about that."

"I know I am." Taking in the space some more, I say, "It looks good in here."

"The budget is pretty big, thanks to the PTA. They have a budget line set aside for dances. It also helps that the head of the PTA is a party planner for Chicago's elite. She gets killer deals."

"Then why do they have it in the gym? They could have it at an event hall."

"Dewitt likes to keep all dances on campus. They did a hotel banquet room once and we quickly noticed the students were filtering off the dance floor and straight up to the rooms."

278

"Oh yeah." I chuckle. "That probably isn't the best idea."

"Nope, and it's not as easy getting alcohol in here since Dewitt has a shake down at the doors and breath tests, as well as a check-in. If you buy tickets, you're required to show up unless we receive a verbal message from the parent that the student can't attend. And there's also a checkout, where parents are informed that the kids left the dance."

"Jesus, that's pretty secure."

"It's why Dewitt always wins Principal of the Year for the state of Illinois. She's about education and safety, and she thinks everything through."

"It's shocking any of the kids still want to come to the dance."

"I thought the same thing, but despite the restrictions, they still want to have a good time. They want that high school experience, so they show up."

"Makes sense. So, what do we do? Just watch them?"

"Yup, make sure no one sneaks off. Make sure all sexual organs are covered on the dance floor."

"Uh . . . what?"

"Trust me, just keep an eye out for unzipped pants. I caught three last year, it's why Dewitt asked me to chaperone again."

"And you willingly said yes?"

He shrugs. "I don't mind helping out. Not a big deal. Plus, Romeo had those tickets and I thought it'd be good for him to go with Stella alone . . . that is, until she invited Cora."

"So you think Romeo likes her?" I ask, excited.

"He obviously does, hasn't said anything to me though. Has Stella said anything to you?"

"No. I think she believes they're just friends."

"I'm sure that will change at some point. Romeo will figure it out."

"Hey." Gunner and I both turn to find Arlo standing

279

behind us. Oh God, he looks sexy. He's wearing a pair of navy-blue chino pants, white button-up, dark-grey cardigan and a navy-blue tie. His sleeves are rolled up and his hair is styled more sexy-messy than normal.

"Hey, man," Gunner says casually as my gut twists and turns. "Ready to find some penises?"

"Why do you have to say it like that?"

"No idea. Hey, there's Dewitt. I'm going to go discuss the game plan with her. I'll report back." Gunner takes off and leaves me standing awkwardly with Arlo, whose eyes are burning up and down me.

"You look beautiful," he says, shocking me.

"Oh . . . uh . . . thank you. You look good yourself."

He adjusts his tie and says, "I can foresee losing this at some point."

"Not a tie kind of guy?" I ask.

"Not so much."

"And I'd have thought you were. You know, since you like your cardigans. Just feels like ties go hand in hand with such mannerly apparel."

"Hate them."

I nod and then stare at the space again, that awkward feeling creeping up the back of my neck. I don't know what to say to him. The thought of talking about different patterns of ties comes to mind, but that would just be embarrassing.

So, Arlo, how do you feel about paisley? Kelvin seems to be a fan of it, as well as short-sleeved button-up shirts. Ever try those?

Lame. Really freaking lame.

Arlo clears his throat and says, "Uh, I think I owe you an apology."

"What?" I ask, flashing my eyes toward him. Did I just hear him right? Did he say he owes me an apology? Did I step into a weird black hole, or an alternate universe?

"For being a dick," he says. "You didn't deserve to be treated the way I've been treating you, and I'm sorry."

Uhhh . . .

"Oh, I . . . um, I didn't know you knew how to apologize," I say. Good God, Greer, not the thing to say. "I mean . . . Jesus, sorry. Thank you."

He chuckles. "That's a fair comment, you know. I can be moody at times."

"Can be? Uh, how about you are?"

"Are you going to pick on me now, after I apologized?"

"Can't take it, Turner?"

He shakes his head. "No, I can't."

"Unfortunate."

"Okay, talked to Dewitt," Gunner says, coming up to us. "We're going to take the west patrol near the food. Since you're new and Arlo doesn't do this often, you're going to take the north side, where the shy students sit. Look for under-the-table rubbing."

"Jesus," Arlo mutters.

"We have two other pairs taking on the east and the south, and one soul who'll be patrolling the dance floor, which I'll swap out on. Students know by now if I'm in there, they need to behave, but I can't be surrounded by sweaty students all night. Hence, the trade-off." Looking serious, he says, "Do you understand the responsibilities of being a chaperone?"

"Yes," Arlo answers, exasperated.

"Good, because the students are starting to file in. Get in your places."

Rolling his eyes, Arlo nods toward the north side of the gym, and we walk over together. "So . . . he takes this seriously?"

"He goes to one hundred whenever he's in charge of something. Dewitt of course thrives off his efficiency, it's why she's always asking him to chaperone. No doubt, we're here because of him. If he asked us, though, I'd have said no."

"Lucky for you Nyema asked."

"Yeah, I can never say no to her."

We position ourselves at the north end of the gym just as kids filter through the doors. Some go straight to the photobooth, others go to the food, and the braves ones head straight to the dance floor, where the music revs up.

"Did you ever go to your high school dances?" Arlo asks.

He seems so relaxed, especially for someone doing something he doesn't want to do. I'm thrown off. I wasn't expecting for him to apologize, and I wasn't expecting him to be nice, either. That's why I was begging Stella to come take my spot, because I really didn't want to deal with a cranky Arlo making snide comments all night.

But that's not what's happening.

And it's confusing me.

"Uh, high school dances," I say, trying to gain my bearings. "Only my senior year, and I went to prom, but that's it. Volleyball took up a lot of my time. I wasn't able to make a lot of the dances."

"So, I take it you were never a homecoming queen?"

I snort and shake my head. "No, I wasn't. Was never that girl. What about you?"

"Prom king."

"Seriously?" I ask turning toward him.

He keeps his attention on the gym floor in front of us, but answers, "Yes."

"Wow, I never would have guessed that."

"Why not?"

"No offense, but you don't seem like a people person, or someone who knows how to let loose and have fun."

"Do you not recall the time I played with your pussy under your classroom desk?"

I swallow hard. "Uh, strike that last comment."

"That's what I thought."

"Does that mean you were popular in high school?"

"Unfortunately, yes. But not for the right reasons. My grandparents had money, so people wanted to be my friend."

"The rich-kid problem."

"Yeah, if you want to call it that."

"Sounds a little sad."

"It is what it is," he answers just as the music picks up. "They gave us a home when they didn't need to, and they left us with an inheritance, with which I've been able to help the school."

That's right, Stella mentioned he donates money to the school.

"That's nice of you."

"What am I going to do with all of the money? I have a house. I don't need much more than that. I'm not much of a technology guy. I'd rather stretch out on a lounger that looks over Lake Michigan and enjoy a book."

"A classic book, right?" I bump his shoulder with mine.

"I do enjoy the classics, but you'd be surprised what's on my Kindle."

"You have a Kindle?"

"Don't you?" he asks, a raise to his brow when he looks at me.

"Yes, but I don't know one guy who has one. Whenever I see a guy reading, it's always a paperback. Thought it was a cool dude thing."

"When you read as much as me, a Kindle is worth it to prevent multiple trips to the bookstore."

"Okay, so what do you read? Wait . . . let me guess." I tap my chin. "Well, I know it's not romance, right? Besides that one series."

He shakes his head.

"Yeah, didn't think so. Ugh, American president autobiographies?"

"I've read a few, but that's not my main genre."

"Of course you've read a few. You have presidential autobiography written all over your cardigan." He chuckles again and, God, it's sexy. He's sexy. This relaxed mood, talking like a normal person, it's refreshing and scary at the same time. Scary because I can easily see myself falling into this man's world if he continues to charm me. I can take the angry, off-putting Arlo, but a charming one? Now that's a completely different story. "Okay, so I want to say you're a suspense guy, that's what my gut is telling me, but it also seems very unlike you. Then again, I think you might surprise me. So, is it suspense?"

"Yup."

"Really?"

He nods. "I'm really into military suspense right now. I love how the stories unfold and always aim to figure them out before the grand reveal."

"Are you correct?"

He laughs again. "Maybe like fifteen percent of the time. If I was ever looking for another profession, detective isn't it."

"I'm shocked. I'd have pegged you as someone who could figure out a storyline. You don't take notes or anything?"

He shakes his head. "No, when I'm reading, I just like to get lost in the pages. Get lost in the world. If I took notes, that would take me out of the story."

"Yeah, I can understand that."

"What about you?" he asks. "Have you started reading that Scot book?"

"Wait." I turn toward him. "You have all those books in your office. You said you read on a Kindle."

"I didn't get a Kindle until a few years ago. I started reading novels in middle school . . ."

"Oh, right." I laugh.

"So, the Scot book—have you read it?"

"Of course. It was fantastic. Made me want to stick my hand up a kilt and see what I find."

"Bet it's a pair of hairy balls." He rocks on his heels with a smirk.

Oh, dear God, he's messing with my emotions. Charming,

cute, smiles, laughter. The music in the background playing like our own personal soundtrack. He's confusing me. I'm confusing me. Tonight the man has showed more sincerity and thoughtfulness than I've seen in him to date. It's as though my forgiveness was extremely important to him. *And I know Arlo Turner isn't a liar.* Which makes this change . . . believable.

I think he might insert himself back into my life . . . and in an all-consuming way.

———

"PLEASE DON'T TELL PRINCIPAL DEWITT," Chuckie, a senior with bright red hair, says, pleading with Arlo.

"And why shouldn't I tell her?" Arlo asks, holding a tiny bottle of vodka in his hand. I still have no idea how Arlo spotted Chuckie on the dance floor with it, but he did.

"Because she's going to suspend me, and my dad . . . well, you know." Chuckie swallows hard. "Please, Mr. Turner."

Leaning in, Arlo says, "Tell me how you got this into the building."

"I found it."

"Lie to me again and I'll send your ass straight to Dewitt." I know that menacing voice. It's scary, and the kid folds right away.

"Basketball practice. We slipped a few under the bleachers before we left."

"Who's 'we'?"

"I can't rat out my bros."

"Then looks like I'll have to rat you out."

"Fuck," the kid says, pressing his hand to his forehead, obviously in distress.

"How about this?" Arlo asks. "I give you five minutes to collect the rest of the bottles and bring them to me. And if I see one bottle out there, or hear of one, I'm turning in your sorry punk ass so fast. Got it?"

"Yes, Mr. Turner."

In a low tone, Arlo says, "Go."

Chuckie scrambles off and inserts himself into the dance floor. Idiot. We can see exactly who he's talking to.

"Keeping track of his conversations?" I ask.

"Obviously. Chuckie, Brannen, and Louis. Could have guessed that."

"Why are you letting him get away with it?"

"His dad is an alcoholic. Unpredictable."

"What?" I ask, turning toward Arlo. "Why don't you report him?"

"No evidence, just conversations. Chuckie is incredibly smart, despite bringing alcohol to the dance. He needs to get the hell away from his dad—his home—and when he gets accepted to Stanford, I'm inclined to put him on the first bus out of here."

"But he's not going to learn anything—"

"Listen, you might not like what I do next, but sometimes, not everything can be by the book, Greer."

Chuckie approaches, hands in his pockets. Arlo stiffens, and I watch him transform into the disciplinarian.

"I have three more bottles," Chuckie says.

"How many did you start with?"

Chuckie swallows hard. "Six, Mr. Turner."

"Where are the other two?"

"Already consumed."

He nods and says, "Hand the bottles to Miss Gibson."

Chuckie hands me the bottles, and I stick them in my dress pocket. As Arlo grips the boy by the shoulder, he bends so he's at eye level.

"You listen to me very carefully, Chuckie. You haven't met your community service hours yet."

"Yes, I have." Chuckie nods vigorously. "I finished them this summer."

"And who has to sign off on those?"

"You . . ." Chuckie says, realizing where this is going.

"Guess who just earned himself twenty?"

"Twenty?" Chuckie's eyes nearly pop out of their sockets. "Why twenty?"

"Ten hours per bottle. Now, I'm only counting the ones that were consumed. I could be a real asshole and give you ten per bottle, making it sixty. Would you prefer that instead?"

"No, tw-twenty is good."

"That's what I thought. See me Monday morning. I'll get you started on those hours. Got it?"

"Yes, Mr. Turner."

He starts to turn away when Arlo halts him. "Look at me."

Chuckie looks him in the eyes.

"I want to remind you of something. Alcoholism runs in your family. Now, you're going to be on your own soon and the choices you make will be yours, but it'd be smart to consider where you come from. You're smart and going places, so make intelligent choices."

Chuckie's shoulders sag and he nods. "Thank you, Mr. Turner."

"Now get out of my face and report back Monday at seven in the morning. No later."

"Yes, sir."

When he starts to walk away, Arlo calls out, "And have some innocent fun. You have forever to be an adult. Enjoy these moments."

Chuckie smirks and then takes off, jumping into the center of the dance floor, where he joins his friends.

And me? Well, I just stand there, jaw on the ground, my heart reaching out to the teachable moment, the way Arlo handled Chuckie, how he spoke to him. It was beautiful, the trust they have in each other.

Clearing my throat, I say, "I was mistaken."

"Huh?" Arlo turns to me.

"Earlier this year, when we were fighting, I said you

weren't a memorable teacher. I was very, very wrong. That, right there, that's a moment Chuckie's going to remember forever, and he'll learn his lesson."

"One can only hope." Arlo reaches out and says, "Hand me the bottles, I'll take care of them."

Chapter Twenty-One

GREER

"Congratulations, you made it through your first chaperoning job," Gunner says, coming up to me. "You did great."

"Thanks. I mean, I didn't really do much."

"Your presence alone is what makes the kids behave." Gunner leans in and asks, "Was Arlo an ass to you the entire time?"

"No, he was actually really nice," I say.

Arlo went to help Nyema make sure kids were getting into their rides safely, while I stayed back and helped the others cleaning up. We didn't have to do much since the custodial staff will be coming in, but we wanted to try to help.

"What did you say? Arlo was nice?" Gunner blinks a few times. "Are we talking about the same guy?"

"Yes." I chuckle. "Trust me, I'm as shocked as you, but he was nice."

"Well, color me surprised. He was bitching to me all week

about chaperoning, and when Nyema wanted me to pair you two up, I felt my ass clench in horror."

I laugh out loud. "Well, nothing to worry about. We got along and there was no fighting."

"Fascinating. Maybe you two are growing up."

"One can only hope." I glance around the gym. Gunner and I the only ones left. "Are we able to leave?"

"Oh, yeah." He chuckles. "Sorry. Take off. I have to meet up with Nyema real quick and then I'm going to head home, but not before stopping at Dairy Queen and grabbing a Blizzard."

"A Blizzard, really?"

"Hey, I earned it." He chuckles. "After every dance I get one. It's congratulating myself on a job well done."

"Smart. I might have to consider something similar. Have a good night, Gunner."

"You too, and, hey, Greer?"

"Yeah?" I look over my shoulder.

"Arlo isn't as sneaky as he thinks he is. We know about Chuckie."

My eyes widen and panic ensues. "Gunner, he—"

"I know. *We* know." He gives me a curt nod. "Nyema assumes Arlo took care of it?"

"Twenty extra hours of community service."

"Twenty, damn. Nyema will be pleased." He waves. "Have a good night, Greer."

"You too."

Walking out of the gym and toward the teachers' parking lot, I take in the quiet school hallway. The lined-up lockers painted teal, the odd teal tiles that are scattered through the weaving of the tiled floors. The bulletin boards, the bullet-resistant doors that lead to classrooms, no longer with windows but with heavy-duty locks to prevent anyone from getting in if, God forbid, that ever happened.

It's peaceful, beautiful almost, knowing that minds are shaped within these walls and I have a part in it.

Arlo's gesture to Chuckie tonight touched me.

There's teaching a lesson.

And there's knowing how to teach a lesson.

Arlo could have taken the easy route and taken Chuckie to Principal Dewitt, who then would have escorted him to her office, where they would have called his parents. Given the situation, Chuckie's dad could have been drinking, and he could have driven drunk to come to the school, which offers up a million different possible outcomes. Chuckie could have gone home and been abused.

Instead, Arlo quietly dealt with the situation. After Chuckie left, he pulled Louis and Brennan to the side as well and offered them the same penance, which they gladly took.

Some might disagree with how Arlo handled the situation. They might say they need to learn real consequences, but I also think we all make dumb mistakes. The grace we find in each other will go a long way. And that's not really something you learn in high school. It's something you learn through living life. *Not simply following scripts from a textbook.* And Arlo's right. That gives a student an advantage in how he or she approaches future mistakes. *Invaluable life lessons.*

I push through the doors and allow myself to take in a deep breath of the chilly night air. Clear sky, stars bright up above, the humid static air of the gym quickly wilting off me.

"Hey." I look to the right, spotting Arlo as he approaches. "Wait up."

I slow down, and when he catches up, he gives me a cute smile. "You made it through your first chaperoning."

"That's what Gunner just said. You both make it seem like these are more traumatic than what I experienced tonight."

"Trust me, they used to be a shitshow, but Gunner and Nyema have put a lot of rules and regulations into place. It shows, because tonight was easier than before. I'll make a note to have them sweep the bleachers before the students filter in next time."

"Smart."

"You spoke to Gunner?"

"Yeah . . . he knows."

"Figured." We start walking toward the cars again. "Does Nyema know?"

"Of course, but he said she trusts you took care of it."

"Good."

"So, does everyone know about Chuckie? And how do you find out about that stuff?"

"Over time. You get to know the students. We found out about Chuckie when I happened to teach one junior-level class last year. He was in it, and he was always falling asleep. I finally got him to confide in me that his dad was an alcoholic. His dad would spend countless hours in the middle of the night raging and throwing furniture around the house. Chuckie wasn't getting any sleep."

"Oh, that's awful."

"Yeah, I spent extra time with him, made sure he was getting the food he needed, and then we worked on his college applications. When he got early acceptance into Stanford, the boys and I took him out to get some ice cream."

"Seriously?" I ask, turning toward him.

"Yeah, nothing wrong with that. Gunner loves Blizzards."

Something I just learned.

"I know, but . . . God, I guess I—"

"Judged me before you got to know me?"

"Hey." I point my finger at him as we reach my car. "You judged me, too. Probably even worse."

He shakes his head. "No, it's my job to make sure you have what it takes to work in our department. At our school. We might live in the suburbs of Chicago, but we still have a lot of struggling families who choose the school because of the advanced placement classes we offer. Nyema has been monumental in making sure we're able to offer seats in our school for everyone. It's why I love working here so much and why it's highly sought after for teachers."

"When I got an interview, I was intimidated. Happy, but intimidated. I still can't believe Nyema hired me."

"She's a good judge of character. Sometimes I don't see it at first, but usually she proves me wrong."

I lean against the passenger side of my car and ask, "Did she prove you wrong with me?"

"Jury is still out." He smirks and says, "I have some cookies in my car and some drinks, if you want to sit for a second."

My brow lifts. "You just happen to have cookies and drinks in your car?"

He shrugs and goes to his car, which is parked next to mine. He opens the trunk and offers me a seat on the edge.

From behind me, he pulls forward a cooler and a box. Freshly made cookies from Crumbl. I very well might die and go to heaven in the back of Arlo's SUV.

"You're trying to kill me with these Crumbl cookies, aren't you?"

"I don't think I've met a person who doesn't like them. I got two chilled sugar cookies and two chocolate chips. Kept it simple." He opens the box, and I pick up a giant chilled sugar cookie. Just having it in my hands is making my mouth water.

"I have some water and seltzer water, too."

"Oh, what flavor?"

He holds up a can. "Uh . . . coconut pineapple. Cora bought them."

I chuckle. "I'll take one of those, please."

He cracks it open and hands me one.

Joking, I say, "Between the donuts and cookies, you might be in for some trouble."

"My running shoes have been lighting up the streets lately. It's helped, though. Helps me think."

"Yeah? What are you thinking about?" I ask, taking a bite of my cookie. Dear God, these are good.

Turning toward me, chocolate chip cookie in hand, Arlo says, "You."

I chew the cookie, swallow, and then say, "Me?"

He nods. "Yeah. I've been thinking about you a lot."

"Oh." I set my cookie on a napkin, and then on my lap, and try to act as calm as possible. "What, uh, have you been thinking about?"

He sighs and looks toward the parking lot. I can practically hear his mind hunting for the right words.

"I didn't handle things right with you and I regret that. I regret not treating you with more respect."

"Arlo, it's not like you were a horrible tyrant."

"Doesn't matter." His eyes connect with mine. "I wasn't fair and I let my body speak for my mind."

"So, you regret . . . the kitchen counter . . ."

His eyes turn dark as the corner of his lip turns up. "No. I don't regret that. But I regret how I handled things after. If I could do it over again, I would."

"Yeah? And what would you do differently?" I ask.

His head tilts ever so slightly to the left when he answers, her eyes trained on mine. "Ask you out on a date. Hold your hand . . . kiss you on the mouth. Treat you the way you deserve to be treated."

"I see." I take a big bite of my cookie. Honestly, what do I even say to that? Everything I said I wanted from him, he's saying he wished he had given me.

This entire night has put me into a perplexed state of emotions. Arlo is not *entirely* the man I built him up to be in my head. He is arrogant, self-absorbed, and self-righteous. But in reality, he's more than that. He's loyal, he cares; he doesn't just see black and white, he sees all the gray in between. And he has the capacity to look at the long-term with the goal of making decisions now that make that long-term better. In other words, he can be empathetic. Judgmental, but somehow thoughtful, too.

And right now, sitting with him in the back of his SUV, sharing cookies and drinks—something he clearly planned ahead of time—it feels sweet, and caring, and thrilling. It lowers my defenses. It causes me to want more.

To yearn for more.

"But I guess I lost my shot, huh?" he says, glancing at his lap.

Oh God.

What do I say?

No, you didn't. Please ask me out. Please, please, please, ask me out?

That doesn't read too desperate.

But that's how I feel.

I want him. I never stopped wanting him. And now there's a chance where something with him might not be a standstill, but might be something more.

I glance at him, and his eyes flash to mine. So much vulnerability in the depths of them. Worry and hope colliding together. It's my undoing.

"There might still be hope."

His brows shoot up to his hairline in surprise. "Really?"

"Yeah, really," I say.

He nods and takes a bite of his cookie. We both turn away from each other and instead stare at the empty parking lot. From the cool night, a chill runs up the base of my spine, causing me to visibly shiver. Arlo catches it and says, "Jesus, are you cold?"

"I'm okay, just caught a chill for a second."

"Here," he says, taking off his cardigan and draping it over my shoulders.

And, oh my God. Someone hand me a tissue, because I'm about to weep from how good it smells.

Like someone bottled up a man and sprayed it all over this

cardigan. All I can really say at this point is the pheromones are on fire.

"Thank you."

"You're welcome."

We both pick at our cookies, when I finally say, "Can I ask you something?"

"Sure."

"Why the change of heart?"

"Because, for once, I listened to a different voice than my own." He pauses and moves a few stray strands of my hair away from my forehead gently. "I felt the absence of you in my everyday routine, and I had no idea that you'd already encroached upon that. I noticed your avoidance, the awkward air between us, and . . . I didn't like any of it. Frankly . . . I missed you. Every smartass, prank-loving, beautiful part of you."

I smile shyly. "I missed the teasing."

"Anything else?" he asks, his voice growing deeper.

"And other things." I don't have to say it for him to know what I'm talking about.

"Good to know."

He smirks, and I melt right there on the spot. There's no denying it, I'm developing strong feelings for this man, and they're charging at me, ready to cling on and hold on tight.

"THANK YOU FOR THE COOKIE."

"Glad you enjoyed it," he says, walking me to my car, which is only a few feet away.

"You didn't have to walk me to my car."

"I know."

"So why did you?"

He reaches out and picks up my hand, linking our fingers

together. My heart flutters from the feel of his palm pressing against me, then how he closes the space between us.

"I wanted to ask you something."

"Yeah? What's that?"

He brings our linked hands up to his mouth and presses a sweet kiss across my knuckles. "Will you go on a date with me this Wednesday?"

"Wednesday?" I ask, sounding breathless.

"Yes. I don't want to wait a week, but figured I'd give you some time to change your mind if you say yes and then realize what a horrible mistake it was once the cookie wears off."

I laugh and smile up at him. "I'd love to go on a date with you."

"Good," he says as his other hand reaches up and cups my cheek. "So Wednesday it is."

"Yeah," I answer dreamily.

His thumb drags over my cheek, and he whispers, "I need to kiss you, Greer."

"I need you to kiss me too," I whisper.

He steps in closer and tilts my jaw up with his thumb, keeping his eyes trained on mine. "I've wanted these lips for a long fucking time."

"Then take them."

He wets his lips and lowers his mouth, leaving an inch between us. I breathe him in, let the moment swirl around us like a tornado of lust as he holds out, taking me to a level of anticipation I've never felt before.

And when I think he won't close the distance, his soft lips press against mine. The lightest of presses, right before he brings me closer, power propelling me against him as his mouth takes charge.

It isn't sloppy.

It isn't awkward.

It's . . . perfect.

Slow, but the perfect amount of pressure that tells me how much he's wanted this. That his yearning matches mine.

I move my hand up his chest, to the back of his neck, where I cling tightly, keeping me in place as his mouth feels out mine.

Dizzying lust consumes me, filling me up from the tips of my toes to the top of my head. Building and building until it almost feels difficult to breathe. Because I know what it's like to have this man's tongue on me, inside me, torturing me.

Divine.

And his hands . . . strong hands that caress with urgency.

Fervor.

His tongue runs along mine, and I have no choice but to succumb to the passion rolling over me in waves, drowning me in his masculinity. I open my mouth and his tongue clashes against mine. And with every swipe, I mirror him with reckless abandon.

He growls against my mouth and presses me against the car.

My hand gravitates to the short strands of his hair.

He unlinks our hands and presses his hand against my hip, pinning me in place.

"Fuck," he whispers, pulling away for a second. "You taste so good."

And then his mouth is back on mine.

Dancing.

Tangling.

Fusing.

His hips press against my leg and I feel his length, hard and long.

I move my free hand to the spot between his legs and grip him through his chinos.

A load groan falls past his lips as his forehead presses against mine and our mouths part.

He swallows hard. "Okay . . . I need to go."

"Are you sure?" I ask, squeezing him.

"Yes," he says, his voice growing stern. He tilts my head up so I'm forced to look him in the eyes. "You know I want you. I know you want me. But I want more between us. I want to try . . . hell"—he takes a deep breath—"I want to be intimate with you."

Understanding what he's trying to say, I nod and remove my hand. "Sorry, I—"

"Don't apologize." He sears me with his gaze. "Do you understand? Don't ever apologize for how much you want me. But let's try to take this slow, to give it a chance."

"Okay."

"And I might need help, because I'm not good at this shit. But I want to try. Shit, I'm desperate to try, because I can't stop thinking about you, Greer. And I want to get to know more of you." He smooths his thumb over my temple. "I want to know more about what's up here."

"I'd like that."

"Good." Exhaling heavily, he presses one more soft kiss across my lips and pulls away. He then says, "I'll text you."

"You will?"

He smiles. "I will."

"About the date?"

"You'll see." He winks and steps away, and as he walks back to his car, I wonder where the hell this man came from and why it's taken this long to see him.

Was I blinded?

Or was he shielding himself from me?

I think it might have been a little of both.

———

ARLO: *Are you ready for some text messages?*

Greer: *You do realize that you don't have to announce you're going to text me with a text. I know you're older than me, but really, Grandpa?*

Arlo: *Is that how it's going to be?*

Greer: *Maybe. Can you handle it?*

Arlo: *If I can handle your sweet, bare ass in my face while you're on all fours on my kitchen island, I'm pretty sure this *grandpa* can handle your ageist jokes.*

Greer: *Had to bring up the kitchen island, didn't you?*

Arlo: *Weren't you the one who marveled over the kitchen island during the teacher BBQ?*

Greer: *First of all, that wasn't a BBQ. Second of all . . . yes.*

Arlo: *LOL.*

Greer: *Dear heavens . . . did Grandpa just say *LOL*? Look at you down with the lingo.*

Arlo: *Pushing your luck, Gibson.*

Greer: *Just getting warmed up, Turner. So unless you can take it, I think we should end this text convo.*

Arlo: *Nice try. I told you I was going to text you, so that's what I'm going to do.*

Greer: *And what is your end goal with this so-called texting?*

Arlo: *Isn't it obvious? Trying to tap into your inner Gen Z with communication.*

Greer: *Uh, excuse me, baby boomer, but I'm a millennial. Thank you very much. Born in 1996.*

Arlo: *You're right on the cusp, which means you hold the traits of both. No wonder you're massively irritating.*

Greer: *Uh, are you trying to woo me with this text thread? Because you're doing a pretty shitty job.*

Arlo: *Consider me a newbie.*

Greer: *Aw, am I your first attempt at wooing?*

Arlo: *Unfortunately, and it seems like you're not going to make it easy on me.*

Greer: *Why on earth would I do that?*

Arlo: *True. Okay, clean slate. Are you ready?*

Greer: *Give it to me . . . Daddy.*

Arlo: *None of that.*

Greer: *Oh, right, I'll save that for the kitchen island. Please proceed.*

Arlo: *Jesus, you're not making this easy.*

Greer: ***bats eyelashes***

Arlo: *You know, I think you're in a mental space of witty comebacks right now. I'm going to try again tomorrow.*

Greer: *Giving up that easily?*

Arlo: *Filling you up with anticipation. I'll text tomorrow.*

Greer: *Again . . . you don't have to inform me of your texting schedule.*

Arlo: *Keep it up and I'll spank that sass right out of you.*

Greer: *Tease.*

ARLO: **Attention* Arlo is going to text Greer.*

Greer: *Good God.*

Arlo: *LOL < - don't make fun of that. What are you doing?*

Greer: *Sitting on my couch, staring at a stack of tests I need to grade but considering just labeling them all a B and being done with it. You?*

Arlo: *Watching my sister try to break her record in hula-hooping.*

Greer: *What? Seriously?*

Arlo: *Yup. She's at twenty loops. Can't seem to pass it. She's blaming, and I quote, her weak, non-childbearing hips.*

Greer: *Why is she hula-hooping in the first place?*

Arlo: *She's on a strong path to find joy and happiness in the little things. I admire it, but it also brings nights on the patio with her attempting to swing her hips back and forth over and over again.*

Greer: *I wish I was there to see it.*

Arlo: *Come over.*

Greer: *No. That would be weird.*

Arlo: *How so?*

Greer: *Uh . . . isn't this like a secret or something?*

Arlo: *Do you *like* want it to be *like* a secret?*

Greer: Don't be an ass. And I don't know. Everyone is so close that maybe it would be nice to just keep it between us for now.

Arlo: You know, I never asked you something.

Greer: What's that?

Arlo: Are you seeing Walker still?

Greer: Are you asking to be exclusive?

Arlo: Are you saying you don't want to be?

Greer: You tell me what you want.

Arlo: You. Only you. I want no one else to have you.

Greer: Okay.

Arlo: Okay?

Greer: Yes . . . okay.

Arlo: . . . okay. So, uh . . . hell, I want to kiss you.

Greer: Then come here and kiss me.

Arlo: No. Keeping my distance. Back to this text conversation I'm trying to have with you.

Greer: Yes, can't forget that.

Arlo: What's your favorite emoji?

Greer: What . . . that's what you've been wanting to ask me? What my favorite emoji is? Turner, you have to be able to do better than that.

Arlo: The little things count just as much as the big things. Work with me here.

Greer: Fine. Uh, I think the obvious answer would be eggplant, but I'm not obvious. My favorite emoji is [thumbs up emoji]. It can be used to express joy and it can be passive aggressive at the same time. Multifunctional.

Arlo: Are you one of those people who gets cut off, and instead of flipping them the bird, you give them a thumbs up?

Greer: Naturally. It's more dickish. Like, "Good job, asshole, you don't know how to drive."

Arlo: Pretty sure I've gotten a few thumbs up in my lifetime.

Greer: Are you a bad driver, Mr. Turns Me On?

Arlo: Mr. Turns Me On?

Greer: Please, as if you don't know you have that nickname. It *floats around the teachers' lounge. Along with Mr. Klein is Fine for Gunner, and Romeo . . . well, his is Mr. Roam Your Hands All Over Me.*

Arlo: *You're objectifying us.*

Greer: *Do you need my breasts to cry into?*

Arlo: *Nah, I prefer a bigger tit to dry my tears.*

Greer: *Oh.*

Greer: *My.*

Greer: *God.*

Greer: *I can't believe you just said that.*

Arlo: *LMAO.*

Greer: *Um, care to rectify that statement?*

Arlo: *I think about your tits all the time. What I wouldn't give right now to have them in my mouth.*

Greer: *Better.*

Arlo: *Coraline wants to get some ice cream.*

Greer: *Uh-oh, another shot to the six-pack. You going to make it?*

Arlo: *No. But she's in a good mood and finding joy, so I'll suffer for her.*

Greer: *You brave soul.*

Arlo: *I'll see you tomorrow, beautiful.*

Greer: *Okay, you made my stomach flutter.*

Arlo: *Good.*

"WERE you really not going to say good morning?" I ask, walking into Arlo's classroom, where he's sitting at his desk, typing away at his computer. He continues to type for a few more seconds before he turns toward me.

His eyes slowly give me a once-over. He's incredibly smooth about it, especially since he does it while standing from his chair and moving to lean against the side of his desk, folding his arms across his chest.

God, he's so handsome. From the scruff on his face, to the

brilliant color of his eyes, to the mess in his hair. He's gorgeous, and I somehow caught his attention.

"Good morning," he says, his voice still carrying a little early morning rumble. "I was finishing up my notes on the community service I laid out for the heathens, and then I was going to stop by quick and hand you this." He reaches into his pocket and pulls out a piece of paper.

"Is that a note?"

"It is." He holds it between his index finger and middle finger, twisting it around.

"You wrote me a note?" I ask, still slightly perplexed.

"Yeah, you have a problem with that?"

"No, it's really cute. So, is that your angle? Trying to make me fall for the grandpa who has resorted to old-fashioned notes now because text messaging failed him?"

He chuckles. "Texting didn't fail me. I just thought this was more your style. Hell, more my style."

I walk up to him and take the folded triangle from his fingers. Yes, folded.

"Don't you know passing notes isn't allowed?"

"I'll bend the rules."

I examine it. "Did you use gel pens? Sparkly ones? Is there a box in there that asks me to check yes or no? Did you draw yourself naked and proportionally?"

His brow furrows. "Did you used to get naked pictures when you were younger?"

"Not me, but my friend did from her boyfriend. She said the pictures didn't match up at all."

"Teenage boys are such morons."

"Tell me about it," Gunner says, coming into the room, Romeo following closely behind him. "They need a detailed roadmap to navigate through high school in order to not come out a nitwit."

"And then they need help folding the map," Romeo says.

Slowly, I distance from Arlo and say, "How was the game, Romeo?"

"It was good." He nods, and that's all he says.

Okay.

Usually he's a lot more talkative than that.

"Coraline said she had fun," Arlo chimes in. "She especially enjoyed meeting some of the players afterward."

"Yeah, they both did," Romeo says, nostrils flared.

Oh.

Ohhhh . . .

I'm going to have a talk with Stella.

"Well, I should get back to my class. Have a good day," I say, not giving Arlo one last glance.

When I return to my classroom, I quickly unwrap the note and read it to myself.

Dear Miss Gibson,

I thought about you all weekend.

I thought about the dress you wore at homecoming.

I thought about the way your hair swept across your shoulders in a ponytail and how I desperately wanted to push it away.

I thought about how your legs looked in those heels, even more gorgeous than normal.

I thought about how I wished I could have taken your hand and shared a dance with you on the dance floor.

And then . . . I thought about our kiss.

And now, I'm thinking about how I can spoil you on our date, so that maybe . . . I can feel your lips against mine again.

Have a great day.

Arlo – Grandpa.

I snort and fold the note back up.

That man has done a complete one-eighty and it's starting to scare me, because not only do I get butterflies in my stomach whenever I see him, get a text from him . . . or read a note, I'm starting to become infatuated.

⊏⊐

"HEY," Arlo says, knocking on my open classroom door.

A huge smile spreads across my face when I see him.

"Hey."

"Love that smile." He approaches me and hands me a note. "Coraline is coming for lunch, but I wanted to give this to you before she does. Also, she's going to want you to join us. Don't feel like you have to."

"Would it be okay if I skip it?" I ask, wincing. "I have a lot of catching up to do."

"That's fine. I'll let you get to it."

He winks and starts to walk away, when I call out, "Date night tomorrow."

He turns and walks backward. "Excited?"

"Thrilled."

"Me too." He smirks and then leaves.

Sighing, I open up the note and delight myself in his perfectly scrolled handwriting.

Dear Miss Gibson,

Tapping into my inner intimate self has been difficult. I decided to go to a marriage counselor session with Coraline—I can tell you more about that later. It's not what you're probably thinking. But I learned something yesterday at my session—not sure if I'll go back, we'll see—but what I did learn, I took it to heart.

There are people on this earth who don't need the touch of another human to be happy. They're pleased with minimal contact and living their own life. And then there are people who need that extra touch. Who crave it. Who—as the therapist says—love love. And if we find ourselves matching up with that person, we need to put in a valiant effort to meet their needs.

I'm not saying you need human touch to survive, but I do believe you're someone who needs altruistic attention. Because you're considerate and compassionate.

And I'm prepared to give it.

But it might take me some time to get used to giving that to you.

Why am I telling you this? Because our date is tomorrow, and if I forget to touch you from across the table, or you don't feel like I'm giving you enough attention, please know, I'm trying.

Arlo

⌐━━▭

"I'M HEADING OUT," I say, at Arlo's door.

He turns in his chair, pen in hand, casual and sexy simultaneously. "Got a big date to get ready for?"

I smile. "As a matter of fact, I do."

He stands, tosses his pen on the desk, and then, from his pocket, pulls out another note. "Here."

I take the note from him. "And I thought you weren't going to write me today."

"Nah, just wanted to save this one for after school." He stuffs his hands in his pockets, as if he didn't, he'd be too tempted to touch me. "Am I still picking you up?"

"If you're okay with that."

"I prefer it."

"Perfect. I'll see you at seven."

"See you at seven."

I want to kiss him.

So badly.

Just a little peck.

Something to tide me over.

But this is not the place. Anyone could walk by and see.

So I muster my self-control and walk away, feeling his eyes on my retreating back the entire time.

When I reach my car, before I even turn it on, I unfold the note and read the simple sentence scrolled across the stark white paper.

I can't wait to take you out tonight. I'm glad you didn't change your mind.

I chuckle. As if I could change my mind at this point. The man has done everything in his power to get me hooked. Although, that sounds almost childish. The man is making more effort for me than anyone else I've known. He's trying to learn how to drive his emotions differently.

I do believe you're someone who needs altruistic attention. Because you're considerate and compassionate.

And he's using his love of words, of expression within text, to help me see that. So, perhaps the correct word I should be using is "swoon." I'm not *hooked* . . . I'm *swooning.*

Chapter Twenty-Two

ARLO

I adjust the cuffs on my sleeves one more time, making sure they're perfectly rolled to my elbows, before knocking on her door.

I spent longer than I care to admit picking out my clothes but decided to keep it simple. Dark jeans, slate-gray button-up shirt, and black vest. I hope I'm not underdressed now. I told her to dress casually, so hopefully she stuck with that.

With a deep breath, I raise my hand and rap my knuckles against the door.

I take a step back, put my hands in my pockets, and stare at my shoes just as she opens the door.

When I look up, my goddamn breath is stolen straight from my lungs.

She's stunning.

In a simple pair of black skinny jeans and heels, she looks tall and toned. Her deep-purple silk tank top floats over her torso while whatever magical bra she's wearing tonight makes her tits look irresistible. And her hair is loosely curled and cascading over her shoulders.

I was afraid I wasn't going to give her enough physical contact . . . Hell, I'm afraid I'm going to touch her too much now.

"Greer, you look fucking delectable."

She smiles, the gloss on her lips making her mouth that much more enticing. "You look really *delectable* yourself. You have that whole 'Justin Timberlake Suit and Tie' era going for you."

"I guess that works. At least it's not 'Justin Timberlake Denim Suit' era."

"True." She snags her purse, a leather jacket, and keys and shuts the door behind her when she joins me in the hallway. When I think she's about to lock up, she presses her hand against my chest and wraps it behind my neck. Standing on her toes, she lifts up and places a soft kiss across my mouth. I barely have time to react before she's pulling away. "I needed to get that out of the way," she says, looking me in the eyes. "After all those notes, I felt desperate to kiss you."

"Then kiss me the right way," I say, right before slowly backing her up against her door, lifting her chin, and connecting my mouth with hers.

It's slow but urgent—the way she grips me. My hold on her chin. I angle her to make room for when I open my mouth, and luckily, she does the same, allowing our tongues to touch.

Fuck . . .

I could do this all night. This could be our date.

Kissing.

This and this alone would be the best night of my life.

"Jesus," I say, pulling away but keeping my face close. "I need to stop, or we're never going to leave."

She smiles and brings my head back down, where she presses a few more kisses across my mouth.

"I love your lips," she says as she releases me and locks up her apartment.

When she turns back around, I hold out my hand for her. She smiles at it and then places her hand in mine.

And just like that . . . we head out to my SUV.

I can already tell it's going to be a good night.

———

"YOU'RE KIDDING ME."

I shake my head.

"Arlo . . ."

"What?" I ask, putting the car in park and turning toward her in my seat.

"We're going sailing?"

"Technically, someone else is sailing the boat, but yes, we are. And I had a dinner catered."

"And you think this is casual? This is probably the fanciest date I've ever been on."

"Good. I like to set the bar higher than the men before me."

"You didn't have to do this. This is a lot."

I reach out and cup her cheek gently. Leaning toward her, I say, "I wanted to do this. I want you to know I'm serious about you, which means I plan on dating you. This is how I date."

"Have you ever taken anyone else out on a boat?"

I shake my head. "No one special enough has come along . . . until you."

The corners of her lips turn up as she presses a short kiss across my lips. "Expect a lot of that tonight."

"I hope so. Now stay right there."

I hop out of the car and go straight to Greer's passenger side door, where I open it up and hold out my hand. She takes it, and I carefully walk her across the pebbled parking lot to the harbor. The sky is dark already, but the stars are shining along with the moon, providing the perfect blanket of romance above us.

"The dock can be slippery, so hold on tight."

We make it down the ramp where there's a boat, lit up and waiting for us. From where I stand, I can spot the dinner table with ample lanterns that provide sufficient glow for me to see Greer.

The staff of two is waiting on the dock.

"Good evening, Mr. Turner," Gary, the captain, says while holding out his hand. I give it a firm shake as he introduces his staff. "This is my wife, Janet. We'll be serving you this evening as you enjoy the beautiful views of Lake Michigan at night."

"Thank you. This is Greer Gibson."

"Miss Gibson, a pleasure." Gary nods. "Let's get you two on board and comfortable, and then we'll set sail."

I get on the boat first and then help Greer. I should have told her to change her shoes but being the greedy bastard that I am, I didn't have it in me, not when they looked that tempting on her.

After a quick tour of the boat, Greer and I decide to sit at the boat's stern while we take off into the lake, and once dinner is served, we'll move to the table.

There's a perfect bench in the back, just big enough for two people. She snuggles into my side, and I wrap my arm around her.

"Would you like a blanket?" Janet asks.

"That would be wonderful," Greer says, taking the wool blanket. She drapes it over her lap, and I'm grateful she brought a jacket, too, because even though I love that top, she'd have been cold with nothing on her shoulders.

Once she's situated, she lets out a long sigh.

"Comfortable?" I ask quietly.

"Extremely. I didn't think my Wednesday night was going to end up on a sailboat, pulling out into Lake Michigan."

"Surprised?"

"A little. A regular dinner at a restaurant would have been just fine." She laughs.

"I'm sure we'll have dates like that at some point, but I figured I needed to go big for the first date."

"Already counting on multiple dates?" she teases.

I kiss the top of her head. "Yeah, I am."

"Not sure how you can beat this."

"I have ideas."

Snuggling in closer, she asks, "Did you tell Cora what you're doing?"

"No. She thinks I'm going out with the boys."

"Smart, unless she contacts one of them."

I shrug. "If she does, oh well. I'll just lie until we're ready. She's been evasive with me ever since she moved in, and it wasn't until recently that she confessed what she's been doing."

"Is that the marriage counseling?"

"Yeah. I won't get into it because, that's her story to tell to you as *her* friend, but to keep it brief, we both seem to have intimacy issues. Cora probably more than I do. Sex has never been an issue, but being affectionate, opening up and letting someone in, that's been harder. She suggested I go to a session with her. I laughed her off until the other day. I thought if I really want to make something of this, then I should put in some time fixing myself."

"You don't need to be fixed, Arlo."

"There's room for improvement, and I became quite aware of that when you walked away."

"It wasn't easy," she says quietly. "I felt like I was giving up on something I barely tapped into, but it started off too strong, too intense, and with a douse of hatred."

"I never hated you," I say quickly. "Did you hate me?"

"Yes," she answers honestly. "And I hated myself for not having any willpower around you. I was tempting the beast and I didn't know how to stop. It brought out a carnal side of you, a lustful side of me—which was great, but it wasn't what I was looking for—and I was mad at myself for taking it to that level."

"You weren't alone in how things changed quickly between us."

"I know . . . but then you dressed up as Jay Gatsby, and I knew there was a part of you that *could* be the man I'm looking for. Not just sexual attraction, but on a different level."

"I can be." I squeeze her tight to me.

"I don't doubt it now. I think we're granted with the perfect chance to get to know each other better now, which is what I'd like to do."

"Ask me anything. I'm an open book."

"Anything?"

"Anything," I say, pressing another kiss to the top of her head, the act coming naturally.

"When I ran into you outside of the restaurant, the night I was going out with Walker, were you upset?"

"*Upset* isn't the correct word. More like indignant. I had no idea what the boys were up to, and when I found out, I saw red. The last thing I wanted was to see you go out with another guy, especially . . . hell, especially when you looked so goddamn fine in your dress. I spent the entire night agonizing over my stupidity. I had a deep conversation with Coraline, and it helped me snap the blinders off and realize what I was missing out on."

"When I saw you that night, it felt absolutely devastating. At the time, I felt vengeful because of everything that had happened between us, but I was devastated because it didn't seem like you cared. I thought maybe I saw a flash of something in your eyes, but I couldn't be sure."

"I cared. Trust me, I cared."

"Is it weird to say that makes me happy?"

I chuckle. "Glad my pain and agony bring you joy."

She pokes my side. "You know what I mean."

"I do, and I understand."

"I do need to come clean about something from that night, though."

Fuck, if she says she slept with him, I'm not sure how I'll handle that. *I'd have no right to be angry. She's irresistible. Walker would be a blind idiot—*

"Walker and I are friends, and friends only."

Thank. Fuck.

"In fact, he talked about someone he's extremely attracted to but can't act upon that attraction, and I . . . well, I talked about you." She's blushing. God, she's adorable when she blushes.

"Me?"

"From the outset. So, you have nothing to worry about there, okay?"

I can't help it. I lean across and kiss her. Gently. *Affectionately.* Because she just showed me enormous kindness and respect. *Not sure I deserve that yet. But I want to earn it.*

The sailboat picks up speed as we head out of the harbor and into the vast darkness of the impressive lake.

"Have you ever had a favorite student?" Greer asks.

"Yeah. Easily. There are students that take a piece of you every year, ones that you'll remember, but there's one student who sticks out above all of them."

"Tell me about him or her."

"Her name is Crystal. Crystal Meyers. She was eager and excited to be in an advanced placement class. She played basketball, was the school spirit type, and participated in every themed day the student counsel came up with. She was happy all the time. That was, until she got her first paper back from me and failed."

"Oh no. You knocked the spirit right out of her with a red pen."

I chuckle. "I did. She was devastated. That lunch break,

she came to my classroom and asked if she could speak with me. Being the asshole that I am, I told her she had five minutes."

"Ugh, Arlo . . ."

"I know. But I've never been one to make friends with students. I wasn't about to chitchat."

"Did she speed-talk to you?"

"Basically. It all came out in one sentence. She was confused, didn't know how she could make the paper better, what she was missing. She just signed a letter of intent to attend University of Connecticut. She received a full-ride for basketball, and she took my class to prepare herself for the higher level of education she'd be facing."

"Like Blair."

"Exactly, but where Blair is surrounded by friends and a support system, I quickly realized Crystal wasn't. She'd come to my classroom almost every lunch break to work on her papers. I didn't think much of it until I started asking around about her. Other teachers never saw her with anyone."

"Oh God, she didn't have any friends."

I shake my head. "No. She had a few friends on the basketball team, but she never hung out with them. She found solace and friendship in my classroom."

"Oh Jesus, you're about to break my heart, aren't you?"

"Depends. We started hanging out at lunch, and of course, Nyema knew, and would frequently pop in to be there, you know, for child protection laws. Or send another female staff member in her place. We followed policies carefully, although, I never feared that Crystal had any feelings toward me, which Nyema and I both monitored. I watched basketball games so I could relate to her, and we talked about what she should expect when she went to college. When the end of the year came, she invited me to her graduation party."

"Please tell me you went."

"I did. I wouldn't have missed it for anything. At the party, she had the 'most significant people' in her life that got her to where she was. Her parents, grandparents, her coaches . . . and me."

"Yup, and here come the tears." Greer dabs at her eyes.

"They served dinner at a table, and she toasted every single person individually, telling the room how important they were to her."

"What . . . what did she say about you?" Greer asks, her voice wavering.

"She lifted her glass of sparkling cider to me, looked me in the eyes, and said, 'Thank you for being the friend I'd never had. Without you, I'd have slipped into another hole of depression. Because of you, I stopped cutting myself, and because of your faith in me, I have confidence going to college.'"

"Oh my God." Greer pulls away to look me in the eyes. "Arlo."

I smile softly. "She has no idea how much that meant to me because, frankly, I think I was lost, too. I cherished those lunches with her. We still email back and forth. She's a junior in college this year. She has a boyfriend who is on the men's basketball team, and they've been dating for a year. She thinks he's 'the one..'" I chuckle. "I told her to be careful and to not forget about why she was in college, to earn a degree and play basketball."

"Ugh, of course."

"But she's thriving, and as an educator, that's all I can ask for."

"I think that's the best teacher story I've ever heard." She cups my cheek and looks me in the eyes when she says, "Thank you for sharing with me."

"No need to thank me, Greer. I want to share everything with you."

She looks momentarily surprised, then smiles and leans in, placing a gentle kiss on my lips. She returns my embrace and together, we watch the wake of our boat disturb the quiet peace of the lake.

A week ago, I'd have mocked and ridiculed any man for giving that level of power to his partner. But ever the avid reader, I've spent time going over the book that the counsellor suggested both Cora and I read. Phrases like emotional attunement, where "turning toward" one another, listening, and showing empathy rather than "turning away," builds trust and safety within a relationship. Something Cora and I never received growing up. We excelled at turning away. *So, I want to try, because Greer is a safe place . . . already.*

"HOW IS EVERYTHING?" Janet asks. She's been respectful of giving us space and attention equally. They're going to be tipped exceptionally well tonight.

The night has been absolutely perfect.

"These crab legs are spectacular," Greer says. "I can't get over how much meat is in them."

"I'm happy to hear that. Would you like some damp towels to wipe your hands with?"

"Shortly, that would be great," I say, as we still have a few crab legs to eat.

"Of course, and the music, is it too loud?"

"Perfect," I answer. "Thank you."

"Very well. Please let us know if you need anything."

She leaves me alone with Greer. The lanterns cast a warm glow around us, adding a beautiful, intimate atmosphere. The instrumental music is quiet enough to make conversation easy, but also soft enough where we can still hear the lapping of the water against the boat.

"This is so amazing, Arlo, seriously. I feel so spoiled."

I smile. "Get used to it."

"Was your childhood like this? Lavish?"

"Depends. Dinners were silent and served to us by my grandparents' staff, so maybe others would call it lavish, but I'd call it cold and uncomfortable. We weren't to talk, just eat."

"Really? That's so sad."

"Yeah, I only realized that wasn't the way families shared dinner when I went to my friends' houses, and I became resentful. I was resentful about a lot of shit, still am, but trying to work through all of that. What about you? What were your family dinners like?"

"Obnoxious." Greer smirks. "Mom cooked, my brother and I set the table, Dad said the prayer at the head of the table, and then . . . well, we'd talk about the most obnoxious things, like different ways you can say the word *fart*."

"What?" I laugh out loud.

"Yup, it was a thesaurus battle. We'd pick one word for the night and go for it. Dad always won, of course, but there was this one night where Mom made porkchops and applesauce, Dad's favorite. He was in heaven, and I think that distracted him, because Mom dominated and took the win."

"What was the word?"

She smiles and, fuck, she's so damn beautiful it hurts. "Penis."

A laugh bubbles out of me and I ask, "How old were you?"

"High school. The words didn't get dirty until we were in high school, and my parents thought it was appropriate to expand our vocabulary so when we were in college, we had new and different ways to not only refer to genitals but to have a colorful bank of insults, as well."

"Give me an example."

"Oh, you know, classic insults like dunderhead, fussbudget, and gollumpus."

"Gollumpus." I chuckle. "Hell, I think that's what I might

start calling every single one of my students until they prove themselves otherwise."

"I'd love to see that."

"Don't tempt me." I wiggle my brows. "Your family dinners sound like the ones I craved growing up."

"Well, if you're lucky, maybe I'll invite you to one some time."

"And where would that be? I have no idea where you're from, which strikes me as odd. I feel like I should know that."

"Well, if you weren't such a bastard at first, maybe you'd have known." She chuckles.

"True. Well, I'm here to learn now. Where are you from?"

"Nebraska. My parents own a farm. They used to sell corn until they realized they could earn big money by having wind turbines on their property and selling renewable energy."

"Smart," I say, rather impressed.

"Yup. They're retired now and living the good life of not having to do very much."

"Good for them. And your brother?"

"Marine. He went straight into the service from high school. He's always had a passion to be a part of something bigger than himself. And let me tell you, the insults we learned at those family dinners come in handy now when he's yelling at his peons."

"I can imagine, that *gollumpus* said in a scary tone could be toe-curlingly terrifying."

"You have no idea." She chuckles and picks up her glass of wine. Head tilted, she says, "I'm having a really great time, Arlo."

"So am I."

"Thank you for stepping out of your comfort zone and trying something new for me."

"No need to thank me."

"Does this mean you'll try my teaching techniques?"

"I want nothing more than to be the man who holds your

hand, but there's no way in hell I'm going to try your teaching techniques."

"And why not? Too rudimentary for you?"

"Too ostentatious."

"Oh my God, no, they're not."

I lift a brow in her direction. "Just last week, did you or did you not perform a one-woman dance routine to help show the timeline of *Pride and Prejudice*?"

"Uh, I didn't. I wasn't showing a timeline; I was showing the class the dance moves from that time period. A little encouragement for homecoming. Clearly no one took my advice."

"You are something else," I say before taking a sip of my drink.

"You like it."

"I like you."

She smiles over her wine glass. "Smooth, Turner . . . smooth."

"I THINK I still have sea legs," Greer says as I hold her hand on our way up to her apartment.

"Technically, they would be lake legs since we weren't out at sea."

"You sound like Keiko."

"No one sounds like Keiko." I chuckle. "She has her own way of speaking."

"Which I love. Sometimes, I just want to sit back and listen to her. I think things are getting hot and heavy with her and Kelvin."

"I can't imagine Kelvin Thimble ever getting hot and heavy."

"He's quite the charmer—at least, that's what Keiko says."

We make it to her apartment and she turns toward me, gripping the bottom of my vest. "Want to come inside?"

I sure as hell do. I want to come inside her.

Really fucking bad.

I want to taste her as she comes on my tongue.

I want to hear her trembling cries as she orgasms around my fingers.

Then eat her again.

And again.

And *fuck*.

"I don't think that's a really good idea."

"Ah, you're horny, huh? Afraid you'll plow your love stick inside me?"

"Do you have to say it like that?"

"It's more fun." She smiles and stands on her toes, pressing a soft kiss to my mouth. "Thanks for the wonderful date. Goodnight." She unlocks her door and reaches for the handle, but I stop her and twirl her around, only to gently push her against the door.

One hand next to her head, propping me up, and the other gripping her jaw, I tilt her mouth up and say, "No way in hell you're getting away with a quick peck."

"No?" Her fingers hook through my belt loops. "So, what are you going to do about it?"

Moving in closer, I lower my mouth to hers and, without answer, I take what I want. I open her mouth right away and dive my tongue against hers. I'm hungry, needy. I want so much from her, but know I need to take this slow, so I focus on her mouth and her mouth only. I don't move my hands from where they are now, even though I want to feel her breast in my palm. I want to rub the silk of her shirt over her stomach, and I want to cause her to gasp by pinching her nipple between my fingers . . . maybe my teeth.

Her hand creeps up my chest, exploring, and unbuttoning my vest . . .

"Greer."

"What?" I feel her smile against my mouth.

"Don't."

"But don't you want to, you know, let me suck you?"

Jesus.

Christ.

I push off the door and put some distance between us as my hand pulls on my hair.

"What's wrong?" She smiles wickedly.

"You're evil."

She chuckles, and it makes me charge toward her again. This time, I pin her with my hand to her hip, and the other slides up her stomach, under her shirt to just below her breast. She gasps into my mouth as I try to leave my print on her. Make her remember exactly who she's dealing with.

She clings to me, opens her mouth, and . . . I pull away.

She nearly falls over from the loss of me, eyes wide, chest heaving. "Wh-what are you doing?"

"Reminding you who has control in the bedroom."

"I don't think I could forget."

"Sounded like you did there for a second." I take another step back. "I'm going to leave, but I'll see you tomorrow, okay?"

She bites her bottom lip and nods as she rests against the door of her apartment.

"Don't look sad," I say.

"Sad the evening is over, but I'll see you tomorrow." She gives me a cute wave. "Night, Arlo."

"Night, Greer," I say, watching her disappear into her apartment.

Hell, I need to get out of here . . . now.

⸺

"SUNDAY—IS EVERYONE COMING?" Gunner asks when I walk into the teachers' lounge for lunch. Greer is already sitting at the table with Keiko and Stella. Romeo and Gunner are sitting at another table but close enough to have a conversation.

"Are we required?" Stella asks before picking up a meatball sub and taking a huge bite.

"Yes, you are."

"Are we practicing at Arlo's house again?" Romeo asks.

I retrieve my salad from the fridge and nod. "Yeah, I have all the gear. It's easier."

"I think someone likes being the Monica Geller of the group," Romeo says.

"What?" I ask.

"Monica Geller, sibling to Ross Geller," Keiko pipes up. "From the popular American sitcom, *Friends*. Within the semi-diverse group of six comrades, she was considered—in street terms—the neat freak, the obsessive, and the hostess with the mostest. To be precise, season four, episode thirteen, properly titled 'The One with Rachel's Crush'—"

"I think we're good on the detail," Stella says. "No need to dive deep into the multi-faceted plots of *Friends*." Whispering to us, Stella says, "She'll go on forever."

"Perhaps you're right. Halt me before I dive into the intricacies of every sub-arc of the storyline."

"Anyway, we're good for Sunday," Gunner says.

Now that that's solved, I turn to Greer and say, "Miss Gibson, when you have a moment, I need to speak to you about Blair."

Her brow furrows, and she says, "Everything okay?"

I glance around the room and say, "In private."

"Ooo, someone's in trouble," Stella says.

Concerned, Greer packs up the lunch she's barely touched and says, "Where should we meet?"

"My classroom should be sufficient."

"Looks like Arlo is about to lay down the law. Look out everyone, Mr. Stick Up His Butt is on the loose," Stella continues. When I shoot her a look, she holds up her hands and chuckles. "Not in the mood for teasing?"

"Never in the mood," I shoot back.

"Got it." She pretends to write something in her palm with an imaginary pen. "Noted: does not like to be teased."

I hold the teachers' lounge door open for Greer, and she follows me. I stay silent the entire walk to my classroom despite her worried questions. When we finally make it to my room, I shut the door and lock it, and she bursts out, "Just tell me, is she going to fail?"

Smiling, I walk up to her, grip her chin, and press a gentle kiss to her lips. "Nothing is wrong with Blair. I just wanted an excuse to get you alone."

She pushes at my chest, but I capture her hand so she can't go far. "Arlo, don't do that. You had me worried."

"Well, you should have known that I wanted to see you at lunch, especially after last night. I didn't see you this morning—"

"So now I'm supposed to be a mind reader?"

"Yup." I smirk and press another kiss to her lips.

"You know, for the alpha male you present to everyone else, you're really just a softy. You realize that?"

"Starting to." I tug her hand and bring her to my desk, where I offer her a chair and pull up another for myself. When she's situated, I slide a note across the desk for her.

She looks at it and her eyes soften.

"More notes?"

"Do you want them to stop?"

She sighs while she opens it up. "Never." She reads the note out loud. *"Dear Miss Gibson. Last night meant a lot to me—"*

"You can read it to yourself, you know," I say, feeling embarrassed and glad no one else is in here.

Smiling, she continues to read . . . but to herself, and when she's done, she looks over the paper and says, "Yes."

I toss her a pen. "You have to check the box."

Chuckling, she checks the box and hands it back to me. I scan the note and say, "I think you should initial it to confirm you're the one who checked *yes*."

"Don't be horrid."

"So you'll go out with me again, then?"

"Yeah, you kind of won me over with the boat."

"Just the boat?"

"Maybe a little more." She winks. She unwraps her lunch again and offers me one of her pretzels, so I take one and pop it in my mouth.

"I planned the first date, so you plan the second."

"Oh, really?" she asks. "I can plan anything?"

I narrow my eyes. "Within reason."

She leans forward and runs her finger along my forearm. The light touch sends a thrill of excitement through me as she seductively says, "How about my apartment? I make you dinner, and you feed it to me while I sit on your lap . . . naked?"

I swallow hard. "Maybe I should plan the date."

"No way, you said it's my choice."

"I take it back."

"You can't take it back. I already marked *yes*."

"But you didn't initial it. How can I be sure it was you?"

"Stop." She laughs. "Don't deny what we have. We can have fun and learn about each other at the same time."

"I won't be able to control myself," I say, feeling fired up at the possibility of what's to come.

"I don't want you to. I loved it when you were spontaneous: the way you made me feel, the look in your eyes when you wanted me right then and there. And now that I know it can go somewhere, I wouldn't mind if that continued."

"Is that right?"

She nods. "But, under one condition."

"What's that?" I ask, loving her tough negotiation skills.

"Next time we're intimate, you get to come. None of this me getting pleasure only bullshit. I want to know what it's like to make you lose control. To see the way your muscles tense when you come. To listen to the growl that stirs up inside you when I take you into my mouth. I want to feel you, lick you, suck you. I want it all. No more denying me."

"You're making me goddamn hard right now."

"Can I—"

"No." I shift on my chair. "Not right now. Not at school."

"Oh really, now that you're involved you don't want to—"

"It's messy as shit for a guy. I don't need cum stains on my jeans."

"You won't . . . because I swallow."

Jesus. Fucking. Christ.

"Not here. But if you want me that bad, you can have me."

"I want you, this Saturday. I'd say Friday, but we have a volleyball game. This Saturday, you come to my place."

I sit back in my chair, studying her. As my chin's propped up by my hand, I say, "Shouldn't *you* woo *me* if you want to take me to bed?"

"Where was the wooing when you locked us in my class-room, pulled up my skirt, and put your face between my legs?" *God, I still get hot thinking about that.*

"It was built up. The small touches, the looks, the promises, the threats. And it worked."

"Ugh, still arrogant." She folds her arms.

"How about this. Starting today, every note I write, you return with a factoid about you. Something I can hold on to, so we still do what I want to do, but you also get my dick."

Looking me dead in the eyes, she says, "If I weren't so horny, I'd be insulted." She sips her drink and then sets it down. "Fine, I'll leave you notes. You know"—she smirks—"if

I knew you were going to be this high-maintenance, I would have second-guessed jumping into something with you."

"You should have known I was high-maintenance from my cardigan collection."

"God . . . you're right."

DEAR MR. TURNS ME ON,

You smell amazing. Just thought I'd throw that out there. Whatever cologne you wear is devastating to my brain. I tend to lose my train of thought and then end up agreeing to something like sending you love notes just so you feel comfortable taking your jeans off in front of me on Saturday.

I want to assure you that seeing your dick for the first time will bring me great joy . . . even if it doesn't live up to expectations. (If you didn't know, the expectations are high. Well, in your case, large.)

Enough about you though. Something about me . . .

I have a fantastic collection of lingerie. I haven't worn any of it in a long time, but I plan to change that very shortly.

Have a great rest of the day.

Greer

DEAR MR. TURNS ME ON,

Okay, okay, so you have a big dick. I think we cleared that up this morning. You don't need to send me text messages while I'm trying to teach. My mistake. I'll never question your length and girth again. Honestly, this is your fault, if you'd have let me test out the dick before I took it for a drive, we wouldn't have this miscommunication.

But thank you for reassuring me this morning in the parking lot . . . where you waited for me, just so you could clarify in person. I noted that you're obsessive about getting your point across.

Anyway, another fact about me . . .

I'm quite adventurous in bed. You're already aware that I swallow, but were you aware that I'm not opposed to using toys . . . in all places?

Yup, so sit on that one for a while (no pun intended) and drum up some fun ideas.

Have a great day.

Greer

—

DEAR MR. TURNS ME ON,

Do you realize how infuriating you are? If you didn't want sexual factoids, you should have been clear when you made the ground rules. And threatening not to come over until you received three facts about me that didn't involve anything sexual? Not cool, man.

Not.

Cool.

But, as I'm sure you're well aware, I'm desperate to see you tomorrow, so here are your three facts:

Tacos are my favorite food. Even though those crab legs were amazing, I love a taco. But we're not talking about fancy tacos you get from a really nice Mexican restaurant. I like straight-up beef soft tacos from Taco Bell. I know, I should be ashamed of myself. But there's something about the unpredictability in the ratios of taco ingredients that really gets my taste buds thriving and wanting more.

I had a lisp until I was ten. I had a really hard time pronouncing Ls. So volleyball always came out va-wee-baw. It was cute for a second, and then my parents realized I needed some assistance. I spent two years with a speech therapist but finally got the hang of it. Sometimes I'll say volleyball like I used to, just to hear it, remind myself how far I've come.

I used to think I was going to marry George Strait. I grew up a country-loving girl—you wouldn't guess that now because there's very little country or farm girl about me—but I truly thought George was going to come swooping in with his cowboy hat and guitar and whisk me off my feet. I realize now that would have been a child-bride situation, but a little girl could dream, right?

And just for an added bonus, because I'm really trying to play my cards right, the first time I saw you . . . you knocked those George Strait fantasies right out the window. You replaced a black cowboy hat with a soft-looking cardigan. And that guitar vanished right out of my head, and instead, a whiteboard marker. You've been a fantasy for a while, even when I wanted to stick a ruler up your ass due to your arrogance. I wanted you.

I still want you.

I want more than just your body, though. I want to date you. Hold your hand. Cuddle with you. Spoon you. Wake up in the morning and see your handsome face on the pillow next to me.

You have me, Arlo.

So come and get me.

Greer

Chapter Twenty-Three

ARLO

"Where are you going?" Cora says, just as I'm about to head to the garage and drive as fast as I fucking can to Greer's apartment.

Her letter yesterday had me wishing she didn't have a game that night, because I wanted to hang out with her. Slowly and luxuriously explore her body while we divulged more secrets. Instead, I texted her last night and talked about the time I almost drowned in Lake Michigan as a kid. It wasn't quite foreplay, but it was just another snippet of my life I was open to sharing with her. Which is still surprising the shit out of me. It's reinforcing how silent I've been for years. How little anyone knew me. Made me wonder how I ended up with gregarious friends like Romeo and Gunner, if I was honest. *And now, Greer.*

"Out," I say, stuffing my wallet in my pocket.

"Where exactly?" Cora leans against the hallway wall, arms crossed.

"Just out."

"Uh-huh. Now look who's being evasive."

"I don't need to tell you everywhere I'm going."

"But I do?" she asks.

"Yes."

She snorts. "You're the worst, you know that?" Pushing off the wall, she comes up to me and sniffs my chest. "Just what I suspected—cologne."

"Oh-kay," I say, drawing out the word.

Her finger motions to my hair. "You've got that messy *I didn't try, but really I did* look."

"Your point?"

"Hand me your wallet."

"No."

"Arlo. Hand it over."

"There's money in the cookie jar in the kitchen if you need some cash."

Her stare grows more intense as she wiggles her fingers at me. "Hand. Me. Your. Wallet."

Rolling my eyes, I give it to her, only for her to open it up and pull out an accordion of condoms.

"Just as I suspected. You're going to go have sex."

I snatch the wallet and condoms away, stuffing them back inside. "You need to start looking for your own place to live."

"Oh no, not now. Not when things are just starting to get interesting. About time there's something juicy going on around here. So, who is she?"

"None of your business"

I move toward the door, but she quickly works her way around me and spreads her arms and legs out like a spider, trying to block me from exiting. "I demand details. You went to marriage counseling with me, you've been giddy at night, attached to your phone, and now you're headed out around date-night o'clock, armed with a militia of condoms. I want to know who the girl is."

"Maybe I'm not ready to tell you. Ever think of that?"

"Yes, but I don't care. I have no boundaries. You should know that by now." She squeezes her hands together, practically praying in front of me. "Pleeeeeease, Arlo. Give me this little nugget to chew on while I sit here, in the dark, lonely and sad because my life is falling apart."

I tilt my head. "No, don't play that game with me. We both know you're past the lonely and sad phase."

"Ugh, you're right. But I still need something, anything. Who are you sticking your dick in tonight?"

"Jesus Christ." I drag my hand down my face . . . just as my phone beeps with a text message. Oh, shit. I didn't grab my phone.

Cora perks up, and terror breaks out across my face as I try to remember where I put my phone. Before I know what's happening, Cora blows past me in an all-out sprint.

"Cora, don't," I say, chasing after her. We reach the joint living room and kitchen area, and we both look around, ready to pounce.

"Ah-ha," Coraline says before pouncing over the couch.

I follow closely behind, tackling her into the cushions.

"Get off me, you gollumpus."

Yeah, I taught her the new insult the other day.

"Ah, that's my boob, you're stepping on my boob."

"Unless your boob is at your feet, I'm not stepping on it," I say, scrambling around just as her elbow connects with my ribs. "Fuck." I curl into my side as she slithers out from under me. From the corner of my eye, I see her reach for my phone on the coffee table. "Don't touch it," I yell as I wallop a throw pillow right in her face, causing her to drop the phone to the ground.

I roll off the couch, still clutching my side, and serpentine my way under the coffee table, where the phone is.

I'm about to reach it when the coffee table turns over and a hulk-like beast rages above me, hair askew, eyes reading like murder as she pulls her elbow back . . . taps it . . . and, oh fuck . . .

She leaps into the air and, as if she just signed a contract with World Wrestling Entertainment, she pummels me with her elbow to my shoulder, and then uses my body to roll away and grab my phone.

Despite my size.

My strength.

My smarts.

I was no match for the psychotic state of my sister.

As if the floor is lava and I'm drowning in it, she hops up on one of the chairs, stands on the armrests, and looks at my phone.

Fuck.

Please let it be Romeo or Gunner. Let it be one of their stupid texts about—

"Mr. Turns Me On?" Coraline says with a huge smile on her face.

Fuck.

Me.

"Oh my God. You and Greer are a thing?"

Coughing, I sit up from the ground and nurse my shoulder while I try to gain my bearings. What the hell just happened?

"I can't believe it. You and Greer. I never would have thought you two would get together. I mean, yeah, maybe there was some sexual tension, but you guys hate each other. Don't you? Well, I guess not, not after all the evidence I uncovered. Wow, you and Greer. She's hot, by the way. Too hot for you, I think. She could easily do better, and I say that out of love." She shakes her head. "Who knows? Do the boys know? Gah. Does Stella know? Keeks? I will scream bloody murder if I'm the last person to figure this out. Straight up, I will stab an apple with a knife. And don't you dare lie to me. Who knows?"

"No one," I say, coughing again.

"That seems like a lie."

I stand from my seated position and snap my phone out of her hands. "It's not a lie. Greer wants to keep it to ourselves right now since our friend circle is so close. We don't want you idiots making it awkward for us."

"Wait." She stands as well, growing serious. "You mean to tell me that I'm the only one who knows about you two?"

"Not by my choice." I adjust my shirt and look in the mirror on the wall by the hallway, adjusting my hair.

"Oh my God. I'm in the know. Look at me, knowing secrets. Teacher secrets. And I don't even work at the damn school."

"Thank God for that," I say, lifting my shirt and examining my ribs. Slightly red, but no serious bruising. "And where the hell did you learn to wrestle like that?"

"While your nose was stuck in a book, I was out earning my street cred."

"I'd believe that if you weren't wearing a pair of Gucci sweatpants."

She glances at her pants and then up at me. "Hey, these pants were a gift from *He Who Shall Not Be Named*, and just because he gave them to me, doesn't mean I'm going to let them eat dust in my closet. Hell no. I'll wear holes in them."

"Good to know." I head toward the garage again. "Not sure when I'll be home. Don't wait up. And for the love of God, don't tell anyone."

"Your secret if safe with me," she says, chasing after me. "And, Arlo?"

I turn around to find her bouncing up and down, hands clasped. "What?"

She smiles and says, "I'm really excited for you. Greer is amazing. Treat her well, okay?"

"That's what I'm trying to do."

"Good, and even though I love her, I love you more. I'm happy you're giving this a shot. You deserve happiness, too."

My anger fades, and I give her a soft smile. Despite what she went through, Cora can still see the positive in relationships. She humbles me. I hope one day she's ready to let someone into her heart. They'd be one lucky bastard. "Thank you."

"Now go plow her into the wall with your penis."

Christi.

I KNOCK on the door and feel the rapid beat of my heart as I wait for her to answer. I'm nervous. I don't know why I'm nervous. I've never been nervous about sex, but something about going into this, knowing that's what she wants, gives me a slight trickle of performance anxiety.

And to hell if I'd ever say that to her.

I can't let her think I'm anything but ready for what she has planned.

I tried to get clues from her earlier, but she didn't budge.

Oh, and her text message that she sent . . .

Yeah, it said: "See you soon, Mr. Turns Me On."

I'd have preferred that my sister didn't read that. Humiliation sank in on the drive over here, and I pray that Coraline has short-term memory loss.

Knowing her, though, she'll never forget it, or the moment where her big brother confessed to being in a relationship.

Well . . . is this a relationship?

I think it is.

The door swings open and Greer greets me, wearing a short white silk robe. Her hair is in waves around her shoulders, and she doesn't have a stitch of makeup on her face.

Mother.

Fucker.

There is no way I'm going to last.

"You're here," she says, pulling me in by the hand.

I kick the door shut behind me and then spin her around so she's pinned against the wall. I caress her face right before I lower my mouth to hers, where I taste the cherry of her ChapStick.

I allow my hands to briefly explore, pushing inside her robe and feeling lace along my fingertips when they brush against the underside of her bra. Looks like she's giving me a brief glimpse of that lingerie collection.

Her hands fall to the hem of my simple white T-shirt and start to pull it up, but I stop her and separate our mouths.

"What are you doing?" she asks.

"Not jumping right into it. Let's talk."

"Ugh, you and your talking. I know I said *open up, be intimate with me*, but I didn't think you were going to want to be so chatty."

I chuckle as she drags me by the hand to her bed.

"Uh, we're not chatting on your bed."

"And where else do you plan on chatting?" she asks, one hand on her hip.

I glance around. "Good point." I kick my shoes and socks off and then get on top of her bed and lean against the headboard, padding myself with some pillows. I expect her to climb in next to me, but instead, she climbs on top of my lap, facing me, and makes herself comfortable. "I'm a chair now?"

"Yup." She smiles and her hands fall to my chest, where they play with the fabric of my shirt. "Now, what do you want to chat about?"

"First things first—Coraline knows."

"What?" Her eyes snap to mine. "How?"

"She was badgering me before I left, and I didn't say anything. But then you sent that text, and I realized I didn't have my phone. In that exact moment, so did Coraline. It's embarrassing to say that we got into a bit of a wrestling match and she came out victorious, but she's scrappy and fights dirty."

"Oh, I don't doubt that." Greer sighs. "Was she mad?"

"Not at all. She actually said you were too good for me."

Greer smiles widely. "I knew I liked your sister. So, what— wait . . . did she read the text I sent you?"

Now it's my turn to smile. I nod and her head falls to my shoulder. "She did."

"Oh my God, that makes me want to die inside. She read the Mr. Turns Me On part?"

"That's how I knew the text was from you, when she said that out loud."

"Wow." Greer laughs and lifts up. "Well, I'll be putting in my resignation for book club this coming week and . . . oh Jesus, Arlo, I have to see her tomorrow."

"She'll be cool." At least, I hope she will be.

"But she'll know. Wait . . . does she know you're coming over here to have sex with me?"

Hell.

"Uh, I believe her parting words to me were 'Now go plow her into the wall with your penis.'"

Eyes stunned, she slowly nods as her lips twist to the side. "Great. That's just great."

She starts to move off my lap but there's no way I'm letting my sister ruin this moment.

"Hey, I promise, she'll be cool. We can trust her."

"I know we can trust her. It's just embarrassing."

"Why? Are you embarrassed of me?"

"What?" Her gaze lands on mine. "Of course not." Her hand strokes the stubble on my cheek that I made sure not to shave today. "It's just that she's your sister, my friend—just makes things slightly awkward."

"It's only awkward if you make it awkward. When you see her tomorrow, own it."

"Or I feign sick and you cover for me."

"Or that," I say, wanting this conversation to be over. "I do have something else I want to talk to you about."

"Yeah? What's that?" she asks while undoing the tie on her robe and pushing it off her slender shoulders, revealing a matching light-pink set of lingerie. A lace bra that barely contains her tits and a matching thong that extends high on her hips, giving new definition to curves.

"Fuck, Greer." I reach out and glide my hands down her sides.

"I've never worn this set before and thought you might like it. Do you?" she asks just as my hands round of the globes of her ass.

I pull her in closer and nod. "It's sexy. Hot. Makes me hard."

"If only these clothes weren't in the way." She tugs on my shirt and I allow her to lift it up and over my head. "Oh . . . wow," she says, blinking a few times. "What on earth?" She looks me in the eyes. "I've seen the donuts and cookies you've consumed. Why are you so chiseled?" Her hand roams over my abs and then up to my pecs. "God, Arlo, you're the most fit man I've ever touched."

I can't deny that makes me feel good.

I move my hand over her shoulder, lowering one of the straps so it dangles by her arm. "That's good to know." I lean in and kiss her shoulder. She lifts her head, giving me better access, and I parade my mouth over her collarbone, lightly sucking, while my thumbs draw miniscule circles on her stomach. I dip a little bit lower, biting down on the swell of her breasts, causing her to gasp as I move to the other side.

"Didn't—oh yes, that feels amazing," she groans, pushing one hand through my hair. "But didn't you want to talk about something?"

I move the other strap down so her bra is barely being held up by her breasts.

"I did." I nibble the swell of her other breast.

"And what was it?"

Pulling away, I look her in the eyes and ask, "Is this a relationship? You and me, is that what we're in?"

The corner of her mouth pulls up as she strokes the back of my neck. "It is for me. Is it for you?"

"Yeah." I swallow. "It is. I, uh . . . I take it very seriously."

"I can tell. I like that about you. I like that a lot, actually."

My hand slides up her back to the clasp of her bra and, with one hand, I flick it open. Her bra tumbles between us and I remove it. Carefully, I tilt her back on the bed and then roll over her so I'm straddling her body.

"What else do you like?" I ask, lowering my mouth to her right breast. I start by slowly licking her nipple until it becomes hard under my tongue.

She quivers underneath me and says, "You're loyal. I know I can trust you."

I lick across the valley of her breasts and move to her other nipple, which is already hard, waiting for me.

"What else?"

"You care for your students. You want to see them succeed, despite the scary-teacher front you put on."

I nip at the side of her boob and she yelps but then hums in pleasure.

"Tell me more," I say, moving down her stomach, to the waistband of her thong. I grip the edge with my teeth and tug on it, only to have her stop me and lift my head.

"I love that you love to pleasure me. But it's my turn. Take your pants off, Arlo."

"You don't call the shots here," I say.

"Fine, then will you please allow me to pleasure you . . . Mr. Turner?"

Fuck . . .

When she looks at me like that, says my name in a sultry, throaty voice, I can't deny her anything.

Running my tongue over my teeth, I lift up and unbuckle my jeans. She sits up, her sexy tits swaying, tempting me, as she reaches out and undoes the zipper to my jeans. Without hesitation, she pushes them down and, as I step out of them, I watch her hand to go my erection, trapped by my black boxer briefs.

She scoots to the edge of the bed and strokes me a few times, the feel of her hand on my length a promise of what's to come. I have so much I need to release, so much pent-up frustration and lust for this woman, that I know when the time comes, I won't be able to hold back.

"Condoms are in my wallet," I say, not wanting to fumble around when I'm seconds away from losing my cool.

She reaches to the side, picks my wallet from my pocket, and pulls out the condoms, which she tosses on the bed. Dropping the wallet to the floor, both of her hands fall to my boxer briefs, and I stand there, watching her every detailed move when she slowly lowers my briefs to the floor. My erection springs forward, large and yearning for her.

When she lifts up to look at me, the most satisfying expression falls over her face. Lust. Joy.

"You're so big," she whispers, taking me in her hand. "Arlo, I needed this so bad. I needed you."

With hands like velvet, she slowly pumps me. It's nothing erotic, I can barely feel her, but it's just enough to help me grow even larger. She moves off the bed and says, "Lie down."

I don't move; instead, I lift her chin with my index finger and say, "I'm not coming in your mouth. Do you understand? You can play with my dick for as long as you want, but when I say I'm going to come, I better come inside you."

"I can handle that."

"Good."

I lie down on the bed and watch as Greer steps between my legs and spreads them wider. I place both hands behind my head to prop me up enough to see what she's doing. Moving her hair to one side, she places one hand on my cock, pressing it against my stomach as she tilts her head and brings her mouth to my balls.

Jesus, not what I was expecting, but it feels amazing as her tongue flicks across the sensitive skin.

"Hell, baby," I say, the term of endearment slipping past my lips before I can stop it.

Moving lower, she sucks me into her mouth, her tongue lapping against my sack, causing my eyes to squeeze shut. I take a deep breath. Releasing me, she replays the movement three more times, and when I don't think I can take it anymore, she moves her mouth up the length of my cock, lightly pressing kisses until she gets to the tip, where she licks my precum right before opening her mouth wide and sucking me in . . . all the way . . . until I hit the back of her throat.

"Fu-uck," I say, clenching my jaw when she does it again, this time swallowing at the same time. "Greer, what the . . . ahh, fuck that feels so good." My hips thrust involuntarily into her mouth and I try to control myself, but her mouth is so damn warm. So damn welcoming that I thrust again. It's been so fucking long since I've been given head. And then she does that again.

And again.

And . . . again.

"Greer, I'm going to come."

She removes her mouth quickly like the good girl that she is and lifts up, leaving my cock glistening with her saliva. Standing before me, she keeps her eyes on me as she lowers her thong to the ground and steps out of it.

"I want to feel you," she says, "bare, for just a second, but I want to feel you bare." She climbs on top of me again and spreads herself over my cock.

Her hands fall to my stomach as she sucks in a sharp breath when her clit presses against my length.

"I'm so worked up, Arlo." Her head tosses back and her teeth roll over her bottom lip. "I'm throbbing already. I can feel my orgasm at the base of my spine, ready to explode, just from sucking on your cock."

"Then make yourself come. Ride me."

She moves her hips, gliding along my length from her arousal. She sucks in a sharp breath and sighs as her fingers move up to my pecs, where they dig in, marking the skin as she glides over me, her pelvis moving fast, her body turning flush, her nipples impossibly hard.

I take her in—the sweat on her brow, the way her beautiful, luscious hair sways with her thrusts, the way her tits are pushed together from the position of her hands.

So goddamn sexy.

Easily the sexiest woman I've ever been with.

"Yes, yes," she chants, her grip on me growing tighter and tighter. "Oh, yes, Arlo." Her head falls back, her mouth parts, and her hips skyrocket into overdrive as a long, loud moan falls past her lips.

She comes, humping my cock, the act so erotic, so satisfying, that I need to be inside her . . . now.

I roll her to the side while she catches her breath, find the condoms, and quickly sheath myself.

"Are you ready for me?"

Her legs fall open and her head tilts to the side. "Please, I want you inside me now."

Restraint gone, I brace myself at her hips, and I position my cock at her entrance. Slowly, I insert myself, letting her adjust inch by inch until I'm fully inside her. Then I pause.

Her eyes find mine, our expressions connect, and an unspoken knowledge transpires between us.

We fit perfectly.

She was made for me.

I was made for her.

Swallowing hard, trying not to sound desperate, I keep my eyes trained on hers when I honestly say, "It's never felt like this."

She licks her lips. "Not for me, either."

"It's never been this warm, this tight, this . . . perfect. Fuck, you're perfect, Greer."

"I don't want you to move, not yet." Her hand comes up to the back of my head and she brings my mouth down to hers. "I just want to feel you inside me. Just for a few seconds."

"Anything you want," I say, desperation to be closer to this woman consuming me. "Anything you goddamn want, Greer." I press my mouth against hers and we spend the next few minutes exploring each other's mouths while we stay connected in the most intimate way possible.

Coming over here tonight, I never expected to feel this overpowering sense to claim her like this. To mark her as mine and no one else's. But as I lie here, cock deep inside of her, I know for damn sure I'm not letting go.

She's mine.

Her tongue dances with mine, twirling and seductively twisting. It doesn't feel like enough. I don't feel like I can get closer but I need to.

"More," I whisper, dragging my mouth to her cheek and down her neck. "I need more, Greer."

"Me too," she says, arching her back when I cup her breast. I pull my hips back and then quickly thrust into her. "Oh God," she moans, her body tensing against mine. "Again."

"You okay?"

"Perfect. More, Arlo."

I drag my tongue up her neck and then thrust again, this time harder, the feeling so delicious that it sends a shockwave through my groin, unleashing the inner beast inside of me. Everything around us fades, and I'm pulsing so fast that I can barely catch my breath.

"Jesus," I say heavily, my legs starting to turn numb. "Greer, it's so fucking good."

"Yes," she whispers, only for her voice to grow louder and

louder with every thrust. "Yes, Arlo, yes. Oh my God, Arlo . . . I'm . . . ahhh." She tenses under me as she cries out in pleasure, her pussy clenching my cock so hard that it almost feels unbearably difficult to keep thrusting.

She convulses beneath me and I ride out her orgasm, pushing harder and harder, my own pleasure taking over as I fall into a numbing abyss.

"Oh shit . . . ahhh, fuck, Greer." My balls tighten, pressure builds in my spine, I bite down on her shoulder, and I come.

My orgasm rips through me like a blazing fire, burning up every nerve ending, blacking out my vision, and sending me into another world as I come over and over again inside her.

"Mother . . . fucker," I breathe out heavily, only to collapse on top of her.

Greer's arms wrap around me and she holds me tight, her hand caressing my back.

Her lips find the side of my cheek, then my cheekbone, then my lips, where I kiss her back. Fierce, claiming her all over again, showing her now through my affection what this means to me. How important this moment is.

"Greer," I say in between kisses and trying to catch my breath.

"Yes?"

"I don't think I can leave, even if you kicked me out."

"Good, I was planning on you staying. I even bought you a toothbrush."

I lift up. "Really?"

She smiles up at me. "Really."

I stroke her cheek softly with the backs of my fingers. "You're so beautiful, just like this, freshly fucked, no makeup, marked as mine . . . so damn beautiful."

"Yours?"

"All mine."

"I like that sound of that, Mr. Turner."

Growling, I dip my mouth against her neck and get ready for round two.

—◼—

"HOW DO YOU FEEL?" I ask. Greer is between my legs, against my chest as I lean against the headboard. I have my arms around her and she's wearing my shirt. We just spent the last four hours fucking.

Slow.

Hard.

We watched each other masturbate. I came before her, and I don't even fucking care. I couldn't hold back, not after seeing her like that, legs spread, her hand doing all the work.

We even fucked on her dining room table, which resulted in breaking it. I promised to buy her a new one.

"Exhausted and full."

After we caught our breath, we ordered some subs, and while we waited, we took a shower and she gave me the best head of my entire life, only for me to return the favor while she was trying to dry off.

Because . . . because it was Greer. *Spectacular, bewitching Greer.*

"What about you?" she asks.

"Tired."

"Want to go to sleep?"

"Not quite yet," I say, even though I yawn. "What do you want for breakfast tomorrow morning?"

"Besides your cock?"

I chuckle. "Besides that."

"Hmm, someplace that's going to deliver."

"Frankie Donuts delivers now."

"Really?" she asks, her voice rising in interest, but the rest of her body's relaxed, completely sated.

"Yeah. Maybe we order a breakfast sandwich, split that and get some donuts?"

"Sounds like a plan." She yawns as well and then turns in my embrace so she's cuddled into me. "Tonight was perfect, Arlo."

"Better than the boat?" I tease.

She kisses my chest. "The boat was the foreplay. But this, this was intimate and just what I needed with you. I needed to make sure you were in this—"

"Hey, I told you I was," I say, lifting her chin and placing a soft kiss on her lips.

"I know, but you were so hot and cold before, so when you changed your mind, it felt like a one-eighty, one that was too good to be true."

"It's not. It's real. I keep checking to make sure it is."

"Did you ever think we'd get to this place, after our first interaction?"

I sift my fingers through her hair as I talk quietly. "Honestly, no. I was attracted to you right away, but your classroom jam sessions really drove me nuts, especially on the first day, when I establish dominance."

"Oh my God, listen to yourself. Establish dominance. These are high schoolers."

"High schoolers that need rules. If not, you lose control of the classroom."

"I haven't lost control." I can feel her tense up, and I don't want to get into a fight about this.

"How about we leave our teaching techniques out of conversation."

She presses up on my chest to look me in the eyes. "We can have a mature conversation about teaching, Arlo. We don't have to shove our differences under a rug."

"I understand that, but I just had one hell of a night with you. The last thing I want to do is talk teaching techniques, especially since we're polar opposites in our style." I rub my thumb over her cheek. "Please, I want to enjoy this quiet time with you."

She places her hand on mine. "Okay. Sorry."

"Don't apologize." I bring my hand back to her hair when she lies down on my chest. "Now tell me a story about your childhood."

"What kind of story?"

"Any kind," I say. "I just want to listen."

For my heart is finally open to hearing someone else's voice.

Chapter Twenty-Four

GREER

"Well, well, well, if it isn't the girl who's boinking my brother."

And Arlo said she'd be cool. I shouldn't have trusted that for a second.

"Cora, please—"

"I'm just messing with you." She brings me into a big hug. "I could not be more excited for you two." Taking me by the hand, she pulls me into Arlo's house and straight to the kitchen, where Arlo is cutting up vegetables. He's wearing simple jeans and a T-shirt. But instead of his hair being styled, he's sporting a Bobbies baseball cap and, for some reason, seeing him in a hat, so casual, makes my stomach flutter.

"Your girl is here," Cora announces.

Arlo's eyes shoot up and connect with mine. The corner of his lips turn up and he sets the knife down to round the kitchen island. Stepping up to me, he lifts my chin and presses a very soft kiss across my lips.

"Oh God, that's so sweet and disgusting at the same time."

"Is anyone else here?" I ask in a panic.

"No, you're the first," he says softly, before returning to the vegetables.

"So, what's the plan?" Cora asks, tossing an orange around. "Are we announcing to everyone? We can throw together a song and dance that introduces you guys. Won't take us more than five minutes. Might be fun."

Arlo eyes me as he says, "We won't be announcing anything."

"But you just kissed her in front of me."

"Because you know. That doesn't mean we're about to tell everyone else."

"So, it really is a secret? Well, then." She rubs her hands together. "I'm ready to hold this in the vault, but I'd like to be compensated at some point for my valiant efforts."

"I think you staying here is compensation enough."

"No way." She stabs the kitchen island with her finger. "I have squatter's rights because I'm your sister. You can't use housing as a bartering technique. Try again."

"She has a point," I say, earning a brow raise from Arlo.

"Okay, how about all the cookies I've bought for you, or the calzones you need to have every Friday night?"

"Squatter's rights. You have to feed the squatter."

"I really don't," Arlo says, chuckling before he sets down the knife again. "Am I going to have to buy you something sparkly?"

"I believe that would be the proper payment at this point."

"Fine."

Clapping, Cora turns to me and says, "And that's how you wear him down. Take note for future reference."

"Trust me, she can wear me down a lot faster than that," Arlo mumbles while putting the vegetables on the plate.

"Oh, I think he's talking about sex. Gross." Cora comes up to me and gives me a hug. "I really am happy for you two.

And be warned. He can be an idiot, so when he fucks up—because he will—be sure to hear him out."

"Thanks, Coraline." Arlo rolls his eyes.

"Anytime. I'm going to go change."

"You're actually going to put on clothes?" Arlo asks with a smirk.

"Don't be an ass, I have a secret of yours," Cora calls out while going up the stairs.

"I can see her using that a lot." After he washes his hands and sets the cutting board and the knife in the sink, he leans against the counter and beckons me with his finger.

I waste no time. When I reach him, he lazily drapes his hands on my hips and leans down for a kiss. I reach up, cupping his cheeks, and give him what he wants.

"How are you feeling?" he whispers.

"A little sore," I say, tugging on the brim of his hat.

"Just a little?"

I chuckle. "Maybe a lot sore."

"Hell, I'm sorry." He draws his hands up and down my back. "I should have taken it easy this morning."

"I particularly liked how hard you were." I wink.

"Your poor neighbors."

I shrug. "Don't know them, don't care." I lift up on my toes and kiss his jaw. "When are we going out again? I'm starting to become addicted to our dates."

"Me too. And whenever you want. I can plan something for Wednesday again."

I rub my hands over his pecs, remembering just how thick and strong they are. His entire body looks like it's chiseled from stone. While wearing his cardigans, you can see that the man is fit, but I never would have dreamed how fit he actually is. I pawed at him every chance I got last night and this morning, hence why I'm so sore. It wasn't really him being greedy; it was me. I wanted more and more of him, and the more I got, the more it set off my need. It's grown so deep that even though it hurts to walk, I want to take him back to his office and let him have his way with me.

"What are you thinking about?"

"Huh?" I ask, smiling up at him.

He squeezes me tight and presses a kiss to my forehead while laughing. "I think you're hornier than me."

"That would be accurate," I say.

"If you weren't so sore, I'd take you up to my bedroom right now."

"Really? If that's the case, I'm not sore at all. I was just playing around."

He laughs into my ear and whispers, "Nice try, babe."

The doorbell rings, and I say, resting my head against his chest, "This is going to be painful."

"Want me to come over tonight?" he asks, surprising me. When I glance up at him, he adds, "Strictly to make out, maybe some over-the-clothes touching, nothing more."

I chuckle. "There better be more, and I'd love that. Think Cora will be fine?"

"Yes, she's a big girl who is blackmailing me. I'm going to take advantage of it as much as possible."

He presses one more kiss to my lips and then walks to the entryway. Infatuated, I watch his backside retreat, remembering how glorious that backside is naked. So many images are floating through my head from last night.

Arlo standing before me, his cock hard as stone, waiting for my mouth.

Arlo in the shower, washing my hair gently, taking his time, growing hard in my hand as he soaps up my breasts.

Arlo in a pair of jeans and nothing else, grabbing our breakfast delivery from the door and then serving me on my bed because we busted my table.

Arlo—

"Are you okay?" I blink a few times and catch Stella, Romeo, and Gunner all staring at me. Arlo is behind them, chuckling to himself. "You were literally just mumbling something about sexy pecs."

Dear Jesus, was I?

"And I think there's drool in the corner of her mouth," Romeo points out.

"And I hate to be that person," Stella continues, "but your nipples are incredibly hard."

Every eye in the kitchen falls to my nipples that, in fact, are very hard.

Looking back at them, and then at Arlo, and then at them again, I laugh awkwardly and say, "Uh, I was, uh, thinking about"—I clear my throat—"well, you know how . . . uh, cucumbers can be very—" I clear my throat again. "Woo, is it dry in here? It's dry, I think. Anyone else need a drink?" I wave my hand in front of my face.

"What's happening with you?" Stella asks. "You're turning red."

"Am I? Maybe I have a rash." I cup my hand over my mouth and pretend to shout, "Call the ambulance, this girl's on fire."

Arlo snorts, while the others look at me as if I've lost it.

"Menopause," I say, lips thinned, nodding my head. "I've hit menopause. At such a young age, too. These eggs are all fried up," I say, motioning to my ovaries. When they stare blankly, I keep talking. "Not really, I can still offer up kin— God, that feels like something Keeks would say." I press my hand against my forehead, then quickly remove it and rub my hand against my shirt. "Oof, that's clammy. Anyone else a little clammy? Just me? Yeah . . ." I swallow hard. "Just me. So . . . anyone ready to play badminton?"

No one answers. They just stare. Their eyes questioning me. Their facial expressions confused . . .

"Are you okay?"

"Fine, just beat it out of me, won't you? Yes, the rumors are true."

"What rumors?" Stella asks.

"Uh . . . Greer," Arlo says, taking a step forward.

"Arlo and I are seeing each other. Are you happy? God, stop badgering me." I throw my arms up in the air and then sink against the counter.

They all turn to Arlo, who is standing there in shock.

A moment of silence falls over us.

Then Gunner says, "Son of a bitch."

"Ha, I fucking told you." Romeo holds his hands out to Stella and Gunner. "Pay up, bitches."

Gunner digs into his wallet, shaking his head, while Stella rifles through her purse. "I can't believe you were right," Gunner mumbles, slapping a twenty into Romeo's hand.

"This is your fault he's right," Stella says to me while she retrieves a twenty. "You shouldn't be taking money from a poor schoolteacher. It's tacky," she says to Romeo.

"I'm a schoolteacher too."

"Who used to play professional baseball and make a lot of money."

"Pfft, for a few years."

"Doesn't matter." Stella pushes at his chest and then flops her purse on the kitchen island. "Honestly, you two couldn't have kept it in your pants?" She points to Arlo now. "You owe me twenty dollars."

Cora comes barreling down the stairs, a giant smile on her face. "Hey, everyone. What's new? Anything happen this past week—"

"Greer and Arlo are together," Romeo says, fanning his face with his two twenty-dollar bills.

"What?" Cora snaps. "I thought I was the only one who knew. Does this mean I don't get something sparkly?"

"Nope," Arlo says with a grin.

"Noooooo."

"Looks like you're ruining everyone's day," Stella says before coming up to me and giving me a hug. "Don't let him push you around, you hear me?" She speaks loud enough for everyone to hear. "I know the cardigans do wicked things to your private parts, but be strong."

"Don't worry, she's already got me wrapped around her pinky," Arlo says, coming up to me and placing a kiss on the side of my head.

All our friends stare at us, bewildered, possibly confused.

"Uh . . . that's going to take me a second to get used to," Gunner says.

"Yeah," Romeo draws out. "I know I called it, but it still feels weird."

"I'm not ready for this." Stella shakes her head. "Nope, I'm going to need a second."

They all file outside, one right after the other.

Cora trails behind and, before she's out the door, she says, "I'm okay with the kissing. Does that get me something sparkly?"

"Get out of here." Arlo laughs.

She shuts the door behind her, leaving me alone with Arlo. I turn toward him and nervously ask, "Are you mad?"

"No." He strokes my shoulders. "Surprised, but not angry."

"I'm sorry, they were staring at me—"

"Because you were acting crazy."

"Because they were staring. Anyway, it felt like they could see right through me and it freaked me out, and before I knew what was happening, I was spilling the beans. I'm sorry."

"It's fine. I'm just glad it wasn't me." He presses a kiss to my lips. "But we should probably tell them not to say anything at school."

"You're right." I sigh and rest my forehead against his chest. "You realize you're going to have to get them all something sparkly."

"I know."

"SO, care to tell me how this happened?" Stella asks while taking a seat, balancing her full plate.

"Yes, I'd like the details as well," Cora says, sitting down. "Minus all the sex stuff."

"You don't know the details?" Stella asks.

"No, I found out last night, when my brother was trying to be very sneaky. Newsflash—he isn't. Oh, I do know Greer calls him Mr. Turns Me On."

Stella chuckles. "Almost every female faculty member does."

"Ew, gross. My brother is not a sex symbol."

I beg to differ.

"So . . . tell us," Stella says.

"Make way," Romeo says squeezing his way in with his plate and drink.

"No." Stella kicks away the chair he's about to sit in. "We're having girl talk. You boys sit over there and strategize our badminton game."

"I want to be a part of girl talk," Romeo complains.

"Well, then grow a vagina," Stella snaps back and then turns to us with a smile. "You were saying?"

"Uh . . . is everything okay between the two of you?"

"Fine. He's just being a nuisance, and I don't have time for that." She looks over her shoulder and shoos Romeo away. "Go on, go over there. That's right, keep moving along. Good boy."

"Do I get a treat for listening?" he calls out.

"Yes, you've avoided a kick to the crotch. Congratulations." Clearing her throat, she picks up her burger and takes a bite. Talking around her mouthful, she says, "Go on, details."

Gunner and Arlo take a seat with Romeo, and before Arlo sits down, he winks at me. That man is going to be the death of me.

"Well, honestly, it started as more of a sexual thing."

"La la la la la la la," Cora says, covering her ears. "I don't want to hear about the sex."

I remove her hands and say, "I'm not going to talk about the sex, I'm just stating, that's how it started. And when it started to get, uh, a little out of control—"

"Jesus, Mary, and Joseph," Cora mutters.

"I asked him where this was all going."

"Oh, famous last words of an enemies-with-benefits arrangement."

"Pretty much. That comment put a halt on everything."

"Ugh." Cora rolls her eyes. "What a dick." Shouting over to the boys, she says, "Arlo, you're a dick."

Arlo raises a brow in my direction, so I shake my head and mouth, "Don't worry."

"Wait, did the halt happen right before you went on a date with Walker?"

"Gah, good point," Cora says, excited. "Did it? Did you make my brother jealous?"

"He didn't like it. At all. And I think it helped him realize that maybe he'd like to give things a chance. That, and some deep conversation he had with you, Cora."

She slaps the table. "I knew he owed me for something. Sparkly item, here I come." She rubs her hands together. "So, he pulled it together, and then what?"

I smile. "Well, at homecoming, I saw a side of him I'd never seen before. It warmed me toward him, and then he and I sat in the back of his trunk afterward with cookies and drinks and talked."

"Crumbl cookies?" Stella asks.

I nod.

"Oh, he got you good. Hard to say no to those."

"That, and his charm. And then he wrote me notes,

wooed me with a date Wednesday night on a boat, and I've been gone ever since then."

"A boat date? God, where do I find myself an Arlo?" Stella asks.

"Romeo is quite the catch," I say with a cheeky grin.

"Brock is a moron."

"Hey, I heard that," Romeo calls out.

Stella turns in her chair. "That's because I said it loud enough so you could hear it."

"You're ripe today."

Oh boy.

Stella's eyes turn into flames. "Go ahead. Call me ripe one more time. See where it gets you."

"Dude, I wouldn't call her ripe," Gunner says out the side of his mouth. "She looks terrifying."

"Are you sure you're okay?" I ask her.

"Fine." She takes a deep breath. "Well, how exciting. Does this mean Walker is available?"

Keeping my voice low to spare Romeo's feelings, since I feel like something is going on there, I say, "He's actually caught up on someone else."

"Son of a bitch," Stella says under her breath.

"Bet you Romeo would take you out on a date," Cora says, loud enough for the boys.

"Over my dead body," Romeo shouts.

And for some reason, I don't believe him.

Chapter Twenty-Five

ARLO

"Look me in the eyes," I demand as I drive into Greer. "Do not close them. I want to watch you come."

"Oh God," she screams, gripping the headboard behind her. "Oh my God, Arlo."

"How close?"

"Right . . . now," she says. Her hips convulse and her mouth falls open, a silent scream causing my orgasm to rip through my body.

"Ah, fuck," I grunt, spilling into her, my hips stilling as she continues to move hers.

Together, panting, we melt into the mattress, me partially collapsing on top of her.

It's been two weeks since our date, and I still look for more and more every night when it comes to this girl. She's only spent one night at my house—as she doesn't want to make Cora uncomfortable—because she *can't* keep her voice down while I fuck her. And the rest of the nights, we've either Face-Timed or I've spent the night at her place.

We spend lunches together.

We walk into school together.

And the weekends, so far, we've spent together.

And I don't have one goddamn complaint.

In a few short weeks, this woman has not only consumed my thoughts, but she's made me think about a different future. One with daily intimacy. No secrets. *No loneliness.*

"God." She laughs and breathes heavily. "I think I blacked out for a second." She turns her head toward me. "I can't feel my legs."

"Same," I say, breathlessly. "Come here." I pull her in close, loving the lavender scent of her hair.

"I told my parents about you."

"Did you?"

"I did."

"What did they say?"

"That they want to meet you." She presses a kiss to my chest. "They asked if you might want to visit for Thanksgiving."

I drag my fingers up and down her arm. "Are you . . . asking me to go home with you for the holidays?"

"Don't tease me."

Chuckling, I pull away just enough to be able to look her in the eyes. I should be terrified. Family events, Thanksgiving and Christmas in particular, were not *fun* times in the Turner household.

So, I *should* be terrified. Greer's family, however, sound warm, inviting, *generous* with love, and accepting. And somehow, through Greer's efforts, I might be a recipient of their affection too. My reward, though, is seeing Greer's face right now.

She wants me there. She wants me to know her family. I caress her soft cheek, lean in close, and say, "Not teasing. I'd like to meet them, babe."

"Seriously?"

I nod. "Yeah. I'd have to make sure Coraline has some-where to go first—"

"She can come. The more the merrier. We can do a road trip."

"Or we can fly first class. A road trip with my sister doesn't sound appealing, no matter how much I love her." She laughs, and I say, "You know, that's a few weeks away."

"I know. Is that okay?"

"Yeah. Just making sure you're okay with attaching your-self to me for that long."

"I don't think I have a choice in the matter. You seem to have dug your arrogant claws into me."

"Damn right." I roll her to her back and hover over her, a large smile on my face. "If you get Thanksgiving, does that mean I get Christmas? Because I can go all-out for the holi-day. I've kept all my grandparents' decorations. We can have a Christmas for all our friends who might not be going home."

"That sounds like so much fun."

"But most importantly, it'll be Christmas with you."

Her hand falls behind my neck and pulls me down to her mouth. "Then it'll be the best Christmas ever."

⊏⊐

"SHOT. EVERYONE TAKE A SHOT," Gunner calls out, lifting a tiny glass.

I suck down the tequila and watch as my girl cringes after setting her glass down.

"I don't think I can do one more," she says. "Oh, dear lord, the burn. How many strikeouts does a team normally get?"

"Anderson is on fire," Stella says, eyes trained on one of many TVs in the back room of the bar.

"Someone call the fire department," Keiko yells right before falling off her stool.

"Jesus," I say, bending down to help her up.

"Maybe we shouldn't be taking a shot for every strikeout," Greer says, swaying next to me.

Holding her finger to the sky, Keiko says, "The probability of predicting thirty-seven strikeouts during one athletic event is one in—*hiccup*—two hundred, trillion billion, ten."

"It's been eleven strikeouts," Stella corrects her. "How many shots have you taken?"

"According to the level of bile that's starting to rise, I'd surmise measurably fifty-two, but can't quite be certain without the proper data analysis of blood alcohol levels."

"If you had fifty-two shots, you'd be dead," Greer says.

"Well, intoxication manifests double vision. Perhaps it doubles one's counting competence."

Talking quietly to Greer, I say, "I think she's one step to the right from puking. We should get Kelvin."

"Kelvin is currently outside, parked in his automobile, waiting for the barf signal." Keiko chuckles. "I mean bat signal."

"Why is he waiting outside? He could join us," Greer says.

"I suggested he not observe me in such a rowdy state of mind." Keiko flops against my arm and clings on. "But perhaps it is time. Bring in the well-proportioned man I call boyfriend. I need his gallant steed to take me home and then ravish my breasts."

"Keep it in your pants," Stella says, right before cheering with the rest of the bar.

"I'll take her," Gunner says. "Lindsay is almost here and I'm going to meet her outside."

"What a modern man," Keiko says, right before kissing my arm and throwing herself at Gunner.

Brow furrowed, he awkwardly walks her through the bar and to the exit.

"I hope she's okay," I say as Greer picks up her water and takes a long sip.

When she sets the glass down, she looks up at me and says, "I'm going to tell you right now, you look incredibly sexy tonight. That's not the booze talking. And I love the way you're holding my hand, and how you spoiled me all week with notes, and our date on Wednesday that seems to be a tradition now for us, and I wore this really slutty bra and underwear set for you tonight, but if I take one more shot, you're never going to see it." *Fuck that. Sexy lingerie and Greer?*

"So, some fresh air then?" I suggest.

She nods.

I take her hand and walk her out of the bar to sit on a bench, where we find Gunner.

"Everything okay?" he asks.

"Just need some air," I say.

"Yeah, Lindsay isn't coming for another ten minutes, but I wanted to sober up a bit before she got here." He holds up a glass of water.

"Smart." Greer sighs against me. "How are things with Lindsay?"

"Great. We told Dylan the other day that I'm his dad."

"Really?" I ask. "How did he take it?"

"Really fucking well. He was excited. Confused a little at first, but then excited. I want to ask Lindsay to move in with me, but not tonight. I want to do something special."

"I get that. It'll mean more if you're not buzzed."

"What about you two?" Gunner asks. "You seem really happy."

"We are," I say. "Right?"

"Hate him, actually," Greer says, using my chest as a pillow. "Can't stand the man. Blech, gross."

"Yeah, really looks like that." Gunner laughs. "How

serious are you guys? Exclusive? Boyfriend, girlfriend? Ready to propose?"

"Are you ready to propose?" I ask Gunner.

"Hell, yeah. I was ready to propose a month ago."

"Well, we're not there yet," Greer says, lifting up and kissing my jaw. "But I think we're headed that way. I sure know more about him than I ever thought I would. Did you know he used to wet the bed up until he was eight?"

"Hey," I snap.

Greer giggles. "Oops, sorry, that must be the alcohol."

"Dude, eight years old? Tough break."

"I blame the lack of parenting in my household."

"My poor bed-peeing boyfriend." Greer taps my cheek, and I turn and nip at her hand. She giggles against me and wraps her arms around my waist. "Gah, I love you."

I go still.

She goes still.

Gunner's head whips around.

"I mean . . ." she stammers. "I love . . . uh . . . you-o-da. I love Yoda."

"Smooth," Gunner mutters.

"Oh God." Greer lifts away from me and puts her face in her hands. "I didn't mean to say that."

"You didn't?" I ask, feeling like I just swallowed my own heartbeat, my throat thick, my emotions bubbling up inside me. She loves me?

That's . . . hell, that's terrifying but also exhilarating.

"I, uh—"

"Oh, this is uncomfortable," Gunner says, and I box him out with my body, forcing Greer to look at me.

"Hey." I cup her cheek and smooth my thumb over her soft skin. "I love you too."

Her eyes widen, and Gunner claps behind me. "Dude, that's—"

"Shut the fuck up, man."

"Yup, gotcha."

"You do?" Greer asks, shocked, elated.

I nod. "I really fucking do."

A gorgeous smile spreads across her face. "I love you, Arlo. I really fucking do."

"And this isn't the alcohol talking?"

She shakes her head. "No, it's not."

"Me neither."

We stare at each other, both smiling, both realizing this is monumental.

"Christ, would you two just kiss already?" Gunner asks.

I bring her lips to mine, opening my mouth, claiming her, just as we hear a very loud "WOOOHOOO" in the parking lot.

We all look up to see a streak of nylon blow by us. Keiko, wearing nothing but a pair of pantyhose and an ironclad bra, streaks by, arms flailing in the air, screaming at the top of her lungs . . . and poor Kelvin chasing behind her with a blouse and plaid skirt in hand.

"This just became the best night of my life." Greer laughs.

Mine fucking too.

"YOU KNOW, I wasn't even a super fan of the Bobbies, but even I feel let down that they didn't win the World Series," Cora says as she hops up onto one of the chairs at the kitchen island.

"Stella is devastated. She called in sick today," Greer says as she helps me make dinner. She's cutting up the veggies for the salad while I shred the chicken from the Instant Pot.

"Really? Man, she must have taken it really hard then."

"Harder than the guys," Greer answers. "It's going to burn her for a bit, but I'm sure she'll get over it."

"Not sure that's ever something you get over," I say,

bumping my shoulder against Greer's. She looks up at me and smiles.

"God, you two are sickeningly cute. I never thought I'd be jealous of my brother, but I kind of am. And before you ask me if I'm okay because I'm getting a divorce—I know you, Arlo—I'm fine. I've really grown to not hate people in successful relationships."

"Growth is important," I say.

"Which is why I need to point out how Greer never stays here. You two said the big *L* word, so why don't you ever stay here?"

Smirking, I say, "Greer moans loudly, and she doesn't want you hearing her." I barely finish my sentence as Greer elbows me in the stomach, causing me to laugh.

"Arlo, things you don't tell your sister."

"It's the truth, and any lie, I'm sure, wouldn't have passed with her."

"He's right," Coraline says, looking at her freshly manicured nails, something she spent a good hour doing last night. I know this because she was doing Greer's nails, as well. "But the moaning thing, now that I believe. You look like a moaner."

"Uh, thank you?" Greer asks.

"You're welcome," Coraline says, now placing both her hands on the counter. "Which brings me to my suggestion."

"Suggestion?"

"Yes, I've been doing some thinking—"

"Never a good thing," I mutter.

"Uh, excuse me, I was talking," Coraline snaps at me. Clearing her throat, she continues, "I've been doing some thinking. Since I got a job—"

"What?" Greer and I say at the same time.

"Ugh, yes, I got a job, nothing to get all huffy about."

"Where did you get a job?"

"At Frankie Donuts."

"WHAT?" Greer shouts and drops the knife. "You got a job at Frankie Donuts? How?"

"It's kind of funny," Coraline says. "I got a box the other day and brought them to my marriage counselor. I took a bunch of pictures and posted them on my Instagram. Kind of like a twelve days of donuts thing and an added bonus, because baker's dozen and everything. Anyway, I tagged Frankie Donuts and they reached out to me, asking if they could use my pictures. I said yes but demanded they meet with me first because I had a thing or two to say about their lackluster Instagram page. Well, I met with the owner, ripped him a new one for missing the mark, and showed him exactly what he should be doing. The guy said if I could turn his Instagram around in two weeks and gain five thousand more followers, he'd hire me."

"And you did?" Greer asks.

"Uh, yeah, his challenge was a joke. I set up a donut photo studio in my room and I've been slaying it. Gained over six thousand followers. And I was hired. So, yeah, I have a job now. I'm also working on branding and customer service, other boring things like that, but, yup, I've got myself a minimum-wage job. I'm excited about it. Anyway, what I was trying to say before you interrupted me is that maybe I should move into Greer's place."

My brow furrows. "She has a studio apartment. Why would you do that?"

Coraline's brow pinches. "Mother of our Lord, guide me." She exhales loudly and says, "Greer would move in here . . . with you. Then you two would have all the loud sex you want."

"Oh, I . . . I don't know how Greer would feel—"

"I love the idea," Greer says. "I mean, if you want your girlfriend to live with you." Greer winces, looking up at me.

Hell.

Smiling, I say, "I would fucking love it if you lived here."

"Yeah?" she asks.

"Yeah."

"God, look at me, advancing a relationship. Looks like you owe me another sparkling item. And if Greer plays her cards right, she might be getting a sparkling item in the near future."

Yup.

She very well might . . .

━━

"HEY, WHERE ARE YOU GOING?" I ask Greer as she power-walks down the hallway.

"Principal Dewitt forgot to schedule an appointment with me. Last minute."

"Okay, I was just checking to see if I was still coming over to help you pack tonight."

"Yeah, sure. I'll order pizza," she quickly says.

"Okay. Coraline was going to come over as well."

"I'll order five pizzas then."

"Five?" I chuckle.

She sighs and pauses, hand to forehead. "Two, I meant two."

"I think one would be fine."

"You know I like leftovers."

True, her life revolves around leftovers.

"Okay, two. But I can order and pay for it."

"No, I got it, you're helping me." She looks over my shoulder and bites her bottom lip.

"Everything okay?" I ask.

"Just nervous." She shakes out her arms. "It's never fun being called in to the principal's office."

I chuckle. "But you're not a student, you realize that, right?"

"I know."

Since it's after school hours, I pull her into a hug and kiss the top of her head. "I'm sure it's nothing serious. Just think, after your meeting, we'll pack you up, and then this weekend, you move in."

I feel her smile against my chest. "Are you sure you want me to invade your space?"

"I already made room in my cardigan closet."

She chuckles. "Okay, I feel less stressed. Thank you." She checks her watch. "I really need to go."

"Whatever it is, I'm sure it'll be okay." I press a kiss to her lips.

"Stella said the same thing." She steps away. "She said her first-year mid-semester evaluation was fine."

Mid-semester evaluation . . .

"I'll see you at my place." She blows me a kiss.

Oh shit.

Oh SHIT!

"Greer, wait."

"I can't. I'm going to be late." She waves to me over her shoulder as she walks quickly down the hall to the office. "Tell me at my place."

"Wait, Greer."

She disappears into the office and my hands quickly go to my hair.

"Fuck." I pace. "Fuck!" I can't believe I fucking forgot. I need to . . . hell . . .

I take off at a run to the office and fling the door open, startling Joanna, the receptionist.

"Arlo, are you okay?"

"Where's Greer?" I look around frantically.

"Meeting with Nyema. They're not to be disturbed."

"Fuck," I mutter and then go up to her desk. "Joanna, I need to talk to her."

"Is it an emergency?"

"Uh . . ."

"If it's not an emergency, then you're going to have to wait."

"Please, Joanna."

"I'm sorry, Arlo. But you're welcome to sit there and wait for her."

I pull on my hair and stare down the hallway that leads to Nyema's office. There's no stopping it. She's going to know. And all I can do is wait and apologize my ass off the minute she comes out of that office.

Anxiety climbs up my spine as I take a seat. My leg bounces beneath me, my teeth practically nibbling a hole in my lip, and I fidget as I wait . . .

And wait.

And wait.

Chapter Twenty-Six

GREER

"Greer, thank you for coming in on such short notice."

"Not a problem." I take a seat across from her and place my hands in my lap, trying not to sweat. After this, fun with Arlo. Packing with Arlo . . . living with Arlo.

"I was waiting to hear back from the school board. One of them was on vacation, so it took a little longer."

I shift uncomfortably. "Oh, I didn't know the evaluations are sent to the school board."

"Forest Heights has its own set of rules, very different than other schools. We hold ourselves at a higher standard, and because of that, we have a multi-layered process."

"Understandable. The prestige associated with working at one of the best public schools in the country is why I felt so grateful I got this job."

"Yes. Before we start, I'd like to say, even though the volleyball team didn't go to State, we still were very impressed with the quick improvement you and Miss Garcia made."

Why does this feel like she's trying to butter me up before throwing a dagger at my heart?

"Thank you. It's been a pleasure working with the girls and Stella. I have confidence we'll reach State next year." *Hoping there is a next year.*

"Yes, well." She places her hands on her desk and takes a deep breath. "As you're aware, when evaluating our new teachers, we take everything into consideration. Comradery with the faculty, teaching techniques, syllabus, even the papers you grade. We like to make sure our teachers aren't just goofing around in class, but providing a brilliant education."

Oh God. I swallow hard. "Yes, I understand that."

"You aren't just evaluated by me and the board, but also by your peers."

"Okay." I nod.

She opens a file on her desk and glances over it. "Overall, your scores varied. Some good, one critical."

"Oh. Well, I'd love to hear all the feedback. I'm always open to constructive criticism."

"We'll start with the good. It seems like your students are understanding the curriculum well. The papers we went over have been exceptional, your comments and feedback insight-ful, and very well-thought-out."

"Thank you. I've loved working with the kids here. They're bright and willing to learn—well, most of them." I chuckle.

Nyema smiles. "There are always a few that push you to try harder to get through to them. But overall, we were pleased with their ability to retain the information. Comradery amongst co-workers is fair. Quite a few faculty members enjoy the fresh personality in the English depart-ment, but there were a few who thought that maybe you were coming on too strong and trying to cause a rift among teachers."

"Oh, goodness, no. That's not been my intention at all."

Nyema holds up her hand. "I understand your eagerness to add value to teaching. Dressing up as a literary character was one of my favorite days of the school year so far."

"Thank you." *Deep breaths. Let her speak. Don't be so defensive, it'll get you nowhere.*

"But the way it came about rubbed some people the wrong way."

"Yes, I don't believe I handled that too well. I apologize, it won't happen again."

She nods and stares at her paper. She runs her hand over her forehead and studies what's in front of her in detail.

My heart sinks.

This entire conversation feels like there's a giant, life-changing *but* at the end of it.

"One teacher in particular has had an issue with your performance."

My back grows stiff.

"I'm honestly surprised with the evaluation they turned in, but I value their honesty."

Oh my God . . .

"They were quite vocal about the way you teach the material. Unorthodox methods that didn't seem to settle well with the school board. Yes, the methods have proven to help the students understand the material, but the methods also don't provide the students a chance to interpret the literature properly, but rather lean on alternative devices to drive home the details. Some of the examples that were brought up were use of movies and CliffsNotes."

I twist my hands together. "Some students need that extra visualization to help them understand."

"I can see how showing a movie that corresponds with the book is relevant, but this teacher is particularly adamant about the nuisance it has caused for classrooms around you."

My heart stutters to a stop.

My breath escapes me.

And every happy feeling drains from my body and pools around the legs of my chair.

She doesn't have to say who this teacher is.

The complaints—I've heard them before. They've all come from the man who loves me, or who I thought loves me.

"You can just say Arlo. I know it's him."

She sighs. "Unfortunately, that's what it has come down to, which surprises me. I've heard through the grapevine that you're a couple, which isn't against school policy, so please know what I'm about to say has nothing to do with that."

What is she about to say?

"But the school board values his opinion greatly. Arlo Turner is one of the top reasons why we're a public school with the highest graduating percentage."

I grind my teeth together to keep them from chattering.

"He's a great teacher."

"And like I said, knowing there's a romantic relationship between you two makes this rather uncomfortable, but I have to give him credit for being able to set aside his feelings and give us honest, critical feedback."

Yeah, what a real hero.

"The school board thought it best that at the end of the semester, we part ways."

Oh fuck. Fuck. Shit. No.

I've never in my life felt such a painful stab to the heart as I do right now.

Tears well in my eyes and betrayal sinks heavily in my heart, turning it into a dark shade of black. His face pops up in my head, and instead of the handsome man I love, all I see is hate.

Hate for him.

For his stupid arrogance.

For his inability to open his mind and see there are other ways to teach students than just standing up front and lecturing them.

Trying to keep my emotions at bay, I say, "I understand—"

She raises her hand. "But that was their suggestion, not the verdict."

"Wait," I say, my throat closing tight. "So, I haven't been fired?"

She sighs and looks me in the eyes. "The reason I hired you, Greer, is because you're unique. Because you don't play by the book. I liked that about you. I also liked your vibrancy. You're captivating, but, yes, I think resorting to CliffsNotes is not how we would prefer our kids to learn. I know there's more you can give. Better ways you can help them understand. Innovative ways like the dress-up day. You bring literature to life, and I know you can figure out how to continue to do that moving forward."

A tear falls down my cheek and I quickly wipe it away. "Thank you, Nyema."

"Of course. You're on strict probation though. Ditch the CliffsNotes and any other online resources you plan to give the kids to read. Stick to the book. The movies are fine, as I know you show short clips right after you read the parts in the book, and then you discuss. I told the board it's bringing that scene to life for them. But start thinking of new ways to help the students learn the literature."

"Of course." I nod. "I'm more than happy to provide you with an updated lesson plan. I'll just need a few weeks."

"Two weeks, please. The faster the better with the school board." Leaning forward, Nyema winks at me and says, "I have your back."

"Thank you."

"And Greer?"

"Yes?" I ask, ready to bolt out of here as quickly as possible.

"I don't want you to be mad at Arlo. He did the right thing. As always, he put the kids first." Easy for her to say.

"Yes, he did." I give her a soft smile, suck in a deep breath, and stand from my chair. "Thank you for being open and honest with me."

"Of course. If you need help with lesson plans and some new ideas, I might have some up my sleeve. I'd be more than happy to sit down with you and chat."

"I'd love that, actually."

"Good, I'll have Joanna set up a time. As for now, deep breaths, everything will be okay."

"Thank you, Nyema," I say as another tear falls down my cheek.

"Are you okay?"

No.

I feel betrayed.

Played.

Like an absolute fool.

"Yes, just a lot to process. I'll be fine."

With that, I give her a quick wave and walk out the door. I stand in the hallway for a few seconds, trying to compose myself, but it's no use—I'm a ball of wretched sorrow, and I need to get the hell out of here.

Wiping at my eyes one more time, I scurry down the hallway, past Joanna, and—

"Greer, hold up."

I glance over my shoulder in time to catch Arlo pop out of a waiting chair and charge toward me.

Oh, hell no.

Turning away from him, I walk more quickly to the exit and hurry down the hallway toward my classroom, wishing I'd taken my things to the meeting so I could go straight to my car. Silly me, though, I was hoping to talk with Arlo afterward.

What a fool.

"Greer, please, wait. Let me explain."

"Go to hell, Arlo," I say, turning in to the English department wing.

"I wrote that before we got together."

I spin around on him. "And that's supposed to make it better?" I yell. Charging forward, I make it to my classroom, Arlo closely behind.

He shuts the door and attempts to approach me.

"I swear to God, Arlo, if you get any closer, I'll scream bloody murder."

He holds up his hands and takes a step back.

"Let me explain."

"Do you realize I was almost fired back there?" I shout at him. "That if it were up to the school board, I'd be packing up a box right now?

"What? They were going to fire you?"

"Yeah, per your evaluation."

"I didn't say to fire you."

"You didn't have to. Let me see if I can get this correct. 'The school board values his opinion greatly. Arlo Turner is one of the top reasons why we're a public school with the highest graduating percentage.'"

"But—"

"No. Wait. There was more. 'I have to give him credit for being able to set aside his feelings and give us honest, critical feedback.'" I point at him. "You knew exactly what you were doing."

"I wasn't doing anything. I was—"

"Can't find the words you're looking for? Let me help. You were a closeminded asshole who couldn't get his way, therefore went crying to the board to do something about it."

"That's not what I did. Hell." He grips his hair. "They asked me my opinion, I gave it to them. If I knew we were going to get together, I would have—"

"Lied?"

"No, I just . . . maybe would have gone easier on you."

Throwing my hands on my hips, I say, "This isn't about the evaluation, Arlo. Screw that. This is about how you truly, deep in your soul, don't believe I'm a valuable educator."

"That's not true."

"It's not? There wasn't one kind thing you said about me. And to this day, we still argue over how to teach. You yourself said we should just sweep the topic under the rug because we'll never agree." I turn away from him, emotion overcoming me, and I let the tears fall.

"Greer, please." I hear him step forward.

"Don't come near me, Arlo. I can't even look at you."

"Baby . . ."

"No," I snap at him. "Don't you dare call me that. I'm not your baby. I'm not your anything. The only thing that I am to you is a colleague and a teacher you share a class wall with."

"Greer." His voice cracks. "You don't mean that."

I spin around again. "What did you think was going to happen? I was going to be okay after being read all the reasons you don't think I should teach and then just jump in bed with you? You might have a good dick, but it's not that good. You hurt me, Arlo. You almost got me fired. I'm on *strict* fucking *probation* and have to rewrite my lesson plans, and I don't care if you filled that out before we were dating. What you wrote were your true feelings—observations—and that hurts more than anything. I've worked hard to get where I am, and yes, it might be a different approach from what you do in the classroom, but it works, and I'm proud of the education I've provided."

"You should be," he says quickly. "I hear about your classroom all the time."

"No." I shake my head. "Do not try to praise me right now because it's going to fall on deaf ears. Just get out."

"Not until you let me explain."

"What's there to explain, Arlo?" I say on a sob. "They asked you what you thought of my teaching. You told them."

"I said there was potential."

"*Potential?* As if you dust some of your stodgy teaching on me, I *might* be able to keep it together long enough to help a student?"

"No—"

"Well . . . fuck you," I say, the words slipping past me before I can stop them. "God . . . fuck you, Arlo. You're such an asshole. I should have known that from the very beginning. I did, actually, but I let my heart get the best of me. Well, not again. You might have been important to me ten minutes ago, but now, you're nothing to me. This job is important. Helping kids is what's important. And my confidence in my ability to shape young minds is important, and I don't need shitty people like you trying to tear me down." I point to the door behind him. "Leave."

His eyes shine, his expression nearly breaking me, but I turn away.

"Greer, I'm sorry. I'm so fucking sorry."

"Sorry means nothing to me." I gather my things, feeling his eyes on me the entire time. "If you're not going to leave, then I will." I blow past him, my shoulder bumping into his just as I realize what I have in my purse. I pause as my lip trembles. I reach into my purse and pull out the key to his house. Turning around, I hold it up to him and say, "I don't need this anymore."

A single tear falls down his cheek as he takes it, and before he can shred my heart apart anymore, I take off.

It's over.

It's so fucking over.

"I DON'T QUITE UNDERSTAND why you're mad. He told the truth," Keeks says while unpacking one of my boxes.

The room stills, and Stella and I look at her.

"Keeks, read the room," Stella whispers.

She looks around, confused. "Read what? There's no literature on the walls."

"Good God," Stella says, going to my dresser and putting my sweaters back in the drawer.

Thankfully, I hadn't packed much because Arlo was supposed to help me, but I'd gotten a jump-start on it. When I got home, I realized I couldn't do this on my own and called the girls over, forgetting how Keeks's brain functions. She sees logic, not so much emotion. It's one of the reasons I love her so much, but right now, I don't want logic.

I want all of the emotion.

"He hurt her," Stella says. "What would you do if Kelvin wrote up an evaluation on you and said you weren't a good chemist?"

"That would be preposterous. He's not in the same field of study as me, which renders his evaluation baseless."

Stella pinches the bridge of her nose. Somewhat humored by her distress—only a little—I take a big gulp of wine from my glass while I sit on my bed, cross-legged.

"Pretend that he's in your field of study."

"Is he a chemist? Physicist? Biologist? Or floating around in general science, unable to figure out which direction he'd like to take, so decides to dabble in every topic?"

"For the love of God, he's a chemist, like you," Stella answers exasperated.

Keeks considers the notion and shakes her head. "Kelvin would never be a chemist."

"I give up." Stella flops on the floor, arms spread, as there's a knock at the door. "It's open," Stella calls out.

The door cracks open, and the first thing we see is a box of Frankie Donuts. Then a voice calls, "I swear, it's just me. I bring donuts. Please don't hate me because my brother is an idiot."

"Come in," I say.

Cora peeks around the door, and I can tell she's been

crying from the red around her eyes and the blotchiness in her cheeks. When our eyes lock, her lips tremble and she says, "I'm so sorry."

I pat the spot next to me on the bed. "Sit. There's nothing to be sorry about. This isn't on you."

She steps over Stella and takes a seat. "I know, but I still feel awful. We share the same blood, after all."

"To be specific, siblings most commonly share fifty percent of their DNA, but half-siblings—"

"Keeks, why don't you grab napkins for the donuts?" I ask kindly. She nods. Turning to Cora, I say, "I'm sorry I'm not moving out. I know you were looking forward to moving in here."

"Why are you apologizing? Don't apologize. This is Arlo's fault. When he told me—God, I've never been so upset at my brother. I wanted to yell and scream at him but there was no chance I could. He was crying, and that just about broke me. I had to leave, or else, I'd have felt sad for him and I didn't want to feel sad for him."

"He was crying?" Stella asks.

Cora nods. "Yeah, he came into the house like that. I thought maybe someone died, but I guess it was your relationship."

He cried . . .

Hard.

Oh God, that makes me feel—

No, it makes me feel nothing. I don't care if he cries. He brought this upon himself.

I flip open the pastry box and pick up the first donut I see. Not caring about the flavor, I shove half the thing in my mouth, taking a giant bite. Cora does the same, followed up by Stella. Keeks is the only one who doesn't partake in a donut; instead, she stands over us, a confused look on her face.

"Why aren't you having a donut?" Stella asks.

"If Arlo cried, then maybe he feels true regret over the evaluation," Keeks says.

"Of course he's regretful—he lost his girlfriend over it."

Still confused, Keeks takes a seat on the floor and says, "But he evaluated you fairly."

"He evaluated me by his own rules, without looking outside his unadaptable and inflexible technique."

"Correct me if I'm wrong, but he's the department head. He evaluates everyone. That's part of his job. Is he supposed to lie because you're now romantically involved?"

Stepping in, Stella says, "Keeks, it's about how he's always thought her teaching techniques don't match up to his expectations. He's always thought that."

"Okay." Twisting her lips to the side, brow furrowed, she asks, "Then why are you surprised by his evaluation? Shouldn't you have already known what he was going to say?"

Why am I starting to feel like I'm in the wrong here? Why is her argument sounding logical?

I don't like it.

This isn't on me.

This is on Arlo.

"I'm not the one who did something wrong," I say, growing irritated.

"You're mad," she says. "I'm sorry, I didn't intend on making you angry. I'm trying to gain an understanding. My first-year evaluation was impeccably difficult to listen to. George Calhoun was head of the science department at the time. Vastly intellectual, quite a curmudgeon, didn't acknowledge contemporary science. I was appraised as frigid with students, awkward while lecturing, and inadequate in expounding knowledge. The school board agreed my personality was ill-fitting for a teaching role."

"Oh God, Keeks, that's awful," I say, my heart reaching out to her.

"I didn't know what to make of the criticism." She pushes her glasses up. "Principal Dewitt graced me with her tutelage and advised me on how to express myself better around the students and how to educate them with my quirks, rather than alienate them." She clears her throat. "Although, as the human race, we consider our individual selves to be astute in our daily practices, perhaps the truth is, we're not. Growth is key to happiness. Growth might hurt at first, but the anguish is worth it in the end."

Hell . . .

"But he told her he loved her," Stella says, letting Keiko's profound words roll right off her. "They were going to move in this weekend. There's a difference. You weren't in a loving, committed relationship with George Calhoun."

"Perhaps not. So what does that say about Arlo?"

"That he's a dick," Cora says, taking another bite of her donut.

"Or that he didn't let his feelings blind him. Instead, he showed true character. I've seen lack of character in a man, and it's unappealing. Intellectually, Arlo Turner isn't blinded by sexual compulsion but rather driven by the impulse to improve. From the inward pucker of your supraorbital ridges, I can observe that I hold the unpopular opinion, but I trust Arlo's intentions were not meant to be ill-willed, but for the betterment of our dear comrade and the school."

The room falls silent, and I wonder if the girls are all thinking the same thing I am . . .

That Keeks sounds like she's making sense right now. And maybe . . . *I* can't see anything past my humiliation and shame.

Because I've never been told I'm not good enough.

⸺

"GOOD MORNING." I don't have to turn around to know who just walked into my classroom. I could feel his presence before he opened his mouth.

I spent the weekend wrapped up in a pair of old sweatpants, nursing a gallon of ice cream, and binge-watching *Friends* because it was the only thing that didn't make me want to start crying all over again.

After the girls left, I felt even more confused than before.

I wanted to be mad.

I had the right to be mad.

But for some reason, what Keeks said made sense, and that was a tough pill to swallow. One I'm not ready to acknowledge.

"I'm busy," I say while writing out essay questions to be answered during class today.

"I know. I don't want to take up too much of your time. I was just hoping that we could speak tonight."

"I'm busy tonight."

"Greer, you can't just shut me out without talking to me."

I glance toward him, and it's the first time I'm catching his distraught appearance. Dark circles under his eyes, hair barely done, and instead of a cardigan, he's wearing a half-crumpled button-up shirt.

Good. He had a bad weekend just like me.

"I can actually do whatever I want. I'm an adult and in charge of my own life."

"Greer, we love each other."

"Yeah, well, that was before you went behind my back and tried to ruin my teaching career." The anger starts to make an appearance again—thank God—and Keiko's words quickly fade into the background.

"I wasn't trying to ruin your teaching career. I'd never do that to someone. They asked my honest opinion. I told them. The intention was to help you."

"I didn't ask for your help," I yell.

"Hey." Gunner comes into my classroom. "I can hear you two down the hall."

I press my hand to my forehead in distress. "You need to leave before I lose my shit."

"Not until you agree to talk to me."

Looking at Gunner, I say, "Get him out of here, now, or I'll cause a scene, and I don't care what happens to me after."

Hand to Arlo's chest, Gunner says, "Come on, man. Dewitt won't tolerate this scene. She's been cool with teachers dating because there's never been drama. Don't let it start now."

His eyes plead with me one last time, but I turn away from him and focus on the whiteboard in front of me.

"Greer . . . I'm sorry," he says, his voice full of regret. "I hope you know just how fucking sorry I am."

I don't look at him. No, I swallow back the wave of emotion that hits me and will myself not to cry.

Today is going to be exponentially harder than I thought.

Not just today . . . but being here in general.

Especially since I can't get the defeated look on his face out of my mind.

Chapter Twenty-Seven

ARLO

"Dude, what the fuck happened?" Gunner asks, shutting the door to my classroom. "Last I knew, you weren't yelling at each other, you were in love, and she was moving in."

I grip the back of my neck, completely distressed.

I spent the entire weekend trying to talk to her. Texts, phone calls . . . at one point I attempted to go to her place, but Coraline stopped me at the door and told me to give her some space.

I didn't want to give her space. I wanted to talk to her. I didn't want her thinking I went behind her back to be manipulative or to ruin her career, which she seems to believe. I wanted to fix things. I wanted to pack her up. I wanted her living with me, damn it.

And now that the weekend has gone by, I can see not going after her was a huge mistake, because when she looked at me, her eyes were lacking the usual sparkle. They were blank, empty, lifeless, and that was scary.

She's vibrant, excited about Monday mornings, ready for a new week of teaching . . .

Fuck, what have I done?

"Arlo," Gunner snaps. "What's going on?"

"We broke up," I say, sitting on the edge of my desk. "At least, that's what I think happened."

"How? What the hell changed?"

"She had her mid-semester evaluation. Nyema referred to my evaluation—"

"And? That's your job as a department head. You told me the other week that you could see some merit in how she structured her lessons."

He's right. I had told him that. But in the midst of getting to know Greer, learning who she is, how she grew up, fucking her every other available moment, falling in love . . . I hadn't even thought about the evaluation or that we butted heads on her style. It didn't seem as relevant.

"Yes. That's correct. But I submitted my evaluation probably four weeks ago, Gunner."

"What did you say?" Gunner asks, taking a seat on one of the desks.

"I don't remember." I pull on my hair. "I mean, nothing that I thought was going to have the school board want to fire her."

"What? They wanted to fire her?"

"Apparently. But Dewitt wouldn't let that happen. I spoke the truth—the only thing I can honestly remember writing is that using techniques like CliffsNotes didn't settle well with me."

"You need to figure out what you said."

"I know. But does that matter now? I can't take it back. I have no idea what to do. I've tried apologizing, I've tried talking to her, explaining myself, but there's nothing I can do. The damage has been done."

He winces.

"What?" I shoot at him. "Should I walk up to Dewitt and ask her if I can see her evaluation so I can refresh my memory on what a dick I was?"

"Pretty much."

"That's not helpful."

"Do you have a better idea?"

"I have no ideas. I honestly still can't believe this is happening." I press my fingers to my brow. "Fuck. I love her—and, what, we're just done now?"

"Only if you give up," Gunner says.

The bell rings, indicating school is starting and kids are going to start filing in.

"Shit," I mumble.

"I have to go, but think about it, okay? This isn't over."

"Then why does it feel like it is?"

———

"YOU LOOK like you want to cry," Coraline says, walking into the kitchen.

"I feel like shit."

"Good, you should."

Living with your ex-girlfriend's friend who knows how to hold a grudge does not make for a good time. I wouldn't wish it upon my worst enemies. Coraline has been relentless about making me feel like the piece of trash that I am. It's bad enough that I already carry around immense guilt and self-hatred, but she loves to pile it on every chance she gets.

"Coraline, I don't need this from you." I press my palm to my eye, not in the mood for food, so I go to the living room couch.

Grabbing a banana from the counter, she joins me, not that I invited her. When I reach for the remote, she kicks it away.

Sighing, I lean my head back against the couch and say,

"What?"

"It's been a week. A week, Arlo, and you've done nothing to fix this."

"There's nothing I can do. She won't talk to me. Pretty sure if she won't talk to me, there's no way I can solve this. She doesn't want to hear me out. She's done, so that means I'm done, too."

"Oh, so you're going to act like a petulant child and just give up because you're not getting your way?"

"I'm not acting like a petulant child. I just know when something is over. I'm not about to—in crass terms—beat a dead horse. It's over."

"Let me ask you this. Do you love her still?"

"No, in a matter of a week I've been able to forget about the only woman I've ever loved and move on," I answer sarcastically.

"Your rude tone isn't going to get you anywhere with me."

"I'm not trying to impress you."

"You should. I'm Greer's good friend. I could put in a good word for you. Mind you, I've been saying some pretty shitty things about you, but I can change that all around."

"Wow, thanks, Coraline."

"Well, don't be a dickhead, and I won't have to try to protect my name because I'm unfortunately associated with you. Trust me, I've bought a lot of apology donuts in the last few days to help hold down my relationship with her. Do you know how awkward it is hanging out with her knowing my brother is the reason she's working her ass off to keep her job? It's not fun. Do you know what else isn't fun? Watching Greer quietly cry to herself while we try to cheer her up. It's painful, agonizing, knowing how much she's hurting."

"She's crying?" I ask, my heart nearly wrenching out of my chest.

"What else would she be doing? Yes, she's angry with you, Arlo, but she also loves you, still does, and that love was shattered. You broke her trust. You made her believe she's not good enough to be an educator. Could you imagine, if the person you're head over heels in love with blindsides you and tells you all the hard work you've been putting into your job isn't good enough? Pretty sure you'd be crushed, too. Honestly, I don't think she's mad about what was said, but more angry about who said it."

"But . . . we've clashed over teaching styles from the very beginning."

"It doesn't matter. You still hurt her."

"I know." Aggravated, I drag my hands over my face. "What the fuck do I do?"

"Well, sitting around doing nothing is not the way to win her heart back."

"Trying to talk to her isn't working either."

"Ugh, you're so dumb." She rolls her eyes. "For the level of education you have on your résumé, you'd swear there would be more than a half-brain in your head." Looking me in the eyes, in all seriousness, she says, "You read those Scottish books, right?"

"What do they have to do with this?"

"It's called a grand gesture, Arlo. You can't win a girl's heart without a grand gesture. And if any moment calls for one, this is it."

"So you think I should ride into school on a white steed and proclaim my undying love?" I roll my eyes.

"With that kind of crappy attitude, you're never going to get her back."

"What happened to just talking? Talking it out? Having a simple conversation?"

Coraline's lips flatten as she stares at me. Nostrils flaring. Why do I feel like she's about to explode?

"Arlo, do you remember that conversation I had with you a while back? Out on the lounger."

"Yes."

"Do you remember how we spoke about intimacy? And it being harder for us?"

"Yes . . ."

"Intimacy isn't just holding someone's hand and kissing them in public. Intimacy is opening your heart to the one you love—opening it up—and exposing it to get beaten, battered, and then loved all over again. You need to open your mind to understand how Greer is feeling. Talking to her isn't going to work. Reason and logic won't work in this moment when her heart is broken. This requires an intimate act, an act of courage on your end. You need to show her not only do you love her, but you honor her teaching as well."

"I do. I've seen her work. I've heard the way the students talk about her. And I said that, but she focuses on the negative."

"Because the negative almost made her lose everything. And the negative—well, it made you lose the most important person in your life." She pats my leg. "So, my suggestion to you is figure out a way you can make it up to her. Show her you value her as a colleague and the love of your life."

"How do you suppose—" I pause, a lightbulb turning on in my head. I sit up on the couch and say, "Oh shit, I think I have an idea."

"Boop," Coraline says, pressing her finger to my thigh. "You're welcome. I'll take another sparkly thing as payment."

"If this works, I'll give you anything you want."

"I hope you realize you just made quite the promise."

⌐━⌐

"THANK you for making some time for me," I say to Nyema.

"No need to thank me. I've been wanting to speak with you."

I shift in my chair, trying to get comfortable. "Let me guess, you want to talk to me about Miss Gibson?"

"Yes." She folds her hands in front of her. "I heard you two have had a falling out."

"I wasn't aware you knew we were together in the first place."

"There's very little I don't know about in my school, including faulty air conditioners." She lifts her brow, and —*Jesus Christ, she knows about that?* Does she know who the underwear actually belongs to? Things I'll never tell Greer . . . that's if she ever decides to talk to me again.

Clearing my throat, I look away and say, "Uh, yeah . . . um . . ." Jesus.

"Now, about Miss Gibson," Nyema says, thankfully helping me out.

"Yes, sorry." I clear my throat one more time. "I was hoping I could chat with you about her evaluation. I know that's confidential, but could I at least be reminded of what I said in her evaluation? I think it'd be helpful in understanding her feelings."

"Are you planning to win her heart back?"

"Yes."

"It's been over a week."

"My sister made me quite aware of that the other day."

"It's going to be more difficult since you've waited so long." She folds her arms over her chest.

"Trust me, I've been trying but realized I'm going to have to make a grand gesture to gather her attention."

"Yes, I believe you are." Nyema smirks and then she studies me. "You know, Arlo, I've known you for a few years now and, I'll admit, I never thought you had room in your heart for more than literature and the love for teaching. But then Greer came along and I saw the way she challenged you, the way you look at her, study her. She fascinated you. So, when you turned in your evaluation, I took it with a grain of salt. I read between the lines. She scares you."

"She doesn't scare me."

"She does." Nyema nods. "Because she makes you question yourself and the way you conduct your classroom."

I go to respond but then quickly realize . . . she's right.

"She's made you uncomfortable, hasn't she? It's why you dressed up for the literary character day. And you liked it."

"It was a nice way to help students explore the deeper intricacies of literary characters."

Nyema chuckles. "You don't have to be proper with me. I know you liked it, Arlo. I sat in the back of your class while you taught your lesson. You were engaged, excited. She brought a teaching angle out of you that you weren't expecting, and that was scary."

I sigh heavily and look down at my hands. "Yeah, she did."

"And your evaluation, although critical, still praised her. It wasn't hurtful, it was what I'd expect from a trusted colleague. The school board took it to heart, but I took it for what it was, an opportunity for her to grow. But she wasn't expecting it, so it hurt her."

"Yeah, I'm aware."

"I'll say this, though, there was nothing in there that wasn't true. I've observed her myself. I allowed her to move forward with her teaching style, and it's been great watching these students absorb the material, but I believe she can do it without the pomp and circumstance. I think as a new teacher, she's relying on easy resources, when I know, deep down, if she finds the confidence, she can lose the resources and rely on her personality to get the material across."

"I agree. That's what I was trying to convey."

"And you did. But you never conveyed it to her, did you?"

"No, I have. I've said that many—"

"In an angry tone? Or a teaching tone?"

I wince.

"I've seen you at each other's throats, arguing." Does she have cameras set up around the school that I don't know about? "You and I both know it's hard to absorb anything when you're put on the defensive."

"And every time we've spoken about her teaching, she's been on the defensive."

"Exactly." She smiles brightly. "So, now you need to figure out how you can show her your appreciation without insulting her."

"I think I have a plan."

"It better be good."

"I believe it is."

***

"QUIET," I say to my fifth-period class.

They quickly settle down, all eyes looking up at me.

Taking a deep breath, I say, "I need your help." They glance around at each other, confused. "You see, I've fallen in love." A few girls make those annoying girl shrieks. "And like every other red-blooded male, I've blown it."

"We can't all be perfect," Chuckie says from the back.

"That's your warning," I point at him.

"Just trying to be supportive." He holds his hands up. "I'm here for you, Mr. Turner."

Ignoring him, I say, "The object of my affection . . . Miss Gibson." I wait as the entire class explodes with shrieks and clapping. When they're settled, I continue, "And like I said, I blew it. Now, I've tried a simple method to communicate with her. But you see, when you mess up the way I did—something I won't divulge to you, so don't ask—a conversation isn't going to do the trick." I lift off my desk and go to the whiteboard, where I snap up the map that's covering it and reveal two words.

Mr. Darcy.

"I'm afraid I'm going to have to go Mr. Darcy on her . . . and I need your help."

Chapter Twenty-Eight

GREER

"Okay, everyone. Hand your papers to the front of the class, where—"

Knock. Knock.

The door to my classroom opens and in steps a student wearing a bonnet. The class erupts in laughter and I have to quiet them down before I can ask what the hell is going on.

"Can I help you?"

"Miss Gibson." She curtseys. "Miss Turner and Mr. Turner are here to see you."

What the hell . . .

Coraline files into the classroom wearing a top hat, while Arlo rounds the corner of the classroom door, shoulders stiff, hands at his side. A student with a phone, recording him, follows closely behind.

Cora bends at the waist, bowing. "Miss Gibson, pleasure to see you. Are you faring well?"

Uhhh . . .

"Dare I say, you look handsome."

Arlo stays silent next to her.

"You must have heard, I'm here in town, staying with my dear brother for a few days."

Okay . . . what the hell is going on?

"I don't know what this is, but you're disturbing my class."

Cora laughs. "Yes, the weather has treated us well."

Arlo stares at me awkwardly, still silent, until finally he asks, "You're well, Miss Gibson?"

The tone of this voice, the short clip of his words, the desperation in his eyes.

The bonnet.

The top hat.

Oh . . . my . . . God . . .

No way.

There is no way this is happening, that he's taking a note from my lesson plans.

He's—oh my God—he's acting out a scene from *Pride and Prejudice*.

Tears start to well in my eyes as I slowly nod.

My pulse skyrockets as I can feel the beat of my heart climb up my throat. The classroom stays silent, all eyes on me.

Slowly, I lower my eyes and answer, "Quite well."

"I hope the weather stays fine for you," he says.

I nod.

Cora looks between us and says, "Well, we must be going."

"So soon?" I whisper.

The girl in the bonnet says, "Miss Gibson looks well, doesn't she?"

Arlo's face stays stoic, eyes downcast, as he says, "She does. Quite well."

Sucking in a sharp breath, Cora says, "Well, we really should be going."

Arlo dips his head and then turns out of the door, Cora following close behind. The girl in the bonnet shuts the door, and after a few seconds, from the other side of the wall, I hear Arlo's class cheer.

And for the first time in two weeks . . . I smile.

"AND WHY WOULD HE DO THAT?" I ask as one student raises their hand.

Knock. Knock.

The door opens, and the student in the bonnet appears, holding the door open. Filtering in behind is Cora in a top hat and Chuckie . . . in a dress.

The class erupts and Chuckie quickly goes to my desk, where he takes a seat.

"Miss Turner to see Mr. Chuckie. Or . . . uh . . . Mr. Bingley to see Miss Bennet?"

The class chuckles, and Cora starts pacing the room.

Chuckie stands, adjusts the ribbon at his waist, and then folds his hands in front of him. Cora whips around and says, "Miss Chuckie, I've been an ass."

Oh, dear God.

I place my hand over my mouth to keep from giggling. From the corner of my eyes, I catch Arlo, standing near the doorframe, looking in, watching. His stare intense, his meaning clear.

Bending on one knee, Cora says, "Will you do me the honor of being my wife?"

Dramatically, Chuckie clutches his hands and pretends to cry as he says, "Yes . . . a thousand times, yes," just like Jane Bingley.

Cora stands and, when I think they might hug, they both hold out their hands and give each other a fist bump, only to run out of the classroom together.

Darcy . . . I mean Arlo, exchanges one more look with me and then the door is shut behind him.

Be still my heart.

"I KNOW WHAT'S NEXT, and I'm terrified," I say, taking a bite of the pizza Stella brought over.

Stella wipes her mouth with a napkin and whispers, "Okay, you know I haven't been a fan of the man because of what he did, but . . . this is freaking romantic."

Glancing at the bathroom where Keiko is, I say, "I know. I keep thinking about what Keeks said the day we unpacked my apartment. About growth and how he was trying to help, not hurt. Do you think there was some validity to what she said?"

Leaning in, Stella says, "Despite wanting to throw her theory into the wastelands, I've known Keiko for a bit, and if there's one thing I know, she doesn't say anything unless there's validity behind it. Her statements have meaning, and even though I don't want to believe it, she was . . . right."

I groan. "Damn it, Stella."

The bathroom door opens and Keiko joins us. "It's surprising that I'm surrounded by two intellectual minds, but your ability to calculate the thickness of the walls and sound-proofing in a small studio apartment is incomprehensible."

"Did you hear us?"

"Every word. And you're correct, there is validity to everything I say." She cuts her pizza with a fork and a knife.

"He's eating away at my resolve. He's using my favorite book against me as a teaching moment for his students and a way to win back my heart."

"It's possible to conclude that he's using the very same teaching techniques he tried to quell from your practice, and instead, proving his theory wrong right in front of you. Quite a noble feat, to not only admit that he was wrong, but also show just how wrong he was."

"See?" Stella nods to Keiko. "Validity."

"So, what happens when it's Mr. Darcy's turn to make a move? What do I do?"

"Depends," Keeks says. "What do you want? If you conclude that life would not be the same without the romantic involvement you once obtained with Arlo, then, I say, play along. But if you believe your life is better, more suitable without him in it, deny his request for your hand."

"From the look in your eyes, I think you know the answer," Stella says.

"Yeah, I think I know it, too."

———

KNOCK. *Knock.*

The door opens and Chuckie once again comes into the room, this time wearing a nightgown. The girl in the bonnet comes up to me and holds open a robe. My class, used to this by now, all sit silently and wait.

With a deep breath, I shrug the robe on and tie it at my waist.

Chuckie lies across my desk and kicks his feet up in the air. "Oh, Miss Gibson," he says, batting his eyelashes. "Can you possibly keel over from happiness?" He smiles and kicks his legs about. "He thought of me as indifferent, that I didn't care for him. Can you believe such a notion?"

Smiling, I shake my head. "Unfathomable."

He shakes his head and sits up. "Miss Gibson, I wish I could see you as happy one day. Happy like me."

"Maybe Mrs. Dewitt has a suitor for me."

The class chuckles as there's another knock at the door.

I turn around to find Romeo walking in, wearing a petticoat.

Oh, dear Jesus.

The class laughs hysterically, and he motions his hands to tamp down their laughter. Once settled, he adjusts his . . .

breasts, and the girl in the bonnet says, "Mr. Romero to see you . . . uh . . . Mr. Turner's aunt, or something like that."

Romeo looks around, lifts his chin, and says, "You have a very small classroom, madam."

The girl in the bonnet says, "Can we offer you some tea, Mr. Romero?"

In a haughty voice, he says, "Absolutely not. I want to speak to Miss Gibson. Alone."

Chuckie climbs off the desk and scurries out of the room.

Once he's gone, Romeo says, "Are you aware of why I make my presence?"

Thinking back to the scene where Mr. Darcy's aunt confronts Elizabeth, I say, "I can't recall why I would have the honor."

"I'm not to be trifled with," Romeo says, stomping his foot. The class chuckles. "You intend on being engaged with my nephew, Mr. Turner. This is impossible behavior, and I've come to let you know."

"If you perceive this as impossible, why are you here?"

"Don't fool with me, girl. Can you confirm you haven't been spreading such rumors of a proposal?"

"You marked such foolery as impossible. How could it be true?"

"Do not toy with me. Mr. Turner is to be engaged to my . . . uh . . ."

"Daughter," I hear Arlo whisper from the door, and when I spot him, my heart leaps out of my chest, right toward him, begging him to take it.

"Right, he's engaged to my daughter."

"If that's the case, he'd have no reason to make an offer to me," I say.

I can feel the energy in the room—all my students, eyes on us, immersed in the moment—and right then and there, I can feel what Nyema was talking about, what Arlo was trying to portray. This is how you make them see it. How you make them understand. This is how you make it come to life and leave an impact. Tears well in my eyes once again.

This man, the one standing silently at the door . . . the proud man, the man full of prejudice—he's opened my eyes in a way I never thought he would.

"You selfish girl," Romeo shouts, bringing me back to the scene. "Your inferior birth will not stand in the way of my daughter getting married. Now tell me, are you engaged to him?"

"I am not," I answer, barely able to see over my own tears.

"And you will promise to never enter into such an engagement?"

"I will not." The class cheers, and I can't hold back my smile. "You have insulted my family and me in every possible way. Now you must leave." I go to the door and hold it open.

Romeo storms off, and when I shut the door, my class erupts into a cacophony of cheers.

        ⎯⎯⎯

GREER: *I'm going to puke. Fifth period starts in five minutes. I know what's supposed to happen today.*

Stella: *You know what you want, right?*

Greer: *I want him.*

Stella: *Then take him . . . take all of him.*

        ⎯⎯⎯

"MISS GIBSON?" Simone in the front raises her hand.

"Yes?"

"Uh, there's ten minutes left before school gets out. Is Mr. Turner going to come in?"

I glance at the clock and try not to show my disappointment.

"I don't know. But let's concentrate on what we're doing

right now, okay?" I take a deep breath and move to the side of the classroom close to the windows. I'm about to ask another question when the door to the classroom bursts open. A gust of wind blows in and Arlo stands in the doorway, wearing a white cotton button-up, brown jeans, and an overcoat. The shirt is open, a fan blows behind him, impersonating wind, and he stands there, proud.

He slowly walks toward me, and in that Darcy-like voice he says, "I couldn't teach . . ."

I love his twist on the storyline.

Getting into character, I say, "Me neither."

The class quiets, and I catch them all leaning forward.

"My aunt—how do I ever apologize for his behavior?"

A few chuckles.

"For I'm in your debt," I say. "For what you've done for . . . Chuckie, and my family . . . for my career. I must be the one who makes amends."

Chin held high, his voice cracks when he says, "You must know. It was all for you." He takes a pause and then says, "If your feelings are still what they were two weeks ago, tell me now. My affection for you has not changed."

There's a slight gasp in the air.

"But if they have changed, I must know, because I need to tell you this." He pauses again, his words almost drowned out by the rapid beat of my heart. "You have bewitched me, body and soul," he says, just like Mr. Darcy. "And I . . . I love you. I never wish to be apart from you . . . from this day on."

Taking a deep breath, I stare him in the eyes, the moment heavy, intense, so palpable that I can feel the truth in his words, the meaning behind them.

"Well then, shall we never be apart again." I say, lifting his hand to my mouth, where I place a kiss on his knuckles.

I look up at him, and our foreheads move in, touching, our noses move closer, and then . . .

The bell sounds off, signaling the end of class.

Collectively, everyone shouts, "Nooooooo."

Chuckie, in the nightgown still, for God knows what reason, says, "Kiss, kiss, kiss."

Laughing, I glance up at Arlo, and he cups my chin. Everyone joins in the chant and before I can decide what to do, Arlo presses his mouth against mine. The cheers fade into the dark, the raucous behavior is out of mind as I get lost in his touch, in the feel of his mouth, in the capturing of his love.

Body and soul. Jane Austen could not have said it more perfectly.

Pulling his mouth away, he brings his lips to my ear and says, "You make me incandescently happy."

Tears fall down my cheeks.

I pull away and cup his jaw. "Mr. Turner, you have no idea."

Epilogue

ARLO

"We're going to win. I can feel it in the air," Gunner says, jumping up and down in ridiculously short cotton shorts.

No man should *ever* wear shorts that length.

But he lost a bet to Romeo—still not sure what that was about—and he showed up to the teachers' league wearing red hot pants. And he's playing it up, big time, bending over and stretching in Romeo's face. I'm pretty sure Romeo is regretting making the bet at this point.

"Greer, are you stretched?"

"Yes," she answers, exasperated.

I kiss the side of her head and whisper, "He'll be worse during the game, so prepare yourself."

"You're lucky you don't have to play. I wish I was the one who broke my thumb."

I hold up my small cast. "I can arrange that. I'll smash it right now with my club hand."

She chuckles and snuggles in close to my chest.

Come to find out, a grand gesture doesn't solve all problems.

Shocking, I know.

After I swept Greer off her feet, Mr. Darcy style, I thought we were going to pick up right where we left off.

Boy, was I foolish.

Nope. There was a lot of talking.

I mean . . . a lot.

We had to hash out every last detail, which made sense in the long run because it has helped us establish a more solid foundation of a relationship, something we can stand on through the good and the bad. It's been hard work, but worth putting the time toward. This might not be a shock to you, but relationships don't come easy to me, so the more we communicate, the more I learn and that's what we've been doing, communicating a lot.

And even with how open we've been with each other; Greer still took it slow with me. She didn't move in right away like I thought she would. Instead, we went back to dating.

Real dating.

I started sending her notes again, telling her how much I love her, entertaining her with dirty poetry (originals), and opening up to her in a way I feel comfortable. We've been spending Friday nights together, focusing on dates and getting to know each other on another level, not just sex. We've hung out with our friends, gone on double dates with Gunner and Lindsay, and have even attended some cooking classes together.

I also pop into her class every once in a while and declare my love for her, especially when she moved on from *Pride and Prejudice* and jumped into *Romeo and Juliet*. I wanted a firm grasp on what a relationship was before trying to move forward with anything else.

For Thanksgiving, I went to her house after all. Talk about nervous. I was a fucking wreck. Greer kept telling me her parents were going to love me but being the guy that broke her heart, I was skeptical. Thankfully, her parents didn't know about the evaluation debacle, as Greer didn't want to taint their opinion of me. When she told me that, I don't think I could have loved her more. She gave me a fair chance to make a good impression. And of course, I took advantage of the opportunity and I worked my charm, while Coraline ate all their pie. We left with full bellies and a welcoming family asking us to come back anytime.

And the sex—well, that was put on hold for a while.

At first, I was okay with it. I knew I had to grow that trust with her again.

But after a few weeks of her kissing me goodnight and sending me out the door, I was growing desperate. It wasn't until she asked me to come over to help her build her new dining room table, a table that I found her spread across in another lingerie set, waiting for me that she relieved me of my torture.

In full transparency, I came hard and quick. Don't worry . . . so did she. After that, we made love several times through the night. The next day, she asked if the invitation to move in was still available. I started packing her up that day. Two days later, she was living with me.

And that's how it's been since.

Christmas is in two weeks, and Coraline and I already have one hell of a holiday party planned, as well as Christmas morning. A special Christmas morning. One that involves a sparkly item, and this one is not for Coraline.

As for my thumb, Gunner broke it last weekend. In a fit of rage while practicing badminton, he swung the racket and chopped my thumb. I swore violently while kicking him in the crotch. We both fell to the ground. I was taken to the hospital,

Lindsay iced Gunner's balls, I wound up with a cast, and Gunner isn't sure if he can deliver any more kids to Lindsay's uterus. His words, not mine.

"Look at them over there," Stella says. "All smug, thinking they're going to win. They have no idea we have a human computer with us."

After we realized having four Division-1 athletes on a team isn't the best idea—since they all go after the shuttlecock at the same time—we enlisted Keiko to help us. She's been secretly studying the teams all tournament and calculating the rate of their trajectory . . . or something like that. I have no idea, except that she's pinpointed all their weak spots and has instructed each player thoroughly on the Forest Heights team about where they're allowed to hit the shuttlecock.

They're ready.

"Are there any questions?" Keiko asks. "I will be quite displeased if I have to repeat myself."

"We got it," Romeo says, bouncing back and forth like a tennis player, racket in hand.

"We're going to annihilate them," Stella roars, lifting her racket to the air.

"And then celebrate with donuts," Cora says next to me, taking pictures.

Everyone cheers and heads to their positions.

Greer turns to me, cups my cheek, and says, "Wish me luck."

"Good luck, babe." I kiss her on the lips and look her in the eyes. "I love you."

She smiles and replies, "I love you." Then she leans in and whispers in my ear, "If we win, I'm sucking you so hard tonight."

I whisper back, "When we win, you're revisiting the kitchen island."

Her cheeks redden and she pulls away. She gives me a

quick wave, and I shoot her a wink as I watch her jog off to the court, her hair swishing behind her.

"God, you're infatuated, aren't you?" Cora asks.

"The proper term would be bewitched, Coraline. Utterly bewitched."

Made in United States
Troutdale, OR
08/15/2023

12111753R10228